The Blue Lotus Tales

MARISA CHENERY

CONTENTS

THE BLUE LOTUS

Kendra Miller finds herself intrigued by the gold pendant her brother sent her from Egypt. She finds the enameled blue lotus flower on it lovely, but the hieroglyphs engraved on the back are a mystery she wants to solve. After innocently translating the glyphs, she sets off a chain of events that can only end in disaster.

Nefertem, drawn to the woman who summoned him, knows his love for Kendra can only lead to heartache. Being bound to the pendant, his stay in her world is limited.

Together they try to stop the disaster Kendra has unwittingly set in motion, and Nefertem fights the changes taking place inside him. If they fail, Kendra might lose more than the love of her live.

CHAPTER ONE

Kendra Miller wiped the sweat-dampened hair from her eyes and cursed the rush-hour traffic on Beale Street. Being stuck in it, in a car with no air conditioning, in hot Memphis during summer, was far from pleasurable. Having just left the art gallery on that street where she worked as a receptionist, she headed home after a long day.

She finally broke free of the heavy traffic, and some of the tension left her body. Though she did this drive day after day, she still hated doing it at a snail's pace in the busy downtown.

Kendra pulled into the drive of her modest two-story house, then parked her car before she headed to the front door. She unlocked it after she flipped open the lid of her mailbox. She grabbed the collection of envelopes, with a mix of junk mail, and then let herself inside.

With a shove on the door, Kendra closed it behind her, then kicked off her high-heeled shoes while she went through her mail. There were the usual bills, but one heavier envelope stood out from among the rest. She threw the others onto the small side table in the entrance hallway and wondered who'd sent her that one. Spying the return address, a smile spread across her lips. What could her brother have given her this time?

Markus was two years her senior — twenty-six to her twenty-four — and was the world traveler of the family. Somehow, he managed to make a career out of it. At each of his destinations, he searched out items of interest and bought them. After he returned to Memphis, he'd sell them to shops that dealt in such things. Sometimes he'd send her a present if he was going to be away for an extended period, which was the case this time. He was on his annual trip to Egypt.

Kendra decided to change into more comfortable clothes before she opened the envelope and went up to her bedroom. She shared the house with her brother when he was home between trips. Since she was the one primarily staying there, she'd claimed the master as her own.

Once free of her restricting dress clothes, Kendra slipped into a tank top and shorts. She stepped into the en suite bathroom and released her tight bun. She pulled out the pins one by one, and her long, light brown hair fell to its full length, reaching the middle of her back.

She caught a glimpse of her reflection in the mirror and stuck out her tongue. She wasn't the type of woman to stare at herself for any great length. Her looks were far from spectacular. The best way she could describe herself was average. Her most distinctive feature was her eyes. They were a startling light green. At the sound of the phone ringing, she quickly gathered her hair into a ponytail.

After picking up the phone that sat on the nightstand beside her bed, Kendra asked, "Hello?"

"About time you got home," replied the woman on the other end.

Kendra smiled at the sound of her best friend's voice. "What do you mean, Tory? You know this is the time I come home from work."

"Never mind. Now get dressed for a night on the town. I'm taking you out."

"Not tonight. All I want to do is sip some wine and watch a bit of television."

Tory groaned. "It's a Friday night. I refuse to let you sit at home alone, feeling sorry for yourself."

"I'll not be doing anything of the sort. I just don't feel like going out is all."

"He's not worth it, Kendra. It's been a month. Time to move on."

Tory meant well, but moving on was easier said than done. Being dumped by her fiancé two days before they were to get married had deeply wounded her.

"It has nothing to do with Greg. Just let it be."

"All right, all right. You win. I won't push you any more. I worry about you. That jerk needs a butt-kicking for what he did to you."

"You're just the woman to do it."

Her friend laughingly replied, "Damn right I am." Tory grew serious. "Promise me you won't let him win. Don't close yourself away because of what he did to you."

"I promise. Now have your fun, and I'll call you later." Having said that, Kendra hung up.

After reclaiming the thick envelope from the bed, Kendra returned to the lower level. Her stomach rumbled, giving her a good reminder that food should be the first order of business. The mysterious gift would have to wait the few minutes it took her to heat up a frozen dinner in the microwave.

Listlessly picking at her food, she shook her head. How low she had sunk? She used to be a good cook. One who enjoyed making a good meal, even if she was the only one who'd eat it, but that was no longer the case. She only cooked when her brother was home.

Kendra gathered up the remnants of her dinner before

pouring herself a glass of white wine, then, with the envelope in hand, went to the living room. After she switched on the television, she ripped open the padded packaging. She tipped it and spilled the contents onto her hand.

At first glance, it didn't look like much, but once she spread it out, Kendra could see why Markus had chosen that piece. She just didn't understand why he'd decided to give it to her rather than sell it to one of his buyers. She hooked her finger through the chain and hung the pendant from its length. Though a bit on the grimy side, the necklace had the potential to be a beautiful bit of jewelry after a little cleaning.

She peered closely at the palm-sized pendant and could vaguely make out Egyptian hieroglyphs etched across the whole surface. Some kind of black gunk seemed to have adhered to the finish of the chain and pendant. With not much else planned for the evening, Kendra decided there was no time like the present to give the whole thing a polish.

Kendra headed up the stairs once more and then to her room where she kept her jewelry cleaner. This piece was more than likely an antiquity, she would have to be careful not to damage it.

Surprisingly, the black stuff came off more easily than she'd thought. What was revealed took her breath away. It wasn't some cheap piece of costume jewelry. What slowly appeared was pure gold. Not the gold-plated junk either, but the real thing.

The thick, rope-styled chain would be worth a fortune, but the pendant was that and much more. Kendra lightly traced the hieroglyphs with her finger. Any Egyptologist would die to get their hands on it, to read the glyphs and learn what they had to say, which sparked an idea. She could try to decipher them herself. Libraries were a wealth of information, and there was always the Internet.

The more Kendra thought about it, the better the idea seemed. For the first time since the Greg incident, some of the lethargy—which had claimed her—dissipated. Tomorrow she would make a start. It would give her a reason to get up in the morning.

* * * *

Waking up from a refreshed sleep, Kendra felt more like herself. She had a purpose now. After eating a quick breakfast of toast, she decided to try the library first, and the Memphis-Shelby County Public Library and Information Center on Poplar Avenue was where she needed to go.

The library was just about deserted on that Saturday morning, so she had the pick of tables. Kendra pulled out a pad of paper and pen from her bag. One of the computers was conveniently located on the counter directly across from her. She accessed the library catalogue before she did a search for books on Egyptian hieroglyphs. After making a mental note of where they were, she quickly grabbed three likely prospects.

She'd thought it would be a no great feat to decipher the hieroglyphs, but she'd been mistaken. There was a standard alphabet that translated each picture, giving it a corresponding letter, but some could be used as a phrase.

After an hour of going through the books, Kendra decided to sign them out and work at home. She hadn't brought the pendant with her, and needed to compare the hieroglyphs directly if she was going to work out what they meant.

It was close to noon by the time she arrived at her house. Much to her surprise, she had a visitor waiting for her. Kendra stepped out of her car and then went to greet the woman standing by her front door.

"What are you doing here, Tory? I thought after a night

on the town you would still be sleeping."

Tory Connor rolled her eyes. "It was hardly a night out on the town once you bailed on me. Thanks to you, I had to stay in."

"Well, come inside, and we can have some lunch." Kendra opened the door before she motioned for Tory to go ahead of her.

Meeting Tory had been one of the best things to ever happen to her. At the time, Kendra had been a very introverted teen, starting mid-year at the high school. After losing their parents in a car crash, she and Markus had gone to live with their maternal grandparents. She'd been sixteen. The loss of her parents, and then facing a new school, had taken its toll on her. There had been one bright light in her darkest time, and it went by the name of Tory Connor. A girl who refused to let Kendra lose herself to her grief. For that, she would always love Tory.

Kendra sighed with envy as she followed her friend inside. Tory had a killer body that attracted men by the droves. Curves in all the right places, long, golden hair, sparkling blue eyes, and a face a supermodel would die to have, summed Tory up. Unlike herself. Kendra had more of an athletic build, and not much in the curve department. The only thing she had the same as her friend was height. They stood equally at five foot eight.

Today, Tory had decided to go with a cutesy look that not many women their age could pull off, but she could and did. Wearing a soft pale pink baby-T and matching short shorts, she could lure any man within fifty feet of her to her side with a glance. If Kendra donned that same outfit, she'd look just plain ridiculous.

Noticing the stack of books Kendra carried, Tory asked, "What are those for?"

Kendra plunked the said items onto the coffee table, then went to the kitchen before she opened the fridge. She pulled out the makings for a salad. Her friend had followed her in.

"Markus sent me a little something from Egypt."

"You know, instead of getting these you should have called me. I know something a whole lot better than these books for translating hieroglyphs. This could take you all day using them."

"What's better than the books I got from the library?"

Tory gave Kendra a knowing expression and smiled. "It just so happens I know someone who works at the museum. He specializes in ancient Egypt. I could give him a call and see if he'd be willing to help you out."

Kendra hesitated answering. She really didn't want an expert to see the pendant. She wanted to keep it for herself. "I don't know if that's such a great idea. Thanks, anyway."

"Okay, out with it. This something your brother sent you must be really special."

"You're right. It's something special. If Markus actually knew what he'd sent me, he would have thought twice before putting it in the mail."

"Now you have me intrigued. Let me see it already, why don't you."

Kendra laughed and then went to her room to get the pendant. Once she returned, Tory had finished making their salads. With a flourish, Kendra spread the pendant and necklace on the kitchen table.

Tory let out a low whistle. She picked up the necklace and examined it closely. "Old Markus must be losing it. This has to be worth a fortune."

"Well, it didn't look like this when it arrived. It was covered in some kind of black stuff. I had no idea what it was. After I cleaned it, this is what I found."

"I can see why you're leery about someone at a museum getting a hold of this." Tory turned the pendant over, appearing to admire the blue enameled lotus flower on the back. "This is magnificent."

"The flower is beautiful, but what the hieroglyphs have

to say draws me more."

After returning the pendant to the table, Tory picked up her fork. "I still think Scott can help you. He knows just about all there is about ancient Egypt." As Kendra opened her mouth to refuse again, Tory interrupted. "I know, I know, you don't want him to see it, but I think we can get around that. After we finish eating, I'll call him and get him to translate this over the phone. I'll tell him it's something I found in a magazine."

"Won't he wonder at your sudden interest in hieroglyphs?"

Tory shook her head and chuckled. "No. He'll think I'm using it as an excuse to call him. I'll have to go out with him on a date in return."

Kendra raised one of her brows and gave Tory a questioning look. "Knowing you, he's already wrapped around your little finger. He must be tall, dark, and handsome. Just how you like your men."

"You got that right." Tory laughed. "Scott is delicious. It'll be no hardship for me to spend some time with him. So once we're done eating, I'll give him a call."

True to her word, Tory called Scott a short while later. He was more than happy to translate the hieroglyphs. In no time at all, he'd completed the task and had dictated to her what they meant. After writing it down, Tory set up a dinner date with him for that evening.

Tory handed Kendra the piece of paper. "Scott said the first part is from the Book of the Dead. A spell for resurrection, the Lotus Spell. The rest, he had no idea what it was for."

"It would have taken me days to figure that out on my own."

"Think nothing of it. Now, I'd better go home and start getting ready for my hot date tonight."

Shaking her head, Kendra walked Tory to the door. Scott was going to be well-reimbursed for his time. With one last wave as her friend backed out of her drive, she shut the door. All she had to look forward to was a long, boring evening plunked down on her couch, watching television.

CHAPTER TWO

The rest of the day passed very quickly for Kendra. After Tory had left, she decided to go to the gym. Weight training was a way of life for her. At least three times a week she made the time to work out. She was, by no means, muscle-bound, but she made sure she kept her body well-toned.

After an hour on the gym floor, Kendra had had enough and went for a shower. On the way home, she decided to do a bit of grocery shopping. She couldn't subsist completely on frozen dinners. Once she paid for the items in her cart, she returned to her empty house.

She put away the groceries, then remembered the paper Tory had written the translated hieroglyphs on. She had only briefly looked at it before leaving for the gym. After retrieving the paper and pendant, she sat on the couch in the living room where the library books still were. To see if she could have done the translation herself, Kendra flipped one open and compared the information in it with what Scott had come up with. Much to her chagrin, it took her ten minutes just to translate the first word. Whereas he had taken that same amount of time to translate the entire set of hieroglyphs. With a snort of disgust, she closed the book.

Kendra picked up the pendant in one hand and the piece of paper in the other and read the translation aloud.

"I am the holy Lotus that
Cometh forth from the light.
I am the pure Lotus that
Cometh forth from the field of Ra.
I herald her coming, the
Mighty one. All those who
Oppose her shall be smote down.
I am her one true warrior.
I do as she bids."

Okay. A little on the pretentious side, but as spells went it sounded pretty darn good. As for it actually creating some kind of magic, she doubted it would work. That is, if she were the type of person who believed in such things in the first place. She put the sheet of paper on top of the books and continued to hold the pendant.

It took her a few minutes to realize it radiated heat. By small degrees, it increased until Kendra feared the pendant might burn her hand. Instinctively, she tried to drop it, but found she was unable to do so. Her fingers wouldn't do what her brain commanded. Feeling some real fear, a trickle of cool sweat dripped down her back. Just what had she done?

A bright flash of light suddenly filled the room, practically blinding her. She threw up her arms to cover her face, trying to shield her eyes from the intense brightness. White spots danced before them. It took a few seconds of blinking to clear them so she could see properly again. What the hell had happened? Kendra knew of no light source in her house that could have caused it. Scanning the room to see what, if any damage there was, her gaze fell on something very disturbing. She was no longer alone.

A man stood in the middle of her living room. At least from the neck down she identified him as male, but his head was that of a large cat—a black leopard's to be exact. She must have made some small sound, because he turned to face her. That caused her to scoot back farther on the couch.

Now that Kendra had the front view of the man, her jaw dropped. He had the most delicious body. His shoulders were wide and thickly padded with muscle, which she could easily see since he wore nothing but a short kilt along with two menet necklaces. With all that male flesh bared for her to look at, she did that very thing.

The man had a killer bod, one a bodybuilder would have taken years to achieve. He was all muscle, right down to his six-pack abs. His legs were just as defined. She ran her gaze up his body, and for the first time, noticed the bow slung over his shoulder. The arrows for it, he carried on his back inside a quiver. She gulped.

She had no idea how long they stared at each other. By now, she realized his head wasn't a real cat's, but a full-head covering, a helmet of some kind, depicting a black leopard's. Through the eyeholes, Kendra saw his light gold eyes were outlined in black kohl. The thing was an exquisite work of art, all black enamel and what looked like real gold.

As he reached up to remove his head covering, Kendra flinched. He slowed his movement, as if he wished not to scare her any further. For the second time, Kendra's jaw dropped once he'd fully removed the leopard head. His face was a perfect match for his body. There wasn't one thing wrong with his hard, chiseled features, high cheekbones, fine straight nose, square chin, and full, seductive-looking lips. His black hair, he wore pulled back in a tail. It fell just past his shoulders in length.

He took a few steps closer, and Kendra's heart jumped into her throat. "Wait...wait, who are you? What do you want with me?"

Her words drew him up short. He cocked his head in her direction, almost as if he hadn't understood what she'd said.

"You don't speak English, do you?" Kendra shook her head and chuckled to herself. "Of course you don't. What a stupid question to ask. Obviously, you're somehow connected to the pendant so you probably only speak ancient Egyptian. Oh, look. I'm talking crazy."

"Yes, but I speak your English now." His deep baritone rumbled over her.

Kendra's gaze flew to his face. "You understand me? What do you mean you know English now?"

He smiled. "You ask many questions, but I'll try to explain how I come to speak your language. To put it simply, you spoke the words in your English to summon me, so I now know it as well."

Kendra left the couch and walked slowly around the coffee table until she stood before him. "Is that what I did? I summoned you?"

He narrowed his eyes. "You possess the pendant. You had to know why it was created or you wouldn't have spoken the words."

Kendra felt her face flush a deep red. "Ah...not exactly." He took a menacing step toward her, and she automatically backed up. Anger flashed in his golden eyes. "I'm sorry I summoned you, but honestly, I thought it wouldn't work."

"Well, as you can see, it did."

"Okay. Let me think here. Since there's a spell to summon you, there must be one to send you back to wherever you came from."

He shook his head. "There is not. What you have started cannot so simply be undone."

"So, you're stuck here then?"

"Yes, at least for the time being."

Kendra relaxed as his anger seemed to leave him. He walked around her living room, touching the television, the phone, her Blu-ray player. She figured it must be a lot to get used to, going to a time so much further in the future. At least she thought he was from another time.

Trying to distract him a bit, she asked, "What's your name? I'm Kendra Miller. Since we'll have to put up with each other until you leave, I should know what to call you." It wasn't as if she could kick him out of her house. The poor guy didn't seem able to cope with her world, and it was her fault he was there, after all.

He stopped the investigation of her lamps and looked at her. "I'm Nefertem." Kendra showed no sign of recognition at the mention of his name, and he sighed. "Where am I?"

"This is my house. I share it with my older brother, but he's away on a business trip right now."

"You are alone here?"

Kendra snorted at his shocked words. "You have a lot to learn, Nefertem." She liked his name. It was so ancient Egyptian, just like the man. "This is the twenty-first century, and lots of women live on their own."

"I will have to take your word for it. Can you tell me what city we are in?"

"I live in Memphis."

A look of hope appeared on Nefertem's face. "If we are indeed in Memphis, we must go to the Temple of Ptah, *Hut-ka-Ptah*."

Kendra cringed. Nefertem wouldn't know there were two cities by the name of Memphis. "We can't do that."

His eyes darkened with ire. "We have to. It is imperative I get to the temple. Once there, I might be able to circumvent the spell. It is the only way."

Sighing heavily, Kendra went to him. "It's not a

question of not wanting to take you there, but more like being unable to go. I don't live in Egypt. I live in Memphis, Tennessee, in the United States. Egypt is another continent altogether."

He closed his eyes, then opened them, staring at Kendra as if seeing her for the first time. Feeling a trifle uncomfortable being under Nefertem's close scrutiny, she swallowed hard. She wasn't used to a man of his caliber staring at her as if he would like to devour her in one gulp. She didn't dislike it. Just the opposite. She liked it all too much. Her nipples tightened, begging to be touched. Her pussy ached and grew wet as a mental picture of his hard cock pumping into her flashed through her mind. If he kept that up, she'd be offering to show him where her bed could be found, which wouldn't do at all. Once burnt, twice shy, as the saying went. Her trust level in men was at an extreme low. Ones like Nefertem didn't offer commitments to women who looked like her.

Kendra cleared her throat and broke his regard. Once she had his full attention, she spoke. "You said there's a purpose for you being here. What exactly would that be?"

"For now, all you need to know is since you were the one who summoned me, I now serve you. In whatever way you desire."

CHAPTER THREE

K endra felt her face flush in response to his words. Nefertem smiled. There was attraction between them. If she were to invite him into her bed, would he accept because she wished it? She was not that type of woman who would use a man in such a way, though.

Nefertem stepped closer. Barely a hand's breath of space separated them. He looked at her. "Anything you wish, I cannot refuse." He dropped his gaze to her lips, then said meaningfully, "Anything." He skimmed down to her breasts.

Her legs trembled, and she had a hard time organizing her thoughts with Nefertem standing near. He was so close she felt his body heat radiating from him. How he smelled did terrible things to her senses. His scent was of sandalwood and man, along with a hint of something floral, which didn't take away any of his masculinity. All she had to do was go on tiptoe, then she could press her lips to his. He was too tempting by far. Her fingers itched to feel his well-defined chest, to reach down and take his cock in her hand, to explore his hard length.

Needing more space between them, Kendra took a step

behind her only to have the back of her knees come up against the coffee table. Not expecting it, she started to fall backward. Nefertem quickly grabbed her by the upper arm. A spark seemed to jump between them where he touched her. She'd never felt the like before. He must have felt it as well. He quickly released his hold on her.

To distract Nefertem, as well as herself, from what had happened, Kendra walked to the bottom of the stairs. "We need to get you some clothes. I think some of Markus' should fit you." In for a penny, in for a pound and all that. If she was going to go with it, she might as well just go with it.

"What is wrong with my attire? It is perfectly respectable."

Kendra took in his pure white linen kilt and shook her head. "Not here it isn't. You'd stick out like a sore thumb if I let you walk outside dressed like that."

"The clothes you wear are acceptable?" He pointed to her cut-off jean shorts and gray racer-backed tank top.

"Yes, it is. Men and women dress in shorts and tanks during the summer." Seeing Nefertem's pained expression, Kendra asked, "What's wrong with my clothes?"

"They are so plain."

Feeling slightly insulted, she turned her back on him and headed up the stairs. He followed. "I don't dress like this when I go to work. So I do wear fancier clothes, but when I'm home, I want to be comfortable."

After reaching Markus' bedroom, Kendra went to his dresser and then pulled out clothes she figured would fit Nefertem. Her brother was over six foot, but Nefertem was three inches taller. There was also the added fact that Nefertem had a slightly bigger build than her brother. It was a good thing Markus liked to wear loose-fitting clothing or Nefertem would have a hard time squeezing himself into them.

Kendra placed the shorts and top into Nefertem's arms, and said, "These might be on the tight side, but they'll have to do for now. Tomorrow I'll take you clothes shopping."

Wanting to give him some privacy, she closed the bedroom door after she stepped into the hallway.

* * * *

Nefertem removed his bow and quiver from his back and then placed them on the bed. He held up the clothes Kendra had given him and skeptically eyed them. He would prefer to wear his kilt, but to fit in he would shed his native land's attire.

The kilt was easily removed, leaving him only in his loincloth. He picked up the shorts before he pulled them up his legs. There was no fastener of any kind that he could see. Some kind of material in the waistband that stretched seemed to be the only thing keeping them on his body. There was one slight problem with them. With the loincloth beneath them, he found it way too tight, especially while sporting an erection. Sighing, he pulled off the shorts and then removed his loincloth. The fit seemed less constricting, but they still did not feel comfortable. He had no idea whether he had donned the offending garment properly or not.

Sliding the shorts down his legs, Nefertem growled in frustration. It came out sounding like a large cat's snarl. His gaze shot to the closed bedroom door. He had forgotten himself. A mistake such as that could cost him dearly.

* * * *

Kendra impatiently tapped her foot while she waited outside the closed bedroom door for Nefertem to emerge.

He took a very long time to put on a pair of shorts and a tank top. Then again, she'd forgotten to show him which way the clothes went on. As she raised her hand to knock, she heard a cat-like growl coming from the other side. She quickly opened the door instead of knocking first. She gasped at what she saw.

The man was totally naked, except for his two menet necklaces draped around his neck. The noise completely forgotten, she closed her eyes and quickly turned her back to him, but she hadn't been quick enough. She'd still managed to see that Nefertem was a large man in every aspect of his person, and he was fully erect. He was too perfect for words, and if she didn't get herself back under control, she would try to ogle his naked body once more.

After clearing her throat, Kendra apologized for barging in on him. "I didn't mean to just walk in on you, Nefertem. I thought I heard a noise coming from the room."

"I heard nothing, but I am glad you came in. I need you to tell me how to put on these clothes."

"That was my mistake. Sorry. I should have told you before I left you alone."

Thinking he had covered himself, because the direction his voice came from implied he stood right in front of her, Kendra once more felt safe to open her eyes. She cracked them slightly open, let out a small squeak, and quickly clapped them shut once again.

"Why will you not open your eyes?"

"Oh, let me see, maybe because you don't have a stitch of clothes on."

"I did not think the sight of me unclothed would offend you. Nudity is nothing to my people. During the hot summer months, Egyptian children wear nothing, girls and boys alike. Could it be you find my body offensive in some way?"

"That's the furthest thing from the truth." Under her

breath, she added, "The problem is I like it too much."

"You may look, Kendra. It would please me if you did so."

She kept her eyes tightly shut. "Can you please cover yourself? Then I'll be happy to open my eyes."

"You may open them now."

Kendra cracked one open. Nefertem had done as she'd asked. He wore his loincloth. Now safe, she opened both eyes and looked at him. "Let me show you the proper way to put the clothes on, then you can meet me downstairs afterward."

Once she left him, and needing to distract herself from the mental picture of Nefertem standing totally butt naked, Kendra went to the kitchen and decided she'd cook a real meal for the two of them. Judging from the size of her guest, he'd need a lot to fill his belly.

Busy with her food preparations, Kendra didn't hear Nefertem enter the room until he said, "Well? Will I fit in now?"

She turned to look at him, and said, "Yes, you'll do nicely."

The shorts weren't too bad, but the tank top stretched tightly across his chest, leaving nothing to the imagination. The only item of his former attire he kept was his menet necklaces. His eyes were still outlined in black kohl, which to her screamed ancient Egyptian.

"I am glad you find me acceptable, even though these clothes are very constricting. Especially the shorts."

To emphasis his statement, Nefertem pulled at said garment, which had Kendra focusing on the one area of his body she had no business looking at. Quickly, she wrenched her gaze away.

"That, we'll remedy tomorrow when I take you to the mall and buy you some clothes in your size."

He nodded and walked to the stove. Nefertem smelled one of the pots sitting on it. He closed his eyes and inhaled deeply, appearing to savor the smell. His stomach growled loudly.

Kendra laughed. "We'll eat shortly. I hope you like pasta and sauce."

"I have never had this pasta and sauce before, but if it tastes as good as it smells, I will like it very much indeed."

"Then I'd better finish cooking it. You can sit at the table while you wait, if you want."

Nefertem went to the table in the center of the kitchen, pulled out one of the wooden chairs, and sat. He watched Kendra as she moved about. She soon placed a heaping plate of pasta in front of him, then took the seat across from him. He slowly copied her movements as she picked up her fork and began to eat. He cautiously put some pasta into his mouth and then chewed slowly. A smile spread across his face.

"I take it you like pasta and sauce, after all." Nefertem seemed to savor every bite like a man who hadn't had a good meal in a very long time.

"Oh yes, I do. It is very good."

"I made lots, so if you want more, just let me know."

They spent the rest of the meal in silence. Once their plates were empty, Kendra placed them into the dishwasher. Nefertem followed her around the kitchen, watching her clean up.

Kendra didn't know when Nefertem's interest switched to only her. Before she realized what he was doing, he'd gathered her into his arms and claimed her lips in a hot, searing kiss. She wrapped her arms around his neck, and he pulled her even harder against his chest and ground his cock into her hip.

The kiss seemed to last forever. Kendra couldn't get enough of Nefertem. The taste, the feel of his body held flush against her own, drove all common sense from her mind. She'd never been kissed like that, not even by her ex-fiancé. It was all-consuming. The sensation of his hard length pressed against her made her body weep with wetness, wanting that part of him pushing inside her. The feel of his tongue sweeping her lips, trying to gain entrance to her mouth, was enough to bring her to her senses with a start. She couldn't do this. She would only get hurt in the end, and she didn't think she could survive another heartbreak so soon after the Greg fiasco.

Kendra pushed on Nefertem's chest with all her might. Not expecting her to push him away, he staggered back a couple of steps. The expression he gave her was so feral in nature she found herself cautiously backing away.

He reached for her once again, but she held out her hands, keeping the small space between them. "No, Nefertem."

He growled deep in his throat. The same cat growl she'd heard earlier. She didn't know what scared her more—the animal-like snarl or his eyes. For a split second, they seemed to change. The pupils contracted to mere slits, just like a cat's, and then they were back to normal. She really wasn't sure whether what she'd seen was real or if she'd imagined it.

Her thoughts were all in a jumble. Kendra could only do what her brain screamed at her to do—she fled. Brushing past Nefertem before he could gather her into his embrace once more, she ran past him and then up the stairs two at a time to the upper level. At her bedroom, she quickly shut the door before she locked it behind her.

CHAPTER FOUR

Drawing in a deep breath, Nefertem savagely tamped down the urge to follow Kendra upstairs. He had to get himself back under control before he faced her once again.

He had scared her. He had seen the flicker of fear in her eyes as she had fled from him. He would somehow have to fix that, but for now, he would let her be.

His reaction while he had held her had surprised him. No other woman had brought that other side of him to the fore so quickly, and he had known quite a few. It usually was not until the time of his leaving that the more animalistic part of him took over. Kendra had unleashed a small part of that with her kiss. Nefertem found it slightly disturbing. What would happen if he were to actually make love to her? He did not want to think of the consequences.

Nefertem stepped into the living room and once more became intrigued with the objects to be found there. Spotting a slim, black rectangular-shaped object that had brightly colored buttons on its surface, he picked it up, wondering what it was for. Curiosity getting the better of him, he pushed on its surface.

* * * *

She lost count of how many times she'd paced the length of her bedroom. What had occurred downstairs, still bothered her. Kendra was pulled in two different directions at the same time. One part of her wanted to play it safe and keep her distance from Nefertem. The other rebellious side, wanted to throw caution to the wind and jump in feet first, not bothering to care who or what the man was. Just the memory of his kiss made her ache for his touch. She yearned for more.

Suddenly coming to a standstill, Kendra made a decision. She needed advice. Man advice. Who better to ask than Tory? She picked up the phone and then quickly dialed her best friend's number. It wasn't until the answering machine picked up did she remember Tory was on her date with Scott. She decided to leave a message, anyway.

After the beep sounded, Kendra asked Tory to give her a call the next day. Before she could explain any further, the sound of the television set at high volume interrupted her. With a curse, she hung up, ran out of the room, and down the stairs.

Kendra grabbed the television remote where it sat on the floor at Nefertem's feet once she arrived in the living room and then quickly brought the volume down to a normal level. She turned to face him.

"What the hell are you doing?"

He guiltily looked at her. "I just wanted to see what that did." He pointed to the remote.

"Well, I suggest next time you wait and ask how to use it first."

He nodded. "I would have, but I did not think you would answer my questions."

Kendra nibbled her bottom lip. "I'm sorry I ran from you. I'll admit it, you scared me a little."

"I promise it will not happen again. It was a momentary lapse of control."

Kendra didn't know whether to be insulted or relieved. "I think we should just start over. Forget it ever happened."

"I agree."

An uncomfortable silence stretched between them. Kendra was the first to break the tension.

"Since you did find out about the television, I should at least show you how it works."

Kendra sat on the couch and patted the spot next to her. Nefertem seat himself where she'd indicated. He kept enough space between them so they didn't touch.

The next few hours, Nefertem became totally mesmerized by the programs on the television. He found it hard to believe there were actors performing their trade and not real life. When a reality show came on, he'd found it all too confusing. Once she yawned largely and suggested they call it a night, he seemed more than happy to comply.

Kendra led Nefertem to the spare bedroom. She wasn't sure if it was such a good idea since it was right next to her own, but her brother wouldn't be too pleased if she allowed Nefertem full use of his room. With that in mind, she had Nefertem retrieve his things from Markus' along the way.

Before leaving him for the night, Kendra showed Nefertem where the main bathroom was and how the toilet worked, which she found extremely embarrassing. In the end, he understood, saving her from having to be too descriptive.

Lying in bed, Kendra waited for the sounds of Nefertem settling down for the night to cease before she closed her eyes and allowed sleep to claim her. She was exhausted. It'd been a very eventful day, and tomorrow would more than likely turn out to be more of the same.

* * * *

Kendra came awake to her doorbell ringing repeatedly. Groaning, she rolled over and looked at her alarm clock. It was nine in the morning. She only took enough time to pull on her housecoat before she went to answer the door.

She pulled it open and was surprised to find Tory standing on her porch, frantically ringing her doorbell. Judging from the way she was dressed, Tory had yet to make it home from her date the night before.

"Why on earth are you ringing my bell at such an early hour? On a Sunday morning, I might add."

Tory threw her arms around Kendra with enough force to push them into the entrance hallway. "Thank god you're all right."

"Of course I am. Why wouldn't I be?"

"The message you left on my machine. You scared the crap out of me."

At first, Kendra didn't know what Tory was talking about. Then it all came rushing back. The pendant, Nefertem's sudden appearance, and her call to Tory after the episode with him in the kitchen.

"I didn't mean to frighten you."

"Well, you did. After I came home this morning and heard your message, I had to rush over here."

Smiling, Kendra pushed her front door shut. "So, you never made it home last night, huh? Your date with Scott must have gone well."

Getting no response from Tory, Kendra turned, thinking to needle her friend some more. She realized Tory was frozen to the spot, staring at something behind her. Kendra turned in that direction. They were no longer alone. Nefertem was on the bottom step of the stairs, silently watching them. Not exactly how she'd pictured introducing her best friend to him, but there was nothing for it.

Kendra linked her arm through Tory's and led her to the man on the stairs. "Tory Connor, meet Nefertem. Nefertem, this is my friend, Tory."

With a nod, Nefertem said, "I welcome Kendra's friend."

Tory's gaze shot to Kendra's face at the sound of Nefertem's heavily accented speech. "Don't tell me he's Egyptian. That would just be way too coincidental."

"Sorry to say, but he is."

"Where did you find an Egyptian?"

"I think you'd better sit down. We have to talk, and what I'm about to say, you might well find unbelievable. I'd be very surprised if you don't call me crazy when I'm through."

* * * *

"Have you gone completely mad?"

"I told you it was pretty unbelievable."

"Oh, this goes way beyond unbelievable, Kendra. Now, let me get this straight. Last evening you said those words Scott translated, and poof, he," Tory pointed to Nefertem, who casually leaned against the wall, "showed up."

"Basically, in a word, yes."

"So, now what? Are you stuck with him?" Tory paused, her gaze sweeping up and down Nefertem. "Then again, that wouldn't be much of a hardship, now would it? The man is hot."

"Tory!"

"What? He could make a fortune with that face."

Having silently watched them as they'd talked, Nefertem interrupted their conversation. "I think I can answer your questions better than Kendra."

Tory came to stand before him. "Okay, I'll take you up on that offer. How long will you be staying?"

"I am not sure. Certain conditions have to be met first, but I have at least a few weeks."

That was the first Kendra had heard Nefertem speak of his eventual departure. "Where is it that you go when you leave here?" she asked.

"A place no living mortal can."

That really didn't explain a whole lot, but Nefertem didn't elaborate any further. Kendra had the feeling there was a lot he wasn't saying, but oddly enough, the more mysterious she found him, the more she was drawn to him. Even now she couldn't tear her gaze from him. His smoldering stare caused her to think he was just as affected as she.

Tory loudly cleared her throat, then said, "I think I'll go home. I hate being the third wheel."

Kendra gave herself a mental shake and brought herself back to reality. "Let me walk you to the door."

Once they reached it and was out of sight of Nefertem, Tory leaned in and spoke quietly. "Are you okay with this?"

"I'm fine."

"You have to admit this isn't normal in any sense of the word."

"You aren't kidding, but I find myself trusting Nefertem. Don't ask me why."

Tory snorted. "Is that another name for lust? Trust?"

Kendra shook her in head in derision. "No, that's not what I meant." At Tory's scowl, she felt herself blush. "All right, I'll admit I'm a little attracted to him."

"That's putting it mildly. All I want from you is to promise you'll be careful. I don't want to see you get hurt at the end of this."

After giving Tory a quick hug, Kendra opened the front door. "I promise. Now go home, and I'll call you later."

"Make sure you do or I'll be here again, banging on your door."

CHAPTER FIVE

After Tory left, Kendra went upstairs for a shower. Nefertem closely followed.

"I like your friend. She has a way about her."

"That's an understatement." Kendra laughed.

"She is very protective of you."

"Yeah, well, she's like the sister I never had."

Having followed Kendra right into her bathroom, Nefertem watched as she brushed her teeth. "Will I get to see more of your world today?"

Kendra rinsed her mouth and nodded. "Yes. First thing on the agenda is to get you clothes that fit. So a trip to the mall is in order."

"I look forward to it."

What Nefertem actually looked forward to was spending the day with Kendra. After retiring the night before, he had spent a great deal of it thinking about her. His body did not require hours of sleep, giving him plenty of time to replay in his mind the kiss they had shared.

The sound of water running snagged his attention. Seeing the rushing waterfall coming out of the wall caused him to gasp and then step closer. He stuck his hand under the stream of water. He found it surprisingly warm.

*

Kendra knew the ancient Egyptians were very conscientious of their person, with a high standard of cleanliness being foremost on their minds. Nefertem would be in for a treat, but she wanted to shower first.

"We call this a shower. You can wash your hair and body in it."

Before she could explain further, Nefertem quickly removed his shorts, the only article of clothing he'd been wearing. Unable to speak, let alone form a coherent thought, Kendra did nothing to stop him as he slid open the other glass shower door and then stepped into the bathtub. He'd given her an eyeful—again. She really had to convince him not to strip naked whenever he wanted to. Especially when he was around her. He would turn her into a blithering idiot if he did it too often.

She regained her composure, and said, "Hey, I started that for me. I thought you could shower after I was finished."

Nefertem slid open the shower door once more. "You may join me if you wish."

He'd done it again. All that bared male flesh blatantly displayed for all to see. She was unable to look away. Water droplets glistened on the hard planes of his chest. One large one slowly ran down it. She followed its descent. Her breath caught as her gaze reached that part of him that set her blood to boiling. It increased in size, growing in length before her eyes. Kendra gasped and looked up at Nefertem.

He smiled seductively. "Join me. We could share the water, along with other pleasures."

Her heart beat at a gallop. Why did he have to look so sinfully good? Kendra licked her dry lips. All the things she could to do to Nefertem rose in her mind. She wanted to lick every inch of his hard body, ending with his cock. She wanted to hear him groaning with pleasure as she took him into her mouth. She fought the urge to take him up on his offer. If she did, she would regret it later. The small, wounded part of her was just not ready to take such a leap of faith.

Kendra collected the shampoo and conditioner bottles from the counter, then shoved them into Nefertem's hands. "Use these to wash your hair." She picked up the bar of soap and handed it to him as well. "This is soap to wash with."

Nefertem juggled the containers and the bar of soap, and Kendra beat a hasty retreat.

* * * *

He was in hell. Whoever had devised this mode of transportation must have been an expert in torture. Nefertem had never been subjected to such a hot, confined space before. He peered at Kendra from the corner of his eye and noticed she showed no sign of the distress he felt. He reasoned part of that could have been from her having ridden in a car many times, and this was only his first journey in one.

"Here we are. Hopefully, the trip wasn't too excruciating for you, Nefertem."

They had reached what Kendra had called a mall. She had brought the car to a stop, turned it off, and they climbed out of it.

He arched a cynical brow. "I do not know how you can ride in that car every day."

"If I made more money, I could afford to buy a larger one with air conditioning, but I don't."

Nefertem followed Kendra when she walked toward the entrance of the mall. "How do you make this money?"

"Ah...well, I don't physically make the money. I work for it. Earn it."

"Does everyone work for it?"

"Most people do. To be honest, the world revolves around it. The more you have, the better your life is."

Money must be cherished, Nefertem thought, almost as if it were revered on some level. Much like the ancient Egyptians had worshipped the gods.

Kendra took a deep breath before she pulled open the heavy glass door. He felt it even before they had completely passed through the entrance. It crashed over him in waves. He had never experienced its like before. The sheer number of mortals in one place was an assault to his senses. The scent of them, the smell of mortal blood, tried to overwhelm him. He ruthlessly fought it back.

Totally oblivious to Nefertem's distress, Kendra grabbed his hand and led him through the mall. The feel of her touching him was the only thing keeping his other part under leash. He had never seen so many mortals together in one place, and he knew this was only a small percentage of the population. What the actual numbers must be, staggered him.

As someone brushed past him, Nefertem had to tightly clench his jaw to keep from growling. He needed to be free of that place, and very soon. "Have we much farther to go before we reach the place you are leading me to?"

Kendra turned her head and looked at Nefertem. "The store is just around this corner." Picking up their pace, she quickly walked around the bend and then entered the store.

It was a tiny measure of relief. The pull was not so strong inside the smaller space. There weren't as many people as there had been in the main part of the mall.

Kendra grabbed what she called shorts, tops, underwear, and socks. Appearing satisfied with all she had found, she took him to the changing rooms.

"Just let me know if something doesn't fit and I'll get another size."

Nefertem quietly shut the changing room door behind him. Safely behind it, he relaxed some of the tight hold he had placed on himself. He looked into the only mirror. His eyes had changed. The pupils were narrow and slit-looking. He clamped down on that part of him, which caused them to return to normal.

To his surprise, all the clothes Kendra had picked fit. After she knocked on the door and asked if everything was okay, he checked his eyes in the mirror before he left the changing room. They were still normal.

"How is the fit?"

"Fine. Can we leave now?"

"Not quite yet. We have to go to one more store to get you some shoes and sandals."

"What is wrong with my sandals?" Nefertem asked.

"Nothing really, except they aren't modern. I promise it won't take very long. Just this one last store and then we can leave."

Kendra did not give him much chance to change her mind. After lightly brushing past him, she collected the clothes from the changing room and then headed to the front of the store. Once she had paid for their purchases, she led him into the mall.

His self-control weakened. It was not a question of if he could control his urges any more. It was a question of when it would shatter completely. He had to leave the mall. Now. Pulling Kendra out of the crowd, Nefertem stopped their travel.

"Kendra, I must leave."

"I know there were no malls in your time, and the crush of people is disturbing to you, but we're almost done."

"No. You do not understand."

The hint of a growl at the end of Nefertem's words made Kendra look at his face. She let out a startled gasp.

Acting quickly, she pulled something from her purse and then placed them on him. It had blackish circles that were dark enough to conceal his eyes.

She took his hand in hers once more and quickly led him to the nearest exit. All the tension left Nefertem's body once they stepped outside into the bright sunlight. She released him. Before he could speak, Kendra walked away, heading in the direction where she had parked her car. Wisely, he silently followed.

CHAPTER SIX

The drive home was just as hellish as the trip to the mall. The only difference was Kendra appeared to mad about something. Why, he did not know. After reaching her house, she collected all the shopping bags from the backseat of her car and then stomped to the front door. She refused to meet Nefertem's gaze as she had walked past him.

Kendra was angry, but he had not realized how very upset she was until she slammed the front door in his face. He tried the doorknob and was happy to find she had at least kept it unlocked. Nefertem stepped inside before gently shutting himself inside. She pounded up the stairs. He pulled the dark lens off, then placed them on the small hall table.

He went into the living room and waited for Kendra to come back downstairs. He would have to do some explaining, but not all. There was a limit to what he could tell her. If she knew the whole truth—he shuddered just thinking about it. For the first time in his long life, he was beginning to care about a mortal, something he had thought would never happen. She was like no other mortal woman he had come across. Others he had used for his pleasure, never caring what they thought of him. Mortals were too far beneath his kind for them to be anything but a means to an end. She did not engender that way of thinking in him. He had feelings for her. Deep ones.

Kendra came downstairs a few minutes later. She glared at him as she walked by the living room. She did not stop, but went directly to the kitchen. Nefertem heard her loudly clang a pot down onto the stovetop. Taking a deep breath, he decided she had stewed long enough. If she was not going to come to him, he would go to her.

Nefertem leaned against the doorframe. Kendra stomped about the kitchen. She muttered angrily under her breath. She was a sight to behold. Her cheeks were stained a lovely shade of pink and her eyes flashed with anger. She seemed more alive, more beautiful. He let a small smile play across his lips, but quickly let it disappear when she looked his way.

"You cannot ignore me forever, Kendra. I realize I have upset you, but we have to talk about it."

"You think?"

"Yes, I think, that is why I said it. Now, tell me why you are so angry at me."

"How typically male. Why is it your sex can never figure out on your own why a woman is mad at you? We must always tell you. Fine. It's your eyes. You should have told me they could change like that."

"I am sorry I did not. I was not sure what your reaction would be."

"Now you know."

"I thought you would react differently. Much differently."

"Like run screaming from you?"

Nefertem nodded. "That is some peoples' reaction." He left out the part about the others having a very good reason to run from him.

"I might have, if it was someone other than you. It just makes me mad that you felt as if you couldn't confide in me."

Nefertem went to stand before Kendra. "I do trust you." He gently ran a finger down her cheek. She shuddered at his touch.

*

Sucking in a breath, Kendra tried to still her rapidly beating heart. "Then tell me, Nefertem. Why did your eyes change while we were at the mall? They didn't here, except for that one time."

He dropped his hand to his side. "There is a reason my helmet is the head of a large cat. It is a part of me. I can control it most of the time, but being in certain situations weakens it. The first sign of the cat taking over is the changing of my eyes."

"So something in the mall caused your control to slip. What was it?"

Nefertem took a few seconds before he answered. "The people. Being around too many at one time caused it."

"The time here?"

He stepped even closer so their bodies just about touched. Kendra was forced to look up at him. "You did."

"You're near me now and your eyes haven't changed." Her mouth went suddenly dry.

"It is because you are not kissing me. I find you very attractive, Kendra."

She gulped. "Does it happen with every woman who attracts your interest?"

Nefertem shook his head. "No, it is only with you. You stir that part of me like no other."

Kendra's knees went weak. No man had ever told her he found her so attractive he lost his control. "So if we kissed, it would happen again?"

"It might, but I think it was a combination of me wanting you, and you refusing me."

He'd brought his arms up and wrapped them around her waist as he'd spoken. Kendra put her hands on Nefertem's hard chest to keep some distance between them. "Then you'd better let me go. I'll admit I find you attractive as well, but I'm just not ready. I've been hurt by a man before. Not so long ago, in fact, and the pain is still there. I don't think I could survive it if you hurt me like that."

Nefertem released her. "Now it is your turn to confide in me, as I did you. What did this man do to you?"

She needed to sit down. Kendra went to the kitchen table, pulled out one of the chairs, and sat. She waited for Nefertem to join her before she spoke again. "I was engaged not that long ago. If things had worked out, I would be married right now, but Greg changed his mind two days before the ceremony."

Nefertem reached across the table and placed one of his large hands atop Kendra's, which she held tightly clenched. "Why would he do such a thing? Any man would feel honored to have you as his wife."

"The lures of another woman made Greg call it off. Apparently, she had all the attributes he found attractive, which I didn't have. Small, blonde, hourglass figure, and not opinionated."

All the hurt rose inside her. She really had thought Greg was the one. He'd been the first man to lavish attention on her. Boy, had she been duped. He'd turned out to be a consummate liar. The words of love he'd spoken had been false. He'd never really loved her. He'd only asked her to marry him because nothing better had come along. That was until he'd met the blonde bimbo.

"Greg didn't even have the decency to tell me in person. He broke up with me over the phone."

"That is the object you talk into?"

"Yes. He wasn't expecting me to be home, and had planned to leave a message on my answering machine. He didn't even respect me enough to break up with me face-to-face."

Hot tears ran down her cheeks. All the pain and anger she felt and had held inside came bubbling out. She told all of it to Nefertem. The things she hadn't been able to say to Markus or Tory. This almost stranger made her feel safe enough to let her guard down, to exscind her grief. At the end, she somehow found herself in his arms.

Kendra felt a change come over Nefertem as he held her. She knew what he was fighting, but now that he'd allowed her to release all the feelings she'd bottled up inside, she couldn't just walk away. Knowing full well she played with fire, she placed her hand on his chest. His muscles jumped beneath her splayed fingers.

"You would be wise to leave me alone, Kendra."

"I'm not always a wise woman."

He growled. "If you do not walk away now, I might not be able to stop later."

"I don't want you to stop." To make him see she was serious, Kendra wrapped her arms around his waist. She laid her head on his wide chest. "Tory was right. I've been using my fear of getting hurt again as a means to push men away. If I do that, then Greg has won. I won't let him have the chance to think I mourn the loss of him. He isn't worth it."

Nefertem gave her the full force of what he'd become. He held her tighter, and with a finger under her chin, forced her to look at him. He slightly opened his mouth, allowing her to glimpse how pointed his eyeteeth now were.

Kendra felt no fear at what he showed her. He tried to use the changes in him to push her away, but she didn't want to leave him. Even though there was no guarantee they could ever form a permanent relationship, she couldn't give up what little time they did have.

She reached up and placed her hand on his cheek. "I'm not running way this time, Nefertem."

Nefertem closed his eyes for a few seconds and took a deep breath. "You know not what you are dealing with. You do not know what I am."

"Then tell me. Whatever you have to say won't change how I feel."

"You are wrong. It would."

"Tell me."

"No. Not yet." He lowered his lips to hers, then said, "Once you accept me, there will be no going back. You will be mine for as long as I am here. No regrets."

"No regrets," Kendra breathlessly whispered.

With a groan, Nefertem claimed Kendra's lips in a searing kiss. Their passion burst into a burning flame of need. He scooped her up into his arms, took the stairs two at a time, and carried her to her bedroom.

He placed her on the center of the bed and then roughly pulled off his tank top before he joined her. He once again claimed her lips. Kendra moaned in response.

The feel of Nefertem touching her in that way was more delicious than Kendra had imagined. He made her feel things she'd only thought existed in one of the many romance novels she read. He proved her wrong.

Kendra grabbed a fistful of his hair and increased the pressure of her lips. She wanted more. Nefertem seemed to know what she needed. In swift succession, he stripped her of her clothing, and his quickly followed suit.

*

As their bared skin met fully for the first time, Nefertem had some serious doubts that this might not have been the best idea. The cat now had full rein of him. Afraid of what he could do to Kendra, he tried to pull away. She did not let him. She tightly wrapped her arms around his waist, and he was lost.

Though the cat had possession of him, Nefertem still kept his awareness, knowing everything he did while under its influence, and everything it did, but this was the first time it had possessed him as he made love to a woman. While he kissed and stroked Kendra to a fevered pitch, he felt no malice from the cat toward her. It wanted to take her, claim her as its mate.

Growling with need, Nefertem left the sweetness of Kendra's mouth and made a trail of hot, wet kisses to her neck. At the spot where her blood pounded, he bit, then licked that sensitive area, making her gasp. He moved lower, inching down her body until he was level with her breasts. He laved first one, then the other with his tongue as her nipples tightened into peaks. He took one into his mouth and grazed the sensitive bud with his sharp eyeteeth. She threaded her hands through his hair, holding him to her.

Kendra moaned once Nefertem released her breast, trailing his lips to her flat stomach. He swirled his tongue into her bellybutton. Then lower he went. At the first touch of him laving her slick opening, her hips arched off the mattress. He put his hand on her hip and pushed her back down. He settled between her legs and nudged them wider apart. She clutched the sheets as he gently nipped her inner thigh with his sharp teeth. She tried to arch her hips into him once again, but he held her in place. Slowly, he nipped his way back up to her pussy. He spread her nether lips. He pushed his tongue into her hot core as she panted.

Kendra grabbed a fistful of his hair and yanked him up to her lips. She sucked on his tongue, kissing him passionately. Gently, she skimmed her fingers across his chest. Going lower, she reached for his cock. She wrapped her fingers around it and stroked up and down. Nefertem growled low in his throat. At the head, she found a drop of wetness. She gently rubbed it into his skin. She released him and shifted so the tip nestled against her pussy. She put her leg around his hip and rubbed back and forth on his shaft, coating it with her wetness.

Unable to hold off any longer, Nefertem took hold of Kendra's leg and slowly slid into her hot, wet core. He moaned as her body stretched to welcome his. He sheathed himself to the hilt, and the cat inside him growled in triumph. It had found its one true mate, and it intended to never let her go.

Nefertem slid in and out of her body. He took her in hard strokes, which pushed his arousal higher. He could not tell where his body ended and hers began. Once the pleasure reached its crescendo, Kendra shut her eyes. She dropped over the precipice and held on to him, moaning as her climax hit her.

Kendra's body spasmodically clenched around him, milking him, and Nefertem's release quickly followed. He threw back his head and growled as he climaxed. Once the last wave of pleasure subsided, he collapsed on top of her, totally spent. Heedful of his much greater weight, he rolled to his back, pulling her against his side. Slowly, his breathing returned to normal, and the cat receded. For once, after making love, he was completely sated. Along with that came the feeling of wholeness. The woman he held did that for him. She completed him. He only wished he could keep her as his.

CHAPTER SEVEN

S till held in Nefertem's embrace, Kendra peered at his face and smiled. "I think you've spoiled me for other men. That was amazing."

A slight smile graced his lips. "A statement like that could very well cause me to become a conceited man."

"You can't tell me another woman has never said those very words to you before," Kendra said in all seriousness.

"No. You're the first."

She propped herself up on her elbow. He was serious. She *had* been the first. "I don't know what kind of women you've known if they haven't thought that."

He really didn't know what to say to Kendra. Telling her he'd never cared if a woman enjoyed his lovemaking, or that he'd never made love using all of himself until her, was not an option. The others were just conquests. He wasn't even sure if any of them had actually wanted to sleep with him. The fear of what he was made them accept his advances. The awful truth was he'd reveled in that emotion. With Kendra, the opposite was true. He never wanted to see that in her eyes caused by him.

Kendra brushed a feather-light kiss across his lips. "You

don't have to answer. I meant it as a compliment. That's why I brought it up in the first place." She kissed him again. "Your eyes have changed. Again?"

"Again." He growled.

She smiled as his cock stirred against her hip. "Who am I to deny you? I'd only be denying myself." She moved so she lay on top of him and passionately kissed Nefertem.

Kendra took hold of Nefertem's wrists and pinned them to the mattress. He could easily break her hold, but he made no move to do so. He looked at her with intense longing. She sucked in a breath.

She ground her pussy on his fully engorged cock. She moaned. Still wet from their earlier joining, he slid into her all the way to the hilt. Kendra arched her hips and moved until he was almost out of her, then pushed down on the hard length of him. She kept up the rhythm until their bodies were slick with sweat and release clawed at him. As her climax surged through her, Nefertem followed her, pumping his seed into her. She released his hands and collapsed onto his chest. She kissed his chin as he wrapped his arms around her, holding her close.

They made love for the rest of the day and most of the night. The one time they came up for air, it was to raid the fridge sometime during the dark hours. What started as feeding tidbits of food to one another, soon turned into another round of lovemaking on top of the kitchen table. Kendra told him she'd never be able to look at it again without remembering.

* * * *

Early the next morning light shone brightly through the half-opened curtains of her room. Kendra stretched, making her aware of the numerous sore muscles she'd acquired during the night. Lazily turning her head to look at her bedside clock, she jumped out of bed, swearing a blue streak. She only had forty-five minutes to dress and get to work.

Nefertem, who'd been soundly asleep next to Kendra, rolled out from under the sheets and surged to his feet. He appeared to search the room for the cause of her agitation. She ignored him and rushed to the bedroom's en suite.

He entered the bathroom while Kendra madly tried to brush her teeth and hair at the same time. "What is the matter? Why the rush?"

After rinsing her mouth, Kendra roughly finished dragging the brush through her long hair. "I'm going to be late for work. I forgot to set my alarm clock last night." She pushed Nefertem out of her way, then hurriedly went to her closet.

"What is this work you speak of?"

"I work as a receptionist at an art gallery. It isn't much of a job, but it pays the bills."

"Must you do this work today? I rather you were back in the bed. With me."

Kendra bit back a moan. Even after all the times they had made love during the night, her body still melted at his words. He turned her into a wanton.

"I really wish I could, but my boss isn't a very understanding man. There really isn't anyone to cover for me if I was to call in sick."

He came up behind Kendra, brushed her hair aside, and kissed the back of her neck. "Stay with me. We could do more enjoyable things together than this work you feel you have to do."

She turned and shoved Nefertem away. She placed the skirt and blouse she had picked from her closet onto the bed before going to the dresser. "I'm sure we could, but the answer is still no."

Nefertem sighed. "All right, you win. How long will you be gone?"

Having donned a bra and panties, Kendra struggled to

put on her pantyhose. "All day. I work until five, so I'll be home shortly after that."

"What am I supposed to do when you are gone?"

Finally finished dressing, Kendra quickly gave Nefertem a kiss goodbye. "Watch television, sleep, whatever you want. Just don't leave the house under any circumstances. Promise me?"

Nefertem shook his head and smiled. "I promise."

"Good. I have to run." With that said, Kendra rushed down the stairs and then out the front door.

* * * *

Nefertem did go back to bed for a few hours until his growling stomach woke him up, demanding food. Unable to ignore it, he decided to shower first, then eat.

The warm water streamed over his body. He had to praise the person who had invented the shower. He definitely could get used to that, warm water at a turn of a dial.

After finding something to eat in the kitchen, he did as Kendra suggested and turned on the television. He found there were different shows on to watch during the day from those at the night. He watched one called the local news. What he saw disturbed him. This world held a lot of pain, which made his circumstance worse. What was to come lived for pain and suffering, punishing all for the few miscreants who committed the worst of sins.

Eventually, he had to change the channel. The more he watched, the more the other part of him found delight in all the pain the mortals went through. The next one took him a few minutes to get the storyline straight. It kept jumping back and forth from one couple's life to another, following the same line. The couples were either making love, fighting with one another, or having to fend off an outsider who wanted to separate them. Nefertem found it entertaining on the simplest of levels.

He spent the remainder of the morning watching one show after another. The only good thing about television was it kept his mind off Kendra's absence. When he did lose interest in what played before him on the screen, she dominated his thoughts.

It was just about two hours before Kendra was expected home when a bell rang. At first, Nefertem did not know what had caused the ringing sound. The bell rang a second time, and he followed the noise to its origins. It had come from the small white box on the wall by the front door. Only then did he notice the two people standing on the other side through the small window next to the entrance. A woman impatiently paced in front of it.

Slowly, he opened the door. Kendra had made him promise not to leave the house, but she had not said what to do if someone came there. Once the door was fully open, the woman walked past him into the house, leaving her companion, a man, to follow.

Nefertem closed it behind them. He recognized the woman. It was Kendra's friend, Tory. "Kendra is not home yet."

"I know. I didn't come to see Kendra. I came to see you," Tory said.

Nefertem had a feeling he knew why Tory was there. Their first meeting had shown him how protective she was of Kendra. Tory wanted to make sure he had not hurt her friend. "I am not sure Kendra would appreciate you coming here to talk to me when she is not home."

"I'm not worried about that. She'll get over it. I'm more concerned about what your intentions are."

Shooting a quick glance toward the man who had accompanied Tory, Nefertem asked, "Did you bring reinforcements in case I would not cooperate?"

Tory rolled her eyes. "No. I don't need any help doing that."

The man chuckled. "Tory does have her ways." He held out his hand. Nefertem did nothing, and the man cleared his throat and dropped his arm to his side. "My name is Scott Burrows. I'm a good friend of Tory."

Nefertem did not miss the possessive way Scott had called Tory a good friend. The man tried to tell him Tory was his. Nefertem looked the other man up and down. Scott stood just under six foot. He had shaggy, dirty blond hair that he obviously did not spend much time worrying how it looked. His dark brown eyes showed intelligence. Looking back at Tory, Nefertem motioned for her to go into the living room.

Once the three of them were seated, Tory turned to look at Nefertem. "I won't let you mess with Kendra's mind."

"I do not understand."

Tory shook her head. "Sorry, I keep forgetting you're Egyptian. I mean, don't make Kendra fall for you. Not unless you intend to stay."

"You know that is not possible."

"Then leave now. Today, while she's at work. Go back to where you came from."

From the corner of his eye, Nefertem watched Scott get up and walk across the room to take a closer look at something. "I cannot do that either."

"Damn it, Nefertem."

The sound of something heavy falling on the carpeted floor drew their gaze to where Scott stood. He looked a trifle pale. His gaze was locked on the object now lying at his feet. "What did you just call him?"

Seeing what it was that Scott had dropped, Nefertem went to retrieve it. The other man had found his helmet. It had somehow been overlooked when his belongings were taken upstairs. Having been set on a small side table in the corner of the room probably was the reason.

Helmet in hand, he answered Scott's question himself. "My name is Nefertem."

Excitedly, the other man pointed at the helmet. "That's real, isn't it?"

"Of course it is. Why would it not be?"

"No, I mean it really is an ancient Egyptian piece."

Tory groaned. "Kendra is really going to kill me now."

"You knew about the helmet?"

"Not exactly, Scott." Tory turned her attention to Nefertem. "Nefertem, by trade, Scott is an Egyptologist. Simply put, he's made it his life's work to study everything to do with ancient Egypt." After taking a deep breath, she added, "He's the one who translated the hieroglyphs."

Nefertem's hard gaze shot to Scott's face. "You were the one? For someone who is so learned, you should have known what those words meant."

"Why don't you tell me what they mean? I recognized the first part from the Book of the Dead, but the last I've never come across."

His challenge was met with silence. Nefertem stood stone-faced, not willing to elaborate on his words. He tightened his grip on his helmet. The faraway look that came over Scott's face heralded trouble. He had seen the intelligence in the other man's eyes before, but now he saw to what extent. He had a feeling it would only be a matter of time before Scott figured out who he was, especially since he was an expert on Egypt of old. Nefertem would be very surprised if the other man did not come up with the answer.

He was soon proven correct. Scott's face went pale as he looked Nefertem up and down. His mouth kept opening and closing, as if he could not get words past his lips. Nefertem stood ready for the axe to fall.

Scott finally stammered, "Y-You can't be real. They're just myths." Slipping into Egyptian, he distractedly recited a part of the Story of Re.

Swiftly, Nefertem grabbed Scott by the throat,

effectively silencing him. "Do not speak her name to me." By the look of fear in Scott's eyes, he knew his words had come out all too cat-like. He released the other man and took a step away. Tory came around him to stand supportively at Scott's side.

"What the hell is the matter with you, Nefertem?" Tory snapped.

Scott found his voice once more and stopped Tory before she could say anything more. "No, Tory. He's right. I shouldn't have said what I did."

"You might find that acceptable, but I don't. I have no idea what you said, and it doesn't matter. He still had no right to grab you like that. What the hell is with the damn cat growling?"

Scott looked at Nefertem for a second before he answered. "Nefertem is an ancient Egyptian god."

Tory burst out laughing. "You can't be serious?" Neither Scott or Nefertem so much as cracked a smile, and her laughter died away. "You're serious."

"I'm dead serious." Gently moving Tory so she stood in front of him, Scott said, "This is Nefertem. He's a member of the holy triad of Memphis. His father is the god Ptah, the creator-god of Memphis. His mother is the lioness-headed goddess of war and destruction, Sekhmet."

Nefertem growled a warning. "I told you not to speak her name before me."

Tory gawked at Nefertem. "Your mother sounds like a real bitch when she wants to be."

"I do not joke about my mother."

"Sorry, I didn't mean to insult you. I'm just finding it hard to get my brain around you being a god."

Scott squeezed Tory's shoulder and interjected, "Even with the knowledge I have about Nefertem, I can't believe it either. That he's real. I get the feeling there's more about him that I don't know." He turned her so she faced him. "I do know you're involved in some way with bringing

Nefertem here, so spill the beans."

"Kendra didn't want you to know about this, and right now, I think I've made a terrible mistake in bringing you here."

"Well, it's a little too late for having such doubts."

"I know, I know, but I'd promised Kendra not to tell you about the pendant."

"What pendant?"

Tory groaned, then said sheepishly, "The pendant that had the hieroglyphs on it."

Nefertem let out a cat growl, drawing Tory's and Scott's attention. He growled once more. "How is it he translated the glyphs if he knows nothing of the pendant?"

Cringing, Tory confessed. "I described what they looked like to Scott over the phone, and he told me what they meant."

Nefertem shook his head. "Fools. You have no idea what you have started. I herald the coming of another. One who will pass judgment on all mortals and mete out punishment. At the hands of my mother."

CHAPTER EIGHT

Kendra pulled into her driveway, glad to have the day almost over. She felt as if a truck had run over her, more than once. Her boss hadn't made her day any easier for her.

Having him impatiently standing at her desk, waiting for her to arrive, hadn't boded well for her day. Being five minutes late hadn't helped either. That was one thing Stan Wilson didn't tolerate from his employees. Lateness.

After pointing out the time of her arrival, he spouted off the huge list of things he needed her to do that day. With important clients coming to the gallery, he wanted her to arrange a catered lunch for them, and he wanted it done now.

The rest of the day pretty much went downhill from there. Grumpy customers, uptight artists, and clients in the gallery to impress, Kendra's nerves stretched to the breaking point. Lack of sleep amplified the feeling.

Once she could finally leave at the end of the day, she had a massive headache. All she wanted to do was get home and see Nefertem. What they'd done the night before kept replaying in her mind. Sex had never been that good for her in the past. With men in other relationships, she'd never felt such an all-consuming need. Not even with her ex-fiancé. Now that she was home at last, she couldn't wait to be in Nefertem's arms again. She already felt addicted to his touch.

Much to her surprise, and dismay, Kendra found company had arrived. Tory had come to visit and had brought a friend, someone who should have been the least likely person to be in her living room. If her assumptions were correct, the man could only be Scott, Tory's date from the other night. A shiver of unease ran down her back. What the hell could Tory have been thinking, bringing him there?

The three people hadn't yet noticed her arrival. They all seemed frozen in some sort of tableau with Scott and Tory staring at Nefertem as if he weren't quite human.

"Can someone tell me why I have two unexpected guests in my house while I was at work?" Kendra looked pointedly at Tory.

Her friend flushed under her regard. "Sorry, Kendra. I only wanted to have a chance to talk to Nefertem when you weren't around."

"You found it necessary to bring Scott along for the ride. It is Scott, correct?"

"Yes, this is Scott." Tory made the introductions. "Scott Burrows, this is my best friend, Kendra Miller."

Kendra reluctantly shook hands with Scott. He seemed like a nice guy, and under different circumstances, she wouldn't have minded getting to know him better, but all she wanted now was for him to leave. Get him as far away from Nefertem as she could.

"Nice to meet you, Scott."

"I you. I didn't know what Tory was up to until we arrived."

Finally turning to look at Nefertem, the bottom of her stomach did a flip-flop. He had his helmet tucked under his arm, out in the open for Scott to see. That was definitely not good.

Nefertem placed his helmet on the coffee table, then took Tory and Scott each by an elbow before he ushered them toward the door. He opened it and waited for them to walk through it.

* * * *

Pulling away from Kendra's house, Tory took a quick look at Scott, who sat in the passenger side next to her. He really was a great guy. Their date the night before last had turned out to be unexpectedly fabulous. She hadn't gone out with him before. She'd met him through one of the girls she worked with at the bank. Cindy had arranged for the three of them to go out for drinks one night. Being a bit of a matchmaker, Cindy had thought Scott and Tory would make a great couple. At the time, Tory hadn't been ready for a new relationship. She'd been taking a break from men, something she did after having to dump a boyfriend. That night out with Cindy and Scott had happened the year before, and Scott had left a very good impression on her. So much so, she'd kept his phone number when he'd given it to her at the end of the evening.

Kendra wanting the hieroglyphs translated had given Tory the perfect excuse to call Scott after such a long time having gone by. She'd known a call from her would be tantamount to asking him out on a date.

The man was a bit of a rarity. He had the mind of a scholar and the body of an athlete. As well as a face that was pure masculine beauty. Tory could quite easily see herself falling head over heels for him. There was only one problem—she notoriously had bad luck when it came to men. She somehow managed to attract guys who only wanted a good time, only to dump her when the shine wore off. Or she dumped them when she felt as if she was being used for only one thing. Scott on the other hand, fit none of those categories.

Taking another peek at him, Tory found Scott staring at her with a bemused look on his face. "What are you smiling about?"

"You. You seemed so lost in thought there. Hopefully, it was me you were thinking of so intently."

"Why would I do that?" Even though she had been, there was no way she would admit it to Scott, at least not at this early stage in their relationship. "If you really want to know, I was thinking about Nefertem. Gee, the man is an Egyptian god for Christ's sake."

"Amazing, isn't it? You, my lovely, have some answering to do."

"Sorry about not telling you where the hieroglyphs were from."

"I didn't mind that so much. What does bother me is that it was the only reason you called me. I've been waiting over a year for you to be ready to call me."

Tory felt herself blush. "That's not totally true. It just gave me something to fall back on if you didn't want to see me. I've been ready for a while now, I just hadn't worked up the nerve to pick up the phone and give you a call."

Scott chuckled. "I'm glad you called about the hieroglyphs." He grew serious. "As for Nefertem, if the story is true about his mother, then we could be in for some trouble."

"Truly?"

"Afraid so. Though I'm still finding it hard to come to grips with the fact it isn't just a legend but real. Nefertem's being here proves it."

"Should I be worried about him staying with Kendra? With her brother away, she's alone in the house with him."

"I don't think you have to worry. What is written about Nefertem doesn't mention anything nasty. He's only described as a sun god of Lower Egypt, identified with the lotus. Paintings of him are usually portraying him wearing a lotus and two feathers on his head. Occasionally, he's depicted as a lion-headed man. Now that I've seen his helmet I understand why."

"His mother? What's said about her?"

"Well, she's another story completely. Sekhmet is the lioness-headed goddess of war and destruction. The god, Re, created her by the fire of his eye. Her sole purpose was to be used as a weapon by Re for vengeance against mankind, because of their wicked ways and disobedience to him. Even her name means to be strong, mighty, and violent."

"She sounds like the mother-of-the-year award winner."

"There's only the one story of when she was set loose on mankind. Supposedly, she slew all who she saw, taking great pleasure in the slaughter and taste of blood. The Nile was to have run red with blood from her victims. Re couldn't control her either. She literally went on a rampage."

"He must have stopped her somehow."

"That he did with a little bit of trickery. You know how much Egyptians love beer, well, so do their gods. Re had red ochre mixed into seven thousand jars of it. He had it poured over the fields so they appeared flooded with blood. Sekhmet, thinking it was indeed blood, drank it all up, getting very drunk in the process. Re was then able to tame her and bring her back under control."

"Do you think all that's true? Just because Nefertem is real doesn't necessarily mean the story of his mother is too."

Scott shrugged. "They do say there are some truths behind the legends."

"In that case, I'd better tell Kendra to stock up on a lot of strong beer."

* * * *

After Scott and Tory left, Kendra went upstairs to change out of her work clothes. Nefertem followed her up. "You do not need to be so worried, Kendra. Scott will not reveal my presence here."

"How can you be so sure? Your helmet would be a valuable addition to the museum where he works, same with the pendant. Thank goodness I kept it in my room or he would have found that as well."

Nefertem refrained from telling her Scott already knew there was a pendant. There really was no point in upsetting her more. "He is a man of honor and would never try to take what is mine." The man knew more than enough about what happened when a mortal angered a god.

"I hope you're right." Finished changing, Kendra went to stand closer to Nefertem. She placed her hand on his broad chest. "I've had a terrible day at work. All I could think of was that you were here, waiting for me."

Taking hold of her hand, Nefertem pressed it so it lay over his rapidly beating heart. All it took was for her to touch him and his body raged to life. "I thought of you."

Nefertem bent his head and claimed her lips, plundering her mouth with his own. He loved the taste of her. Her scent washed over him—a heady smell that was all woman. He released her hand, then wrapped his arms around Kendra and pulled her hard up against him. That was how he had had wanted to greet her on her return from work. Not having to banish her fear of his being found out.

After breaking the kiss, Kendra looked at Nefertem. "Before this goes any further, what exactly did Tory need to talk to you about without my being around?"

"Only to warn me not to hurt you or she would hunt

me down."

Kendra groaned. "She promised she would stop doing that. That would be the reason she came while I was at work."

"She meant well." He tried to claim her lips once again, but Kendra pushed his face away. He growled in frustration. Obviously, she was not going to be easily put off.

"What did you tell Scott? How did you explain having possession of your helmet?"

Nefertem sighed in defeat. "I told him it had been in my family for generations."

"He accepted that?"

"Of course. That is enough about Scott. I have waited all day to make love to you and I will not wait any longer."

Nefertem scooped her up into his arms and took Kendra to the bed. Before she could ask another question, he claimed her lips in a searing kiss. Like the first time he had made love to her, the cat rose within him, taking control. She was his mate. He did not have to question that. Knowing the cat would not hurt her, he let it fully join with him.

It did not take them long to strip each other of their clothing. Neither one of them wanted to draw out this joining. Later would be time enough for slow, tender lovemaking. Unable to wait any longer, Nefertem tested Kendra's readiness. Finding her wet and more than ready, he slid his cock into her, relishing the feel of her body embracing his. She clutched his back and pulled him closer. He moaned/growled in response. Her release came hard and fast, making her cry out. He soon followed.

CHAPTER NINE

The dream claimed him while he slept next to Kendra. He did not normally dream while in his mortal form. This one took him by surprise, causing warning bells to go off in his mind.

He found himself in the middle of a lavishly adorned temple chamber. Gold and jewel tones were painted on all the walls and furnishings. At the end of the space, there was a raised dais with a gold throne on it. The woman who sat on it smiled warmly.

"My son, will you not come and greet your mother properly?"

Preparing himself for what was to come, Nefertem slowly walked across the room until he stood before his mother. He kissed the top of the hand she held out to him.

"Mother. Why have you summoned me this way?"

An enraged snarl bounced off the temple walls. He looked at his mother to find anger flashing in her gold cat eyes. Unlike him, she was cat and woman combined at all times. Her body was that of a woman's, but her head was a lioness'. On it she wore a black, braided wig, which fell just past her shoulders. She also wore the solar disk and *uraeus*, a cobra. Those two objects stated her role as the protector of the sun against the destructive elements that might attack it during the night. Her gown was red and semi-transparent. Nothing but a length of sheer cloth wrapped around her body.

Sekhmet growled once more. "Do not question me. You left me no other choice. You will not answer my calls while you are awake."

"I ask for your forgiveness." Nefertem bowed his head, hoping to make his mother see he was contrite, which was the furthest thing from the truth. He had to tread warily. "I was not ready to report to you as of yet."

"Why not, Nefertem? Two days have passed since you were summoned. That is more than enough time to determine what the punishment should be."

"The one who summoned me did not do it purposely. There is no enemy to defeat."

"How could a pharaoh not know what the pendant invoked?" his mother snapped.

"It was not the pharaoh who summoned me." Nefertem paused, taking his time to carefully think out his next words. "We have been too long out of touch with the mortal world, Mother. The reign of the pharaohs is over. They no longer rule over Egypt."

Snarling in rage, Sekhmet surged to her feet. "How can this be? The pharaoh was as much a god as you or me."

"The mortal world has changed." Flashes of what he had watched on television, of all the pain and destruction the mortals did to each other in this time, came to the forefront of his mind. He quickly tamped them down before his mother could pick up on them. Her next question told him he had not banished the thoughts quickly enough.

"It has changed for the worse. Has it not, my son? Do not bother to deny it. I can see it in your mind."

Now came the tricky part. He had to convince his

mother she was not needed in the mortal world. "Yes, in some ways it is worse, but in others it has vastly improved. The quality of life is much better. Mortals live to a far greater age. Their lives, for the most part, are good."

Moving with the quickness only a god or goddess could display, Sekhmet came to stand directly in front of Nefertem. "You defend mortals now? Never before have you ever said such things about them." She sniffed the air around him. "You even smell like one of them."

He ignored her last comment. "I feel the mortals should be left alone. We need not interfere with them."

His mother backed away and once more seated herself on the throne. "There is one thing you have not told me about the mortals. Do they still worship us?"

That was something he could not circumvent. His mother would sense the lie even before it left his mouth. "No, they do not worship us any longer. There are new gods, but one stands out among the rest. A lot of mortals worship this one god."

In response, his mother's eyes flashed fiery red. "Their fate is sealed. Nothing you say can save them. Punishment must be meted out for scorning us. Let them feel the power and destruction of the goddess Sekhmet. Once more I will slack my thirst on the blood of mortals. None shall be spared."

Before he could at least try to dissuade his mother from that course of destruction, he awoke. His was covered in sweat and his heart raced. For the first time while being in mortal form, he felt actual fear. There would be no stopping his mother. In little more than two weeks, she would come. All would fall before her, a victim of her rage. Reaching to where Kendra lay blissfully asleep, he pulled her against him so her back was to his chest. He was going to lose her, and there was nothing he could do about it.

* * * *

Kendra was having a hard time keeping her mind on her work. Her thoughts kept straying to Nefertem and how oddly he'd acted that morning. Something wasn't right, and he was as closed-mouthed as he could be about certain things.

After her alarm clock had gone off—which she'd thankfully remembered to set the night before—she'd awakened to find herself tightly clutched in Nefertem's arms. Even in sleep, he wouldn't relinquish his hold. She'd had to forcibly break free, waking him in the process. Which caused him to jump from the bed with a look that seemed very much like fear. Fear for her.

Lost in thought, Kendra nearly jumped out of her skin when her boss slapped a file folder onto her desk. Looking up, she found him scowling down at her.

She pasted on a smile, and asked, "What do you need, Stan?"

"For you to pay more attention," he answered sharply.

"I'm sorry. There have been a lot of things happening at home the last couple of days."

"That should have no bearing on your ability to do your job here."

"Sorry." Kendra apologized once more. "I'll try not to let it happen again."

"See that it doesn't." Before letting her get back to work, he asked one last question. "How long have you worked for me now?"

"It's just been over a year."

He nodded in response. "By the way, I'm expecting someone for a meeting in the next couple of hours. Be sure to inform me when she arrives."

"I will. Is she a prospective client?"

"No. There's no need to concern yourself about it."

Stan walked away, and she had the feeling that person

was something more than a normal, scheduled meeting. She looked at the appointment book on her desk and couldn't find one for that time. She distinctly remembered Stan telling her last week to keep that time slot open and not to book anything for then under any circumstances.

The next two hours passed quickly. A tall brunette, dressed in an expensively-tailored skirt and blazer walked in. Kendra did as Stan had instructed and buzzed his office, telling him the woman waited at the front desk. No sooner had she hung up, then Stan was out of his office and walking at a brisk pace toward her desk.

Without sparing a glance in Kendra's direction, Stan shook the woman's hand and then led her to his office. Kendra just managed to hear him tell the woman that all had been arranged before he closed the door behind them.

Another hour went by during which Kendra answered the phone when it rang and finished a couple of letters on the computer. Once Stan's office door finally opened, her jaw dropped. The woman held him by the arm that had been handcuffed behind his back. Reaching Kendra's desk, she handed Stan over to the two uniformed police officers who had managed to slip into the gallery without Kendra noticing.

The woman turned her attention to Kendra. "Sorry to inform you, Miss Miller, but as of today, you no longer have a job. Your boss is under arrest."

"What for? What exactly has he done?"

"He's charged with shipping stolen goods outside the country." At Kendra's look of concern, the woman smiled reassuringly at her. "We already know you've had no involvement in this. We've been watching your boss for many months now, and did a thorough investigation."

Kendra breathed a huge sigh of relief. "I had no idea."

"This started long before you started working for Mr. Wilson." She passed Kendra a business card. "My name is Detective Peters. We already have more than enough evidence against Mr. Wilson, but just in case we need to talk to you, please keep my card. We have your phone number from your boss' files."

"I'll be sure to do that. I guess I'd better pack up my things and go home."

After putting the few items she kept at work into a small box, Kendra handed over her keys to the gallery to the detective. She stepped through the door for the final time and felt no great loss. She really hadn't liked her job all that much, and she'd liked her boss even less.

Kendra put the box onto the passenger seat of her car and decided a few days off were in order before she started looking for another job. Maybe she would even wait until Nefertem had to leave. Each day she had with him was precious. She had a bit of a savings to get by. A new employment could wait.

* * * *

Nefertem paced the living room, his movements imitating those of a caged, wild animal—something he felt he was slowly turning into. The dream had done more than just put him in contact with his mother. It had started the change in him, the one that would slowly turn him into his mother's child—an animal lusting for mortal blood.

He resisted the change, another first for him, and it made it that much worse. As he paced, he racked his brain for ideas on how to stop his mother, but he kept drawing a blank. Once called, there was no way to stop the coming of Re's punisher. Feeling helpless and frustrated, Nefertem paced all the more.

That was how Kendra found Nefertem, pacing, so deeply in thought he did not at first even realize she was there, watching him. Her clearing her throat drew his attention. He spun on his heel and turned in her direction.

She spoke first. "All right, Nefertem, it's time you start

talking. Your eyes have changed again. I know you aren't telling me everything about yourself. I think I have a right to know."

Nefertem tried to suppress the cat, but it was now too strong to let him have full control once again. Which meant his eyes would not return to normal. Kendra was right. He owed her an explanation, but he wanted someone there who understood his world to help her accept him for what he was. He was quite sure she would not take this well.

"You are right. I do owe you some kind of explanation, but I am afraid you will not like what I'll tell you."

"Your eyes aren't changing back. Why?"

"They will not. Before I say what must be said, I want you to have Tory bring Scott here."

"I don't think involving Scott in this situation any more than he already has been is such a great idea."

He clasped her hands in his and tried to make her see why he wanted Scott, in particular, there. "Kendra, he is the only one I know in this world who will understand where I come from. I feel he might be able to help."

Kendra looked him in the eyes. "Fine. I'll call Tory and see when they can come over. Since you won't say any more until they show up, I'm going to get out of these work clothes."

Nefertem released Kendra's hands, then watched as she went and picked up a box sitting on one of the chairs. "What do you have there?"

Kendra chuckled. "All my belongings from work. It turns out my boss was involved in some illegal activities. The police came and arrested him today. So I'm now out of a job."

"Does that mean you no longer have to leave each morning?"

"You got it. I've decided a bit of a vacation is in order as well. I won't be doing any job hunting for the next couple of weeks, at least. I'll be here every day, all day long."

"Hmm, that is very good news. I know just what we can do to pass the hours." Nefertem took a step closer with a glint in his eyes.

"Oh no, you don't. I won't be sidetracked that easily. I'll change and call Tory. Now behave yourself and stay down here." Kendra clutched the box closer to her chest, then quickly went and climbed the stairs.

CHAPTER TEN

Tory and Scott arrived on Kendra's doorstep exactly a half hour after she'd called them. Scott had already been at Tory's place. Kendra would have to have a little chat with Tory the next time they were alone. Some good-natured ribbing was in order, but for now, she settled for giving her friend a poke in the ribs as she walked by.

They decided to order some takeout Chinese food before getting down to the business of why Kendra had invited Tory and Scott over. While they ate, Kendra told the others about the eventful day she'd had. Sitting next to her on the couch, Nefertem silently ate his food. He wore her dark sunglasses, keeping his eyes hidden from their guests. Much to Kendra's surprise neither Tory nor Scott made any comment about it.

Once the leftover food was packaged up and put away, they returned to the living room. A short silence ensued. Tory was the first to break it. "This was a great idea having Scott and I over like this, but I'm getting the distinct impression there's more behind your invitation than just getting together for the evening."

69

Kendra looked at Nefertem only to find him in stoic silence. She turned back to Tory, and said, "Yes, there's a little more to why I called you both to come over. Actually, it was Nefertem's idea."

"So you've decided to tell Kendra who you really are." Tory directed her comment at Nefertem.

Kendra stiffened at Tory's words. That, she hadn't expected. She'd been racking her brain since they'd arrived, trying to figure out how to explain the change in Nefertem's eyes. Obviously, no such explanation was needed from her, after all.

Nefertem gained his feet and went to stand in the middle of the room, effectively catching the others' attention. "You are correct, Tory. Now is the time for me to tell Kendra. I can no longer hide or ignore what I am." He turned his head and looked at Kendra. He reached up and removed the dark glasses before his gaze briefly touch each of them.

At the sharp intake of breath Scott took, and the gasp Tory made, Kendra realized they hadn't known that part about Nefertem. To be perfectly honest, Scott looked as if he wanted to put Nefertem under a microscope. He seemed unable to take his gaze off the other man's face.

"All right, Nefertem, enough delays. I want to know what you've been hiding from me," Kendra said.

Nefertem stared intently at Kendra. "I'm not a normal mortal man."

Kendra grunted in response. "I already know that. I think your eyes are a dead giveaway, don't you think?"

"I mean, I am much more. What I am trying to say is that I am immortal."

"What do you mean immortal? As in not-ever-going-to-die immortal?"

"Correct."

"How can that be? It isn't possible. I know you're from ancient Egypt, but I thought the pendant plucked you from your time and dropped you into mine."

"That is not how it works, Kendra. I am a god, and the pendant summons me."

Kendra felt as if she'd been punched in the stomach — very hard. "A god? You're a god? One of the many Egyptian gods written about in hieroglyphs?"

"Correct."

"If you're a god, why do you have to sleep, eat, and do everything else a mortal body needs to do?"

"Once I'm summoned, I become mortal for the duration of my time here."

She really was having a hard time digesting all that Nefertem told her. Being one of those people who didn't believe in an all-powerful god, let alone any other true gods existed, Kendra's mind balked at what he claimed to be. "Okay, you're a god. God of what?"

Finally able to pull his gaze from Nefertem's face, Scott answered Kendra's question. "Nefertem was, I mean is, an ancient sun god of Lower Egypt. He's part of the holy triad of Memphis. Son of the god, Ptah, and the goddess, Sekhmet." At Nefertem's warning growl, he quickly added, "Whom I'll from now on call the lioness-headed goddess."

Hearing Scott confirm that Nefertem was indeed who he claimed to be helped Kendra somewhat. There was still one big, unanswered question bouncing around in her mind. "I can now see why you wanted Scott here, but he can't answer all my questions." She pinned Nefertem with a hard stare and continued. "You say the pendant summons you. What exactly are you summoned to do?"

All the life seemed to leave Nefertem's eyes. They turned hard and emotionless. "Once summoned, I am to judge."

"Judge what?"

"Mortals. Usually, the one who possesses the pendant is the pharaoh. In turn, he can use it to smite down Egypt's enemies."

"Obviously, I'm not Pharaoh, and we aren't in Egypt. There are no enemies here. What can you possibly be judging then?"

If it were possible, Nefertem's eyes turned even colder. "The entire mortal race."

That was the last thing Kendra thought any of them had expected to hear. An eerie silence settled between them and the otherworldly being standing before them.

Kendra could only stare at this man, this god, whom she'd welcomed into her home, and her bed. At this moment, Nefertem didn't resemble the man whom she was coming to care for. All the tenderness and protectiveness he'd displayed before had vanished. In their place was only hardness. Being perfectly honest with herself, she found this personality made her feel uneasy.

Clearing her throat, Kendra tried to speak. Her voice came out little more than a croak. She cleared it once more. "Who are you to judge us? You know practically nothing of our world. Only the little I've shown you."

"You forget you also showed me television. What I have seen on it was more than enough."

"I explained to you that not everything on TV is real."

"Yes, you did. I understood that. So I know what was broadcast on the news were indeed actual events."

By this time, Tory had seemed to have heard quite enough. "It sounds as if you've already judged us." Nefertem's silence said it all, and with it her temper rose. "How dare you? You bastard. You have no right."

Scott reached across to where Tory sat and grabbed her hand, trying to calm her down. "Enough, Tory. Give Nefertem the chance to explain himself."

"By calling me forth that right was placed into my hands. Judgment has been made."

Tory wouldn't be so easily placated. "That's total and utter bullshit." As Scott squeezed her hand once more, she shoved it off hers. She stood before Nefertem, appearing not willing to back down an inch.

"You might be a god, but that doesn't mean we have to go on bended knee and kiss your butt. Take back your judgment."

"I cannot. Re's punisher will come."

"Not good enough for me. The punisher is your own mother, for god's sake. Can't you at least try to stop her?" At Kendra's sharp intake of breath, Tory went to her and sat, putting her arm around her. "Sorry, hon, we shouldn't have kept all that from you."

Kendra shook her head. "No, you shouldn't have." She felt someone intently staring at her and looked up to find Nefertem watching her. "How long before she comes?"

"A little over a week's time."

"That'll be the same day you leave?"

Nefertem focused his gaze on the wall just behind her. "I do not exactly leave. It is the day I truly become my mother's son. A weapon of the punisher."

Thinking of the weapons Nefertem had brought with him, Kendra now realized what they were for. The thought sickened her.

"Can't your father intervene? Ptah is no minor god." That last question came from Scott.

"If we were in Egypt and I was able to go to his temple, maybe. No one has tried to stop my mother before, after using the pendant."

"There's no temple to Ptah here, but we do have something from his temple in Egypt. Right here in Memphis there are two large quartzite fragments from the gateway to the Apis House. Would those suit your purposes?"

"I really do not know. It might."

"It's worth a shot. I think the sooner you try, the better. If it doesn't work, other plans will have to be made. Time is not something we have a great deal of."

"I am willing to try."

Scott gained his feet, held his hand out to Tory, and pulled her up onto her own. Before leaving, he turned a steely gaze on Nefertem. "You don't have any say in the matter, Nefertem. You'll go tomorrow with me even if I have to hog-tie you and throw you into the back of my car. God or no god." Not giving Nefertem a chance to reply, Scott led Tory out of the house.

With just the two of them left in the room, Kendra had no idea how she was supposed to react to all that had transpired. She certainly hadn't expected the evening to turn out that way. She hadn't felt this bad since the day her ex-fiancé had called off their wedding. She hated having to feel that way all over again.

Still standing before her, Nefertem continued to avoid looking directly at her. Which hurt even more. "You should have told me. Especially on the night you arrived."

"I did not want to." He finally looked at her.

"I really don't know you at all. I thought I did, but I don't."

"Yes, you do. Kendra, you know me better than anyone else has before. There is something about you that lets me be what I want to be as a man."

Kendra laughed. Even to her it sounded close to being this side of hysterical. "Meaning I bring out the killer in you? Just what I really needed to hear."

Nefertem shook his head. Some of his former warmth had returned to his stony features. "No, that is not what I meant. When I am with you, I feel things I was unable to before. I actually care about a mortal. I understand your kind better because of it."

"With your newfound understanding, you were still able to condemn us to death. Excuse me if I don't take that as a compliment."

Kendra jumped to her feet. She had to get away from Nefertem for a while. Before she could take two steps, he snaked out his arm and hooked it around her waist. He dragged her hard against his chest. Fiery-gold eyes stared at her.

"You keep misconstruing my words. All the other times I have been in the mortal world I thought they were beneath me. To be used however I wanted. They had no feelings or rights where I was concerned. Now, I know how I treated them was demeaning. I know that."

Kendra swallowed back the tears that threatened to come to the surface. "Yet you condemn us still."

"No, I did not. Not really. My choice was taken from me. I usually contact my mother after the first day or two of my arrival. This time I did not. I hoped she would wait until I was ready. She contacted me."

"When?" Kendra remembered how Nefertem had been that morning with her. Not wanting to let her out of his protective embrace. "It was last night, while you slept."

He nodded. "Yes. Only when I sleep are my defenses down, and she can be in contact with me. Even if I do not wish it." He placed a finger under Kendra's chin and made her look at him. "She took what information she wanted from me, involuntarily I might add, and passed judgment."

Some of the pent-up tension left her body, and Kendra's head fell to rest on Nefertem's chest. "So, what happens now?"

"Now all there is to do is wait for her coming. I will try my best to stop her, but this Memphis is so far away from Egypt."

"You? What happens now to you?"

"The changes will happen gradually, increasing closer to the day of her coming." Nefertem rested his chin on top of Kendra's head. "Near the end, I will not recognize you, nor remember what you are to me. You will have to get very far away from me. I wish never to hurt you."

Kendra tightly wrapped her arms around his waist and

breathed in his scent. She would forever remember the way he smelled. A mixture of heady musk, almost flower-like, and something totally male.

"Is it really necessary?" Trying to lighten the mood a little, she said, "I could always tie you up. In my bed."

"No." There was no humor in his voice whatsoever. "No. When the change is complete, nothing can stop me." Nefertem forced Kendra to look at him once more. "You have to be far away from me. Promise me you will do that."

Reluctantly, Kendra nodded, but that was one promise she wouldn't keep. She had no intention of giving Nefertem up.

CHAPTER ELEVEN

The drive to the University of Memphis where the quartzite pieces from Ptah's temple resided was a quiet one. All of what had transpired the evening before appeared to be still fresh in their minds.

Scott and Tory had picked them up shortly after they'd finished their breakfast. Since Scott was the only one who knew where the pieces were housed, he had offered to drive to their destination. Within minutes they'd been on their way, Scott and Tory sitting up front, Kendra and Nefertem in the back. Dark glasses once more hid Nefertem's eyes from view.

The university had an extensive collection of ancient Egyptian artifacts. The most well-known piece was a two-thousand-year-old mummy called Iret-irew. Scott had been the one to provide that bit of information. He knew quite a bit about the university's collection since it was his old alma mater, thus his knowledge of the pieces' whereabouts.

After reaching the main campus, they headed to the university's art museum where the pieces were displayed with the rest of the collection. Even though it was summer, there were a few students taking classes. They passed by them without causing undo notice.

As they wandered through the exhibit, they paused to look at the various items on display. Jewelry, metal and stone statues, clay votives, stelae, and amulets made up the majority on display. It was the amulets that seemed to snag Nefertem's attention more than the others.

Noticing Nefertem hadn't followed as they moved off to the next display, Kendra went back to stand beside him. He appeared to be staring intently at the amulets, or at least she thought he was. It was hard to tell since the dark glasses hid his eyes so well.

Slipping her hand into his, she asked, "What is it? You recognize something?"

"Yes, the two amulets at the back. I know those very well."

Kendra peered at the two he'd pointed out and read the small description of each one. It became all clear. They were amulets made in the likenesses of Nefertem's parents.

The image of Ptah was gilded and inlaid, made of bronze. His body was the form of a mummy with a human head. Only his hands seemed free of wrappings. In his grasp, he held a scepter. He wore a skullcap. The image of his wife was a glazed, decorated type of earthenware. She was depicted having the head of a lioness and the body of a woman. She wore the sun disc upon her head. The description of her amulet claimed Sekhmet represented the two sides of a cat—the lovingness of a mother, along with the destructiveness of a lioness. Kendra snorted to herself. What kind of mother would ever turn her offspring into a killer and still be claimed as protective? That seemed a contradiction in terms to her.

With a squeeze to Nefertem's hand, Kendra pulled him away from the amulets. Scott and Tory patiently waited for them. Once they reached the display where the other two stood, Scott pointed at the contents inside the glass case.

"These are what we came for."

To Kendra they really didn't look like anything spectacular. They were very large, she had to give them that. On closer inspection, she faintly saw the hieroglyphs carved into the stone. It was a muted gold-color much as one expected the blocks in the great pyramids to look.

Nefertem stepped closer and placed his hands, palms flat, against the glass of the display case. After a few moments, he opened his eyes and sighed. His arms fell to his sides.

"Well?" Scott asked.

"Nothing. It did not work."

"Try again."

Nefertem slowly turned his head to look at the other man. "The stones are empty. They are no longer consecrated. They are no longer connected to Ptah."

Scott shook his head. "Not good enough. Try again. There has to be a connection. Try harder."

With cat-like swiftness, Nefertem grabbed Scott by the shirtfront and pulled him so they stood nose to nose. "Do not order me, mortal."

Kendra sensed the change in Nefertem almost immediately. His stance, the feral look that came over his face, signaled the change. Having gone through something very similar with him during their trip to the mall, she knew she had to step in.

She placed her palm on his cheek and turned Nefertem's face to her. She went on tiptoe and claimed his lips in a kiss. Once he responded, she slowly slid her hand down his arm until she reached his hand that was still tightly fisted in Scott's shirt. Gently, she pried Nefertem's fingers open, freeing the other man. After he was released, Scott put a large amount of distance between himself and Nefertem. Kendra ended the kiss.

Kendra stared at Nefertem. Some of his feral part had

left him. "Scott meant no insult to you, Nefertem. He would just like you to try again." He seemed to hesitate, and she added, "Please, for me then. One more time is all I ask."

Nefertem briefly rubbed his thumb across Kendra's lower lip before he turned to Scott. "I apologize for my actions. I should not have reacted that way."

Scott wrapped his arm around Tory, who stood beside him, and nodded. "Apology accepted. I could be partly to blame. I shouldn't have sounded so forceful."

"I will try one more time and that will be all. I must leave this place soon. There are too many mortals here and their presence is sapping my control." To prove his words correct, a group of five people, who also viewed the collection, passed by. Nefertem instantly stiffened in response to their nearness.

Kendra wrapped her arm around Nefertem's waist, leaning against his side. He slowly relaxed. "One more try, then we'll leave."

*

With a slight nod, Nefertem once more turned to the glass display case that held the pieces from his father's temple. He placed his hands against the cool, glass surface, and focused his mind on the stones. As before, he could not sense anything, but for Kendra, who stood at his side supporting him with her presence, he concentrated harder. Going deeper, he searched for any sign of Ptah's spirit.

There, at the very center of the thick stone, he could just faintly detect a glimmering of what it had once possessed. The question was, would it be enough? Latching on to it, Nefertem sent out a silent call.

Why do you call for me, my son?

The question could only be heard inside Nefertem's mind. Using his thoughts only, he answered his father's question. *I need your help.*

You know I cannot aid you with the task you must do in the mortal world.

I know. That is not why I called you. I do need your help with why I am here. A long stretch of silence ensued, making Nefertem wonder if his father had broken contact with him.

What is it that you want?

Nefertem silently breathed a sigh of relief. His father had not abandoned him, after all. *The one who summoned me knew not what the pendant was for. There is no enemy of the pharaoh here. There is no pharaoh. How can I stop what is to come?*

There is no way.

There has to be! Nefertem growled in his mind. *Re would not allow Mother to be set loose on the mortal world again without a way to control her. Not after what happened the first time she walked among mortals.*

Why do you ask this now? You have never cared about protecting the mortals before.

His father gently nudged Nefertem's mind, trying to seek out the answer himself. In response, Nefertem shielded his thoughts. *I have learned more of this world. They have been judged wrongly.*

There is one mortal you wish to protect more than the others.

There was no use in denying it. Hiding the truth from his father was impossible. It was the one ability his parents shared. They could get the answers they wished from him, no matter how hard he tried to shield his thoughts from them.

Yes, there is. A woman, the one who possesses the pendant.

A mental image of his father smiling filled Nefertem's mind. *So you have finally found a mortal who has melted your cold heart. It was not always encased in ice. This pleases me.*

Then how can I stop Mother?

Your woman is safe. Even though she is not pharaoh, she still possesses the pendant, and therefore, is safe as long as she wears it.

At one time, that answer would have satisfied Nefertem, but not now. It was important that he save Kendra, but she would not forgive him so easily if he gave up on the rest of the mortal world. *That is good to know, but I still need to know how to stop Mother.*

There is one way. It has never been tried before…

Nefertem strained to hear the rest of what his father said, but the power in the stones was draining away. Straining to catch the last bit of it before it shrank completely to nothingness, he called, *What is it? What do I do?*

Egypt…library…scroll…of the ancients…hidden… The connection was lost.

Nefertem slowly dropped his hands to his sides and turned to find the three expectant faces of Kendra, Tory, and Scott staring at him. He gave them a slight nod. "It worked. I was in contact with Ptah."

"And?" Kendra asked softly.

"The stones failed at the end, and I lost contact before my father could tell me exactly what I must do, but I did hear some of what he tried to tell me. The rest we must figure out on our own." Feeling his control starting to slip once again, Nefertem added, "Let us leave this place. It would be better if we discuss this at Kendra's house. I cannot stay here any longer."

Kendra threaded her fingers through his and walked them to the exit. Scott and Tory followed. Wisely, they did not push Nefertem any further.

CHAPTER TWELVE

Once more safely ensconced in Kendra's house, Nefertem gained full control of himself. Even the addition of Tory's and Scott's presence in the house did not lessen it. Kendra's home had become his sanctuary from the outside world—a place where he did not feel his mother's gift inside him. A great deal of it was caused by just being with Kendra. Looking at her now, a warmth ran through him.

Kendra must have felt his gaze on her. She smiled sweetly at him and patted the cushioned seat of the couch beside her. Not taking his gaze from her, Nefertem slowly went to sit next to her.

The living room had unofficially become their strategy room. For when they arrived, they all automatically headed for that particular room and found places to sit. Nefertem, who had taken part in a number of councils of war, found this a bit amusing. Their small group did not mimic any of the posturing or grandstanding the pharaoh's generals had performed at each council.

Scott was the first one to speak. "Okay, you spoke with your father. That's a good thing. Now tell us exactly what he said. If we're to figure out what we're to do next, we need to hear all that was said to you before you lost contact with him."

Being in a calmer state of mind, Nefertem took no exception to Scott's brisk manner of speaking. "Ptah said there was one way to stop my mother, but it had never been tried before."

"As long as there's a way is all that really matters."

"The only problem is, he never got to finish telling me how to go about it before the stones completely lost their power."

Scott frowned in response. "Hmm...that could be a problem. So this is what you meant by our having to figure out the rest on our own."

"Yes. All I was able to understand was Egypt, library, scroll, of the ancients, and hidden."

"In that exact order?"

"Yes."

Scott's brows furrowed as he became lost in thought. After a minute, he shook his head. "This, I'm afraid, will be no easy riddle to crack. I think some research will be in order."

Rising to her feet, Tory matter-of-factly said, "Then let's get a move on. I'll help if you wish. I might not be as smart as you, but I can read."

Scott smiled warmly up at her. "I gladly accept your offer. I have a feeling this is a two-person job, anyway." Having gained his feet while speaking, Scott motioned to Tory that he was ready to leave.

*

Before Tory left, she caught Kendra's eye and jerked her head in the direction of the door. Kendra stood as well and followed them out of the living room. Once out of sight of Nefertem, Tory questioned Kendra.

"Are you sure you're going to be all right alone with him?"

Kendra knew which "him" Tory referred to. "I'll be perfectly safe. Nefertem would never harm me."

"How can you be so sure? Twice now he's gotten a little rough with Scott."

"I'll be fine."

"I wish I could feel as sure as you do. There are moments when Nefertem can be downright scary."

"She'll be okay, Tory," Scott interjected. "As for what he did to me, I might have brought that on myself. I sometimes forget who and what he is. He comes from an environment where class was everything. In ancient Egypt, I would have been miles beneath Nefertem. It would have been very injudicious of me to speak to him, let alone order him about."

Tory shook her head. "I still don't feel comfortable leaving Kendra alone with him."

Smiling, Scott chuckled. "Tory, because Nefertem is the type of man I just described, he would never hurt Kendra. Especially since she's his woman."

"What do you mean his..." Tory's voice trailed off when she had to have seen the blush that Kendra felt stain her cheeks. "Oh...I see. It's like that, is it?"

Nodding, Kendra stammered, "Y-Yes."

"I'm glad you've gotten over that other jerk, but I wish you could have picked a man who can stay with you permanently."

"So do I, Tory. When you're in love, you can't choose."

After giving Kendra a quick hug, Tory smiled. "Well then, Scott and I will make our exit and leave you two alone. If he makes you happy, then all I can do is wish you the best."

Once he opened the front door, Scott motioned for Tory to go out first. "Stop worrying, Tory. Let's get a move on. We have a long day ahead of us. I hope hours of reading won't bore you stiff."

"I look forward to it." Giving Scott a saucy wink, Tory stepped past him and walked out the door. Scott followed closely at her heels.

After returning to the living room, Kendra found Nefertem on the couch, staring off into space. "A penny for your thoughts."

Nefertem turned to look at Kendra. "I have no such penny to give you."

Kendra shook her head. Even though Nefertem had the English language pretty well down pat, he still didn't know the sayings that had grown more widely used as time went by. "Sorry, that's just something you say when you find someone lost in thought."

"Oh, so you really do not want a penny?"

"No, I don't want a penny." Kendra sat beside him and brushed Nefertem's lips with her own. "You can tell me what makes you look so serious."

"I was trying to see if I could recall anything that would help us figure out what Ptah tried to tell me."

"Don't push yourself too hard. It'll come when it comes."

Nefertem nodded slowly. "You might be right. There was one thing my father told me, something I did not want Scott or Tory to know about just yet." He left Kendra's side and headed out of the living room.

Perplexed, Kendra listened to the sound of Nefertem's footfalls on the stairs leading up to the bedrooms. A few seconds later, she heard him returning. When he was once more within sight, she arched a questioning brow. "Okay, now what was that all about?"

Nefertem opened his right hand to reveal the necklace. He stepped in front of her and slipped the heavy gold chain over her head. The pendant came to rest between her breasts. Kendra looked at him, feeling even more confused.

He sat on the edge of the coffee table in front of Kendra and gently brushed the pendant with his index finger. "I want you to wear this at all time. Do not remove it for whatever reason you feel you should."

Kendra shook her head. "Nefertem, I can't go outside wearing this. It's a much too expensive piece. I would stand out in a crowd with it on."

"You must. That is what Ptah told me. As long as the pendant is around your neck, I cannot harm you."

"It isn't necessary for me to wear the pendant. I know you wouldn't hurt me."

"How do you know that? I...I do not even know that myself. Just wear the pendant. Please?" Nefertem asked pleadingly.

Sighing deeply, Kendra nodded. "All right, I'll wear it, but I can't see how a mere pendant will keep me from harm, unless I use it to knock you over the head. Even at that, it doesn't make much of a weapon."

"That is not what the pendant is for," Nefertem remarked lightly. "Since you now possess it, and as long as you wear it, I cannot harm you, because you were the one who summoned me."

"In other words, I started all this, and therefore, am immune, so to speak."

"Yes."

It finally dawned on Kendra why Nefertem hadn't divulged that new information in front of Scott and Tory. "You mean, it'll protect me and only me."

"Correct." After gently caressing her cheek, he spoke once more. "So please leave the pendant on. At all costs."

* * * *

Scott's apartment was that of a typical unmarried man's place. The furnishings were utilitarian and not over abundant. The color scheme was browns, tans, and beiges.

Not a single pastel was in sight. Tory plunked herself onto one of the couches and wearily rubbed her eyes.

Scott shook his head. "Quit your worrying. You're worse than a mother hen. Kendra is an adult and can look after herself. She doesn't need you fretting over her."

"I can't help myself. Ever since we first met, I've felt I should watch out for her. If you could have seen Kendra when she was the lonely, withdrawn teenager who'd just lost her parents, you would understand better."

"You're a good friend to her, Tory. I'm sure Kendra knows that, but I don't think she'll take too kindly to you interfering in her relationship with Nefertem."

Tory snorted. "I know I told Kendra I would be happy for her, but why did she have to pick Nefertem?" Scott gave her a look that said she must have been joking. She backtracked a bit. "Okay, I can understand some of the reasons. I'll admit the man has a face that would have any woman panting over him, and a body to match, but those eyes... They really do creep me out. Cat eyes don't in any way, shape, or form can be considered normal."

"No, but you can't put Nefertem in the category of being a normal man. He's an altogether different animal entirely."

"You got that right—he's an animal."

Scott scooped up four large volumes that sat on a bookshelf hung on the wall, then returned to Tory. "Okay, enough of that. We have a lot of work ahead of us, and I don't expect the answers to jump right out at us. I think we could be at this for at least a couple of days. So let's get cracking." He dropped all the books onto Tory's lap. She grunted in response.

Tory moved the books so they sat on the couch beside her, then picked up the top volume and read the title. It was a book about the ancient histories of Egypt. The next one was about the ancient Egyptian gods and the myths surrounding them. Inwardly, she groaned. The size and thickness of just those two books were enough to send her running from the room. School had never been her passion, and studying had been a chore. How would she even last an hour reading those? What had she gotten herself into?

Finally realizing Scott still stood in front of her, watching her reaction, Tory pasted on a smile and looked back up at him. "I guess I'll start with these two." She grabbed a second textbook.

"If you would prefer not to do this, Tory, then you don't have to. I can manage on my own."

"No...no, I don't mind. Really."

"But?"

She gave Scott a sheepish grin. "If I fall asleep, please don't take it personally."

Scott laughed. "I won't. How about I make you a deal? We work on the research for a few hours, then I'll take you out for a nice dinner."

"You have a deal." Opening the first text, Tory settled herself more comfortably on the couch and read.

CHAPTER THIRTEEN

She ended up getting a headache. Not just a slight throbbing pain, but a massive, feel-like-someone-is-pounding-on-your-head-with-a-hammer ache. Rubbing her eyes, Tory tried to focus once more on the open book on her lap. She finally gave up. She took a quick glance at her watch and found that two hours had gone by since they'd started that arduous task. She looked at Scott, who sat on the loveseat across from her. He was totally immersed in what he was doing, completely oblivious to anything going on around him. She smiled to herself.

Once again, she thought about how different Scott was from the other men she'd dated in the past. Contrary to what Kendra might have thought, Tory hadn't slept with Scott yet. Their first date hadn't ended with them having sex. Even though she had stayed the night at his place. All they'd done was talk for hours.

Tory closed her book with a snap to signal she was done. Scott raised his gaze from the page he'd been reading. "Had enough, have you?"

"More than enough. I need a break."

"Sorry, I tend to get a little lost in the past when I do

research."

"I could tell." Tory put the book on the couch, then went to sit next to Scott. "You did have a faraway look on your face."

Impulsively, Tory reached out and moved a stray lock of hair off Scott's forehead. She trailed her fingers down to his temple and over his stubble-roughened cheek. Finally, they came to rest on his square jaw. Her gaze became riveted to his firm, chiseled lips. Leaning in slightly, she softly brushed his with hers, then once again. She left her hand cupped around his chin and pulled back a bit to peer into his eyes.

The faraway look was most definitely gone. It'd been replaced by one so hot she could almost feel her skin sizzling under his regard. Tory swallowed hard. That stare caused her body to respond at a most alarming rate.

Scott pulled Tory into his arms, crushing her against his chest. With a moan, he claimed her lips in a soul-searing kiss. The book he'd been holding fell to the carpeted floor, unnoticed. The whole apartment could have come crashing down around them and she wouldn't have cared. For a self-confessed bookworm, he knew how to kiss a woman senseless. She wrapped her arms around his waist and held him close.

It was a long time before they surfaced for air. They panted. There would be no going back if they continued.

Seeming to know what she wanted, Scott pulled Tory closer, stood, and picked her up off her feet. He kissed her as he walked, heading toward his bedroom. Once he reached his destination, he broke their kiss.

"Tell me now, Tory, if you want this or not. I won't make you do anything you're not ready for."

Just his asking was all she needed to hear. That he would and not just take, was more than enough for her to make her decision. "Don't stop. I want this as much as you do."

Scott took two steps to reach the bed, and set Tory onto it. He only paused long enough to rid himself of his shirt before joining her there.

Tory sucked in a breath. Scott had been hiding a well-toned chest under his loose-fitting T-shirt. Even though he wasn't as muscular as Nefertem, he still had well-defined pecs and abs. She couldn't resist skimming her hand across his washboard stomach.

"Though my chosen profession has me sitting behind a desk most of the time that doesn't mean I'll allow myself to turn into a fat slob."

"Well, I do like surprises." Tory grabbed a fistful of his hair, pulled Scott's head down, and claimed his lips, effectively stopping any further conversation.

In short order, their clothing found their way to the floor. They kissed and explored each other's body until their passion reached a fevered pitch. Only then did Scott join his body with hers. It didn't take long for them to reach the pleasure they strived for.

* * * *

Kendra was in that in between place. Not really in a deep sleep and not really awake. It didn't matter which sleep realm she inhabited, she just didn't want to wake up and leave it.

She bit back a moan as the hand caressing her body delved into a sensory-overloaded spot, rubbing the little nubbin of flesh between her legs. Even though they'd made love before going to sleep, Kendra could never get enough of Nefertem. If he wanted her again, she was more than willing to comply. She craved his touch like a flower craved the sun. Like the sun, he made her body burn for his touch.

Kendra rolled into her lover's caress and went to wrap her arms around him. Instead of encountering Nefertem's reclining form her hand came in contact with something else, something hard and unyielding. Slowly allowing herself to wake up to awareness, she blinked a few times before opening her eyes fully.

Focusing on what her hand rested on, Kendra blinked again, hoping her eyes were deceiving her. That the scabbard she touched was just in her dreams, a figment of her imagination. That it wasn't attached to a man whom she'd never met before, who was even now stroking her body—intimately. Unable to stop herself, she followed the length of the scabbard up, across the large expanse of naked male chest, then to a face that was breathtaking. She gasped. She reached for his roving hand and tried to push him away. He chuckled in response, but did nothing to remove it.

Nefertem must have heard her, for one moment he laid beside to her, and the next, he held the stranger's wrist in a vice-like grip. Giving a warning snarl, he forced the other's hand from her body. He said something she didn't understand in a warning tone.

Kendra looked at Nefertem and then back at the other man. It was obvious they knew each other. The one other telling clue was the stranger's clothes. He wore the same styled kilt Nefertem had worn when he'd first arrived. Nefertem hadn't spoken in English. She could only assume he'd used ancient Egyptian.

The two men continued to speak in the same language, then a full-throated growl reverberated off the bedroom walls. Starting to get more than a little worried, Kendra shifted into a sitting position. She held the sheets tightly to her chest. Not being able to understand what they said was doing nothing to settle her mind either.

The two men glared at each other with Kendra between them. After a few minutes of being subjected to this silent display of male posturing, she couldn't keep silent any more. "Nefertem, who is this?"

Without taking his gaze off the man in question, Nefertem said, "No one important. He won't be staying."

Their visitor switched to English. "You do not mind if I stay, do you, sweet lady? You were quite welcoming not so long before."

Kendra wasn't at all surprised by how quickly he'd mastered speaking her language. Nefertem had been the same. Even the heavily-accented English they spoke sounded the same. "If Nefertem wants you to leave, I think you should do just that."

"My, my, what a warm welcome I am getting now."

Nefertem left the bed, not giving his nudity a second thought. He walked to the other side of the bed and grabbed the other man by the arm before dragging him from it. "I did not call for you. This is the last time I will tell you, Mahes. Leave!"

"Do I need a reason to come and see my brother?"

Now that Nefertem and Mahes stood next to each other, Kendra realized there was more than their shared way of speaking that was similar. Both stood well over six foot, and had the same muscular build. Also, they were drop-dead gorgeous. She could now easily see the family resemblance as well. The only difference was Mahes' eyes. His were not like a cat's as Nefertem's were.

Both men were silent for so long Kendra managed to finally drag her gaze off the great deal of naked male flesh displayed before her and looked up at their faces. She felt her face flush a bright red. She'd been caught staring.

She gave a slight shrug. "Sorry, but what do you expect? If you're both going to walk around half-clothed, or in your case, Nefertem, butt naked, I'm going to look."

Her words caused Nefertem to mutter something under his breath as he pulled one of the covers off the bed before he wrapped it around his narrow hips. Mahes only chuckled.

"Well, brother, are you going to introduce me to your

companion? Or do I have to get back into that bed with her and introduce myself?"

"You do and you will be very sorry you did." Nefertem growled. "I can see you will not let this go. Kendra, this is my younger brother, Mahes."

Still holding the sheet loosely to her chest with one hand, Kendra stuck out the other to shake Mahes'. As she leaned forward, the pendant around her neck swung free. Mahes' gaze latched on to it.

"So it is true. It was a woman and not Pharaoh who summoned you, Nefertem."

Stiffening, Nefertem asked, "Who told you that?"

Mahes shifted his gaze from the pendant so he could look at his brother. "Mother did. She is the one who sent me to you."

"Why?"

"Why else but to make sure you do what you are supposed to. She has sensed a change in you, and is not pleased."

"I do not need you watching over me. You know as well as I do when the change is complete I have no choice."

"I can see it has started." Mahes looked pointedly into Nefertem's eyes. "Be that as it may, you are different." He slid his gaze knowingly toward the bed where Kendra still sat.

Nefertem closed his eyes for a few seconds and uttered a string of words in what Kendra thought were Egyptian. The air in the room suddenly became charged with some unknown energy, causing the hair on her arms to stand on end. A split second later, an eerie blue light surrounded Mahes. After it disappeared, he gasped, much like someone who'd been holding his breath for a long period of time and could finally fill his lungs once again.

"What have you done?" roared Mahes.

"You should have left when you had the chance. You

were always too smart for your own good, Mahes. I cannot have you running back to mother, filling her mind with tales. This was the only recourse open to me. So I used it against you."

"There was no need to go to such extreme measures."

"Oh yes, there was."

"What goes on here, Nefertem? Mother was right. There is something different about you."

Nefertem's gaze strayed to Kendra. "You are right, Mahes. I have changed. For the better."

"You are up to something. If you were not, why else would you have done what you did."

Nailing his brother with a stern look, Nefertem took a step closer. "If I am? You will not stop me. I will not allow it."

"What is it you are trying to do?"

"I plan on stopping Mother. I refuse to set her loose on innocents. Now that you are stuck here, dear brother, you are going to help me."

Not sure what had happened to Mahes, and feeling left in the dark for far too long, Kendra cut into their exchange of words. "Nefertem, what's going on?"

Nefertem dragged his gaze from his brother and sat beside Kendra. "To stop Mahes from returning to tell my mother what I do not want her to know, I made him mortal. He is now trapped in this world and cannot return home."

Kendra saw that Mahes was still not at all thrilled with what Nefertem had done to him. "I guess that means another trip to the mall is in order for me then."

Nefertem brushed Kendra's forehead with a feather-light kiss, then smiled. "Afraid so."

"I figured as much. Just tell me one thing, do you have any other siblings who could pop in unexpectedly?"

"No. Why do you ask?"

"If I have to go clothes shopping for everyone in your

family, you're going to put me in the poorhouse." Kendra wrapped the bedsheet around her more firmly, then got out of bed. "If I'm to make Mahes look more like a mortal man, I'd better get a move on. One last thing, try not to kill each other while I'm in the shower. I don't need to be cleaning bloodstains out of my bedroom carpet. So the two of you had better play nice."

CHAPTER FOURTEEN

Kendra had been all prepared to go to the mall by herself. Mahes had the same build as Nefertem so she already knew what size clothes she needed to buy, but that wasn't to be. Nefertem had wanted Mahes to experience this new world firsthand. So after properly attiring his brother in some of his newly purchased clothing, Nefertem had pushed them out the door.

This trip to the mall was decidedly different from the one she'd experienced with Nefertem. Mahes drew the eye of every woman who passed them by, but whereas Nefertem ignored them, Mahes seemed to thrive on it. He met their glances with an appreciative look of his own. The man was a walking, talking, sex magnet. If she'd left him alone, Kendra was sure he would have found some woman who would take him to her place. He exuded enough sex appeal to fell a woman within fifty paces.

Surprisingly, Kendra felt nothing for Mahes. He looked like a sex god, but he wasn't Nefertem. They might look very similar, because they shared the same blood, but something about Nefertem called to her. Which was not the case with Mahes.

Having to pull on Mahes' arm for the umpteenth time to get him to peel his gaze off yet another woman who'd walked by, Kendra was ready to scream. Plus, it didn't help that she had to yank twice before he actually acknowledged her presence. Even though she felt like kicking herself for doing it, she turned to look behind them to see whom Mahes had been ogling so intently. She rolled her eyes. It figured. The woman was a tall, lanky blonde, wearing tight-fitting shorts and a tank top.

"Mahes, if you don't stop that, I'm going to leave you here and make you find your own way home."

"What am I doing that bothers you so?"

"Don't play stupid with me. You know exactly what I mean."

Mahes flashed Kendra a sexy smile. "Would you rather I looked at you instead?"

Kendra elbowed Mahes in the ribs, hard enough to make him grunt in reaction. "No, I don't. I'd need to take a shower after you did. I'd feel dirty."

Wrapping an arm around her shoulders, he pulled her against his side. "Come now, you cannot say you do not find me attractive."

She shoved him away. "I will say you're handsome. I would have to be blind not to notice that, but you do nothing for me." At Mahes' puzzled look, Kendra amended, "I mean, I'm not attracted to you in that way."

Mahes looked insulted by her remark. "What if I were to try to change how you feel about me? I can be very persuasive when I want to be."

"I'm sure you can, but no thanks."

Not willing to give up so easily, Mahes pulled Kendra down one of the mall's service corridors. As luck would have it, it was deserted. He pushed her against a wall with his body and lowered his lips to hers. A second later, he yelped in pain.

Kendra gave the fistful of Mahes' hair she still held

another hard tug and shot daggers at him with her eyes. "That's enough. Your first couple of attempts at trying to seduce me, I let slide, but I won't be so nice any longer. Get it through your thick head. I don't want you. I only want Nefertem. I'll not betray him. No matter how little time we have left to be together." Much to Kendra's shame, tears welled in her eyes.

Mahes followed the trail of one fallen tear down Kendra's cheek with his finger and sadly shook his head. The seductive, laid-back mien he'd worn previously was gone. "You love him, do you not?"

Kendra nodded, then quietly whispered, "Yes. Very much."

"I am sorry for what I did before. I just wanted to see how deep your feelings for Nefertem really were. I can see now that they are indeed true."

"You could have asked instead of putting me through a test."

"Once again, I am sorry, but I felt it was necessary. You are not the first woman to proclaim her love for my brother."

From the way Mahes had said it, she could tell it hadn't ended happily. "What happened?"

"Takhat was a priestess in our mother's temple. The first time she saw Nefertem appear there, she decided he would be hers. In the beginning, it started out innocent enough, but the more hours Nefertem spent with Takhat, the more grasping she became. At that time, Nefertem had not had much congress with mortal women, so he did not realize her words of love were contrived. He believed her."

"Then what happened?"

"In the end, Takhat seduced Nefertem. She figured if she got him into her bed she would be able to get whatever she wanted from him."

Kendra was almost afraid to ask, but she needed to know. "What did Takhat really want if she really didn't want Nefertem?"

"Immortality. She thought Nefertem would be so enamored with her that he would want her by his side forever. How wrong she was. Nefertem enjoyed their bed sport, but he did not want her permanently in his life. He refused. In a fit of pique, Takhat ran to my mother and told her Nefertem had forced himself upon her and she wanted him punished for it."

"Did your mother believe Takhat?"

Mahes shook his head. "No, she did not. She did punish Nefertem in the end, though."

"Why? If she knew Nefertem was wrongly accused, why punish him? She should have punished Takhat for telling lies."

"Oh, she did, and not so much for telling lies, but for having slept with Nefertem."

"Aren't you allowed to be with mortal women?" Kendra asked, not really understanding.

Mahes chuckled. "On the contrary. I can see you do not know much about those who serve in the temples. During that time, the priestesses must stay celibate for the entire duration. Takhat did not, so she violated Maat."

"What did your mother do?"

"Well, for Nefertem, for daring to sleep with one of her priestesses, she made him what he is today. Bound to the pendant you wear around your neck. Summoned to punish mortals, and to live as one until her coming. As for Takhat, her punishment was death."

Kendra swallowed loudly. "How?"

Mahes took a step away from Kendra. "I killed her."

Feeling all the blood drain from her face, Kendra sidled farther away. "Why did it have to be you who killed her?"

"Just as Nefertem has a duty, so do I. I am the one who punishes those who violate Maat. I punish all transgressors. Maat is universal order, and it must be protected from wrong-doers."

"I don't think I'll ever get used to the idea of you and Nefertem being actual gods. Wrathful gods when called to do so."

"Well, for the moment, we are not all that much different from you. I did not tell you all this to make you fear us. I only wanted you to understand why Nefertem is the way he is."

Kendra nodded, then walked back into the main part of the mall. Mahes followed her. He'd given her a lot to think about, especially about Nefertem's relationship with Takhat. He'd, of course, told her nothing of that before. Right now, she had no idea how to feel about the whole thing.

Slowing, Kendra allowed Mahes to draw up next to her. "Let's get you some proper clothes so we can leave here." She noticed he drew stares again from any woman who passed them.

"I sense you are displeased with me."

"Yes. No. Not really. I just don't know what to think."

"Maybe I should never have told you. It really was not my place to discuss that with you."

"Maybe not, but it has given me a little better understanding of Nefertem."

* * * *

The rest of the shopping excursion went relatively well. Though there were a couple of salesladies Kendra had to almost beat off with a stick. They'd trailed Mahes like lovesick puppy dogs. One even going so far as to follow him into a changing room. Only Kendra's loud throat clearing and pointed stare had chased her away. Which Mahes, of course, found vastly amusing.

Once sufficiently outfitted and a couple of hundred dollars more charged to her credit card, Kendra dragged Mahes out of the mall. Much to her surprise, no hoard of women lusting after him followed in their wake. As she pulled out of the parking lot, she made a mental note to never go to the mall with him ever again.

Just the same as the ride to the mall, Mahes sat staring out the car window, watching the scenery as it went by. Unlike his brother, he was more inclined to readily show his emotions. He didn't hold himself under such tight restraints.

After they arrived at the house, the sight of an agitated Nefertem confronted them. He paced from the kitchen to the living room and back again. The television was blaring in the background. It was set at such a loud volume the sound drowned out any other, and because of that, Nefertem didn't hear Kendra or Mahes' return.

Kendra could only stare at Nefertem in shocked silence. She'd seen him in bad straits before, but this was nothing compared to that other time. He held himself so tightly the veins that ran down the sides of his neck stood out. His jaw was clenched firmly as he fought whatever demon struggled inside him.

Mahes dropped the shopping bags at his feet, then covered his ears with his hands. He crossed swiftly to where Nefertem paced, took hold of his brother's shoulder, and pulled him to a halt.

"Be at ease, Nefertem. You cannot continue to fight it." The words had barely left his mouth when Nefertem turned on him. He flipped Mahes onto his back in a matter of seconds. Nefertem used his knee to pin Mahes to the floor. A look of pure animal rage was on his face.

The speed in which Nefertem had brought Mahes down caused Kendra to gasp, but seeing the look of rage he wore caused her to act. Having no thought for her own safety, she rushed to the men. She caught Nefertem by the chin and forced him to look at her.

"Enough, Nefertem. Let Mahes up." At first, he didn't seem to recognize her. Speaking more insistently, she said,

"Nefertem, it's me, Kendra. Now let Mahes up."

Nefertem gave a shake of his head and seemed to come back to reality. He looked at Kendra. He scrambled off Mahes. "I did not mean to do…"

"It's okay, Nefertem." Kendra smiled warmly. He appeared deeply agitated.

"No, it is not. I should not have reacted that way. The only excuse I have for it is I let my imagination get the better of me."

Mahes, now on his feet once again, brushed non-existent specks of lint from his clothes. "What were you picturing I was doing? I know it had to do with me or you would not have jumped on me like that."

"Most of my thoughts were hardly unfounded, Mahes. I know what you are like, especially with women."

His brother chuckle, then said, "You fretted for nothing. My charms, as it turns out, do not work on all women."

Kendra rolled her eyes at Mahes. "Like you have to lay on the charm very much to get whatever woman you want." Turning to Nefertem, she said, "You could have warned me about the effect your bother has on women before we'd left. It gave a real boost to my ego to watch Mahes lust after every female who happened to walk by while I had to fight to gain his attention."

She decided to leave the brothers alone for a while and collected all the shopping bags Mahes had dropped. "I'll put this all away upstairs in the spare bedroom for Mahes. I'm sure the two of you can amuse yourselves while I'm gone." Before either of the men could protest, she headed up the stairs.

CHAPTER FIFTEEN

"She will stay true to you, Nefertem," Mahes said, as he stared at the stairs where Kendra had disappeared to the upper floor.

"How can you be so sure?" Nefertem scowled.

"Do not look at me that way. I did it for you. I had to know how Kendra really felt about you."

"What exactly did you do, Mahes?" Each word came out forced and full of menace.

"I tried to kiss her." As Nefertem snarled and advanced on him, Mahes held out his hand to stop him. "Let me finish before you grind me into a pulp. When I said my charms do not work on all women, I meant one in particular. Kendra. She would have nothing of me. She almost snatched me bald for my efforts."

Nefertem fell back. "Kendra rejected you?"

"Amazing as that may seem, yes, she did. You could not have really thought Kendra would do that to you?" His question was met with silence. Mahes shook his head in wonderment. "Nefertem, she loves you. You cannot tell me you did not already know that."

Nefertem stiffened at Mahes' offhand remark. "Kendra

told you this? Or are you just assuming this from her reaction to one of your famous tests?"

"She told me so herself."

At Kendra's footsteps moving around upstairs, Nefertem stared at the ceiling. "Why could you have not just left things as they were?"

"I thought you would be pleased to know you have the love of your woman."

"Pleased? What good does it do me to know Kendra loves me? You know there can be no way for the two of us to be together."

"What if you were to—"

Nefertem cut him off before he could finish that particular sentence. "No. Do not even say it."

"It is possible, Nefertem. You still have the power to do it."

"I said no. Would you have her tied to an animal, a killer of her kind, forever?"

Mahes sadly shook his head. He could not believe Nefertem would give up so easily. "You cannot just let her go."

"That is precisely what I have to do." Nefertem cocked his head. He must have heard Kendra returning as well. Quietly, he added, "If you have any love for me as a brother, you will keep your big mouth shut and tell Kendra nothing about this."

Mahes wisely held his tongue. He could not very well tell Nefertem that Kendra already knew about his power to grant immortality. Nor that he had told her all about Takhat. He loved his brother, but in instances such as this, he thought him the biggest fool.

* * * *

Stretching her arms over her head, Tory pulled the kinks out of her body. She was completely satiated. The night she'd spent with Scott was one she wouldn't soon forget. She turned her head and found the bed next to her empty. She placed her hand on the spot where Scott had been lying and found it cool to the touch. The faint sound of a page turning reached her ears.

Tory held the sheet to her chest and propped herself up on one elbow. She peered at the desk set up directly across from the bed, finding the source of the noise. A smile crept across her lips. Scott sat at the desk, reading one of his history books. What made her smile was the splendid sight that met her eyes. He was in the chair, not wearing a stitch of clothing. The way it was positioned, he didn't face her. She roamed her gaze over his broad, muscular back. The man did have a killer bod, and she'd explored every inch of it during the night.

Wanting to gain Scott's attention, Tory yawned loudly. If she could drag him away from his books long enough, maybe she could entice him back to bed. She smiled seductively once he turned in the chair to look at her.

"Awake, are you? I thought you might sleep the whole day away."

"If I did, I would have had just cause to do so."

Scott's gaze grew downright steamy in reaction to her remark. "Very true."

Tory patted the bed next to her. "Well, I didn't sleep the day away, so come back here."

"Oh, what a greedy woman you've turned out to be."

Tory gave a throaty laugh, and dropped the sheet she clasped to her chest until Scott got a glimpse of her breasts. "I'm only greedy when it comes to you."

In response to Tory's very blatant invitation, Scott shot to the bed, practically knocking over the chair in his haste to reach her. His lips claimed hers in a passionate kiss a second later. She groaned deep in her throat.

Scott lifted his mouth from hers by a mere hair's breadth, and said, "Far be it for me to deprive a lady of something she wants. All you have to do is ask."

"Then I'm asking," Tory said huskily. She pulled his lips back to her own.

It was much, much later when they became aware of the real world once again, though it was with great reluctance on both their parts that they did.

Tory snuggled close to Scott with her head pillowed on his chest. His heart still raced beneath her ear, and hers matched the tempo. Slowly, their breathing returned to normal. He gently caressed her back.

"You know we can't stay in bed all day. Even though you're a greedy woman and are never satisfied."

"I guess you're right. I think I can wait a few more hours to have you again."

Scott's laughter rumbled inside his chest. "That's good to hear." Giving her bottom a smack, he said, "Time we got out of this bed before I change my mind."

Tory groaned. "You party pooper. All right, you win. If it was for anyone else besides Kendra, I'd be saying who gives a damn."

"Well, it is for Kendra, so we have work to do. You can have the shower first if you'd like."

Tory slipped from the bed, completely unabashed with her naked state, and stretched largely. She gave Scott a saucy wink, then left the bedroom and headed for the bathroom down the hall.

* * * *

Having finished her shower and feeling much more refreshed, Tory returned to the bedroom to find Scott lost in the book set before him. She rolled her eyes in his direction. She guessed she'd have to get used to the idea of being forgotten by him once in a while, but just so long as it wasn't all the time. She had her ways to ensure that didn't happen. For the moment, she could let it slide.

After his shower and a couple of hours more of research, they decided to see Kendra and Nefertem. On the way out the door, Scott grabbed the newspaper that lay on his doorstep. He added it to the pile of books and papers he carried.

They arrived a short time later. Tory rang the doorbell. Before anyone came to answer the door, she stole a quick kiss from Scott.

"What was that for?"

"I couldn't resist any longer."

"Well, I can do better than that." He hooked his free arm around her waist, then pulled Tory closer and proceeded to give her a kiss that was in no way considered a quick peck.

"My, my, I had no idea I would be treated to such a display. Almost makes me want to join in."

Scott and Tory jumped apart. Tory's fluster soon turned to surprise when she saw who stood in the now-open door. Seeing the large Egyptian framed in the doorway, and knowing that was what he was from his dark good-looks, she imagined all kinds of terrible things that could have happened to Kendra. Having another one of Nefertem's kind in the house, and answering the front door, no less, could in no way be considered a good thing. At least in her way of thinking it wasn't. Without saying so much as a single word, she barged past the stranger and rushed inside the house.

Tory stepped into the hallway, and yelled, "Kendra! Kendra, where are you?"

Kendra came rushing out a few seconds later. "Tory, I'm here. What's wrong?"

"Oh, thank goodness you're all right."

"Of course I am. Why on earth wouldn't I be?"

Jerking her head in Mahes' direction, who now stood a short distance behind her, Tory said sarcastically, "Well, let me see now, could it be because of the tall, strange

Egyptian who answered your front door, do you think?"

"No cause for alarm. Mahes is harmless."

"Excuse me, but I could take great exception to that comment. I am hardly considered harmless, especially when it comes to a lady's virtue."

Kendra rolled her eyes. "Shut up, Mahes," she admonished. "Ignore him, Tory, he thinks every woman who sees him can't resist his purported charm."

Relieved Kendra was indeed okay and not in any danger, Tory turned to get a better look at Mahes. She saw why he would have such a big ego when it came to his charms. He was good looking enough to make any woman's mouth water in longing. She had to wonder how two such drop-dead gorgeous men like Nefertem and Mahes could exist. If she'd met Mahes before she'd met Scott, she would have been very tempted, but not now. Her gaze instinctively slid to Scott. She was surprised to find him staring at Mahes with a look of awe.

"Scott, can you please tell me why you're looking at Mahes like that?" Tory was almost afraid to ask.

"It's just…it's just, he's Mahes."

It was Tory's turn to roll her eyes. "Here we go again."

Mahes turned to look at Scott. "Yes, I am Mahes."

There was excitement in Scott's voice when he spoke. "Since you're here at the same place as Nefertem, then you must truly be his brother. It's only been assumed that you were, but you being here is the proof. I can't believe the one called The Lord of the Massacre, the punisher of those who violate Maat, is standing in front of me."

"How do you know so much about me?"

Kendra was the one who answered that question for Scott. "He's an Egyptologist. Which means he's made a career in the study of everything to do with ancient Egypt."

"Truly? Are there many such people who do what he does?"

"Yes, there are many people who do. So excuse Scott if he stares at you. He did the same thing with Nefertem when they first met."

"Interesting. I see there is much to learn about this world of yours."

"I, in turn, could learn much from you," Scott added.

"Be that as it may, Scott is here for another reason all together."

*

Nefertem had spoken those words. He had silently listened to the conversation taking place in the hallway. He had been in the kitchen with Kendra when Scott and Tory had arrived. The easy camaraderie between his brother and the others reaffirmed just how different from them he was becoming. The feeling of being emotionally detached was getting stronger inside him—another sign that time would all too soon run out for him.

"Have you found out anything, Scott?"

Scott shook his head. "I'm really not sure, but I can show you what I have so far." Preceding the others, he went into the living room and placed his papers on the coffee table. The rest of them filed in after him.

"What exactly do you have him searching for, brother?" Mahes asked.

"It is of no concern of yours."

Scott interrupted. "I beg to differ. He could help. He might be able to come up with some ideas about what your father tried to say."

Mahes shot Nefertem a surprised look. "You were in contact with Father? I thought you told me that was not possible. That there are no temples of Ptah here."

"There are not. Let us just leave it that there had been one way, but it has been exhausted and no longer of any use. You can forget about trying to use it yourself."

"You can stop worrying, brother. I have decided to help in your plans to stop mother. Besides, it is not as if I have much choice in the matter. You made that decision for me when you trapped me in this realm."

Nefertem gave his brother a hard stare. He trusted Mahes, but there still was that one truth that hung between them—Mahes had come there at their mother's behest. "Am I to only take your word for it? You came here for a purpose."

"Yes, but once again, you voided that. I cannot very well tell anything now, can I?"

"Fine, I guess I do not have much choice. Just try to behave is all I ask."

Mahes chuckled. "I will try, but I cannot tell you I will be on good behavior at all times."

Nefertem gave him a fierce scowl, not finding any humor in what Mahes had said. Deciding to ignore his brother for the time being, he turned his attention back to Scott. He expected to find him still riffling through the papers he had brought, but was a bit surprised to find Scott staring at a newspaper. He seemed absorbed in a particular article.

"What are you reading, Scott?"

Not taking his gaze from the newspaper, Scott shook his head. "All those hours of pouring over textbooks and all I had to do was look in today's newspaper. I would have saved myself a lot of time."

"What do you mean?"

"I've been looking through all my books and have come up with nothing. Which was obviously a big waste of time. I should have been reading newspapers, it would seem." He pointed at a small article found on the last page of the first section of the newspaper. "This one tiny article is the biggest clue I've found so far."

Nefertem moved so he could look over Scott's shoulder, then read the article the other man had pointed out. The more he read, the more he saw what Scott had been referring to.

It held great significance, at least it did to them. It was written about the Sphinx and the possibility of there being a hidden chamber buried beneath the two front legs of the monument. One theory went so far as to state that a long-forgotten library, from the lost city of Atlantis, could be housed there. It told of two Frenchmen's theory of a secret chamber to be found inside the Great Pyramid called Khufu or Cheops. The so-called "structure" was likely to be located in an area below the queen's burial chamber inside the pyramid.

That wasn't something they could take lightly. The idea of either theory proving to be true was something they could not easily dismiss out of hand, especially since both hidden rooms—if they existed—were within a stone's throw from each other. The pyramid, Kufu, was the only one of the three Great Pyramids in close proximity to the Sphinx. Could those rooms be what his father had tried to tell him about?

CHAPTER SIXTEEN

Neither Scott nor Nefertem seemed to deem it necessary to let the rest of them in on what they'd found. Kendra decided she'd pry the information out of them.

"Are you two going to keep us in the dark, or do I have to snatch that newspaper from you?"

Scott answered. Nefertem seemed to be lost in thought and unable to do so. "Well, it just so happens an article in today's paper might be able to point us in the right direction. Apparently, there's a possibility of there being two hidden rooms, one beneath the Sphinx and another hidden inside one of the Great Pyramids."

"In Egypt?"

"Yes, of course, in Egypt."

"Okay, that's all very well and good, but I have one question. Does that mean we would have to be in Egypt to have this information be of any use to us?"

Appearing at a loss for words, Scott didn't answer right away. The silence stretched.

Finally, Nefertem spoke. "If they are to be found in Egypt, then Egypt is where I must go. I can do nothing here."

Kendra narrowed her eyes at Nefertem. "What do you mean by you? Shouldn't you have said we?"

"No, I meant exactly what I said."

It hurt to hear him say that. All she could think of was how could Nefertem even think to leave her behind? The time left to them was finite. It hurt that he would choose to cut it even shorter.

"Just how do you plan to get to Egypt? It isn't as if you can drive there. Unless you have another power at your disposal, which can pop you there in a matter of seconds."

"In this form, as a mortal, no, I have no such power."

Tory broke into their conversation. "Yeah, Nefertem, Kendra is right. You do need us. We know how to get you to Egypt, and we have an inside contact, sort of. Kendra's brother is already there."

"You did not tell me your brother was in Egypt, Kendra."

Kendra shrugged. "It wasn't as if you ever asked, now was it? I didn't think Markus being there held any relevance to our problem."

"It might not have before I spoke to my father, but now it does."

"So Markus is in Egypt. I doubt he could be of much help, anyway. The only contact information I have for him is the return address on the package he used to send the necklace to me. By now, he could have already moved on to another hotel. As for owning a cell phone to contact him that way, Markus never takes it away with him in case he loses it, which is a pain."

Mahes went and slipped an arm around Kendra's shoulders. He pulled her against his side. "If you have well and truly decided to not take Kendra with you, Nefertem, I will gladly stay behind with her." With his free hand, he forced her to look at him. "I am more than happy to take your place in her bed." He bent his head to kiss her.

Nefertem let loose with a loud cat howl of rage. In one smooth motion, Mahes shoved Kendra away so he could dodge the fist that had been about to slam into his face. He easily avoided the next, and the next, that flew in quick succession. Nefertem's rage made him sloppy, and with each miss, the angrier Nefertem became.

The next punch aimed in his direction, Mahes caught in his open palm. Closing his hand around Nefertem's fist, he kicked a leg out, knocking Nefertem's out from beneath him. Acting quickly, Mahes jumped on the now felled Nefertem. He positioned himself so he sat on his brother's chest and arms, effectively pinning him to the floor.

"No more, Nefertem. You needed me to do that."

Nefertem let loose with another ear-piercing growl. "Damn you, Mahes, and your tests."

"If not for my tests, dear brother, you would never learn anything."

"Get off me. Now!" Twisting, Nefertem tried to displace Mahes.

A bit distressed at what had just taken place, Kendra couldn't watch Nefertem and Mahes any longer without interrupting. "Please, Mahes, let him up."

Mahes cocked his head in her direction and shook it in denial. "Not just yet. I do this for his own good." After saying that, he redirected his attention back on his brother. "I will let you up when you get it through your thick head that you need Kendra. Like it or not, she is now part of you. Stop hurting her with your self-sacrificing words."

"All right, I admit she has some sway over me. Is that good enough for you?"

Giving a quick nod, Mahes relented and eased off his brother. Nefertem quickly gained his feet.

"Do not do that again, Mahes. I will not tolerate any more of your useless tests. Do you understand?"

"As you wish."

Now that the ruckus was finally over, Kendra went to

Nefertem. "Is it true what Mahes said? Am I a part of you?"

"In some respect, it is. You are the best bed partner I have ever had. If you are referring to that aspect of our relationship, then yes, you are a part of me. I will not find anyone as good as you to take your place."

Not giving it a second thought, Kendra curled her right hand into a fist and slammed it into Nefertem's stomach. She was no weak woman. There was power behind her punch. A combination of her strength and his not expecting her to react so violently had him bending over and gasping for breath.

It hurt more than when she'd been dumped by her ex-fiancé. She'd thought Nefertem was different, and that what she saw was what she got. How wrong she'd been. She had to get away and be by herself to think things through. Staying in the same room, let alone the same house, with Nefertem, she could no longer do. Kendra slowly backed away from him.

"I can't do this right now. I have to leave for a while." Turning around, Kendra avoided looking in the faces of the three other people in the room as she walked by them. She picked up her purse and car keys from the table in the front hall, then calmly walked out the front door.

* * * *

"You bastard! How could you do that to Kendra? If I were a man, I would teach you a lesson you wouldn't soon forget," Tory said with barely contain her fury.

"Calm down, Tory." Scott put a reassuring arm around her shoulders. She just as quickly shrugged out of his embrace.

"No, I won't calm down. He hurt her. Badly."

Scott looked at Nefertem. He saw what Nefertem had said to Kendra had cost him dearly. The man was stiff as a board, and his face had become an equally stiff mask, displaying not one single emotion. Scott didn't agree with what Nefertem had done, but he knew the reasoning behind it and so sympathized with the man.

"I think we should go, Tory, and let Nefertem and Kendra work this out by themselves."

Tory was about to protest, but Scott turned her away from Nefertem. Before he led her out of the house, Scott paused to say one last thing to Nefertem. "Now that we have at least a little more to go on, I'll dig up all I can on those supposed hidden chambers."

Nefertem bowed his head in Scott's direction. "Thank you. The sooner you find out more, the sooner you can help me get to Egypt."

"I'll do that." Having said all he wanted to say, Scott steered the still-fuming Tory from the house.

* * * *

Kendra had no idea where she was going. All that mattered was getting farther away from the house, and farther away from Nefertem. His harsh words still echoed inside her mind. They still cut her to the very bone.

Driving down streets with no real destination in mind, she was surprised when she ended up at the mall. She pulled into a parking space way at the back of the parking lot, then shut the car off. Kendra laughed and cried at the same time as she thought about the irony of it all. She'd wound up at one of the very places that'd been a turning point for her. Where she'd found out exactly what Nefertem truly was, where she'd actually admitted to Mahes, earlier that very same day, of her love for Nefertem. She leaned her forehead against the steering wheel and let her tears fall.

The length of time she sat there and cried her eyes out, Kendra couldn't guess. It could have been anywhere from a few minutes to an hour that easily passed before her tears ran dry. She straightened again, then reached for her purse and fished around inside it until she came up with an unused tissue. Using it, she roughly dried her eyes and then blew her nose.

Now that she'd given in to her tears, she was done with them. It was time for her to show Nefertem she wasn't going to let him hurt her like that so easily and get away with it.

Starting the car motor running, Kendra pushed back her hurt. She pulled out of the parking lot and then drove home with a purpose. It didn't take very long for her to arrive at her house since she was no longer driving aimlessly.

Kendra slammed the front door behind her before she went to look for Nefertem. She found only Mahes, sitting in the living room. Nefertem was nowhere to be found. "Where's Nefertem?"

Mahes, who'd been busily flipping through all the stations on the television, jumped at the sound of Kendra's voice. "I did not hear you come in."

"I can see that." Kendra nodded in the direction of the television to back up her simple statement. "Where is he?"

"Which 'he' are you referring to?"

Kendra scowled. "Are you deliberately being obtuse to piss me off even more?"

Mahes smiled. "That is what I wanted to hear. Being angry is a good thing."

"Do you ever stop testing people, Mahes?"

"Sometimes, but I find it much too entertaining to stop all the time."

Kendra shook her head in dismay. "To each his own I guess. Now where the hell is your brother?"

"He went out to what you call your backyard."

Kendra left Mahes to continue with his channel surfing and headed for the dining room where the sliding glass doors opened to the backyard. She paused just long enough to see where exactly Nefertem was before she pulled open the slider.

Her backyard could in no way be described as artistically landscaped to perfection. Gardening was not her forte. Even so that didn't mean she totally neglected it either. She kept the grass neatly trimmed, and managed to stay on top of the weeds in the one small patch of flowers she'd planted. Roses, irises, and a few tulips were what she'd decided would do the job of adding a dash of color to the back. That they needed very little care had been a bonus.

Kendra stepped through the door and onto the deck, then crossed it in a few strides. She took the two steps down to the lawn before she headed to the very back of the yard where a large maple tree grew. There Nefertem sat on the grass at the base of it. He had his face lifted to the rays of sunlight that filtered through the branches. His eyes were closed.

Kendra skimmed her gaze over his handsome face. Why couldn't he have been different? Why did she have to fall for men who ended up trampling all over her heart? Another fresh wave of tears reared inside her. Ruthlessly, she pushed them away. Weakness wasn't what she needed right now. She recalled all of Nefertem's hateful words and grew angry once more.

"Wake up, Nefertem. You had your chance at taking potshots at me, but no more."

Nefertem cracked one eye open. "I only but spoke the truth."

"So what we've shared was a lie. When you told me you'd never before felt like this with a woman, that was an act?"

Closing his eye again, Nefertem turned his face back into the sunlight. "Of course. I learned that telling mortal women such tales opened their arms to me, along with other parts of themselves."

Seeing red, Kendra did what would hurt Nefertem more than mere words ever could. It was something her brother had taught her when she'd reached her teenage years. With one swift kick to a certain part of Nefertem's anatomy, she effectively unmanned him. He writhed in pain. She had to admit it gave her a small measure of pleasure.

"If that's truly how you feel, I can guarantee you'll never be welcomed into my bed again. We're finished, you and I, from this moment on. Since it was I who started this whole mess, I'll see it to the end. Contrary to what you want, I'll be going to Egypt with you. Not you, nor anyone else, for that matter, is going to stop me. When this is over, you'll never have to set eyes on me again."

She turned her back on Nefertem, who was still curled in a ball, and left him in pain. Her days of caring for a man were over.

CHAPTER SEVENTEEN

It was some minutes later before Nefertem could uncurl his body. That was one pain he would never have felt had he been in his immortal form. Being mortal had too many weak spots for his liking.

Finally able to breathe without panting, he slowly sat up. Kendra had surprised him with that move. He had not expected her to react so violently. He had not known she knew how to fight so dirty either. He silently commended her for it. He deserved what she had done to him. It had been all a lie, and it turned out to be an all too effective lie at that. Already a part of him mourned the loss of her.

Nefertem gingerly moved to his feet, then went inside the house. Much to his dismay, Mahes waited to confront him as Nefertem stepped through the glass door.

"Not one word out of you, Mahes." Meaning to walk past his brother, Nefertem found his path blocked by Mahes' outstretched arm.

"Not this time, brother. What game are you playing at here?"

"You of all people should know why I do this."

"Yes, I do, but I do not agree with it."

"What else would you have me do? Spout words of undying love to Kendra, then turn around and leave her? It is not as if I can return to her once I am back to my true self."

"I still think you have made a monumental mistake."

"I think not. Even if we do manage to stop Mother, I still cannot keep Kendra as mine. I will have to leave her behind."

Mahes shook his head sadly. "All right, I will say no more, but you have managed to make the rest of our stay here a tad uncomfortable. Kendra was furious when she came back in from talking to you."

"I bet she was." The pain she had inflected on him proved that.

The sound of feet stamping around on the floor above them could suddenly be heard. Nefertem and Mahes looked at the ceiling.

"I would say Kendra's temper has not cooled off one bit, Nefertem."

"From the sound of it, you are right. I think I should at least see what she is doing up there."

Nefertem left his brother, who wore a bemused grin, and went upstairs. He could still hear Kendra stamping about in her bedroom. He could not see what she was doing in there, because the door to the room was shut tight. He wanted to go in and comfort her, tell her he was wrong and did not mean what he had said, but doing that was out of the question. It was for her own good that he had done what he had done.

Startled when the door suddenly opened, Nefertem jumped back. Kendra was in the open doorway with her arms loaded with most of his belongings, things that had been stored in her room until now.

"Oh good, you came up. You can now take these and save me from having to make two trips." Unceremoniously, Kendra shoved what she held into

Nefertem's arms.

Kendra turned back into the room before she walked to the bed and gathered up another pile of his things. She marched past him, then went to the spare bedroom and dumped what she carried onto the bed there. Nefertem quietly entered behind her.

"Here's how things are going to work, Nefertem. You'll now be bunking with Mahes for however long you're here. My bedroom is, as of this minute, off limits. So get used to the idea of sleeping with your brother."

Kendra walked out of the bedroom with her head held high. She did not even spare Nefertem a backward glance on her way out.

* * * *

That night sleep did not come easily to Nefertem. It did not feel right not having Kendra sleeping beside him. Mahes was a poor substitute by far. To reinforce the differences between the two, Mahes snored very loudly. Something his brother had been doing for most of the night. To get away from the noise, Nefertem rolled onto his side to the very edge of the bed.

This was worse than any punishment his mother could ever inflict on him. The ironic thing about it all was that it was one of his own devising. He closed his eyes and tried to make sleep come and claim him for the hundredth time that night. Surprisingly, it did.

With it came a dream. This time he was not in his mother's lavishly decorated temple. He found himself surrounded by a thick mist that obscured all that was near him. There was only complete silence. Not liking where he had been taken, Nefertem prepared to meet whatever was to come. It would not be pleasant.

"You have a lot to answer for, Nefertem." His mother's voice boomed all around him.

"What do you want with me, Mother?"

"Do not speak to me in that manner. You know exactly why I have brought you here. By what right did you have to change Mahes into a mortal? He should not be with you."

"Of course he should not. I am to suffer this punishment alone."

"As it has always been."

"Well, Mahes came to pester me. Place the blame on him rather than me."

"Are you trying to keep something from me? Is that why you kept Mahes with you? Did he find out something you do not want me to know?"

Nefertem ground his teeth. His mother was too close to the truth for his liking. "No, Mother, I am not trying to hide anything from you. Mahes just picked a time to visit when I was not in a very forgiving mood."

"So you decided to keep him with you. I would think you would have sent him away instead, if he was bothering you so."

"You know I cannot do that in this form. I did what I could at the time."

"I see."

For a time, his mother fell silent. He knew she wasn't finished with him yet. If she had been, he would have been released from the dream.

"I can feel your pain, Nefertem." His mother paused dramatically, then said, "Ah, it is caused by a woman."

Nefertem stiffened. "The pain is mine to feel."

His mother laughed. "How self-sacrificing of you, but totally unnecessary. What kind of mother would I be if I did not take it away?"

"I do not want you to do that." Nefertem growled.

"You are feeling too much lately. I like it not, but that can be fixed."

Before Nefertem could respond, the dreamscape slowly

faded around him. The sound of his mother's laughter was the last thing he heard before he returned to himself, and the last thought he had was that his mother had defeated him. When he came awake with the morn, whatever she had done to him would be revealed.

* * * *

Stretching, Kendra winced at the pain in her head. Lack of rest always gave her a pounding headache. Her sleep during the night had been fitful at best. It was hard knowing Nefertem slept in the spare room just down the hall. She missed not having him in her bed to snuggle with. Each time she'd reached out for him, and found the place next to her empty, she had awakened. Subconsciously, she couldn't let him go.

Kendra rolled over and squinted at her alarm clock. It was hours past the time she usually got up in the morning. She groaned to herself.

She got out of bed, then took a quick shower, hoping it would help clear her head. The warm water relieved some of the pain. As she dressed afterward, she strained to hear if anyone else moved around in the house. She couldn't detect any sounds coming from the other room.

Gingerly, she opened her bedroom door, poked her head out, and looked up the hall. It was deserted. She opened the door wider, stepped through it, and headed down the stairs.

Completely bypassing the living room, she went straight to the kitchen. A couple of cups of tea were in order to fix what remained of her headache. After reaching that room, she found Mahes was already there, at the open fridge. He seemed to be looking for something.

"Can I help you, Mahes?"

Having had his head stuck deep inside the fridge, Mahes cracked the back of it when he jumped at the sound of Kendra's voice. The door had blocked her entrance.

He straightened and rubbed the abused spot. "Kendra, you shouldn't sneak up on a person like that."

"I was hardly sneaking around." Kendra laughed.

"Fine, whatever you say. Since you are here, I am starved. What is there to eat?"

Kendra shook her head. "Typical male you are. Filling your stomach takes precedence over everything else."

"Well, that is not exactly the first thing I would have liked this morning, but I doubt you would be willing to satisfy that baser need for me."

Kendra shook her head again. "You really are incorrigible, you know."

"Someone around here has to be."

She pushed Mahes out of the way, reached into the fridge, and pulled out eggs and a loaf of bread. "Since I won't do the one, I can at least do the other. I'll whip us up some breakfast."

Mahes moved aside so Kendra could get to cooking without him being in the way and sat at the table. "How are you doing, Kendra?"

"Fine. Why wouldn't I be?"

"Maybe because you had your heart trampled on by my idiot brother."

Just about to crack an egg into the frying pan she'd set on the stove top, Kendra froze at Mahes' remark. "What of it? I'll get over Nefertem just as I did my ex-fiancé."

"Will you still help us?"

"Of course. I hold myself responsible for starting this whole mess. I'll do what I can to clean up after it."

"I am glad you will not abandon us. There is much about this world of yours neither Nefertem nor I understand."

"Speaking of your brother, where is Nefertem?"

"He is still sleeping. He did not have a very peaceful rest last night. I decided to let him be and sleep longer."

Kendra stilled once again. "Why would Nefertem have trouble sleeping? The man has a heart of solid ice."

"Do not believe everything he said to you yesterday."

At Mahes' words, Kendra spun around and glared at him. "Stop it. Stop trying to convince me Nefertem is a better man than he is. Stop confusing me. You say one thing, and Nefertem tells me another."

Mahes came around the table, took Kendra by the shoulders, and slouched so he looked her squarely in the eyes. "That is not my intent at all. I know you care for Nefertem, deeply, just as he does you. What he said to you yesterday was not truly how he feels for you. He is trying to play the gallant. He figures if he gets you to hate him before he leaves, then your parting will not be so painful for you."

"You don't know how much I wish what you said was the truth."

"Believe it."

After saying those words, Mahes looked at something over her head. "Well, hello, Nefertem. You are in time for breakfast. Kendra has kindly agreed to make some for us."

Kendra turned to look at Nefertem. Her heart beat faster at the sight of him, something it did every time she saw him. She found him as devastatingly good-looking as she had when she'd first clapped eyes on him. Wanting desperately to believe everything Mahes had told her, she smiled tentatively at Nefertem. All he did was stare back at her coldly. The smile fell from her lips.

Nefertem walked farther into the room and went to the stove to see what was cooking. He sniffed and scowled.

"I guess I can make do with this for now, but I expect better meals than what you have cooked."

At first, Kendra couldn't tell if Nefertem was serious or making a crack about her cooking. He sat at the table and then snapped his fingers at her to serve him. She realized he was indeed serious.

Feeling a sense of shock over Nefertem's behavior, Kendra flashed a questioning look at Mahes. He shrugged.

Kendra decided to just let it go and went to the stove. She dished up some eggs and toast for Nefertem. She placed the plate in front of him, then made plates of the same for herself and Mahes. Once they were all seated at the table, she decided to broach the subject of what Nefertem had said to her the day before. She needed to hear him say they were all lies. She couldn't think otherwise until he told her yes or no.

"Nefertem, I need to ask you something, and I want you to answer truthfully."

He gave her an exasperated look and put down his fork before he sat back in his chair with his arms crossed over his chest. "I hope this thing you are going to ask is important enough that you had to interrupt me when I am eating."

"I feel it is, and I should think you would feel the same."

"Well, get on with it before my food becomes inedible."

His tone words gave Kendra some pause. Nefertem had never spoken to her in that manner before. It was quite different, even from yesterday's behavior. "It's about what you said to me the day before. Did you mean what you said or did you say that to push me away? So I wouldn't be devastated when you left at the end of all this?"

Nefertem threw his head back and howled with laughter. It took him a few seconds to get himself back under control enough to be able to talk. "You stupid woman. Why would I wish to spare your feelings? Who would put such drivel into your mind?"

Unable to respond, Kendra helplessly looked at Mahes. Once again Nefertem's hurt-filled words had floored her. Was it Mahes' job to set her up for Nefertem, only to have him knock her back down again?

Nefertem shook his head. "I see my brother is even a

bigger fool than you are."

If Nefertem had planned to say anything further, Mahes didn't give him a chance to finish. He sent his food flying, clambered across the table, and slammed his fist into his brother's face. They ended up on the floor after that single punch. Kendra sat helplessly in her chair as the two men fought. She silently hoped they'd kill each other.

CHAPTER EIGHTEEN

Over the sound of Nefertem's and Mahes' fists connecting with flesh, Kendra heard the phone ringing in the distance. She left her chair, carefully stepped around the two men, and went to answer it. She hoped it wasn't Tory calling to see how she was holding up. She wasn't ready to have a friend-to-friend chat at that precise moment.

Kendra picked up the phone and distractedly said hello. The person on the other end spoke, and tears came to her eyes.

"Hey, baby sister. I thought I'd call and see if you got the present I sent you okay."

"Oh, Markus, you have no idea how happy I am to hear the sound of your voice."

"All right, out with it, Kendra. Something is wrong, and don't tell me there isn't. That idiot Greg isn't bothering you, is he?"

After swallowing hard, Kendra pushed back her tears and forced herself to chuckle. "Hardly. As for your gift, I got it all right." At that moment, a particularly loud crash came from the direction of the kitchen.

"What the hell was that, Kendra? Are you sure you're okay?"

"Yes…no. I wish you were here."

"That's it, I'm coming home. I'll catch the next flight out of here."

"No. No, don't do that. Right now, the best way to help me is for you to stay in Egypt."

"Kendra, either you tell me what's going on, or I'm coming home, no matter what you want."

Kendra briefly closed her eyes and thought through what she could tell Markus without having him come running home. "Let's just say your present turned out to be something other than a simple pendant. I got a lot more than I bargained for." She briefly outlined her plans to go to Egypt.

Markus didn't say anything for a brief span of time. "Okay, so the inexpensive piece of jewelry turned out to be not so inexpensive. Is that it? That still doesn't explain why you have to come to Egypt, and I presume, with the pendant in tow."

"Um…it doesn't have to do with how much it's worth as to what I inadvertently released with it."

"You've lost me now."

Suddenly realizing the noise that had been coming from the kitchen had ceased, Kendra could only wonder who had turned out to be the victor of the battle royal that had taken place.

"Look, Markus, I have to go now. I promise to call you when everything has been arranged. Please try not to worry. I'll explain it all when I see you in person. Before I go, give me the number and address where you're staying."

Markus gave Kendra his contact information. After she hastily scribbled it on a scrap piece of paper, she hung up. She stuck the note into the pocket of her jean shorts as she decided she'd better check out what kind of damage had been done to the kitchen.

At first, she couldn't see the two men. The table was knocked over onto its side and obscured her view. Obviously, that was what had caused the loud crash before. She stepped around it and found Mahes sitting on the floor so out of breath he panted. Nefertem was prone beside him. He seemed to have been knocked out cold.

"Looks as if you were the victor, Mahes. I hope you didn't kill him in the process."

Mahes flashed Kendra a crooked grin, and said, "Close, but I decided I had better hold back." His expression turn serious. "We have a major problem here. What I told you before about Nefertem trying to push you away was the truth, no matter what you think. Now, that was no act on his part. Something changed him during the night. Or I should say *someone* changed him."

"You mean your mother got to him again through a dream. Just great. So, what has she done to him now?"

Mahes sadly shook his head. "From the way Nefertem acted, I can only assume she took away his ability to feel, to care. Sorry, Kendra, this is entirely my fault. If I had not come, Nefertem would not have been forced to keep me here, and my mother would not have known anything was wrong. She must know he changed me to a mortal."

Kendra's heart dropped, but she made no outward sign that it had. "Now what? Does it mean I'll have to tolerate an obnoxious Nefertem only or is there more?"

"Much more, sorry to say. We will have to watch Nefertem very closely. The first sign of him wanting to commit any kind of violence, we have to tie him up, and that time will come all too soon."

"Then we'd better get to Egypt as soon as we can arrange it. Before it's too late."

The still-unconscious Nefertem was placed none too gently on the bed in the spare bedroom. Mahes had hefted his brother's dead weight up the stairs and into the room.

Kendra had trailed him. Now that Nefertem had been moved, she motioned for Mahes to follow her. She closed the bedroom door behind them.

After returning to the main floor, they headed for the kitchen. Mahes righted the table while Kendra cleaned up the food mess. Once the room had been restored to its former condition, she poured them each a cup of tea from the pot she'd made earlier. She took a fortifying sip and then handed Mahes his.

"While you and Nefertem tried to kill each other in here, my brother phoned. He's still in Egypt. I told him as little as I could without having him totally freak out. How things stand now, he'll be expecting us to meet him there."

Mahes took a sip from his mug and scowled. "You enjoy this weak drink? I would much rather have a beer."

"Sorry, we don't drink beer in the morning, at least not in this house. Settle for having tea. Now keep to the subject at hand. Getting you and Nefertem to Egypt is going to be no small feat."

"I got the impression from what you said earlier it would not be so problematic."

"For me or Tory or Scott even, it wouldn't be. You and Nefertem are different. It isn't so much how we'll get there, as the paperwork you both will need to have access to it."

Mahes scratched his head. "Paperwork?"

"Yes. You see, anyone who wants to leave this country to travel to another is required to have a valid passport or they can't leave. To get one you need proof you were born here or have citizenship."

"Since neither Nefertem nor myself were, we cannot get this passport."

"That and the fact you're both thousands of years old."

The phone rang once more. Kendra rolled her eyes and went to answer it. "I hope this isn't going to be more bad news. I've already had my share of excitement for one day."

Kendra returned a short while later. Mahes looked at her questioningly. She shook her head in response.

"No more bad news, thank goodness. It was Tory, checking in on me. I explained what's going on with Nefertem and the need to go to Egypt very soon. Apparently, getting both of you passports won't be as hard as I'd originally thought. Scott was at Tory's place, and he said he has a friend who can take care of them for us. A byproduct of a misspent youth it would seem."

Mahes wore a blank expression, and Kendra chuckled. "Scott knows someone who can make passports for anyone for a price. Which is actually against the law."

"Is it wise that we do this?"

"It isn't as if we have much of a choice. I admit it isn't something I condone, but there's nothing else for it. If we were to do it officially, not only would it take months, but they would lock us away in the looney bin for our troubles. No one would believe you and Nefertem are what you say you are."

"So, what must we do now?"

"Tory and Scott are on their way here as we speak. Scott is bringing his digital camera to take yours and Nefertem's picture for the fake passports."

"Hopefully, Nefertem will be in a better frame of mind when they get here or we will have another battle on our hands."

Kendra sighed. "Let's hope a part of him remembers what he truly is and cooperates."

* * * *

"If he's that unpredictable, how exactly will I be able to take a half decent picture of him?"

"I will make him cooperate," Mahes replied.

Scott shook his head. "Okay. Before we tackle that

problem, let me take your picture." After positioning Mahes so he stood with his back to the one white wall in the living room that was devoid of pictures, Scott took aim with his digital camera and snapped the picture. "One down and one more to go," he muttered.

Blinking, Mahes headed for the stairs. "I will bring Nefertem down. He should be revived by now."

After Mahes disappeared up the stairs, Tory wrapped an arm around Kendra's shoulders. "Now that the three of us are alone, we need to talk. Scott and I think with Nefertem the way he is now, it really isn't safe for you to remain here anymore. I want you to stay with me until we leave for Egypt."

"We?"

"Of course, we. Do you really think I'd let you run off to Egypt without us going along? After all, Scott and I have been involved with this from the start. We want to see how it ends."

Kendra gave Tory a weak smile. "I'm not going to say I'm unhappy about that, because I'm not. Having you and Scott along will be welcome company."

"You agree to stay with me until we go?"

"I can't, Tory. Even though he isn't the same man, I can't give up any of the days we have left together."

Tory nodded in understanding. "I won't force you then."

"Which I'm thankful for. I have enough on my plate already without having to fight with my best friend on top of it all."

Just at that moment, the sound of heavy footfalls coming down the stairs reached her ears. *Let the fun begin*, Kendra thought as Mahes and Nefertem rounded the corner. From the look on Nefertem's face, he seemed not in any better frame of mind.

CHAPTER NINETEEN

"Mahes says you need to take my picture. Why?" Nefertem had not lost any of his arrogant manner after being knocked out cold by his brother. If anything, he was worse. Kendra gritted her teeth in anticipation of the fight that was to come. She came to stand in front of Nefertem to confront him.

"Yes, we need your picture. If you don't do this, you won't be able to go to Egypt."

"Why would I want to go home to Egypt? It matters not where I am. She will still come."

It was obvious when his mother had taken away his emotions, she'd also inadvertently erased Nefertem's memory of what they'd planned to do. "Yes, that's true, but wouldn't you rather be on Egyptian soil when she does?"

Nefertem seemed to study her face, almost as if he weighed the truth of her words. He gave a curt nod. "Fine. I will allow my picture to be taken. For some reason, I have an urge to see my homeland again. I feel as if I have something in particular to do there."

So, with no ensuing fight, Nefertem allowed Scott to

position him against the wall. The picture now taken, she breathed a sigh of relief. Not noticing any of the under currents of emotions swirling around him, Nefertem went to the couch and switched on the television. Not wanting to set him off now that he seemed to be in an agreeable mood, Kendra motioned for the others to follow her to the kitchen.

"How long will it take to get the passports, Scott?"

After viewing the pictures on the camera, Scott nodded. "I called in a favor, so they should be done by tomorrow."

"Okay, good. I'll start calling around to book us flights to Egypt. Markus is taking care of getting rooms at the hotel where he's staying. I'll call him later as well and tell him another one needs to be set aside for you and Tory."

"We'll leave you to it then," Tory said. She turned to Mahes. "You look after Kendra. If anything should happen to her..."

Mahes held up his hands. "No harm will come to her. Nefertem is forbidden to touch the one who summoned him. Myself, on the other hand, is not so well-protected from him." Gingerly, he touched the now visible black eye he sported.

"At least that's reassuring, that he won't hurt Kendra. As for you, I'm sure you can hold your own."

Tory gave Kendra a quick hug before leaving, and whispered into her ear, "Remember, my door is always open. You can make the phone calls from my place as well as you can from here."

Kendra shook her head and squeezed her friend in return. In equally hushed tones, she said, "Stop playing the part of worried mother hen. I'll be fine. If what Mahes says is true, I'm in no danger."

"I'm not just talking about physical danger."

Kendra stepped back and gave her a slight smile. "I'll be fine, physically and mentally."

Tory held up her hands in submission. "Okay, I give.

Call me when you have everything arranged."

"I'll be sure to do that. Tory, thanks."

"For what?"

"For not walking away. Let's face it, this isn't exactly what you'd call normal."

"Are you kidding? I wouldn't miss this for the world. I should be thanking you. If not for all of this weirdness, I wouldn't be with Scott today. For that, I'm very grateful."

Kendra was happy to hear her friend say those words. Tory needed a good man in her life, and it looked as if she'd finally found him. Seeing Tory and Scott out the door, Kendra thought at least one of them would have a happy ending.

* * * *

Scott had dropped Tory off at her place before he'd headed for the downtown section of the city. After parking his car in one of the parking garages, he headed to a tall high-rise office building. He took the elevator to the top floor and then entered the offices of one of the city's largest advertising agencies.

At the reception desk, he asked the woman there to let his friend, Peter Graves, know he was there to see him. The woman happily buzzed to the right office, and a few minutes later, Peter came to meet him.

Peter shook Scott's hand before he motioned for Scott to follow him. Scott occasionally met Peter for drinks when both of them managed to find time from their busy work schedules. They'd first met when they'd started university, and had stayed friends ever since. Scott still found it hard to accept that the Peter from those days was now a straight-laced advertising executive. Peter had been a wild child during their schooling.

Once they reached the office, Peter shut the door behind them and closed the blinds on the one glass wall, giving them more privacy. He took a seat behind his desk and motioned for Scott to take one of the chairs in front of it.

"Okay, Scott, what have you got for me? Before we go any further, let me say I'm only doing this for you since I owed you one. After this, I won't be doing anything like it again."

Scott smiled. "No problem. I wouldn't have asked you if there was any other way, which there isn't." He took his camera out of the case he carried over his shoulder and handed it to Peter. "I need passports for the two men in the pictures."

Peter reviewed the pictures. Scott waited for his reaction when he got to Nefertem's. As expected, Peter looked at him with an incredulous look on his face. "You've to be kidding? Why is he wearing contacts to make his eyes look like that?"

"Those aren't contacts, Pete. I need you to doctor the picture a bit so they look normal."

Peter ran his hand through his short-cropped, reddish-brown hair and sat back in his chair. "I can do that. I won't ask you what you're up to or who these guys are, because I don't think I want to know. Just don't get your ass arrested and have the phony passports traced back to me. I was an idiot when I did a few of these for extra cash in university, but I don't have the balls now that I had then."

Scott laughed. "Tammy was the best thing for you, Pete. She finally tamed the wild child." Scott stood, and added, "Tell your beautiful wife I said hi. I'll drop by tomorrow for the camera and the passports. You're a lifesaver."

* * * *

Kendra spent the rest of the day on the phone. Even though they needed to be in Egypt sooner rather than later, she wasn't going to pay through the nose for airplane tickets. Tory and Scott would cover the cost of their own, but she had to pay for Nefertem's and Mahes' as well as her own. Her poor credit card was going to take another beating.

Finally getting a price she could handle, Kendra booked them all on a flight leaving for Egypt in three days. It would be cutting things a little close, but it was the best she could do. She wanted to allow for all contingencies. The main problem that could arise would be whether or not the passports would be ready when Scott said they would. Feeling a bit better for having accomplished that much, she dialed Tory's number at home.

* * * *

Nefertem had not a worry in the world. What happened on his arrival until now was just a vague, foggy, distant memory, one he could not readily bring into focus. With Kendra, he felt somehow connected, and not just because she possessed the pendant, which he felt more intensely as the day grew on.

He watched her as she made numerous phone calls throughout the day, arranging for transportation to Egypt. He still did not know the reason for the great urgency to go there, but it did not weigh heavily on his mind. There was no force that could get in the way of the punisher.

That his brother was there as well, and in mortal form, he vaguely remembered was caused by his own hand. There again, he could not fathom the motive behind it.

Now alone in the living room while the television's bright light lit the space, Nefertem felt the need to go to Kendra. Not as the coldhearted beast he was, but as he would be with his mate. The longer he sat, the stronger it became. Unable to resist the pull any longer, he switched the television off and then headed up the stairs to the bedrooms.

He did not go to the room he shared with Mahes, but

continued down the hall until he came to Kendra's closed door. He rested his hand on the doorknob. His body, his very soul, cried out for that mortal woman, but unbelievably, he hesitated. He could have her, possess her, but one small part of him resisted. It knew if he took her this night, he would hurt her. Not physically, but mentally. With great reluctance, he walked away. If he had stood there much longer, he would not have been able to keep to the decision of leaving her alone.

*

On the other side of the bedroom door, Kendra released the breath she'd held. Sleep had eluded her so she'd still been awake when she'd heard Nefertem's footfalls coming up the stairs, which she'd recognized. He'd come to her door, and she'd held herself as still as possible, not because she felt if he'd heard her moving he would have come in. No, it was herself she was afraid of. He was no longer the man she loved, but that didn't stop her from wanting to be back in his arms again.

Nefertem hadn't stepped away too quickly, and Kendra's will of resistance had eroded. It'd been a close one in the end. If he hadn't walked away then, she was pretty sure she would have opened the door for him. Luckily, she hadn't had to test the limits of her resistance.

Once she heard the spare bedroom door shut behind Nefertem, Kendra settled herself back in bed. It was going to be a very long night. She punched her pillow down and hoped what they found in Egypt would solve everything, for better or worse.

* * * *

Scott's friend turned out to be true to his word. Nefertem's and Mahes' new passports were finished the next day. Scott dropped them off, along with the plane tickets he'd agreed to get the day before. Kendra had thanked him for the help. It gave her one less thing to worry about, which was a good thing. As it turned out, Nefertem and Mahes had left all the packing to her. Not that it really bothered her, for it wasn't as if either one of them had had to perform that task before. It was just easier if she did it herself.

The rest of the day proved uneventful, and Nefertem behaved himself, which was a plus. Neither he nor Mahes decided to start World War Three under her roof. To make sure Nefertem did nothing untoward, Mahes had kept him company all day. If Nefertem had turned violent, Kendra had no idea what she would have done. The real test was to come, though. How would Nefertem react while in the air on the plane? She cringed to think what he'd do in such close quarters.

Thinking it might be better to be safe rather than sorry, Kendra made a trip to the drugstore. Since Nefertem would react badly having to be around a large number of mortals, she'd decided that to suppress the cat side of him a sleeping pill or two would be in order. The trick would be to get him to take them in the car on the way to the airport or shortly after arriving there. He had to be alert enough to go through customs or they possibly wouldn't allow him to board the plane. Ideally, he would sleep for most, if not all, the time they were in the air.

The pharmacist accepted the story she told him of her boyfriend suffering from major anxiety attacks while flying. After telling him the size of Nefertem, he suggested a brand of over-the-counter sleeping pills and told her what dose a man that large should be given.

After paying for her purchases, Kendra left the drugstore with a little bit of a lighter step. Nefertem would take the pills, even if she had to get Mahes to sit on him while she shoved them down Nefertem's throat.

CHAPTER TWENTY

The night before they were due to leave, Kendra spent the last couple of hours before going to sleep checking she hadn't forgotten anything. She had a bad tendency to get all in a tizzy when she had to prepare to go away. Her stress level would hit the roof hours before the scheduled time to leave. That was part of the reason she didn't accompany Markus on his many excursions. She only ended up driving him nuts.

So this night, not being any different from other times she'd traveled, Kendra kept flitting about the house. Upstairs one moment, and the next, running down the stairs to check she'd packed an item, which she'd thought she might have missed.

After about the sixth such trip down the stairs, Mahes blocked Kendra's path to the luggage that sat waiting for their departure in the living room. "Enough, Kendra. You are going to wear yourself to a frazzle before the trip has even begun."

"I just...need to...check..." Kendra tried to sidestep around Mahes, but he kept blocking her way.

"Everything is there. It was there the last five times you

checked. Now go to bed."

"If I don't look, I won't be able to sleep."

Mahes took Kendra by the shoulders, turned her around, and walked her to the foot of the stairs. "Go to bed. All is at the readiness for our departure tomorrow. Now go or I will be forced to stand guard on the luggage all night. In this form, I need as much sleep as any other mortal. So please let me rest tonight."

Kendra turned to face Mahes and shook her head as she smiled. "Okay, you win. I'll go to bed and stay there all night. I would hate to have to deprive you of your beauty sleep."

Mahes arched a brow. "I think my looks would not change for the worse that quickly."

Kendra laughed. As if Mahes' looks could ever change that drastically. "Of course not. Never mind."

She threw her arms around Mahes' neck and gave him a kiss on the lips, then hugged him close. He turned out to be a strong bulwark in her time of need. She only wished Nefertem could be that to her again. She sighed as Mahes returned her hug.

The sound of a deep-throated growl broke them apart. Kendra turned to stare at Nefertem. His handsome face was twisted with a snarl of rage. Mahes reassuringly patted her shoulder and pushed her toward the stairs once more.

"You go on up, Kendra. We will be fine." She hesitated. Mahes leaned closer and whispered, "He will calm down after you go upstairs. I think seeing you in my arms has set him off."

Understanding what Mahes had said, Kendra couldn't suppress the thrill that ran through her. Somewhere deep down inside, Nefertem must still have feelings for her. After sliding a quick look in his direction, she did what Mahes had asked.

* * * *

Once Mahes heard the sound of Kendra's bedroom door closing above, he turned to face his brother. "What is wrong, Nefertem?"

"Keep your hands to yourself. She is mine."

Mahes smiled to himself. Their mother must not have removed everything inside Nefertem. He still cared about the woman who was upstairs in her room. That could be a good thing for them.

"So proprietary you sound."

"She is mine," he said again.

"Just because she summoned you, and is in possession of the pendant, does not mean she is yours. Kendra is her own woman."

A range of emotions passed across Nefertem's face. There was definitely a deeply buried memory inside his brother's mind. It just had to be dug up and brought to the surface.

Nefertem snared at Mahes. "That is not why she is mine."

"Then enlighten me. Give me a good reason she is yours, and why I should not claim her as my own."

"I do not know," Nefertem said distractedly.

Mahes smiled. "If you do not know, I suggest you think long and hard about it. Your time grows short. Let Kendra at least have a memory of you not being a coldhearted bastard at the end. Look deep inside yourself. It is there, my brother. The answer you seek is inside you."

Hoping what he had said planted a seed that would grow, Mahes turned and went up the stairs. Tomorrow would be a very long day for them all.

* * * *

Flying from Memphis, Tennessee, to Cairo, Egypt,

would be no small undertaking. They couldn't just board one plane and fly directly there. It would take not one but three flights before they reached their final destination. After leaving Memphis, they would first fly to Chicago. After a two-hour flight, they would have a six-hour layover. Their next destination would be London, England. They would be in the air the longest then. It would take six hours to reach London. Once there, they would have another layover of eleven hours. Finally, they would arrive in Cairo after a four-hour flight.

Kendra had known how exhausting it would be from Markus' visits to Egypt, but she'd never done the trip herself. It turned out to be more horrendous than she'd expected. She now knew why Markus only made that trip once a year.

Unlike Markus' trips and what he usually went through, she had the extra stress of worrying whether or not Mahes and Nefertem would make it through customs. Especially Nefertem. Scott had the guy who'd made the passports change Nefertem's eyes back to normal in his picture, which was a good thing. If the customs officer wanted Nefertem to remove his dark glasses, how would they explain the change in them. She ended up stewing about it during the cab ride to the airport.

Tory and Scott met them at the check-in desk. They'd already checked their luggage, so after the rest of them had done the same to theirs, and since they had a couple of hours to wait before departure, it was decided coffees were in order.

Kendra kept an ever-watchful eye on Nefertem as Scott and Tory picked an almost deserted coffee shop at the terminal. Being inside the airport with large amounts of mortals milling about would be the first test of Nefertem's control. That is if he wished to control himself. The way he was now, he was unpredictable. She'd had Mahes explain to Nefertem that he had to control his cat side while they traveled, but she wasn't sure he'd taken to heart what he'd been told.

After finding a table to accommodate their numbers, they all settled to sipping hot coffee. Kendra fiddled with hers, unable to calm her thoughts. A large hand closed over hers, and she looked up to find Nefertem was the one who'd stilled her anxious movements.

"What bothers you so?"

Kendra wished she could see his eyes through the dark glasses. If she could, would she find them staring back at her with warmth or cynicism? "If you must know, you have me worried."

"Whatever for?"

"You know perfectly well why. If you do something to mess this up, we could all be in serious trouble. Not just you. Then, there are your eyes. They might want you to take off the glasses."

Nefertem waved away Kendra's concerns with a flick of his hand. "You worry overly much about nothing. I can handle that situation if it should arise."

Kendra didn't feel reassured by that statement one single bit. If anything, it increased her apprehensive feelings, but there was no point in questioning Nefertem on what he'd meant exactly. He'd already turned away. He'd dismissed her as he would a lowly servant.

After the coffees were drunk, things pretty well progressed according to schedule. Even Nefertem seemed to be on his best behavior. Once the time came to go through customs, Kendra found out what he'd meant.

As she'd feared, they asked Nefertem to remove his dark sunglasses. Kendra had to fight the urge to grab him by the arm and run them out of the airport. Instead of doing that, though, she settled for holding her carry-on bag in a death grip as Nefertem slowly pulled off his glasses. It was over in a matter of seconds. Once the glasses were removed, the officer compared Nefertem to the picture in his passport, gave him a nod, then gave the passport back. Kendra's breath, which she hadn't realized she'd been holding, left her in a rush.

Still feeling bewildered on how Nefertem had managed to get through with no questions asked, Kendra approached the customs officer. As if in a daze, she handed him her boarding pass and then accepted it back after he looked at it.

After moving to stand beside Nefertem, Kendra walked beside him as they went to board the plane. "How the heck did you manage to pull that off?" she quietly asked under her breath.

He gave her a crooked grin, making her believe the old Nefertem was back, but he opened his mouth and the illusion shattered into a million pieces. "I managed it easily. Unlike you weak mortals, I have the ability to make one see what I wish them to see. That one's mind was easy to sway."

Kendra mouthed the word "oh" and made a mental note to have a nice long chat with Mahes to find out what exactly were Nefertem's powers as a mortal. She didn't want to have Nefertem springing any nasty surprises on her.

CHAPTER TWENTY-ONE

Not long after boarding, they taxied down the runway. Being seated between Nefertem and Mahes, Kendra got the pleasure of watching each man's reaction as the plane left the ground. She couldn't keep the smile of amusement from her face. For such large, strong men it was humorous to see them grip the armrests on their seats hard enough to turn their knuckles white as they steadily went higher in altitude. Once they leveled off and the seatbelt light turned off, they still held on as if their very lives depended on it. Releasing her buckle, Kendra laughed softly.

Mahes turned his head to look at her and said through clenched teeth, "I am glad you find this amusing, because I do not in the slightest."

Kendra laughed again, then in turn released Mahes and Nefertem from their seatbelts. "I'm sorry, Mahes. I really don't mean to laugh at your expense."

"That is nice to hear. You could have at least warned us, you know."

"I thought I'd explained it well enough."

"Oh yeah, saying the plane will go quickly down a

large stretch of pavement, then take to the air, staying up for a while, then land again at our destination, was very helpful indeed," Mahes said sarcastically. "You forgot to mention the loud roaring sound this monster makes, and when it takes to the air, your stomach feels as if it has dropped to your feet."

"Okay, I admit I left out a few minor details." As Mahes cocked a brow at her, Kendra quickly added, "All right, they might not be minor details to you, but the worst of it is over for now. Enjoy the ride. Take a look out the window. Don't the clouds look spectacular when flying above them?"

Mahes turned to look out the window, then quickly looked away again. "I would rather not, if you do not mind."

"I like this not." Nefertem who'd remained silent up until then spoke stiltedly. "I do not wish to be here."

Kendra wondered if she'd made a mistake having Nefertem sit in the window seat. It was obvious the view outside the plane agitated him. She reached across him and quickly pulled down the window shade, blocking the view from sight.

"You can't get off the plane, Nefertem, until we've landed."

"Is this your idea of torturing me?" There was a slight growling undertone to his words.

Kendra stiffened. Had Nefertem's control finally run out? She reached for her purse on her lap. The package of sleeping pills was in it still. "No, I didn't do this to torture you. This is the fastest way to get to Egypt."

"There was no other mode of transportation?"

"Yes, but it would take weeks to reach Egypt that way. We would have had to take a cruise ship, and even then, there would be one airplane flight to get to the ship."

To Kendra's relief, her explanation seemed to set Nefertem somewhat at ease. He seemed to slowly relax.

She in turn loosened her grip on her purse.

"Try not to let it bother you, Nefertem. This leg of the journey will be over soon."

He only grunted in response. Kendra had the distinct feeling he didn't believe her last statement. She settled back into her seat and hoped he would keep the good behavior.

* * * *

The rest of the journey was sheer torture for them all. Kendra just thanked the stars above that Tory and Scott traveled with them. Kendra was never one to handle lack of sleep very well, and having to deal with the time differences on top of it all, made it that much harder on her. If she'd been alone, she would have been in tears more than once.

The only plus side of it all was Nefertem's behavior. Not once did his control slip, which in itself was a bit worrisome. Where had that newfound control come from, and when would it disappear? Because she'd bet all the money she had in the bank that disappear it would. The big question was when.

Deciding she didn't want to be left in the dark as to when Nefertem would slip up, Kendra managed to pull Mahes aside from the others during the layover in London. She took him a short distance from the others and confronted him.

"All right, Mahes, spill it."

"Spill what?"

"About Nefertem. When do we get the very nasty surprise?"

"I do not know what you mean," Mahes said with all innocence. Too innocently, Kendra thought.

"You know perfectly well what I mean. No games now. When is Nefertem going to stop playing nice?"

"No more games. You are right. Nefertem's time is running short."

"When?" Kendra's stomach dropped now that Mahes had confirmed her fears.

"Once we reach Egypt. After he steps onto the land of our birth, the change will become complete."

Kendra swallowed loudly. "You mean the urge to maim, kill, and basically do major damage to anyone mortal?"

"Something like that."

"I can't allow him to do that. You said the pendant prevents Nefertem from harming me, does it give me some power over him as well then?"

Mahes shook his head. "No. My mother will have full control of him. Kendra, he'll be more cat than man."

Kendra closed her eyes for a brief moment as her heart broke. She would lose Nefertem, not when this was all over, but much sooner. The man would be lost to the cat inside.

"I still can't allow him to hurt anyone. I guess I'll have to use what I brought from home. A safety net, so to speak."

"It will have to be a pretty strong net if you are to use it to restrain Nefertem."

Kendra shook her head. "It's not a net of that sort." She took a quick look behind her to make sure Nefertem hadn't come to see where they'd gone, then opened her purse and pulled out a small box. "This is our safety net. These are sleeping pills. If I can slip Nefertem a dose of these before we land in Egypt, it should knock him out for a few hours at least."

Mahes smiled. "You thought of everything, did you not? Smart and beautiful. I can see why Nefertem fell in love with you."

With more force than was necessary, Kendra shoved the pills back into her purse. "Don't, Mahes. This is eating me up inside as it is. I don't need you reminding me of what I'm about to lose."

"That was not my intent. I apologize."

"Whatever. Let's get back to the others before Nefertem comes to find us. I'm not sure Tory was happy with us leaving her and Scott alone with him."

* * * *

The flight from London's Heathrow airport, luckily for them, wasn't delayed. Extremely jet lagged, one and all, that last stretch of their travels was the light at the end of a very dark tunnel.

Once more, just as they had for the first flight from Memphis, Kendra was seated between Mahes and Nefertem. By design, she maneuvered Nefertem into the window seat. If things ended up turning nasty, she wanted him in a position where he could do the least damage to those around them.

The four-hour flight seemed to be passing much too quickly. At least it was for Kendra. As each minute ticked by, she became wound as tight as a spinning top. She kept looking for indications that Nefertem was starting to change.

About thirty minutes before they were due to land at the Cairo airport, Nefertem displayed the signs Kendra had wished wouldn't come. He no longer sat quietly, but shifted around, looking at the other passengers. She could tell from the wicked-looking smile on his lips that it wasn't avid curiosity that made him stare. Deciding now was the time, she elbowed Mahes and discreetly cocked her head in Nefertem's direction. He peered at his brother. He turned back to her and gave a curt nod.

Having prepared for that moment before boarding the plane in London, Kendra ever so calmly reached for her purse. There would be no chance of getting Nefertem to swallow a pill without telling him what it was for so she'd managed to get the needed dose ground to a powder. A quick trip to the washroom had kept her actions a secret from him.

Mahes handed her the small bottle of soda he'd kept from his meal. After getting up, she walked to the airplane's washroom. Once safely inside with the door shut tightly behind her, Kendra pulled out the tissue in which she'd wrapped the ground sleeping pills. She opened the soda, dumped in the powder, and gave it a gentle shake to dissolve it. She replaced the lid, then went back to her seat.

Kendra took a deep, fortifying breath and turned to Nefertem. "I think you should drink this." She held out the bottle of soda.

Nefertem looked at it. "Why should I take that?"

"Because you haven't had anything to drink for a while and we'll be landing soon. It could be some time before you can get another."

"I soon will not need to worry about trivial things such as that."

Kendra tried to keep the anxiety growing inside her from her voice as she spoke again. "Please, just drink it." This time she removed the lid before she offered it to him.

He hesitated for a brief moment, then took the bottle from her. "I will do as you wish this time. Only because I must prepare for what is to come. I have no wish to have you bothering me in this way."

He placed the rim of the bottle to his lips and proceeded to down the entire contents in two large gulps. He handed the now-empty bottle back to Kendra.

"I have done as you have asked, now speak to me no more, mortal."

Kendra cringed at the overbearing manner Nefertem had used to speak to her. She could only hope the ground-up sleeping pills would take effect soon.

In the end, the wait turned out not to be very long. It only took a few minutes before Nefertem nodded in sleepiness. After another ten minutes, he was out cold. As he slumped to the side, Kendra grabbed him and positioned him so his head rested on her shoulder.

"I see your safety net worked perfectly," Mahes said quietly.

"It might have worked too well. How are we going to get him off the plane in this condition? It'll be questioned as to why we're dragging him out of here."

"Not to worry. Nefertem is not the only one who can get others to see what he wishes them to. I too have the same ability. To all who see us, they will think he is awake and alert. Only to us will he be as he truly is."

Sure enough, when the flight attendant came to make sure they had their seatbelts fastened in preparation for the landing, she didn't seem to notice Nefertem still slept on Kendra's shoulder. After landing, Mahes dragged Nefertem to his feet, put his brother's arm around his shoulder, and walked to the airplane's exit.

Kendra, Tory, and Scott followed Mahes out. They went through customs smoothly, with the still sleeping Nefertem held upright by Mahes. After collecting their luggage, they stepped into the terminal. Kendra scanned the crowd as she passed through the gate doors, looking for the familiar face of her brother.

Being slightly over six foot tall, Markus was easy to pick out of the mass of people milling about. Letting her companions follow, Kendra rushed to her brother and threw her arms around him. She needed him more now than she had needed him for many years. She savagely pushed back tears that threatened to come to the surface.

"What's this? My little sister missed me that much?"

Kendra pulled back and gave Markus a weak smile. "Of course I missed you."

Markus looked passed Kendra. "I see you brought your

friends as planned. A couple of new faces as well."

"I'll tell you the whole story once we get settled into the hotel."

Markus gave a curt nod. "I won't push you now. I imagine all of you must be exhausted. I see the jet lag has hit one of you the hardest."

Kendra turned her head to look behind her. Mahes give her a wink. "That can be explained as well."

"You'd better, Kendra." Markus picked up the suitcase she'd placed at their feet, then led them out of the airport and into the city of Cairo.

CHAPTER TWENTY-TWO

The hotel where Markus stayed, and where he'd managed to book extra rooms for them all, turned out to be very comfortable. It was, by no means, a four-star hotel, but it was nice enough. The biggest asset was its being located in close proximity to the Great Pyramids at Giza, and in turn close to the Sphinx.

Once Tory and Scott were ensconced in their room, Markus brought them to the one Mahes and Nefertem would share. Kendra had thought she'd stay with them, but her brother had another opinion about that.

After firmly shutting the door behind Mahes once he'd walked through it, dragging Nefertem with him, Markus took Kendra by the arm and pulled her into the room right next to theirs. He placed her suitcase on the bed that would be hers.

"You can sleep here with me."

"I would prefer to share Mahes and Nefertem's room. I don't think it's wise to leave them on their own in a hotel room."

Markus sat in one of the two chairs and crossed his arms across his chest while he gave Kendra a hard stare.

"Why should I allow you to stay with them?"

Kendra stared equally hard at her brother. "That isn't your decision to make."

"What the hell is going on?" he asked softly.

Sighing deeply, Kendra searched Markus' face. She knew the look he wore. He wouldn't relent until she gave him a very good reason to do so. She loved him dearly, but in situations such as this, he could be a tad overprotective. "Let's get this over with before something unpleasant happens in the room next to us."

After taking a deep breath, Kendra launched into the unbelievable story that had become her life. She only left out the part of how close her relationship with Nefertem had been, but Markus was too astute not to pick up on the truth.

"So, when did you sleep with this ancient Egyptian god?"

Kendra rolled her eyes. "After what I told you, about what's going to happen, all you can think to ask is when I slept with Nefertem?"

"Yes. I'll get to the rest of it after you answer my question."

Kendra seldom got angry with her brother, but today was an exception. Her temper flared to life. She stalked to where he sat and glared down at him. "That is none of your business. I won't be interrogated by you about my sex life."

Markus shook his head. "You just answered my question in a way. You definitely slept with him or you wouldn't be so indignant about me asking. You really do know how to pick them."

"Shut up." That only caused her brother to laugh, making her ire toward him increase. Markus must have seen the flash of anger that had to be in her eyes and wisely stopped laughing.

"Okay, I'll let it go for now. I must say I never expected

this turn of events to come about by me simply sending you that pendant. It really wasn't in the best of condition when I bought it."

Now that Markus had given up on his line of questioning, Kendra's anger died. "Well, it did, and the pendant's real worth was hidden beneath grime of centuries."

Kendra pulled out the pendant from inside her shirt and left it to hang on the outside. Doing what Nefertem had told her, she hadn't removed it.

Markus sucked in his breath as he caught sight of it. After getting up from the chair, he reached out and lifted it from where it rested on Kendra's chest. "This is worth a fortune. I could sell this, and we could be set for a very long time."

Kendra slapped Markus' hand away. "Like hell you will. The pendant is mine. You can't take back the gift you sent me, and as long as Nefertem and Mahes are here, it can't leave my neck."

"Why?"

"Nefertem won't harm me then. He made me promise not to take it off before the change took him over."

Markus sighed. "Fine, keep it. I wouldn't dream of taking it from you." Kendra wrapped a hand around the pendant. "Okay, bring me to them. I want to meet these 'gods.'"

Kendra gave Markus a quick kiss on the check, then smiled. "Thanks for at least trying to understand. It's what I need from you now. Your understanding."

* * * *

After Kendra's brother had left with her in tow, Mahes had settled Nefertem on one of the beds. He prowled around the hotel room all the while keeping a sharp eye on Nefertem. There was no telling when he would awake, and with Kendra still in possession of the sleeping pills, there was no way he could get Nefertem to take more if he did wake up before she returned. He hoped Kendra did come back to the room. Mahes had seen the look on her brother's face as he had shown them to their room. The man was not at all pleased with this whole situation.

Coming to stand before the only window in the room, Mahes looked out at the city he had once known so well. It was now almost unrecognizable to him. He had not expected it to have changed so much. A knock on the door pulled his gaze from the view outside.

"Come in."

Behind the door, Kendra's voice sounded muffled as she said, "You have to open the door, Mahes. It locks automatically once it shuts. We don't have a key for it."

After crossing the room, Mahes pulled the door open. He smiled at Kendra and nodded in her brother's direction. "Come in, please." Stepping aside, he made room for them to come inside.

Mahes turned and found Kendra standing over Nefertem while her brother hovered closely behind her, ready to pull her away if Nefertem made a move, or so it seemed to Mahes. He joined them.

"You told Markus everything." Mahes did not say it as a question but as a statement of fact.

Taking her gaze from Nefertem's sleeping form, she turned her attention to Mahes. "Yes, but Markus being Markus has to see things for himself."

"Nothing like talking as if I'm not in the room."

Kendra rolled her eyes. "Let me make the formal introductions then. Mahes, this is my brother, Markus. Markus, you already know who these two are. Is that good enough for you?"

"Kendra feels she needs to stay here with you and your brother instead of in my room. After the story she told me, I want to hear from you that she'll be okay."

"Of course she will be safe. Kendra possesses the pendant. No harm will come to her."

"All right, I can accept that. What about Nefertem? You can't keep him doped up on sleeping pills twenty-four/seven."

Mahes looked at Kendra. "Do you have those sleeping pills with you now?" At her nod, he answered Markus. "For the time being, it is for the best if we keep him in this state. I need to get to what is left of my father's temple and see what else can be done to keep Nefertem under control."

"Fine, I'll take you there in the morning. It's too late to go today."

A low growl from the direction of the bed instantly drew their attention. Nefertem, now fully awake when just a second before he had been in a deep sleep, now sat up, eyeing them intently.

Mahes stepped closer to the bed. His brother was primed to attack. Having another mortal besides Kendra in the room was all it would take to set Nefertem off.

"Kendra, I think it would be a very good idea if you left with Markus."

"No, Mahes. I think you and Markus should leave."

"You can't be serious!" Markus shot back.

Kendra ignored Markus and spoke to Mahes instead. "I won't let you beat him. The other method worked earlier."

"Kendra, being here has intensified the change. He is beyond reasoning." As if to prove Mahes correct, Nefertem growled menacingly.

"Please, Mahes, trust me. I can do this."

Mahes studied Kendra's face. He knew what she wanted to do. He did not know if it would work, but he did not have the heart to deny her that last chance to be with Nefertem.

"All right. I will be right next door. If things go wrong for you, I will break the door down if I must."

162

Kendra smiled. "Thanks. Now get out of here."

Markus protested. "I won't allow you to do this, Kendra."

Grabbing Markus by the arm, Mahes began to drag him from the room. "The decision is already made. Leave Kendra to do what she has to do." Even though the other man dug in his heels, his strength was no match for Mahes'. He easily propelled Markus toward the door.

Before closing it behind them, Mahes spoke to Kendra one last time. "If all goes well, I will come back in the morning. No one will interrupt you." With the still-protesting Markus in tow, Mahes closed the door behind him with a click.

CHAPTER TWENTY-THREE

Being left alone with Nefertem, Kendra wondered if she'd been a little too hasty in her decision. He'd showed signs of interest in the room now that Markus and Mahes had left, but it wasn't as a man would. It was more like an animal searching for a means of escape.

Kendra took a deep breath to boost her nerve and sat on the bed beside Nefertem. His head snapped in her direction as he eyed her warily. Slowly, she reached out and gently caressed his cheek.

"I know the real you is in there somewhere deep down, Nefertem, the one I fell in love with." Not one emotion flickered in his gold eyes. At least he hadn't outright rejected her touch. Emboldened, she stroked his cheek again. He closed his eyes and pressed her hand flat against it. He let out a low rumble of what sounded like pleasure.

Kendra's heart beat a little faster. Not with fear, but with desire. It was the cat that reacted to her, but that knowledge didn't stop her from wanting him. Encouraged, she leaned forward and gently brushed her lips across Nefertem's.

He released Kendra's hand and gathered her hard

against his chest. He kissed her thoroughly. As she moved her lips beneath his, he growled softly. Her body melted in response to being held by him. She wrapped her arms around his neck. He demanded more from the kiss, and she allowed him entrance to her mouth. There was no going back now, which wasn't something she wanted. Soon she needed much more.

Kendra unwrapped her arms from around him and slowly ran her hands down Nefertem's shoulders and then across his chest. As she reached the bottom of his shirt, she slipped under it. A thrill shot through her as his stomach muscles quivered beneath her fingertips.

Nefertem twisted with Kendra still in his arms and moved so she lay on the bed. He stretched out beside her. He released her mouth and slowly undid her blouse. Every inch of skin he exposed he pressed his lips to. She shivered beneath his touch. He popped open the front clasp of her bra, then sucked her nipple deep into his mouth.

He roughly pulled off her blouse and the skirt she wore. Her bra and panties quickly followed. Nefertem's gaze raked over Kendra's body. She longed to touch him. She pushed on his chest and rolled him onto his back before she straddled his thighs. Taking hold of the bottom of his shirt, she pulled it up and over his head, leaving his broad chest bare. She leaned forward and trailed kisses across his bronzed skin. At his flat nipples, she grazed her teeth across them. He bucked under her. Feeling the power she had over him, she moved down his body until she reached the waistband of his pants. She made short work of undoing them and sliding them off. Now free from the constricting confines of his jeans, his cock stood at the ready.

Kendra wrapped her fingers around his thick shaft and slid up and down. Nefertem grew even harder. Needing to taste him, she leaned forward and stroked his entire length with her tongue. He shuddered. As she took him fully into her mouth, he threaded his fingers through her hair, holding her to him. She alternated between sucking and laving his sensitive tip. She looked up and found him watching her. Her body clenched at the raw expression of desire he wore.

Nefertem took hold of her and pulled her away from his body. He surged off the bed and moved her so she kneeled on all fours in the middle of the mattress. He came up behind her, spread her body open, and pushed into her hot opening. He held on to her hips as he pumped his cock in and out of her. Kendra rocked back, matching his strokes.

Kendra moaned softly at the sensation of Nefertem filling her, stretching her. Having him take her this way, he hit her cervix with each thrust. It'd only been a matter of days since he'd last made love to her, but it'd felt more like an eternity. No man but him made her body crave his touch so, and no other would.

As he pumped inside her, Nefertem reached around and rubbed her clit in time with each hard thrust. He pushed her ever higher until one of the most intense climaxes she'd ever had claimed her. Kendra couldn't hold back the moan of pleasure that slipped past her lips. She climaxed around him, milking him, and he threw back his head. With a deep-throated growl, he quickly followed suit. He rolled onto his side and pulled her close as his eyes slowly drifted shut.

* * * *

The new day's sun hadn't long begun to brighten the sky when Markus was jerked from a deep sleep by someone pounding on the door to his room. His first reaction was to look at the other bed. Mahes lay there, watching him.

"I guess I'll answer it," he said grumpily. Markus threw

off his covers, then got out of bed before crossing the room to the door. He opened it and was roughly pushed aside as Tory barreled inside.

"Where is she, Markus?"

"Not here, obviously."

Scott, who'd entered at a more sedate pace, said, "Sorry about the early hour. I couldn't keep her away any longer. If Tory had had her way, she would have been knocking on your door a lot earlier than this."

There was no question of Tory leaving them to sleep any longer. From past experiences with her, Markus knew he'd never be able to oust her. The woman could be as stubborn as a mule. Most especially when it came to situations where Kendra was involved.

"Relax, Tory." Markus rubbed the sleep from his eyes as Tory scanned the room. "Kendra is with Nefertem."

"Alone?"

"It was her decision. Not mine, believe me."

"Tell me you at least tried to change her mind."

"Of course I did, but Kendra is all grown up. I have to respect her choices in life. I might not like it, but I'll accept it."

Tory gave Markus a hard stare. "Why is Mahes here with you instead of being with Nefertem?"

Mahes chuckled. "What Kendra and Nefertem were doing did not require an audience. It would not have been something Kendra would have appreciated me being in the bed next to them."

Markus waited for the blasting Tory was sure to give him and Mahes. Surprisingly, it never came. Instead of ripping a strip off them, she just walked to a chair and plopped down into it.

"What's this? No ranting? No raving?"

"There's no point in doing any of that. What's done is done."

"I think you're losing your touch in your old age."

"Stuff it, Markus. Far be it for me to take this last chance Kendra has with Nefertem away from her. Since nothing terrible happened during the night, she must have been able to calm the savage beast in him. Okay, before one of you checks on Kendra, what do we do first today?"

Mahes sat up with the sheet covering the lower half of his body. "I have to go to Ptah's temple. It is imperative I try to contact my father. Sooner the better."

"All right, then what are you waiting for? Get your ass out of that bed."

Mahes gave Tory a crooked grin. "If you insist." He threw the sheet back and stood. He crossed his arms in front of his chest and stared at her. Tory's face turned red.

Quickly putting her head down, Tory looked at the floor. "I can see you need a few minutes to get ready. I'll wait for you in the hall." She kept her face averted as she left the room.

After the door closed shut behind her, all of them laughed. Mahes grabbed the pajama bottoms he'd stripped off before going to bed the night before and pulled them on. "I must apologize to you, Scott. I could not resist."

Scott chuckled. "Tory did walk into that one, I'll admit. She'll think twice the next time."

"Don't count on it." Markus laughed. "I must say it looked good to see her so flustered. That doesn't happen very often."

"I guess I had better change, then check on Kendra and my brother. I do not think it is wise for any of you to go near Nefertem. It will probably undo what Kendra tried to do during the night." Scott and Markus nodded in agreement.

CHAPTER TWENTY-FOUR

K endra awoke to the sensation of being held close by a pair of strong arms. She smiled to herself and snuggled closer. The night she'd spent with Nefertem was everything she could have asked for. Though he hadn't spoken a single word, it turned out not to be necessary. He'd shown her how he felt about her, more than once, in a way mere words couldn't express. Wishing this wouldn't end, she cuddled as close as she could get into his arms. His only reaction was to hold her tighter.

Before Kendra could drift back to sleep, the sound of the room door being quietly opened brought her back to wakefulness. She cracked open her eyes. Mahes slipped through the door and then softly closed it behind him.

Mahes came to kneel by the side of the bed Kendra lay and held a finger to his lips so she wouldn't speak. "We are leaving to go to Ptah's temple." He spoke in a soft whisper. "Do not let Nefertem leave this room, and do not let anyone else in here besides me. He is calm now, but that will change in an instant if another mortal comes near him. I know you can keep him controlled. You have the touch, Kendra. I will return as soon as I can." Kendra silently nodded. Mahes brushed her cheek with a finger. "I will not come back until I get an answer." He left the room as silently as he'd entered it.

* * * *

It was only a short trip from Cairo to Memphis. Since Kendra and Nefertem were staying at the hotel, Markus, Scott, Tory, and Mahes were able to pile into one taxi. The journey was a hot and dusty one. Tory spent the time staring out the window, watching the scenery go by. Being the only one who had never been to Egypt before, she appeared fascinated by all she saw. She commented on how she could not help but feel a sense of awe to be in a place that had survived through the ages and had such ancient roots.

Mahes also watched out the window. The land of his birth had changed so much, but there still were aspects of it he found familiar. The closer they came to Memphis, the more he felt as if he were going home.

After reaching their destination, Markus paid the taxicab fare as the rest of them started walking to the ruins of Ptah's temple. It was situated in the center of Memphis. In its prime, it had been enormous, but today it was only a ruin. Though it had been brought so low by the passage of time, it still was an impressive sight. There were fallen blocks from the once massive hypostyle hall, huge remains of statuary, and a few well-preserved structures. One such structure was the burial house of the Apis bulls where the fragments in Memphis, Tennessee, had come from. That was where Mahes had decided to try to contact his father.

It was still fairly early in the day so there were not many people visiting the ruins. Even if there had been a crowd, it would not have bothered Mahes. The conversation he hoped to have would take place in his mind. No one would overhear what was said.

Moving a short distance away from Scott, Tory, and Markus, who were now investigating the ruins, Mahes mentally called his father's name.

I am here, my son.

Mahes was pleased to hear his father's voice coming through strong and clear. *Nefertem needs your help, Father.*

I will offer what I can, but what I can do is very limited, as you know.

Yes, I am aware of that. All I ask is for you to tell me what you told Nefertem about the hidden library. The power in the stones he had used to contact you was very weak, and he did not hear all of what you told him.

There was a long pause before Ptah spoke again. *You do realize time has almost run out.*

Yes, that is why we have come to Egypt. Nefertem was able to get that part about where to find the library.

You have brought him to Egypt! Do you know what you have done?

We have him under control, for now.

How? No one has been able to control him when he reaches this stage. Not even Pharaoh, who possessed the pendant, could.

Mahes made a chuckle only his father could hear. *Well, Pharaoh was never the woman Nefertem loves.*

So it is true. Nefertem has finally lost his heart to a woman.

Yes. It would seem because of that very reason Kendra has kept him reined in, but I do not know for how much longer.

All right, I will tell you what I told Nefertem when he had contacted me. What you do with this information is up to you.

Mahes spent the next few minutes listening as his father told him exactly what they had to do. Once Ptah reached the end, he broke contact with him. Mahes watched the others of his party as they moved about the ruins, allowing the information Ptah had given him to sink in. Despite the thousands of years of life he had lived, this was one secret he had not known. Scott would be over the top when he found out. Only it was a shame he would not be able to use the newfound knowledge to further his career. For this secret was one the rest of the world could never learn.

* * * *

Nefertem came awake with a woman in his arms. He brought her to instant wakefulness as he pulled her bottom closer to his hips and kissed the back of her neck. She purred with pleasure, reached up behind her, and buried her fingers into his hair. He filled his lungs with his mate's scent. She smelled of woman and sex. For him, there was no stronger aphrodisiac. All he wanted to do was bury himself within her warm embrace. An eternity of having her would never be long enough.

Before he could join his body with hers, a voice boomed inside his mind. *Nefertem! Why are you not doing what I have charged you to do?* Even once he reached the stage where he no longer understood others' speech, he always understood his mother and could communicate with her, but that ability was very limited at best.

Something more important.

His mother's anger washed over him. *How dare you! Whatever you feel is more important than the task I set for you, do away with it.*

No.

You will do what I say. I will not be denied.

No, he said again. *She is my mate.*

Have you not learned from your past, Nefertem? His mother growled. *A mortal cannot be your mate. It is only because she is the possessor of the pendant. I have rid you of your feelings for this woman once before, I can do it again.*

Not this time. I will not allow you.

That, my son, is beyond your control. I will not allow you to be distracted by a mere woman. Let alone a mortal one.

Nefertem tried to fight his mother's will, but in the end, she proved to be more powerful than he. Just before the memory of the past night spent in his mate's arms was taken from him, he shoved Kendra away.

*

Deeply submersed in a haze of sexual arousal that Nefertem had woven around her, Kendra was unprepared when he pushed her away. One moment he caressed her, next he abruptly stopped.

The mattress moved beneath her. Kendra rolled onto her back to see why Nefertem had broken contact with her. She found him sitting up, staring at her. "What's the matter?"

He continued to stare at her, and a sense of unease traveled through her. Something wasn't right. His behavior was nothing as it'd been during the night. Hoping to dispel her feelings of wariness, she reached out to caress Nefertem's face. He quickly batted her hand away before she could make contact with his skin. He gave her a warning growl and slowly got out of bed. Kendra's feeling of unease quickly changed to fear.

Kendra moved with slow and easy movements as she wrapped the bedsheet around her before she went to stand before Nefertem. The expression he wore was anything but kind. It was hard and feral-looking. His upper lip curled into a snarl as she stepped closer.

"Everything is all right, Nefertem. Calm down." Kendra reached out and placed a shaky hand on his bared chest. Her touch had calmed him before, and it should work now, at least she reasoned to herself.

Once again, Nefertem's reaction wasn't what she'd expected. As soon as she made contact with his chest, he roughly grabbed a handful of her hair, pulling her head to the side, and growled menacingly. He yanked her hard against him.

Biting back a moan of pain, Kendra held up the pendant she wore around her neck and showed it to him. "Let go of me, Nefertem. You know you can't hurt me as long as I have this."

Nefertem's gaze slowly slid down to the pendant, then he gave her a snarl of disgust. For the second time, he shoved her away. This one he used enough force to knock her off her feet. She ended up sprawled on the carpeted floor. Clutching the sheet tighter around her, Kendra looked up at him with hurt in her eyes.

*

Ignoring the woman at his feet was easy. She meant nothing to him. The pendant was the only reason he hadn't ripped her throat out with his teeth. He ran his tongue over his now fully extended, sharp, canine teeth. It would have given him great pleasure to have sunk them into her soft flesh.

Nefertem grabbed up the clothes he had worn the day before and donned them. It was time to leave. His mother's call echoed inside his mind. Once fully clothed, he turned back to look at the woman. She was no longer on the floor. She stood before the only door that led to the outside world, as if her slight form could stop him from going through it. He shook his head and smiled, showing her his fangs.

She tucked the sheet she wore more tightly around her and held her arms out on either side of her body to block the door more effectively. Nefertem only smiled again. He simply vanished.

CHAPTER TWENTY-FIVE

A sense of wrongness hit Mahes as they neared the halfway mark back to the hotel. It could only be caused by something pertaining to Nefertem. He kept that to himself, just as he had kept silent about the information his father had given him, much to Tory's chagrin. If she had had her way, he would still be at his father's temple, explaining what had been said to him. Only his unwillingness to be browbeaten into talking made her grudgingly relent and get into the taxi for the trip home.

Once they at last reached the hotel, Mahes made sure he was the first one to get out of the taxi. Not stopping for the others to catch up, he headed for the room where Nefertem stayed. He did not bother to knock before he used the extra room key, which he had pocketed the night before to let himself inside.

He pushed open the door and knew without even looking that Nefertem was no longer there. He next searched for Kendra, who was easy to find. She sat on the floor not far from the door and appeared to only be wearing a sheet.

After quietly shutting it behind him, Mahes went to Kendra. He crouched beside her. "Are you all right?"

Kendra blinked. "He's gone."

Mahes knew whom Kendra meant. "I know. What happened?"

"I don't know really. One minute we were about to…" Kendra blushed profusely.

"I think I can guess what you and Nefertem were doing," Mahes said with a chuckle.

"Well…um…one minute he was all loving and then the next he shoved me away."

"I had hoped you could keep Nefertem preoccupied enough so he could ignore my mother's demands. She must have been too persistent for him to be able to refuse her."

"I'm really starting to take a great dislike to your mother."

Mahes chuckled again. "She does tend to engender that emotion in people at certain times."

"Where did he go, Mahes?" Kendra asked quietly. "He acted as if he didn't even know who I was."

Mahes wrapped his arms around Kendra and kissed the top of her head. "Nefertem has gone to my mother. As for not knowing you, she could have taken the memory from him."

Kendra craned her neck so she could look at Mahes. "How much time do we have left?"

"Less than thirty-six hours."

"That's it? We need more."

Mahes gave Kendra one last kiss on the top of her head before he stood. There would be no more time allowed. "I will leave you now to get dressed. Once you finish, come to your brother's room. We have much to discuss."

* * * *

A short time later, feeling a little better after having a quick shower, Kendra went to Markus' room. She knocked on the door and waited to be let inside. It ended up Tory was the one who opened it for her.

Taking Kendra by the hand, Tory pulled her into the room and gave her a hug. "How are you holding up? Mahes told us Nefertem has left."

"As well as can be expected."

Kendra released Tory, stepped away from her, and went to sit on the bed next to her brother. "All right, Mahes, time to tell us all you know."

Mahes nodded and waited until he had everyone's attention before he spoke. "Our time has just about run out, and what needs to be done to stop what will come is very risky at best."

"I, for one, am willing to take that risk," Kendra assured him. The others nodded, giving their assent along with hers.

"I did not expect any of you to refuse now that we have come this far." Mahes took a deep breath, then plunged on. "It turns out, Scott, you were correct in your assumption about the location of the library. It is indeed to be found beneath the Sphinx."

Scott perked up at that. "They were right about there being a hidden chamber to be found in that location. This will be the find of the century. Only problem will be how to get permission to dig on such short notice."

"That will not be necessary," Mahes said woodenly.

"I'm afraid it is. The Egyptian government won't look too kindly on us digging around one of their national monuments."

"You do not understand. We will not be doing any digging of any kind. I can gain access to the library using another method. One not so obvious and not so detrimental to the Sphinx."

"Okay, so you can somehow get us in with your special

abilities. I guess after we accomplish the task at hand, I can see about getting permission to dig at a later date."

Mahes shook his head. "No."

Scott scowled. "What do you mean no? The contents of that library can't just be left buried there to rot. It's a part of the ancient past and should be preserved."

"I know that would be your greatest wish, Scott, but in this case, the library must remain hidden from the rest of the world. My father stressed that to me."

"What exactly is this library that it must be kept as a close-guarded secret?"

Mahes nailed them all with a hard stare. "It is the collected knowledge of the ancient Atlanteans. What we need from it is only a very small piece of the whole. The Atlanteans were a brilliant race, which in the end, was the death of them all. Within the library's works is the very knowledge that brought about their downfall. Ptah does not want that knowledge given to you mortals or the same fate that befell the Atlanteans will be yours."

Absolute silence reigned after what Mahes had said. Scott slumped in defeat, appearing to finally accept what he couldn't change. If an Egyptian god wanted the library kept out of the hands of mortals, then there would be no way around it.

Kendra felt some small measure of amazement that such a library, and to who it had belonged to in the distant past, had remained a secret over the centuries, but that there was something in it they needed held more of her interest. "Then what are we waiting for? We know where the library is, and that we have access to it. We can go to it now."

Mahes shook his head. "Sorry, Kendra, it will not be that easy."

Feeling no small amount of desperation, Kendra pounded the bed with her fist. "Why the hell not?"

"If I was not in my mortal form, it would be no problem

at all, but I am, and my powers are limited. For me to get us all into the library, I must be standing directly above it, or very close to it, which means we have to be at the Sphinx. What I have gathered, during the day it will be crawling with tourists. We must wait until late at night when no one is around. Unless you know of a way to conceal the fact that five people can seemingly disappear in a blink of an eye before hundreds of onlookers."

"I can't just sit here and do nothing when Nefertem is god knows where. I just can't do it."

Kendra looked at the others and could easily read their pity written on their faces. Markus put an arm around her shoulders to try to comfort her. It was almost too much to bear. She didn't want or need them to feel sorry for her.

She shrugged off her brother's hold, then stood and paced. She clenched and unclenched her hands, which she held at her sides.

She was soon brought up short by Mahes when he stepped directly into her path. "Do not do this to yourself, Kendra. I need you to be clearheaded when the time comes. We will be working against the clock."

"What kind of timeframe are you talking about here?" Markus asked.

"We will have until just before dawn two days from now. Once dawn's light hits the horizon, my mother will come. If we have not stopped her before that, there will be no way of doing so her."

Kendra looked at the clock sitting on the one bedside table situated between the two double beds. The number of hours until they could act was far too great. If those hours didn't pass quickly, the fragile hold she placed on herself would surely break. Even now, it slipped. Ruthlessly, she pushed back the urge to let go of her emotions and cry her heart out.

* * * *

Nefertem appeared before his mother. Now that the change within him was complete, he could will himself back to the immortal realm. He would do whatever Sekhmet wished.

Sekhmet sat on her gilded chair and looked at him. She raked him from head to foot with her gaze. With a mere thought, she stripped him of his garments, and in their stead, clothed him in a snow-white linen kilt. She smiled at her handy work. Nefertem now looked the way an Egyptian man should. Standing, Sekhmet went to him and kissed his cheek.

CHAPTER TWENTY-SIX

The intervening hours until they could go to the Sphinx ticked by slowly. They all ended up congregated in Markus' room, which had been silently nominated as their meeting place — to Kendra's great pleasure. She didn't want to be in the one where she'd shared the night with Nefertem. It would have made the waiting unbearable. The memories would be too fresh, too new.

The early evening arrived none too quickly for Kendra. If she could have managed it, she would have herded the others out the door and to the Sphinx, but that wasn't going to happen. Right now, dinner was the topic of discussion, weighing heavily on the males of the company, who only had food on their minds. Taking her anxiousness into account, room service was ordered instead of subjecting her to a crowd inside a restaurant.

Dinner conversation was light. Markus voiced an idea he had. "Perhaps we could leave earlier than planned and see the sound and light show at Giza. It really is spectacular, and is something everyone should make a point of seeing when in Cairo."

Scott nodded enthusiastically. "That's a great idea. I've seen it, and more than once. I think Tory and Kendra will enjoy it. Even you will like it, Mahes."

"I look forward to it," Mahes said. "I have seen the pyramids in the distance. I would like to see them up close. That they have survived through the ages says much for them."

"Yes, it does. To this day people stand in awe of them, but they're far from looking as they did after they were first built."

Mahes nodded. "Very true, but they still are an impressive. Khufu's pyramid had been a sight to see. Standing at four hundred and eight-one feet, the Great Pyramid sits on nearly thirteen acres of land. The outside of the pyramid used to be covered entirely with Turah limestone, giving it a smooth surface. An enclosure wall and paved courtyard had been made from the same limestone. Now, all that is gone, just leaving the bare bones of the pyramid to stand throughout the ages."

They silently sat as Mahes got a faraway look on his face, then Markus elbowed Kendra who sat next to him. "So, sis, are you game to see the show tonight?"

Kendra smiled wanly. "If it'll get us out of this darn room and closer to our destination, I'm up for it."

"That a girl. I knew you wouldn't disappoint me."

* * * *

Though most television documentaries give the feeling that the pyramids are situated in the middle of the desert, in actuality they aren't. The truth is, the great pyramids can be found near the city limits of Greater Cairo, just a short trip heading east on the Pyramid Road. With civilization encroaching, it was a real threat to the pyramids. Scholars, aware of that fact, took steps to prevent any damage to the ancient structures.

Now that the sun was setting, the heat was not nearly as bad as it'd been during the day. It still was very warm, but not scorching hot, so many people took advantage of that fact and came to the nightly show at the pyramids.

Blending into a crowd of other tourists, their group decided to split up and regroup when the show was to start. Scott and Tory went off in the direction of the Great Pyramid. Holding hands, they looked like any other couple doing some sightseeing. Mahes, Kendra, and Markus walked to the Sphinx, which was only a short distance from Khufu's pyramid.

Mahes grabbed Kendra's hand, mimicking Scott and Tory. At her questioning look, he gave her a saucy wink. "Relax, Kendra. It is only for those others around us."

She cocked an eyebrow at him. "Are you sure? Or are you just using that as an excuse to hold my hand?"

Shaking his head, Mahes chuckled. "Maybe it is a little bit of both. It was either hold your hand or hold Markus'. I much prefer to hold yours."

"As would I," chimed in Markus.

Not to joining in Mahes' banter, Kendra asked, "What exactly are we looking for, anyway?"

Mahes pulled her along and nodded toward the Sphinx. "Scott said there are security guards around. I want to see how many. I have to locate the exact location of the library chamber below. There is a chance there is more than one beneath the Sphinx. I would hate to pick the wrong one. Who knows in what state the empty chambers might be in?"

Kendra nodded. They couldn't risk that happening. She shuddered just thinking of what it would be like if they ended up in the wrong one and it collapsed on top of them.

The Sphinx didn't sit alone. There was an old temple, from the New Kingdom era, as well as other smaller structures, but it was the Sphinx that dominated. Sitting between the its paws was the dream stele, the stone slab Thutmose IV had made. On the stele, Thutmose described a dream he'd while still a prince as he'd slept in the shade of the Sphinx after hunting. In the dream, the Sphinx spoke to him, telling him to clear away the sand that engulfed it. If Thutmose did that task, then he would be rewarded with the kingship of Egypt and become Pharaoh. That was exactly what he did, and what the Sphinx had promised became fact. Thutmose did indeed become Pharaoh.

Mahes stopped their meandering stroll once they reached the Sphinx. They ended up in front of the dream stele.

Kendra looked at Mahes. He seemed to be staring off into space. "Is it there?"

With a nod, Mahes gave Kendra a smile. "Yes, it is. This is the one. It is just beneath the feet of the Sphinx. I will be able to get us inside without any problems."

"Good. If only you could get us in there now."

Markus walked to Kendra and put his arm over her shoulders. "Patience, little sister. The time for that will be upon us before you know it. For now, relax and let's enjoy the show. It's just about time for it to start."

Markus was correct. After leaving the Sphinx and rendezvousing with Scott and Tory at the Great Pyramid, they were greeted with the start of the show.

A voice over a loudspeaker boomed, "You've come tonight to the most fabulous and celebrated place in the world. Here on the Plateau of Giza stands forever the mightiest of human achievements. No traveler, emperor, merchant, or poet has trodden on these sands and not gasped in awe."

So began the nightly sound and light show. Kendra only paid half-attention to the spectacle going on around her. Any other time she would have immensely enjoyed the show, for it really was an impressive sight. This night it was only a distraction to help make the minutes tick by more quickly.

Once the time finally arrived, Kendra's nerves were stretched to the breaking point. Knowing that a possible way of undoing what she'd started, and maybe just maybe there was a slim chance of getting Nefertem back, her patience was at an all-time low. She would even settle for just seeing him again as he was now.

They wandered around the pyramids after the show until they were the only ones there. With only a couple of security guards left, Mahes used his ability to make them think all the sightseers had departed.

Now they were before the Sphinx, a short distance from its gigantic paws. Mahes took control of the situation. "To get us all into the chamber at the same time, I need you to hold hands. Do not, and I cannot stress this more strongly, do not let go until we are all safely inside. If you do before we reach the chamber..." Mahes let his sentence go unfinished.

Doing as they were instructed, Kendra, Markus, Tory, and Scott linked hands. Mahes nodded and then took the free hands of Kendra and Tory. Closing his eyes, he seemed to call up the power within him to get them all inside the chamber below.

The ground shift beneath Kendra's feet, followed by a sense of disorientation. That quickly passed. Blinking, she slowly took in her new surroundings. Her jaw dropped as her eyes became adjusted to the muted lighting inside the chamber.

It didn't in any way match the picture she'd conjured inside her mind. She'd expected the chamber to be a dusty, moldering room with a thick layer of grime coating everything inside. How wrong she'd been in her thinking.

In no way did the chamber appear to have been buried beneath the sand for centuries. Large pieces of opaque crystals placed strategically throughout the chamber mutely glowed, giving off feeble light. Not a speck of dust could be found anywhere, not even on the slab stone floor. How, or more importantly who, kept the chamber in such pristine condition, Kendra could only wonder.

It was quite large, which it needed to be to house all the objects amassed within. There were a number of large scrolls in large, decorated clay urns. A big, solid marble table sat in the middle of the chamber. The rest was an assortment of chests and objects that weren't recognizable at first glance.

Kendra took a deep breath and was surprised to find the air fresh, not stale or musty-smelling. That surprised her the most since they were under the sand with no direct opening to the chamber anywhere to let in air or light.

"Mahes, why is it we aren't suffocating down here from lack of oxygen?" Kendra had to ask.

"It is the crystals. Not only do they emit light, they produce oxygen. My father has spoken of them in the past, but I have never seen one firsthand before."

Kendra nodded, then looked around for the others. Markus and Tory were slowly turning in circles so they could look at everything. Scott appeared frozen in place, almost as if he was afraid to move, afraid the chamber would disappear before his very eyes.

After giving them a few minutes to adjust to their new surroundings, Mahes called them together. "I am not exactly sure what we need to find here, but anything that mentions or alludes to my mother will be our best bet. Time is limited, so move as quickly as you can, but do not pass by anything."

Kendra nodded once again and headed off to what she felt was a likely spot to hunt. She was determined to find what they needed to stop Sekhmet.

CHAPTER TWENTY-SEVEN

Rubbing her eyes, Kendra tried to get rid of the gritty feeling in them. Hours of scanning ancient scrolls and lack of sleep took their toll on her. It didn't help that she searched for the proverbial needle in a haystack. Of course all the scrolls were written in a language she didn't understand. Luckily for them, Egyptian hieroglyphs were peppered throughout the ancient text. That being the case all she had to look for was hieroglyphs that referred to Sekhmet or Nefertem. She had their glyphs memorized.

They were all clustered around the marble table, each to his or her own separate space, not wanting to mix all the scrolls together. Scott, being what he was, watched them like a hawk as they opened each new one. Even though they were in pristine condition, he still wanted extra care taken.

As the hours ticked by and not one of the scrolls made any mention of Sekhmet or Nefertem, Kendra felt her last hope start to slip through her fingers. She wasn't ready to give up just yet, though.

She gathered up the scrolls she'd finished perusing, then returned them to where they'd come from. She turned back to the table and found the other occupants of the room watching her. "What?"

Mahes took a deep breath before answering. "I will go back to my father's temple and tell him we found nothing. Maybe he knows of another way to stop this."

Kendra's temper rose. "So, that's it? You're going to give up just like that?" She snapped her fingers to stress her point. "Ptah says there's something here, then it must be here. We just need to look harder."

Markus shook his head. "Be reasonable, Kendra. Dawn is fast approaching, and we have to leave before it gets so late tourists are around."

"Leave me behind then."

"We cannot," Mahes said wearily. "The crystals only work while I'm in the chamber."

"Another safeguard against mortals, I take it," Kendra said snidely.

Tory went to Kendra's side. "Come on, hon. We're all tired and need some sleep. Tomorrow is another day."

"No. No, I'm not leaving here until I find what we came for," Kendra yelled in defiance.

Markus walked around the table until he stood in front of Kendra. "Since you won't listen to reason, I guess we'll have to do this the hard way."

Making a grab for Kendra, he wasn't at all prepared for the swift kick to his shin she gave him when he reached for her.

"I'm not giving up." Kendra backed away from Markus.

Markus rubbed his abused shin and scowled. "There's nothing here. You'll only be chasing something that doesn't exist. I won't allow you to harm yourself over it."

"I'm not a witless child. Don't treat me as such."

"I never said you were. It's just you aren't thinking straight right now."

Circling around Markus, Mahes, Tory, and Scott,

Kendra put the table between her and them. It was then she noticed the design on the floor. The table stood in the center of it, almost completely covering what was depicted there.

Ignoring Markus who was still trying to convince her to give up on her search, Kendra peered closely at one section of the design that showed. Her breath caught. A renewed sense of hope soared through her. She grabbed the edge of the table and pushed with all her might.

Markus stopped mid-sentence. He scratched his head. "What in blazes are you doing now?"

Smiling broadly, Kendra pointed to the three men in the room. "You, you, and you, get your muscles over here and help me move this thing." They made no move to help her. She pointed at the floor. "It's been under our very noses all night. Look at the design in the floor."

Scott was the first to come to where Kendra stood, who was still trying to move the table on her own. He shook his head. "Good god, all the hours we wasted. We looked in the wrong spot all along. It wasn't the scrolls Ptah wanted us to find, but the floor." After giving Kendra a kiss on the cheek, he pushed with her. The table shuddered in response.

Quickly, Mahes and Markus joined Scott and Kendra, adding their strength to the endeavor. Tory fell in beside Kendra and pushed as well. With their combined effort, the huge table surprisingly slid across the stone floor with ease.

Now with it no longer sitting on top of it, the design could be easily made out. A large set of Egyptian hieroglyphs had been set into the floor. They were the glyphs that represented Nefertem's name. Kendra walked around each of them. One looked like a long-handled spoon and the next two sat one on top of the other. And the next one looked like half a circle sitting on top of what she thought seemed like a reclining layout chair. The last one depicted an Egyptian man seated, wearing a wig and Pharaohic beard.

"Thanks to Kendra our night has not been a total waste of time, after all," Mahes said. "I am glad one of us decided to stay firm and not give up."

Scott kneeled to take a closer look at the legs. He ran his hand down one, then crouched. "I think I've found something we needed to find."

"What have you uncovered?" Mahes kneeled beside him.

"I'm not sure, but here," he pointed to the spot on the table leg, "has hieroglyphs that spell Nefertem's name, a perfect match to the ones in the floor."

Mahes nodded. "So it would seem. That begs to question why are they there and what is their purpose?"

Scott ran his fingers over the glyphs, then pushed on them. The marble shifted beneath and slid out, leaving an opening in the leg. He reached into what was obviously a hidden compartment. Slowly, he pulled out a small scroll. Carefully, he unrolled it to read what had been transcribed upon it. As Scott looked at the glyphs, Mahes looked over his shoulder.

Having reached the end of her patience, Kendra couldn't keep silent any longer. "What is it? What have you found?" Mahes and Scott meaningfully looked at each other, which she didn't miss. Her feeling of hope all too quickly changed to apprehension. "Okay, give it to me. I can tell what's written on that scroll must be bad in some way. Your faces say it all." She steeled herself for the worst.

Scott stood and looked at Mahes. He nodded, and Scott answered. "This is a spell, another summoning spell, to be exact."

"To summon Nefertem?"

"Yes, but there's more to it than just that."

"Of course it couldn't be as simple as that. Don't leave

me hanging. Tell me the rest of it."

Scott walked past Kendra and stood in the center of the hieroglyphs on the floor. "Kendra, you have to stand in this exact spot, and while holding the pendant, you have to say the spell out loud. Nefertem will be brought here whether he wishes it or not. He'll be bound to the glyphs. He'll only be able to move to where they extend on the floor."

Swiftly pulling the pendant free of her top, Kendra went to take Scott's place on the hieroglyphs. "Okay, translate the spell for me and I'll summon Nefertem now."

Mahes put his hand over Kendra's as she moved to draw the pendant over her head. "You must not remove the pendant, especially when you say this spell. We have to wait, though. The spell cannot be performed now."

"There's more. Something you have to seriously consider before you do this," Scott added.

Kendra shook her head. "There's nothing to consider. I'll do it."

"Scott is right, Kendra. You cannot jump into this lightly." Mahes looked at her intently. "This spell could very well cost you your life."

"Whoa there," Markus interjected. "There's no way you're going to do this, Kendra."

This time it wasn't Kendra who objected to what Markus had said. It was Mahes who rejected his worries. "Kendra is the only one who can perform this spell."

"Not if it's going to cost her so much." Markus vehemently shook his head.

"There is a greater chance of nothing like that happening at all. I feel Kendra will not be at risk, but she must know what consequences she might face."

Tory came to stand next Kendra for support, crossed her arms over her chest, and glared at Scott. "Okay, mister, spill it. You and Mahes have kept us in the dark long enough."

"Your wish is my command." Scott winked at Tory. She becomingly blushed, and he smiled and turned to address Kendra. "I don't know if I would say you have nothing to worry about, but Mahes does know Nefertem better than any of us." At Kendra's nod, Scott continued. "The validity of the spell hinges on Nefertem's feelings for you. He must accept you as his mate or the spell will fail, and you could pay a heavy price for your actions."

A chill ran down Kendra's spine. She really didn't have any idea if Nefertem thought of her in that way or not. If she had to judge from the way he'd acted the last time she'd seen him, then she'd say no, he didn't.

"What will happen to me if Nefertem doesn't accept me as his mate?"

Mahes answered Kendra's question when Scott looked at his feet, seeming unable to tell her what he knew. "Nefertem will kill you."

"How will he do that?"

"For the spell to be complete, you and he must have a blood exchange. Nefertem being the first to drink yours. If he doesn't claim you as his mate, he will rip your throat out. We will not be able to stop him either. Once the spell has begun, it will not only keep Nefertem bound inside the glyphs with you, but it will keep us out."

Kendra wrapped her arms around herself as she shook. She didn't know if she was brave enough to put herself in such jeopardy. "When does the spell have to be performed?"

"Just before dawn on the day of my mother's coming."

Kendra nodded. The chamber she'd once found large enough, now felt as if the walls closed in around her. She needed the openness of the surface above. "Can we get out of here? We found what we looked for. That's enough."

Mahes nodded. After motioning for the others to hold hands, he reached for Kendra. A few seconds later, they were all on the surface, standing before the Sphinx with the dawn's early light just beginning to glow on the horizon.

CHAPTER TWENTY-EIGHT

K endra fell onto the bed in the hotel, and within seconds, went to sleep. The room where she slept was not her brother's, but the one she had shared with Nefertem.

Mahes gently removed Kendra's sandals and then tucked her in. Once he had her settled, he stretched out on the other bed. Just like Nefertem while in mortal form, he did not always need long hours of sleep each night.

Even though the day had dawned, sleep would be hard to find. The spell was touchy at best, and that worried him. He did believe Nefertem's feelings for Kendra were true and he would do her no harm. The one thing that plagued his mind was how their mother would react to being thwarted, which was the other aspect of the spell that could turn out for the worse.

Mahes turned his head and looked at Kendra. She was strong enough to see this to the end, and if she should falter, he would be there to see she did not.

* * * *

After four hours of deep, dreamless sleep, Kendra roused herself. Her mind wouldn't settle for any length of time. Even asleep, subconsciously she'd kept going over and over what she'd have to face. It became so bad those thoughts had leaked into her dreams where she couldn't tell if what she experienced was real or not. It was after such a dream she'd finally pushed herself to wakefulness.

Kendra rubbed the sleep from her eyes and sat up. She had a headache from lack of sleep and was very out of sorts. It didn't help her temperament any when her stomach decided to growl loudly. The sound of Mahes chuckling caused her to look at the other bed.

"I see you're in a fine mood this morning, Mahes. I wish I could say the same thing about myself."

Mahes chuckled again. "Let us order some room service. I know I could do with some food. After you eat, you can try to get a little more sleep. You will feel better after that."

Kendra shook her head. "I'll take you up on your offer of food, but I don't think I can sleep another wink."

"Do not fret so." Mahes went and sat on the bed next to her. "It will turn out all right."

"Can you promise me that it will? That you're a hundred percent sure I'm Nefertem's mate? If you can't, I don't know if I can do it."

Mahes reached out and brushed a lock of hair behind Kendra's ear. "I am positive you are. If you were not, Nefertem would not have spent the night in your arms after we landed in Egypt. You tamed the savage beast, so to speak."

"Yes, that might be true, but in the morning, all that changed. What if he doesn't remember me or what we shared?"

"My mother can do all she likes to Nefertem. She can take his memories of you from him, but deep down inside his heart he will remember what you mean to him."

Kendra so wanted to believe that. "I hope you're right, because I'm risking my life on that very assumption."

"You will do it then?"

"Yes. I love Nefertem enough to do it. I can only pray he feels the same about me." Kendra's stomach growled loudly once more.

"I think we had better get you fed before you wake up the people in the room beside us." Mahes laughed. He kissed Kendra's cheek. "Thank you. Just remember you will not be alone." After hopping off the bed, he went in search of the room service menu.

Kendra pushed herself up so her back was against the headboard and absently rattled off the items she wanted from the menu to Mahes. He could say she wouldn't be alone, but the truth of the matter was she would be. The spell would make sure of it.

* * * *

"No, no, and no. I won't let you do this, Kendra."

Beyond exasperated at that point with Markus' refusal to see reason, Kendra stood firm. "This is my decision to make. We aren't kids any more, where I'll let you bully me into changing my mind."

"Why do you have to be so stubborn?" Markus turned and slammed the flat side of his fist onto a wall. He kept his back to her. "You're the only family I have left. Don't you see? If anything happens to you, I'll be alone."

Kendra crossed to where Markus stood and took him by the shoulder to turn him to face her. There was fear in his eyes. She pulled him into her arms.

"You know I wouldn't voluntarily leave you, Markus. I love you, but I also love Nefertem."

"I can see I'm only wasting my breath. You won't be swayed from doing this." Markus pulled out of Kendra's hold and nailed Mahes with a hard stare. "I need to know exactly what will happen once Kendra starts that spell. Everything. Since she's so bent on this madness, I want to know even the smallest thing that could possibly go wrong, and what can be done to fix it."

Mahes gave a short nod. "As you wish. An hour before dawn, Kendra must start the spell. If it is performed too soon, it will fail, the same if it is done too late. As I said before, once she steps onto the hieroglyphs and begins, we will not be able to cross them."

"A fat lot of good that will do us if Nefertem decides not to cooperate," Markus said snidely.

"Even though we cannot get to them, they will still be able to see and hear us. If need be, I will distract Nefertem, but I still feel it will not be necessary."

Seeming not entirely reassured by Mahes' statement, Markus asked, "Okay, say Nefertem does recognize Kendra as his mate, what will happen then? You said something before about a blood exchange taking place. How exactly is that going to happen?"

"Nefertem is going to bite me." Kendra knew those fangs he now sported had a purpose other than making Nefertem appear scarier.

"Yes, you must let Nefertem drink from you," Mahes said flatly. "That will be the test to see if he claims you as his mate. If he does not..."

"He'll kill me."

Mahes nodded. "Which will not happen. Once he takes some of your blood, he will offer his to you."

Kendra swallowed hard. The prospect of drinking blood, even it if was Nefertem's, she didn't find at all appealing. "Okay, I think I can do that."

"You are not required to take much, Kendra, only a small amount. Even one drop would be sufficient to complete the spell."

"Then?"

"Nefertem should return to normal with the cat fully

subdued. My mother will no longer have access to the mortal world." Mahes paused. "The end of the spell is a ceremony. After it is completed you and Nefertem will be mated. It is the equivalent of a marriage ceremony."

Kendra's spirits soared. Nefertem would be her husband. "He'll be able to stay with me, after all."

Mahes sadly shook his head. "No, he will not. He will still be bound to the pendant and my mother. Nefertem will return to the realm of the immortals, unable to walk among mortals once again. He will only be able to return if summoned with the pendant."

"Which would start all this craziness all over again." Kendra fought back tears that burned behind her eyes. "I won't do that even if it is the only way for me to be with Nefertem again."

Kendra wouldn't, no matter how tempting it could be. She would rather live the rest of her life alone than put the world in danger again, and she would be alone. There would be no other man in her life. If Nefertem was to be her husband, then he always would be. Even if it sentenced her to a life with no man by her side and no children, she would always think of him as such. She would have to cherish the time spent with him for long and lonely years to come.

* * * *

The time drew nearer. Nefertem took a deep breath, relishing the strong, heady scent of mortal blood. Soon he would be able to appease his thirst for it. For now, he could wait. His patience would soon be rewarded.

Moving silently among the mortals, they in no way acknowledged his presence. He had no wish to be seen by them. It was a simple matter to manipulate their weak minds to believe he was not really there. No one so much as batted an eye when he walked past them. Once again properly attired in a linen kilt, he would have done more than just draw a few curious looks from the passersby.

He really did not know why he came there, to Giza. For some unexplainable reason, he felt pulled to come to this spot. He took another deep breath as he walked near the Great Pyramid. Nefertem caught a scent. That was why he had come there. The smell of the mortal woman still lingered. It grew stronger the nearer he drew to the Sphinx.

As he inhaled huge drafts of air, her scent filled his lungs so it invaded every fiber of his being. Even though it was hours old, it still was a potent mix. He closed his eyes and drew in more of it. Kendra. Nefertem's eyes snapped open. That was the mortal woman's name.

With that recollection, came a series of images that quickly flashed through his mind. They sped by so quickly his brain didn't have time to retain them. Nefertem shook his head. They made no sense. Why he should feel a connection with the mortal woman, other than her being the one who possessed the pendant, was beyond his knowledge. What disturbed him the most was the feeling of longing the scenes had left in their wake. He longed to hold the woman in his arms, to protect her, to claim her as his.

Ruthlessly, Nefertem pushed those feelings away. He had no need of a mortal woman. He was a god and far superior to her kind. She, and the rest of her kind, would all too soon learn just how superior he actually was.

Nefertem came to stand in front of the Sphinx, before its large paws. The woman's scent was stronger there. Before he could stop himself, he drew in another large breath. His blood surge in want. Realizing what he had just done, he snarled in irritation. This weakness he had when it came to the woman he would not tolerate in himself.

Giving the mortals who milled around him one last look, Nefertem willed himself to his mother's side. With the coming of dawn, all that would change. Their punishment was at hand. Then he could exorcise the unwanted feelings he had for the mortal woman. The blood of her kind would be the cure from her he sought.

CHAPTER TWENTY-NINE

Knowing she wouldn't be good company to the others, Kendra elected to stay in her hotel room for the remainder of the day. There really was no point in having the others strung out as she was. As well, she didn't think she could endure Markus' looks of concern. That was something he'd done more than once during her time with him during the latter part of the morning. She loved her brother dearly, but this was something she had to face by herself.

Now alone, Kendra stretched out on the bed and tried to will herself to sleep. She was drained, and for what she had to do that night, she needed her wits about her.

She tossed and turned for what felt like hours before sleep finally claimed her, but it was nowhere near a restful, untroubled rest. It was full of dreams much like the ones she'd had during the early morning hours, only there was one that bothered her more than the others.

This dream took place in the hidden chamber, with her standing on the hieroglyphs set into the floor. *Unlike reality, the chamber was full of dark shadows, and where she was, it was the only spot brightly illuminated. Turning in place,*

Kendra sought out the others, but they appeared not to be in the chamber with her.

Kendra gripped the pendant and spoke out loud to the empty chamber. What she said, she couldn't discern. She only knew she'd said something, and it caused a reaction. There was a blinding flash of light that lit the whole chamber for the briefest of seconds. Once her eyes adjusted to the dimness, Kendra saw she was no longer alone. Nefertem stood before her.

He was dressed as he'd been when she'd first used the pendant to summon him. Even right down to him wearing the leopard-shaped helmet. As she watched, he removed it. Nefertem held his hand out to her.

Kendra smiled and cautiously placed her hand in his larger one. Nefertem smiled in return, giving her a better view of the fangs he possessed. He drew her closer. She lifted her face to accept his kiss. Passion instantly flared to life as their lips met.

Her heart beat a little faster. The spell was going to work. Nefertem wouldn't be kissing her so passionately if he hadn't accepted her as his mate. Breaking the kiss, she pulled back and looked lovingly at him.

Nefertem stared back. The love she'd expected to see wasn't there in his golden cat eyes. Kendra tried to free herself from his embrace. Moving with a speed no mortal could possibly manage, he grabbed a fistful of her hair and wrenched her head painfully to the side, giving him better access to the throbbing vein at the side of her neck. He bared his fangs and sank them into her flesh. She screamed.

Bolting upright, Kendra gasped for breath as the last vestiges of the dream receded. She closed her eyes and tried to push away the feeling of panic that coursed through her. A hand gently rubbed her back, and she nearly jumped out of her skin. She screamed in response.

"Relax, Kendra. You are okay. Did you have a bad dream?"

With her hand clutched to her chest, Kendra turned. Mahes sat next to her. "Do you mind not doing that again? You almost gave me a heart attack. Yes, I did have a bad dream. One of several I've had since we were in the hidden chamber."

"I apologize. I did not mean to scare you like that. I came to fetch you. It has been decided that we are all going out to eat this evening. Tory thought it would be best if I told you. She figured you would want to know ahead of time, and for us not to just spring it on you at the last minute."

Kendra shook her head. "I think I'll pass. I don't really feel like eating, anyway."

"I am afraid you might not be able to get out of it so easily. Tory was quite insistent about you going with us."

"I'll still pass. Tory will just have to take no for an answer. How long before we go to the Sphinx again?"

"In a few hours."

Surprised by that, Kendra looked outside. The sky was already darkening to twilight. She hadn't realized she'd slept so long. She rose from the bed and went to the window. She took a long, shuddering breath when she spied the large, hulking shapes of the pyramids in the distance.

"What did you dream about?" Mahes asked from where he stood a short distance behind her.

Kendra crossed her arms across her chest and rubbed them as she recalled parts of her dream. "About Nefertem. About what will happen tonight."

"You are a strong woman. Do not let your mind play tricks on you." Mahes came directly behind her.

"I won't, but it's hard not to." Turning so she looked at Mahes, she asked. "What happens to you if the spell works in the end and we're able to stop your mother? Will you leave with Nefertem since he was the one who tied you to the mortal world?"

Mahes nodded. "Yes, I leave when he does."

"Are you able to come back afterward?"

"Yes. I have no such restraints on me as Nefertem does.

I can come to the mortal world any time I wish. Would you like me to visit you? Is that what this is all about?"

"I would like that. I've grown kind of attached to you as I would a brother." Kendra tried to swallow the lump that suddenly developed in her throat. "That way I won't feel completely cut off from Nefertem. You can tell me how he's doing."

Mahes kissed Kendra on the tip of her nose. "I too have come to think of you as a sister. I would be happy to see you again under normal circumstances. Now with that having been said, I really do think you should reconsider your decision about going out to eat. You need the distraction. At least take some pity on Markus. He is worried sick about what the outcome will be tonight. He is afraid he is going to lose you."

Mahes was right. She did need the distraction. Sitting alone in the hotel room, replaying her nightmare in her mind would only cripple her. "Okay, I'll go. Just let me shower, then I'll meet you all at Markus' room."

Mahes smiled. "That a girl. You have made the right decision. I will let the others know." After giving Kendra a quick peck on the cheek, he turned and left her to get ready.

* * * *

Kendra gave herself one last once over in the bathroom mirror before she went to meet the others. After showering, she'd pulled out the one dress she'd brought with her from home. She really didn't know why she'd packed it, but she figured tonight would be the night to wear it. If she was to be married to Nefertem, she'd be damned if she did it in a tank top and shorts.

She ran her hands down the full length of the dress and tried to smooth out the few wrinkles that remained from being packed in her suitcase. It was one of very few she owned that was on the slinky side. It was pale pink and made out of brushed silk-looking material. It had thin spaghetti straps and only reached to just above her knees. The strappy high-heels she put on her bare feet matched the color of her dress.

Satisfied with what she saw in the mirror, Kendra took a deep breath and let herself out of the room. She walked the short distance to Markus' and then knocked on the door. It opened before she even had a chance to lower her hand to her side. Markus stood in the open doorway, looking totally dumbfounded.

"Are you just going to stand there gawking at me, Markus, or are you going to let me in? I'm starting to feel as if I made a mistake wearing this dress."

Coming around from behind Markus, Troy pushed him aside. "Don't you dare change, Kendra. You look stunning. I knew you'd look great in that dress when I convinced you to buy it."

"You're sure I don't look ridiculous?" Kendra asked as she walked into the room.

"Absolutely not. You'll have every man you walk by staring at you, wishing you were his."

"That's what I am afraid of," Markus added dryly.

"Don't listen to him. There's nothing wrong with attracting a little bit of male attention."

Kendra slowly backed toward the door as she started to have second thoughts about the whole dress idea. "Maybe it would be best if I did change. I don't think I'll feel all that comfortable thinking everyone is watching me."

"Please do not change, Kendra." Reaching out to her, Mahes took her hand in his and pulled her back into the room. "Tory is right, you look stunning. I know Nefertem would love to see you dressed this way."

"Truly? You aren't just saying it to be nice?"

"Yes, I mean what I say. If you are worried about a little unwanted attention, I will stay by your side and keep the other men at bay."

"All right, you and Tory have convinced me not to change, after all."

The main factor behind her decision was being able to have Mahes by her side. He would garner the most attention from men and women alike. With his great height and dark good-looks, he'd easily draw the eyes of everyone around him. The women would want him, and the men would hate him for it.

With her arm firmly threaded through Mahes', Kendra let him lead her out of the room. The rest of their party closely followed. Their destination was the restaurant situated in the hotel.

Luckily for them, it wasn't very crowded so they were quickly seated at a table. After that, at least for Kendra, the meal pretty well passed in a daze. She went through all the motions of ordering her and eating, but it all really didn't register in her senses.

She really couldn't recall precisely what she'd had to eat, only that the main part of her meal had chicken in it. Her dinner companions' conversation washed over her. If she was called upon to contribute, she only answered in monosyllables.

Sipping on her glass of wine, totally lost in thought, Kendra didn't notice when everyone was ready to leave the restaurant until Markus took the now-empty wineglass from her hand.

"Time to go, Kendra."

Kendra smiled sheepishly. "Oh, already? Sorry, I wasn't paying attention."

"You haven't been with us mentally at all." Markus leaned closer so only she heard his next words. "You don't have to do it. I hate seeing you like this."

"Then don't look at me. I'm doing it, Markus. If I back out now, I'll never forgive myself. The consequences would haunt me for the rest of my life."

Markus nodded in defeat. "I know it would. I just think you're taking an awful risk. I don't know Nefertem as well as you do so I have reservations."

"I wouldn't expect anything less from you." Kendra pulled Markus into a quick hug, then went to Mahes, who waited for her, effectively ending the discussion.

CHAPTER THIRTY

The time was fast approaching. The need, the hunger, pulsed through his veins in a rush of hot blood, and was something he could not easily ignore. Why he tortured himself by walking among the mortals when the time for him to spill their blood was so near, he could not find the answer. Usually, he would have avoided them until his mother arrived, but one mortal woman drew him still. He had not been able to rid his mind of her, and her scent haunted him. At times, the need to be with her overpowered the need to taste mortal blood. That was something he found hard to accept.

Wandering aimlessly among his oblivious intended victims, hidden from their view, Nefertem went on full alert when he spied a group of mortals leaving a hotel a short distance away. He closed his eyes and breathed deeply as her scent rolled over him. Even from afar, it was potent enough to have the longing he had for her become almost unbearable.

He focused his full attention on the woman and gave little heed to the other mortals who were with her. Not even his brother's presence with her sparked much interest in him. He followed her movements with his gaze as she climbed into a waiting taxicab. As the vehicle pulled away from the curb, Nefertem closed his eyes and followed it with his mind until it reached its destination. He willed himself to that spot.

He materialized just as the woman got out of the cab. As Mahes took her hand and led her toward the Great Pyramids, Nefertem fought back the urge to strike his brother down. The sight of another man handling the woman infuriated him. The mortal female was his.

He kept himself hidden from their senses and followed the small group as they looked at each of the pyramids. Once they stopped to watch a show of light and sound, he stayed near, even though the music hurt his sensitive ears. After the performance, as the crowd thinned, Nefertem followed the woman to the Sphinx.

After the group disappeared, he knew Mahes was responsible. He did not like how his brother interfered with the mortals. He was just about to use his powers to find out where Mahes had taken them when his mother's voice filled his mind.

Nefertem, return to me. The mortals' time is almost up. You must prepare.

His mother would not tolerate him disobeying her wishes. Something in the back of his mind told him it was not wise to draw attention to the mortal woman. After taking one last whiff of the woman's scent, he willed himself to his mother's side.

* * * *

Being inside the hidden chamber once again, Kendra found all her scattered thoughts were becoming focused. It came down to this. All that was left to do was wait for the appropriate time to perform the spell.

To pass the long hours ahead, Scott decided to have a

better look at the contents of the library. Their first visit hadn't allowed him the time to really investigate what was hidden in the chamber. As it turned out, Mahes was just as curious to see what secrets the library held so he followed Scott.

After the second sound of exclamation that was heard coming from Scott, Markus joined the other two men and left Kendra and Tory alone. They sat side by side on one of the intricately carved benches. The one they were on was carved in the semblance of a leopard. Ebony wood and gold inlay mimicked that particular cat's spotted coat. Markus had been busily admiring the craftsmanship just moments before.

"Alone at last. Well, as alone as we can get in here, anyway," Tory said lightly.

Kendra arched a brow at her friend. "Don't tell me you've grown tired of being around Scott day after day."

"Hell no," Tory said vehemently. Kendra's lips twitched, Tory laughed. "You got me good."

"Looks like I did," Kendra said, laughing. "About bloody time too, I might add. I thought you'd never find someone who's right for you."

"You and me both. All I have to say is that pendant of yours was what I needed in my life."

In response to Tory mentioning the pendant, Kendra closed her hand around it. "That's the only good thing I can say about it. It led us to the men of our dreams."

Tory changed the subject. "I wonder if old Mahes over there would notice if we pocketed something small from here as a souvenir. I know Scott would never do it, but I'd like to have something as a keepsake from this grand adventure we've been on."

Kendra chuckled. "I doubt you'd get away with it. I think Mahes has eyes in the back of his head. Either that or he just heard what you said. He's watching you. Rather intently."

Tory stuck out her tongue at him and then turned back to Kendra. Mahes' deep, baritone laugh could be heard right after.

"Guess you're right, Kendra. That one doesn't miss much. Oh well, was worth a shot."

After that, Tory decided she and Kendra should do some exploring on their own. Besides housing ancient scrolls that were treasures in themselves, there was an assortment of small statues, amulets, and carved slate tablets. Some of the statues and amulets were made from pure gold.

Tory, deciding she wanted to have some fun with Mahes, picked up a gold amulet that was about the size of her palm and calmly shoved it into her jean shorts pocket. She nonchalantly moved on to the next item that caught her fancy. It wasn't very long before Mahes came up to her and silently stuck out his hand.

"What can I do for you, Mahes?" Tory asked sweetly.

"Hand it over, Tory."

"What would 'it' be exactly that you're wanting?"

With his hand still outstretched, Mahes said, "Give the amulet to me or I will take it from you myself. I would not mind. I would enjoy it, as a matter of fact, but I think Scott would be a trifle angry with me afterward. It is your decision."

Smiling just as sweetly as before, Tory fished the amulet out of her pocket and then plunked it onto Mahes' open hand. He gave her a quick nod before he returned the amulet to its rightful place.

The next couple of hours, Mahes and Tory played that little game. Kendra was hard pressed at times not to break out in laughter as Tory managed to look innocent of any wrong-doing, and Mahes would oh, so patiently wait for her to hand over whatever she'd hidden on her person. They did that mostly for her benefit, to help lighten her mood, and she loved them for it.

It was Mahes who finally called their game to an end. He calmly came to Kendra and held out his hand to her. "It is time. Are you ready?"

Kendra silently nodded and placed her hand in his. Her stomach suddenly became filled with butterflies, but she didn't hesitate when Mahes led her to stand on the hieroglyphs on the floor. Scott was already there, waiting.

"I've translated the spell, Kendra, and wrote it out for you." Scott handed her a small piece of paper. "All you have to do is read it."

She nodded again. Kendra couldn't bring herself to speak. She didn't trust her voice not to crack and give away what she felt inside.

Sucking in a fortifying breath, Kendra wrapped her hand around the pendant. She met Markus' gaze where he stood at the very edge of the glyphs. He nodded once in her direction. That was all she needed to let herself finally look at the paper she held and read the spell out loud.

"I stand inside the words that hold him. I call him to my side. I lay my fate in his hands. My blood he takes to make his choice. I give it to change the past. Come to me now!"

Just as the first time, the pendant warmed in her hand. A blinding flash of light followed shortly thereafter, the same as before. After her sight cleared, she found she wasn't alone. Nefertem stood on the hieroglyphs with her.

He was dressed as he'd been on that fateful night when they'd first met. The black leopard helmet covered his face. His bow and quiver of arrows were slung over his shoulder. The kilt he wore low around his hips was pristine white.

Kendra swallowed the nervousness that welled inside her. This was Nefertem, she reminded herself, and he would never hurt her. As he turned his golden gaze upon her, and his eyes seemed to bore right through her, she had to repeat that assurance to herself more than once.

He soon lost interest in her. Nefertem removed his

helmet and took in his new surroundings. His gaze lit on each of the other individuals just outside the hieroglyphs. In response to finding three mortals before him, he smiled, giving them each a clear view of his fangs. He lunged toward them, only to be brought up short when he tried to step off the glyphs. He snarled with rage. He tried again, only to have the same result, which enraged him all the more.

"Be easy, Nefertem." Mahes' softly spoken words drew his brother's attention. "We mean you no harm." Nefertem growled.

"Why doesn't he speak to you, Mahes?" Tory asked as she sidled a little closer to Scott.

"The change is finished. Speech is beyond him now. The cat is in complete control, but I can still make Nefertem understand what I say to him."

"That puts my mind to rest," she said sarcastically. "If he can only understand you, how will he understand Kendra?"

"She possesses the pendant. Whoever wears it, even if he or she is a mortal, Nefertem will understand them."

"What now, Mahes?" Kendra didn't know what to do next. So far, Nefertem wasn't paying the least bit of attention to her. He seemed more interested in trying to get to Tory, Scott, and Markus. He repeatedly threw himself against the invisible barrier that kept him trapped with her.

"Your guess is as good as mine. The instructions with the spell did not say anything about him ignoring you."

"I see. I guess I'm not enticing enough to him. I must be losing my touch."

Mahes chuckled. "Hardly. Just give him a few minutes. He will soon grow weary of trying to break free."

The prediction Mahes made about Nefertem soon tiring turned out to be way off the mark. Ten minutes later, and Nefertem was still trying to gain his freedom. He tried from every angle, even going so far as to shove Kendra out of the way so he could reach the space behind her. By now, her nervousness was completely gone. She actually found his attempts at escaping quite funny. The man was stubborn to a fault.

After being rudely shoved aside for a second time, Kendra had had enough. "This is ridiculous. Will he not accept that he can't get away?"

"Obviously not," Mahes said dryly.

"All right then, I have to take matters into my own hands."

Kendra marched to where Nefertem stood, pushing at the invisible barrier, grabbed him by the arm, turned him to face her, and took his face in both hands. Not giving him a chance to push her away, she yanked his head down and proceeded to kiss him thoroughly.

She wasn't sure whether he would accept her advances. His first reaction was to hold himself stiff as a board, but Kendra refused to let him go. She wound her fingers through his hair, holding him to her. She slipped her tongue into his mouth and ran it across the pointed tips of his fangs. Nefertem groaned in response and wrapped his arms around her waist, pulling her flush against him.

Mahes chuckled again. "Seems you have his attention now, Kendra."

She vaguely heard Mahes. By now, the only thing that existed in her world was Nefertem, and the only thing she wanted was for him to keep kissing her. Nothing else mattered.

Just as it had been in her dream, the area outside the glyphs seemed to dim, leaving only her and Nefertem bathed in a soft, glowing light. Their kiss went on and on. Still haunted by the rest of the events that had taken place in her sleep, Kendra knew she had to end their passionate exchange. She had to look into his eyes and see how he was reacting to her being in his arms. Slowly, she lifted her lips from his and looked at him.

A wide smile spread across her lips at what she saw. It was nothing like it'd been in her dream. There was such a look of possessiveness on Nefertem's face. As if he didn't want to leave her with any lingering doubts, a single word, *Mine,* echoed inside her mind.

Kendra smiled once more and said out loud the same word he'd mentally told her. "Mine."

Her response must have pleased him. Once the word left her mouth, Nefertem threaded his fingers through her hair and claimed her lips in an ardent kiss. A state of euphoria washed over her. All the anxiety she'd felt previously had been for not. He had accepted her.

Nefertem's lips left hers as he made a trail of kisses across her jaw. Reaching her ear, he traced its outline with his tongue before he gently nipped her earlobe. Kendra sucked in a breath.

As his lips left her ear and slowly headed down to the side of her neck, Kendra held her breath. She locked her arms around Nefertem's waist and held on as tightly as she could. She knew what was to come next. She bent her head to the side and happily gave him better access.

CHAPTER THIRTY-ONE

E ven though she'd been expecting it, Kendra still gasped as Nefertem sank his fangs into her exposed neck. It wasn't from pain, but from the sudden rush of senses that overwhelmed her. Everything he felt, she did as well. Every sensation, every emotion, she experienced as if they were her own, and she knew he had the same experience as she. She allowed all the love she felt for him well within her to silently let him know. In return, he flooded her mind with the full extent of his feelings for her. He loved her too. Her heart soared with that knowledge.

Then it was her turn. Nefertem released his hold on her and stepped back, letting some space come between them. He intently held her gaze, and used his fangs to break open the skin at his wrist. Blood welled from the cut. She didn't hesitate when he stuck it out for her to take. She closed the small distance between them and brought his arm to her mouth. Just as when he'd taken her blood, Kendra felt the same rush of emotions and sensations.

Being as connected as she was to Nefertem, at that moment, Kendra felt the changes begin inside him even before she lifted her mouth away from his wrist. The coppery taste of his blood lingered. Impulsively, she wiped her lips with the back of her hand.

The changes in Nefertem increased. His fangs slowly receded in length until they returned to normal size. They still retained their sharp appearance, as they had when Nefertem had first arrived. His eyes changed back, losing the slit-like pupils. She looked into them and waited for a sign to let her know the change was finally complete.

"Kendra?" Nefertem asked slowly, as if he hadn't spoken in a very long time.

"Yes, it's I." Kendra wrapped her arms around his waist and placed her head on his broad chest. Nefertem gathered her close. "We did it, Nefertem. It's finally over."

"How..." Nefertem's words trailed off. He kissed the top of Kendra's head. "How could you have taken such a risk for me?"

She lifted her head to look at him. "Do you really have to ask that? I would do anything for you. I love you, Nefertem. I would walk through fire if it was what I had to do to be with you."

"As I love you, and would do the same for you." Lowering his head, Nefertem kissed Kendra with all the love he had for her.

The sound of someone loudly clearing their throat broke them apart. For the first time, Nefertem seemed to realize he and Kendra weren't alone. His gaze rested on the four other people standing a short distance away. Scott held a teary-eyed Tory in his arms, and Mahes had a massive grin plastered on his face.

Nefertem led Kendra to Markus. He stuck out his free hand to the other man. "You must be Kendra's brother. I am Nefertem. Sorry our first meeting was not what it should have been."

Markus accepted Nefertem's hand and shook it. "Yes, I'm Markus. I'm happy to finally meet the real Nefertem."

He turned his attention to Kendra. "Are you okay, sis?"

"I'm perfectly fine."

Markus relaxed his stiff stance. "Mahes said once the spell was completed you two would be considered mated. Is that correct?" he asked Nefertem.

"Yes, that is right. Kendra is now mine."

Nodding, Markus fished around in his shorts pocket. "Then you'll need these."

Kendra's throat closed with emotion as Markus pulled his hand out of his pocket and revealed what he held on his open palm. He had two plain gold wedding bands— one a man's and one a woman's.

Throwing herself into Markus' arms, Kendra hugged him. "Where did you get those?"

Markus hugged Kendra in return, then released her. "I knew you'd like to have them. I bought them earlier today when you were napping. I know you always wanted a big, fancy wedding, Kendra. Since that's not to be, the least I could do is make sure you had a wedding ring to wear."

Kendra took the rings from Markus and turned to Nefertem. "It's tradition when couples get married they exchange rings when they take their wedding vows. Will you do that with me now? Will you wear the ring I give you?"

At Nefertem's nod, Kendra slipped the larger gold wedding band onto his ring finger on his left hand. It was a perfect fit. Giving him the second band, she held out her left hand for him to slip it onto hers.

"You may now kiss your bride," Markus said with a smile.

Nefertem pulled Kendra into his arms and kissed her while the others cheered. Once the kiss ended, the other people in the room gathered around them.

Mahes kissed Kendra's cheek. "Welcome to the family. I always wanted a sister." He turned to Nefertem. His face grew serious. "I hate to bring this up, but time is running out."

"How long do we have?"

"A half hour at the most, I think. Since this spell has never been done before I am not exactly sure what timeframe we have left, but I think once dawn comes, we leave."

"That's not enough time," Kendra said sadly.

Mahes caught Nefertem's eye. "We will give you a little time alone." He and the others quietly went to the opposite side of the chamber.

"I just got you back. I can't let you go now."

Nefertem caressed her cheek. "You look beautiful in that dress." His gaze drifted down the length of her body.

Kendra felt herself blush. "I don't usually wear dresses like this, but I wasn't going to my wedding day in a pair of khaki shorts. You really like it?"

"Yes. I like it a little too much for being in the company of others."

At Nefertem's words, a thrill raced through Kendra's body. She in turn looked appreciatively at his bared chest. "I must say seeing you dressed only in your kilt is making me wish we were alone as well." She dropped her gaze to the said garment. There was no mistaking what the bulge was that pushed out from the front of his kilt.

Nefertem groaned as he followed where Kendra's gaze had drifted to. "If you do not stop staring at me like that, I am likely to give our brothers and friends much more to see than what they bargained for."

Kendra laughed. "We can't have that now, can we?" She wrapped her arms around Nefertem's neck and looked lovingly at him. "I think Markus would have a fit if you did what I think you want to do."

Nefertem smiled. "Mahes, well, let us just say he would find it very entertaining and would be giving me suggestions."

Kendra laughed again. "Very true. Your brother really

is a piece of work."

After she said what she had about Mahes, Kendra realized Nefertem didn't know what she'd meant by the confused look he wore. She had to remember her husband was still not totally familiar with modern sayings such as that. She was about to explain what she'd meant when a loud cat growl reverberated off the walls of the chamber. Nefertem instantly stiffened in her arms.

*

Quickly releasing Kendra, Nefertem turned and deliberately stood in front of her so his body shielded her. He looked at the woman who stood a few feet away. "Hello, Mother." He spoke in Egyptian.

Sekhmet growled with rage. "What have you done?"

"What needed to be. You would not listen to me. I had to take matters into my own hands."

"You had no right to interfere with me. No one has ever been able to stop my coming."

"Well, this time you were."

Mahes came to stand beside Nefertem. His mother turned her hard-eyed gaze on him. "You. Why did you not stop him? I did not send you to the mortal world to play at being one of them and go against me."

"It was not my decision to stay in the mortal world. Nefertem made that choice."

"You then had to take his side?"

"Yes. Nefertem's decision to save the mortals was the right thing to do. There is much good here."

"The pair of you have grown weak."

Sekhmet's sharp eyes had already found the three mortals cowering across the room. It did not surprise Nefertem that she had known about the fourth he'd tried to protect from her.

"Who is it you seek to shield from my sight, Nefertem?"

"You will leave her alone."

Sekhmet curled her lip. "I only wish to see the one who managed to thwart me." Nefertem made no move to step away. She pushed him aside with her mind.

*

Suddenly being out in the open, Kendra could only stare at Sekhmet. She swallowed hard. Nefertem's mother was like no other being she'd ever seen before. She was indeed half-lioness and human-woman. The sharp cat's eyes seemed to bore right into her.

Sekhmet moved so she stood in front of Kendra. She walked around her until she once more stood before her. Sekhmet pointed to the pendant that hung around Kendra's neck and said something she didn't understand.

Kendra turned to beseechingly look at Nefertem. He tried to move back to her side, but his mother seemed to have frozen him to the spot where he now stood. He groaned in frustration. "It will be okay, Kendra." He then said something to his mother in what Kendra assumed was in Egyptian.

Sekhmet curled her lip in disgust. "Do you understand me now, mortal?"

Kendra nodded. "Yes."

"Good. Before I leave this place, I have one thing to say to you, mortal. You might have won this simple victory, but in the end, it is I who has truly won. Nefertem will return to me. He always will be mine, and do my bidding. He might have mated with you, but you will never again lie in his arms once he leaves you."

Nefertem pulled the bow and quiver from his shoulder and threw them a short distance away. They clattered loudly on the stone floor. "No more, Mother. I will no longer do your dirty work. Release me so I can at least spend the remaining time I have left with my mate."

Sekhmet calmly said, "So be it."

With a wave of her hand, she released Nefertem from the hold she'd had on him. He rushed to Kendra and gathered her into his arms.

Sekhmet walked to where Nefertem had thrown his bow. She picked it up along with one of the arrows from the quiver, nocked it, and pulled back on the string. She took aim and released it.

CHAPTER THIRTY-TWO

The arrow caught Kendra on the left side of her back, lodging just under her heart. At first, she didn't know what caused her to be thrown hard against Nefertem or the sudden sharp, blinding pain that followed. It was his look of horror and Tory's cry of anguish that made her realize something was very wrong. As her legs gave out on her, he clutched her to him and slowly lowered her so they kneeled on the floor. He supported her with his body.

Gasping for breath, Kendra asked, "It's bad, isn't it?"

He shut his eyes for a brief moment before he answered her question. "Yes. It is."

"You should not have disobeyed me, Nefertem. You only brought this on yourself." Sekhmet snarled.

Nefertem turned a look of pure hatred on his mother. "Do you not think you have made me suffer enough? Just having to leave Kendra forever was sufficient punishment. You have gone too far this time. Do you think Re will not know what you have done? You have harmed the one who possesses the pendant."

The mention of Re being greatly displeased with her

actions seemed to give Sekhmet some pause, but she quickly recovered. "I will make Re see that I am justified in my actions."

Nefertem shook his head. "No, Mother, you are wrong. You have broken his decree that the bearer of the pendant must not be harmed in any way. Maybe he will not be quite so hard on you if you fix this. In this form, I do not have the power to heal Kendra, but you do. Do it now before it is too late."

"No, I will not. She will die, and you will finally be free of her." Not saying anything more, Sekhmet threw down the bow she still held and then vanished from the chamber.

Growling with rage, Nefertem looked at Kendra. Her eyes grew heavy, and she blinked to keep them open. He gave her a gentle shake.

"You must not sleep, Kendra. Stay with me. I am not going to let you go without a fight. Do you hear me?"

After Sekhmet's disappearance, the three others rushed to Kendra's side. Markus wore a distraught expression as he looked at the arrow protruding out of her back. He turned a steely gaze on Nefertem and Mahes.

"You two are gods! Do something to help her!"

Mahes sadly shook his head. "We cannot. Nefertem was right when he said we cannot heal her in our mortal forms."

Kendra force her eyes to stay open at the sound of her brother's voice. "It's okay, Markus. It's better this way." She was now so weak her voice was barely above a whisper.

"No, it's not!" Markus bellowed. "Somebody do something."

Nefertem gently passed Kendra to Markus and stood. "That is exactly what I intend to do. I have not given up yet." He stood to his full height, and yelled, "Ptah! Come to me now." A split second later, his father stood before him.

"I have come, my son. What has caused you to call me so urgently?"

"Help her. She does not have much time left."

Nefertem took Ptah by the arm and pulled him to where Markus held Kendra. Ptah's face clouded with anger when he saw the arrow in her back. "Who did this to your mate?"

"Mother." That one simple word spoke volumes.

Ptah nodded in understanding. "I see. Let me take a look."

Kendra gathered her rapidly flagging strength to look at Ptah as he kneeled beside her. He smiled. She quickly realized it was their father that Nefertem and Mahes took after in looks. Ptah didn't look any older than his two sons. If she hadn't known Ptah was their father, she would have thought he was their brother instead.

After giving the arrow a cursory inspection, Ptah nodded. "I want you to hold her, Nefertem. The arrow has to come out first. Sorry to say I will not be able to save her from the pain of removing it." After Markus gingerly handed Kendra to Nefertem, who was now kneeling beside him, Ptah squeezed his shoulder. "Your sister will be all right."

Once Nefertem had Kendra firmly held in his arms with her head cushioned on his chest, he gave a curt nod to his father. Taking hold of the arrow, Ptah pulled it free of Kendra's body. Her cry of pain filled the chamber.

Acting quickly, Ptah placed his hand over the now gushing wound. Kendra fought the blackness that rose to claim her after the arrow was pulled out. The pain of it had been unbearable. She would have lost the battle if it hadn't been for Ptah. He helped her push back the darkness even as he worked to repair the damage done to her body by the arrowhead. In a semiconscious state, she heard him speak to her inside her mind.

You and the new life you carry inside you are safe.

Afterward, she didn't know if what Ptah had said only to her was real or her mind playing tricks.

Once his father moved away, Nefertem looked at her. "Kendra?"

She smiled. "I think I'm okay now."

Claiming her lips in a searing kiss, Nefertem seemed to pour all the love he felt for her into it. He broke the kiss and stood while he still held Kendra in his arms. He looked desperately at his father.

Ptah sadly shook his head. "I cannot change your fate, my son."

Just as suddenly as Ptah had appeared in the chamber, he disappeared.

Mahes was the next to speak. "You have all come to mean a lot to me. I shall miss our times together." He stepped to Kendra, then gave her a hug and a kiss. "I will miss you the most of all. If you still wish it, I will come to visit, but not right away I think."

Kendra nodded. Mahes was going to give her time to grieve over losing Nefertem before she saw him again. She just hoped he didn't stay away too long. "I'd like you to."

Mahes turned to Scott and Markus and shook each of their hands. To Tory he gave a kiss. Then he too disappeared, leaving Nefertem behind.

Clutching Nefertem's hands tightly in her own, a sense of panic overtook Kendra. "I can't let you go."

Nefertem held her hands just as tightly. "I wish I could stay, but I cannot. I will love you forever. Try to be happy, Kendra." He disappeared, leaving Kendra to hold nothing but air.

They were brought to the surface before Kendra had time to even wonder how they were going to leave the chamber. One minute they were in it, and the next they stood outside in front of the Sphinx.

The sun was just breaking over the horizon. He was

gone. She'd never see him again. At that moment, it hit her, and hard. Tears streamed down her face. She could no longer keep them at bay. All her hurt and pain spilled out of her. She was racked with heart-wrenching sobs, and Markus gathered her close and let her wet the front of his shirt.

As the sun rose higher, Kendra by slow degrees pulled herself back under control. Once she managed to stem the flow of tears, she felt utterly spent. Leaning heavily on Markus, she allowed him to lead her from the Sphinx and the Great Pyramids. Scott and Troy fell in beside them.

The taxi ride to the hotel was a quiet one. They were all lost in their own thoughts. Kendra replayed the scenes from the night over again in her mind. It was still early morning hours when they reached the hotel so they were able to slip up to their rooms without attracting undo notice. This was something they'd hoped to accomplish. The back of her dress would have compelled them to answer some questions they could in no way answer with any kind of truth.

Unable to stand being in the room she'd shared with Nefertem, she said nothing when Markus took her to his. After telling Scott and Tory they would meet with them once they all got some sleep, he let Kendra into the room. She ended up in the middle of it, staring at nothing.

Markus grabbed one of his largest T-shirts and then came to her side. "Here, Kendra, take this and change in the bathroom. You need to sleep."

Kendra looked blankly at the shirt Markus had put in her hand. It took her a few seconds to come out of her stupor. She closed her fingers around it nodded before she silently went into the bathroom.

She came out wearing his shirt, which reached her knees. She climbed into the bed next to Markus'. Once she was settled, he flicked off the light.

CHAPTER THIRTY-THREE

They ended up staying in Egypt for another week before booking flights to Memphis. The delay was due partly to Markus having to finish his work there, and partly because Kendra wasn't ready to go home. After waking from a fitful sleep after that eventful night, she'd come to a decision—she wasn't ready to let Egypt go.

Markus went to the local markets and antiquity stores, and Kendra went along with him. She immersed herself in the country's culture and ancient past. Somehow, it lessened her pain over losing Nefertem. She soaked it up like a sponge.

At first, Markus was worried Kendra was becoming obsessed, but after a few days, he realized she had a genuine interest. She was using it as a therapeutic method to get over Nefertem. Markus came up with something that would help the both of them in the long run.

On their last night of staying in Egypt, after Tory and Scott had returned to their room, Markus broached the subject of his idea to Kendra. They were sitting on his bed, watching television when he turned to her.

"Kendra, I've been thinking about something for the last couple of days. Something that'll be good for the both of us."

Switching off the television, Kendra turned to face Markus, giving him her full attention. "All right, you've piqued my interest. What is it?"

Markus smiled. "Well, since you've become so interested in all things Egyptian and you've turned out to be a fast learner, I wonder if you'd like to work with me. Be my partner. It'd be our own family business. I need the help, and you don't have a job to go back to, so it works out perfectly."

"Are you serious? I'd love to work with you. This last week has shown me why you love doing what you do. Besides, I don't think I could handle getting another job I hate. The last one was enough for me."

"Then it's settled." Markus stuck out his hand. "Shall we shake on it, partner?"

Kendra took hold of her brother's hand and pumped it up and down. She could go home now with a purpose to her life. Part of the reason she hadn't wanted to leave Egypt was she couldn't have faced being in the house all day with no job to distract her rambling thoughts. It would hold too many memories of Nefertem as it was.

* * * *

The next morning, sitting in the airport, waiting to board the flight to London, Kendra told Tory and Scott about her decision to work with Markus.

Tory was thrilled by the news. "Way to go, Markus. I knew you'd think of something to get Kendra to turn back into her old self."

Markus smiled and put his arm around Kendra's shoulders. "Hey, I didn't ask her out of pity, you know. She has a genuine interest. Seems as if it runs in the family, after all."

Kendra shook her head at the praise Markus heaped on her. "Now let's not go overboard here." She snagged Scott's attention. "I have something to ask you."

"Okay."

"How would you feel about teaching me how to read hieroglyphs and speak ancient Egyptian?"

Tory groaned and rolled her eyes before Scott could answer. "Oh, god, Kendra. I think you've just made his day. You've given him someone new he can indoctrinate in everything ancient Egyptian."

Scott chuckled at Tory's theatrics. "Kendra, I would be more than happy to teach you all I can. I have to agree with Tory, though, you've just made my day."

Kendra's lessons began. Not wanting to waste any more time, she had Scott begin her lessons during the long hours of travel it took to reach Memphis. It made the trip less horrendous for her, and by the time they landed in Tennessee, she had a pretty good understanding of the hieroglyphs and ancient Egyptian. She only wished she could have used her newly learned talent on Nefertem.

* * * *

After returning home, Kendra settled into a new routine for her daily life. She slipped into her three-times-a-week workout at the gym, which had been something she'd neglected while Nefertem had been with her. With the working out, taking lessons from Scott a couple of times a week, and learning the business ropes from Markus, she really didn't have time to think what might have been. Which was exactly what she'd hoped to accomplish.

Though she didn't want to dwell on what kind of life she could have had with Nefertem, that didn't mean she wanted to totally forget him either. She clung dearly to the memories she'd created with him. Even though the ceremony was in no way orthodox, Kendra still considered herself married. The simple slim, gold wedding band he had slipped onto her finger she wore every day. Along with it, she wore the pendant. She could now read the hieroglyphs, which she, of course, did silently to herself.

Now with Markus home, Kendra went back to cooking proper meals again. That evening she decided to make one of Markus' favorite — roast chicken with roasted vegetables. She chopped a carrot, and her knife slipped, accidentally cutting her finger. Much to her surprise, she felt no pain, but when the cut seemed to heal before her very eyes, she grew alarmed. After going to the kitchen sink, she stuck her finger under the running water to wash away the small amount of blood that remained. There wasn't a mark on her skin to show where the wound had been.

Kendra went back to the cutting board where she'd been working and grabbed the knife. Not giving herself a chance to think about what she was going to do, she used the tip to slice a shallow cut across the palm of her left hand. As before, she felt no sensation of pain, and the wound healed itself in a matter of seconds.

To make sure it was actually happening, Kendra cut her palm over and over again. Each time the result was exactly the same. What was happening to her?

She managed to finish the dinner preparations and then dished up the food after Markus had come home, but what had happened earlier kept her feeling distracted.

Markus sat at the table and ate with relish. After he downed a couple of mouthfuls, he asked, "What did I do to deserve all this?"

"I just decided to treat you is all," Kendra answered softly.

"I get the feeling you aren't really with me. What's troubling you?"

Kendra looked up and gave Markus a sheepish grin. "I

can never hide anything from you."

"Of course not. What kind of brother would I be if I couldn't pick up on your feelings? Tell me."

Kendra pushed back her chair and went and retrieved a clean steak knife from the cutlery drawer before returning to the table. "I think the best way is to show you instead."

She drew the sharp edge of the knife across her palm. "What the hell are you doing, Kendra?"

Kendra held her palm out for Markus to see it better. "Relax. Just look."

A look of shock came over his face as the wound Kendra had inflicted upon herself healed. It only took a matter of seconds for her flesh to knit together, leaving no sign of an injury behind.

"How did you do that?"

Kendra shook her head and chuckled. "I haven't the faintest idea."

Markus grabbed her hand and pulled it closer to take a better look at it. "That's amazing. I wonder if it's a side effect from Ptah healing you."

"I never thought of that. You could be right. It isn't as if he stuck around for very long after he healed me to tell me if there would be anything I should know about."

"Well, that's one side effect I wouldn't mind having. Now that you've gotten that off your chest, I'm going to eat this delicious dinner you made before it gets cold."

Kendra smiled as he once more returned to eating. She picked up her fork and did likewise. Markus had managed to set her mind at rest. She'd felt as if she were going a little nuts. As he'd said, it wasn't that bad of a side effect.

* * * *

It was after a month had gone by since she'd come home from Egypt that Kendra had the dream. In it, she replayed the moments inside the hidden chamber, which in itself wasn't so strange since she'd done so more than once after returning. What marked this one as different was at the point where Nefertem left her, Ptah returned.

Once she took the hand he held out to her, she found herself alone with him. Darkness surrounded them on all sides. She could only see him in front of her.

He smiled. "I am happy to see you again, Kendra."

"Is this real or just a part of my dream?"

Ptah smiled again. "Nefertem told me you would be full of questions."

Kendra looked at Ptah expectantly. "He did? Is Nefertem here with you now?"

Ptah's smile disappeared and he shook his head. "No, he is not. It is not allowed."

"Then why have you come?"

"To see you, of course. To make sure you are moving on with your life."

"I'm finding some kind of direction, if that's what you call moving on."

"What of other men? Is there a new one you care about?"

Narrowing her eyes, Kendra gave Ptah a hard look. "How dare you ask me that? There's only one man in my life now, and he is my brother. There's no room in my heart for another. Nefertem has it all and always will." She held up her left hand and showed Ptah the wedding ring she wore. "I already have a husband, and no one will ever take his place."

"That is all I needed to hear." Ptah began to fade from sight as a thick mist seemed to rise and cover him. Before he totally disappeared, he said, "Remember, Kendra, you are not alone. Remember what I said to you in the chamber."

Kendra woke up with a start. Had the dream been real or was it only a figment of her imagination? What had Ptah said to her in that chamber back in Egypt? She swung her legs over the side of her bed and racked her brain, trying to recall all he'd told her. Then it came to her.

With a shaking hand, Kendra opened the drawer of her bedside table and pulled out the small daily calendar she kept there. She frantically flipped the pages. She went back one month and then a second. It was there she found what she looked for. She didn't know whether she should laugh or cry.

Kendra returned the calendar to the drawer and decided she'd better have her suspicions proven correct before she got her hopes up. If they were right, it would seem Nefertem had indeed left a part of himself behind for her to cherish—he might have given her his child.

CHAPTER THIRTY-FOUR

After having a quick shower, Kendra raced down the stairs and then out the front door. Markus, who was in the kitchen at the time, didn't even have time to ask what the hurry was all about before the door slammed shut behind her. He shook his head. Kendra was developing quirky behaviors she hadn't had in the past.

A mere twenty-minutes later, Kendra returned home and ran up the stairs. Deciding to ignore what she was doing, Markus continued to sip his morning coffee and read the newspaper. A few minutes later, he nearly jumped out of his skin when she shrieked upstairs. He left the kitchen at a run and quickly went to her bedroom.

Thinking an attacker had somehow gotten into the house, Markus was surprised to find Kendra jumping about the room, laughing like a lunatic while tears streamed down her face. He came to the conclusion his sister had finally lost it.

"Okay, Kendra, first you nearly give me a heart attack screaming like that, and now I find you acting like a total nut case. Can you explain what it is you're doing? I would like your explanation before the men come with a straight jacket and take you away to a padded cell."

Kendra went to Markus and gave him a loud, smacking kiss on the lips before she raced to her bathroom. She returned with a plastic stick. She held it up for him to see while she grinned from ear to ear.

Markus had seen enough commercials on television for that particular item to know what it was. He sucked in his breath and quickly looked back at her. "Is this what I think it is?"

Nodding, Kendra said while giggles bubbled out of her, "It sure is. I'm going to have Nefertem's baby."

"About time one of us extended this family," Markus said as he gathered Kendra into a big hug.

"I'll have something of Nefertem to hold, and to love now." Tears of happiness welled up in Kendra's eyes.

Markus wiped her tears away and grinned. "I'll be an uncle." He grew serious. "Don't worry about anything. I'll help you every step of the way. You don't have to feel as if you're a single parent. I'm not going anywhere."

"I'll hold you to that. When the time comes, I'll want you in the delivery room with me."

Markus swallowed. "That, we'll see about. I can't make you any promises, though."

* * * *

Unable to keep her good news to herself, Kendra called Tory that very same day. Knowing her friend was rarely at her place any more, she dialed Scott's phone number. Tory picked up after the second ring.

"Don't you think it's a bit early to be calling, Kendra? It's a Saturday, you know."

"It's hardly early. My clock says it is eleven in the morning." At her friend's silence, Kendra chuckled. "Had a long night, did you?"

It was Tory's turn to chuckle. "Well, let's just say we

were celebrating. Scott has the stamina of an ox."

"Ah, that's way too much information." Kendra laughed. "How am I ever to look Scott in the face now that you've let me in the know on that bit of information? What exactly did you celebrate?"

"I think I've even shocked myself with this one. I've gone and done it. Scott asked me to marry him last night, and I accepted." Tory was quick to add, "Only on the condition we stay engaged for at least a year."

"Oh, Tory! I'm so happy for you. Scott is the perfect man for you." Kendra meant every word she'd said. She was happy for her best friend. She might have felt a bit jealous in the past, but now that she knew she had a part of Nefertem with her, she felt nothing but joy for Tory.

"You don't think I'm being rash in my decision, do you?"

"Of course not. It seems today is ending up being full of nice surprises."

"I feel a bit better about the whole thing now that you've said I haven't made the biggest mistake of my life. What was the other surprise you spoke of? Don't leave me hanging here."

"It's just one more surprise. I got some good news myself this morning. It would seem I'm pregnant." Kendra had to quickly pull the phone away from her ear as Tory screamed.

"This day is just getting better and better!" Tory bellowed.

Kendra winced as Tory continued to scream. "If you keep bellowing like that, I'll be deaf in one ear before we've even finished this conversation."

The sound of Tory taking a deep breath could easily be heard before she spoke once more. "Okay, I promise I have myself back under control now. All I have to say is that your news definitely tops mine. A baby is what you need. I was getting worried about you."

"Well, you don't have to fret over me any longer."

"I might, just a little," Tory said with a laugh. "To let you know, when the time comes, I'll be at the hospital by your side. You can't count on that wuss Markus to go in with you. When Ptah pulled that arrow from your back, Markus didn't know whether to puke his guts out or faint. He'd be no use to you laid out on the delivery room floor."

"Markus will be greatly relieved to hear you volunteered to take his place. He wasn't too enthusiastic about it when I asked him to come to the hospital with me."

"When it comes to seeing you in pain, the man is a wimp."

Kendra chuckled. "I'll make sure not to tell Markus you called him a wimp. I'm going to let you go now, but we'll talk later. We have a wedding to plan. Tell Scott I said congrats."

"I will. You go and put your feet up. We can't have you wearing yourself out."

"Yes, Mom."

Kendra shook her head as she hung up. Now that she was expecting, she could count on Tory watching her like a hawk. She'd have to think of something to distract her friend. Helping Tory plan her wedding should hopefully do the trick.

* * * *

The knowledge that she was carrying Nefertem's child kept Kendra on a permanent high. Going to see the doctor and having him confirm she was indeed pregnant only increased the feeling.

A week after finding out about the baby, Kendra had an evening on her own. Markus had arranged to meet a couple of his friends for a guys' night. So she didn't expect him home until the early hours of the morning, if at all that night. She wouldn't be surprised if he decided to crash at one of his friend's places.

To make the most of her evening by herself, Kendra planned to watch a movie and made herself one of her favorite meals. In lieu of wine, she opted for a bottle of sparkling white grape juice.

She finished eating her meal and settled in the living room to watch the movie. She couldn't help but be reminded of another evening she'd spent almost the same way as this one.

Kendra quickly became involved in the movie. It was one of those sci-fi action flicks she loved to watch. She didn't hear a knock on the front door right away. A second came much louder than the first, and it was then Kendra finally noticed there was someone at her door. She put what she watched on pause and went to answer it. She wondered who could be coming for a visit at that hour of the day.

A knock came again before she could reach the door. Kendra took hold of the doorknob and pulled it open. Much to her surprise, she found her old boss, Stan Wilson, standing on her front porch.

"Stan, what a surprise. I thought you were in…"

The older man finished her sentence for her. "In jail? I have a very good lawyer and he managed to get me out on bail. My trial isn't for a few months."

"I see. Is there something I can do for you?"

"As a matter of fact, there is. May I come in? I promise not to take up too much of your time."

Kendra couldn't think of a good enough reason to say no so she stepped back and allowed Stan to walk through the open door.

Once inside, Stan gave the hallway a cursory look. Kendra made no move to invite him farther into the house. He cleared his throat, then said, "How have you been, Kendra? I know your termination was a bit of a shock.

Have you been able to find another job?"

"Actually, I have found something else. I now work with my brother."

"Ah. Markus is back from Egypt?"

Kendra became a little uneasy, especially when Stan peered around her as if he checked to see where Markus was. She decided to play it safe.

"Yes, he's back at home. He just stepped out for a while. I expect him any minute."

"I'm sorry I missed him." Stan brushed past her before Kendra could protest. "You have a lovely home."

Kendra followed Stan into the living room. "Thanks. You said you needed me to do something for you?"

Stan turned to face her. "Yes. You can tell me what you told the police."

"I didn't tell them anything." She didn't like the turn the conversation was taking.

"Really now? I find that hard to believe. The police had a lot of information about me. Things you could have quite easily gotten your hands on. Did they pay you well for the information you provided? Is that why you're now working with your brother?"

Stan's tone changed from being polite to accusatory. Kendra had enough. "I have no idea what you're talking about. Believe me, it came as a very big surprise to me when you were arrested. Now I think it's time you left."

"I'm not going anywhere until you answer me."

"There's nothing else I can tell you. I didn't have anything to do with the police finding out about your illegal activities." Kendra backed from Stan, but he quickly grabbed her by the arm before she could get too far out of reach.

Stan tightened his grip as he dragged her back into the living room. Roughly, he shoved her onto the couch. Once released, she rubbed her abused arm. For someone of his stature, he was far stronger than he looked.

He stood so she couldn't get off the couch without him easily stopping her. The expression in his eyes made Kendra's mouth go dry in fear. His was a look a man wore who had nothing to lose and couldn't accept the hand fate had dealt him.

"What do you think you're accomplishing here, Stan? Hurting me won't change what happened to you."

"Maybe not, but I'll get a measure of satisfaction from it. You've destroyed me financially and socially by playing the stool pigeon for the police. I'll take great pleasure in making you pay for what you did to me."

It wasn't hard for Kendra to realize her former boss had lost his sanity. Being arrested must have been the catalyst that pushed him over the edge of reason. Knowing she dealt with a mad man did nothing to dispel her mounting fear. Sending out a silent call for help, she hoped someone out there would hear. Without some assistance, she could all too easily see this ending badly. For herself.

CHAPTER THIRTY-FIVE

After moving the coffee table out of his way, Stan paced back and forth in front of the couch. Kendra followed his movements with her gaze, unsure of what he intended to do next. If only Markus would come home. He could easily take care of Stan and throw him out of the house.

Stan stopped his frenetic pacing and turned to face her. "I'm really disappointed in you, Kendra. I thought very highly of you. I never expected you to turn on me as you did."

"I didn't turn on you. I wouldn't have even known where to find the evidence against you."

He waved away her excuses with a flick of his hand. "You can stop lying. I know you had your hand in this. All I want to hear from you is why you did it. If it was for the money, I would have willingly paid you more than the police did. If you had proved your loyalty to me, I might have brought you into that side of my business."

"You aren't listening to me." Kendra spoke in a soft, even tone, hoping Stan would actually hear what she told him. "I'm not lying to you."

Stan took her roughly by the chin and stared at Kendra, giving her a hard look. "I can see it in your eyes that you are. So, what's the point in continuing with these untruths?"

The lights in the room flickered once and then a second time. That was all she needed, to have the power go out. She didn't relish having to deal with a crazy man in the dark. "I think you're only seeing what you want to see. Not what's really there."

The backhanded blow Stan gave her caught Kendra on her cheek. Much to her surprise, she only felt a small twinge of pain. It was nothing near to what she should have felt, considering he'd hit her with enough force her head had snapped to the side.

Before she could think more about that particular anomaly, the lightbulb in the lamp closest to the couch suddenly exploded. Glass shards fell to the floor, littering the carpet with sharp points. The room was plunged into semi-darkness. The remaining lamp still lit threw only the smallest amount of brightness and didn't do much to banish the shadows.

The lightbulb's shattering drew Stan's attention from Kendra. Using it to her advantage, she carefully inched along the couch to the opposite end. Her luck didn't last very long, though. He noticed her movements and blocked her escape.

"Oh no, you don't. I'm not through with you yet. Let's try this again. I'll have an answer from you, Kendra, and by any means necessary to hear the correct one."

Deciding that playing the part of a submissive victim was getting her nowhere, Kendra attempted to clamber over the arm of the couch. It would have worked too if only Stan had possessed slower reflexes. He managed to snag a handful of her hair and roughly yanked her back onto the cushions.

As he raised his hand to strike her once again, a loud

cat growl filled the room. Stan slowly lowered his arm and searched for the source of the sound.

Kendra's breath caught at the growl. She recognized it, and her heart beat faster. Frantically, she looked for the one being she knew who could make such a sound. She found him standing in the shadows. She fought the urge to fly off the couch and into his arms. There was still the small matter of ridding herself of Stan first.

Moving with the grace and stealth of a sleek hunting cat, Nefertem closed the distance between himself and the man who meant Kendra harm. Dressed as he had been when summoned, along with the helmet depicting the head of a black leopard completely hiding his face from view, he was an impressive sight. He growled with menace, pulled his sword free from its scabbard, and advanced on his intended victim.

Stan backed away. He seemed to forgot all about Kendra. He held his hands out in submission, trying to increase the distance between himself and Nefertem. The tip of the sword held in his direction never strayed from the mere inches that were between it and his chest.

Nefertem silently forced Stan away from her and out of the living room. All the while, a litany of, *Please let him really be here*, became a desperate plea that kept repeating itself inside her mind. Not moving from her spot on the couch, she waited for the sound of the front door shutting that would herald Stan's departure. It eventually came, and she sailed off the couch and ran into the hallway.

To her dismay, the entranceway was empty. After yanking open the front door, she looked outside to see if Nefertem had chased Stan all the way out of the house, but he wasn't on the porch either. All Kendra saw was Stan's car speeding off as if the hounds of hell nipped at his heels.

Kendra turned around, slammed the door, and hurried to the living room. It too was empty. "Nefertem! Where are you?" she called. There was no reply.

Her heart sank. Nefertem was gone again. She didn't know if it was a blessing to have him back only to save her from Stan, or a supreme torture to see him and not be able to touch or speak to him.

With spirits low, Kendra set about cleaning up the glass mess from the shattered lightbulb. Once finished, she replaced it with a new one, and the gloom of the room was quickly banished. After the events of the evening, she no longer felt like sitting through the rest of the movie she'd been watching before Stan's arrival. Kendra shut down the DVD player, switched off the television, and headed upstairs.

On the way up to her room, she decided not to report what took place between her and Stan to the police. She was afraid too many questions she didn't want to answer would be asked. After reaching her bedroom, Kendra went into her bathroom and took a look at her face. It was what she was afraid of. There wasn't a mark to show where Stan had hit her. If she called the police, they would want to see the bruising she most assuredly should have had. This ability she now possessed to somehow quickly heal herself was really freaking her out. It wasn't at all natural.

Sighing, Kendra switched off the light inside the bathroom and then returned to her bedroom. What she found sitting on the middle of her bed brought her up short. Her heart skipped a beat at the sight of them.

Hoping beyond hope they were indeed real, Kendra quickly closed and then opened her eyes. That changed nothing. They still sat on her bed. She went to the bed and tenderly touched the leopard's head helmet and blue lotus flower placed in front of it.

She picked up the lotus and inhaled its heady scent. It reminded her of Nefertem. It was the smell of that flower that always seemed to be with him.

Having a feeling about who could have put those two items in her room without her knowledge, Kendra took another whiff of the lotus, and said to the room at large, "If you did this as a joke, Mahes, I'm going to kick your butt the next time you show yourself here. God or no god."

"It was not Mahes who left those for you." The voice that came behind her was deep and rich.

Kendra tightly clutched the lotus and slowly turned in the direction from where the voice had come. Tears welled in her eyes and spilled over the top, uncontrolled. It was Nefertem who stood behind her.

"How can this be?" Kendra asked. "You said you'd never be able to come back to me."

Nefertem took the two steps needed to reach her and swept her up into his arms. He held her so her feet no longer touched the floor, and claimed her lips in a searing kiss. He released them, but kept his arms firmly around her.

"All that has now changed," Nefertem softly answered.

"I don't understand."

Nefertem went to the bed. He lowered himself onto the mattress and arranged Kendra so she sat sideways across his lap. She kept her arms wrapped around his neck.

"The edict placed on my ability to move in the mortal realm has been removed."

"For how long?" Kendra looked into Nefertem's golden eyes, still unable to believe he was truly with her.

Nefertem gave her a wide smile. "It is forever. Once Re heard about what my mother had done to you, he acted against her. She broke one of his dictates when she struck you down. As her punishment, he released me from the spell of the pendant. I am no longer bound to it."

With shaking hands, Kendra lifted the pendant from where it hung from around her neck. She flipped it over so she could read the hieroglyphs engraved on the other side. She gasped in surprise. The original spell was no longer there. In its place was something more meaningful.

"What does the hieroglyphs say now, my love?"

Nefertem urged.

Kendra swallowed audibly. "It says, a love born out of strife. Where there was only one, there are now two. Their love, the lotus shall ever keep." Kendra swallowed once more. "It's beautiful."

Nefertem brushed a lock of hair behind Kendra's ear. "As you are. I love you, Kendra, and always will. I know our mating was not what you expected when you decided to take a husband, so I want to make it right for you. Will you marry me?"

Kendra shook her head. "No." When Nefertem opened his mouth to protest, she placed a finger across his firm lips. "No, I won't. Our mating will always mean more to me than a marriage ceremony ever could. You already are my husband, Nefertem." Lifting her left hand, she showed him the gold band that circled her finger. As he held up his, Kendra saw the matching one on his. "You know the inscription on the pendant is wrong, Nefertem."

"In what way?"

"Well, it's the part about there now being two. That's incorrect." She placed Nefertem's hand on the small swell of her tummy. Kendra smiled. "Soon there will be three of us."

Nefertem looked down to where Kendra pressed his hand and then back up at her face. "A child? We are going to have a baby?"

At Kendra's nod, Nefertem claimed her lips once more. As he kissed her, he slowly laid back on the bed and moved her so she was sprawled on top of him.

Wanting nothing more than to complete what she and Nefertem started, with great reluctance, Kendra pulled away. A hundred questions whirled inside her mind. Most could wait for another day, but some she needed answers to now.

"I want to know a few things before you make me incapable of coherent thought, Nefertem."

Shifting on the bed so Kendra lay on her side, facing him, Nefertem acquiesced. "I knew you would have questions. It is part of your nature. Ask away."

"Okay then. Firstly, where are you going to live? Will you stay here with me and only spend a little time in the immortal realm? I know me being mortal I won't be able to follow you there."

"I will stay here with you. There might be times I must go to the immortal realm, but I will never leave you for long."

"That does put my mind to rest about that particular subject. Now, what about your mother?"

Nefertem chuckled. "My mother will no longer be a problem, my love. When Re broke the spell on the pendant, she returned to her normal self. Like me, she only became what she was when the spell was invoked. She is normally a loving and caring person."

Kendra found that hard to believe, but if what Nefertem said was true, she would have to rethink how she felt about Sekhmet.

"I guess I'll have to take your word on that."

"I can see you find it hard to believe, but you will see for yourself the next time you are around my mother."

"Whoa there, one step at a time. I'm not quite that ready to forgive and forget what your mother did to me. She did try to kill me, after all, and would have succeeded too if it hadn't been for you father."

After kissing Kendra's forehead, Nefertem said, "I will not push you into doing something you are not ready for."

"Speaking of your father, when does the side effect from his healing me wear off? It's really doing a number on my head."

Nefertem's brows furrowed. "What do you mean by a side effect? I have never heard of such happening after a person has been healed."

"I mean this ability I seem to have to heal myself in a

matter of seconds. Not to mention the fact I don't feel any pain worth speaking of. Even when Stan hit me, it didn't hurt as it should."

Nefertem quickly sat up and looked closely at Kendra. She too sat up as he stared intently at her.

"What is it, Nefertem?"

A second later, Ptah appeared in the room. "I think it is best we have this conversation face-to-face. I did not tell you, because I wanted you to find out on your own."

"It was when you healed her that you did it. Is it not?"

"Yes. You had chosen Kendra as your mate, so it seemed to be the most logical thing to do at the time. I knew Re would make things right for you both in the end."

Not understanding what Ptah and Nefertem said about what Ptah had done to her, and it was obvious he'd done something, Kendra broke into their conversation. "Hello, I'm still in the room. Now that I have your attention, can someone please tell me what all this is about?"

Nefertem closed his hands around Kendra's. He seemed a bit lost for words. "Your ability, to heal yourself, is no side effect. My father made you an immortal that day."

Kendra's jaw dropped. She quickly closed her mouth and turned to look at Ptah. "I'm immortal now? As in I'll never die?"

Ptah smiled. "Yes." He stepped closer to her and kissed her cheek. "Welcome to the family, my daughter. Before you can ask, the child you carry is also immortal. I will leave you both alone now, but your mother and I expect to see you very soon." He disappeared.

Immortal. She was now immortal. It dawned on Kendra exactly what that meant for her and Nefertem. They would be together forever. Letting out a shriek of joy, she launched herself into his arms and kissed him. Nothing would ever come between their love again.

* * * *

Eight Months Later

Standing at the entrance to her living room, Kendra watched her husband and their one-month-old daughter. It was a sight she never got tired of seeing.

Nefertem was slouched on the couch with little Cleo fast asleep on his broad chest while he watched television. One of his large hands gently rubbed the baby's back. Cleo had her little legs drawn up under her, quite happy to be where she was.

It'd been Nefertem's idea to name their daughter after the famous Egyptian queen, Cleopatra. Kendra had consented only after it was agreed the baby's name would be shortened to Cleo.

Markus was in the room with his brother-in-law and niece. Ever since Nefertem's return to her life, he and Markus had hit it off. Markus had even managed to get Nefertem hooked on watching sports. Something they tended to do a little bit too much for Kendra's liking.

After stepping farther into the room, Kendra sat on the couch beside her husband. "Would you like me to take Cleo from you?"

Nefertem kissed the top of the baby's soft downy head. "No, she is perfectly fine where she is."

Kendra slouched to the same level as her husband and rested her head on Nefertem's shoulder. "Where's Mahes? I thought he'd be here by now."

Mahes came to visit them at least a couple of times a week, and on sports night, as Kendra liked to call nights like this, he never failed to show up. It wasn't so much that Mahes enjoyed watching the game as he enjoyed the beer drinking that went with it.

Markus shrugged. "I have no idea. If he doesn't show

up, that just means there will be more beer for me."

Kendra rolled her eyes. "Like you don't get enough of the stuff as is. Have you heard from him, Nefertem?"

Nefertem shook his head. "No, but I would not worry overly much. Knowing him, he might very well have found something that sparked his interest more than the idea of coming here."

At that moment, Cleo stirred. After stretching largely, she rooted around on her father's chest, looking for something he couldn't provide.

Kendra chuckled. "Come here, my little girl. Daddy will have to give you up now before you start getting upset." She picked up the baby and stood. Kendra patted her daughter's behind and grimaced in response. "I think a diaper change is in order. Someone has very soggy drawers indeed."

Getting to his feet, Nefertem followed Kendra out of the room, leaving Markus to continue watching the game. "I'll change Cleo and then you can nurse her."

Kendra walked into what had once been the spare bedroom, but now had been turned into a baby's room and placed her daughter on the change table. As Nefertem came to put a dry diaper on Cleo, Kendra sat on the rocking chair to wait until he finished.

Nefertem made short work of the diaper change, and then with reluctance, passed Cleo over. Kendra adjusted her top and settled the baby to her breast.

Once Kendra shifted Cleo to her shoulder to burp, Nefertem said, "I hear Stan Wilson's trial finally took place the other day."

Kendra nodded. "Yes. He won't be a free man for a few years. At least he never came back here again. I think you gave him a good scare."

"He deserved more than that for what he did to you," Nefertem said harshly.

"That's water under the bridge. He's out of our lives,

and that's all that really matters."

Nefertem let the subject of Stan Wilson drop. "By the way, we are expected to visit my parents tomorrow."

"When you say expected, don't you mean there's no choice in the matter?"

Kendra had finally relented to see Sekhmet a month after Nefertem's return. She'd dreaded the meeting with her mother-in-law, but as Nefertem had said, the woman from the hidden chamber was far different from the one she'd now become. Kendra had not forgotten what Sekhmet had tried to do, but she was slowly warming up to her mother by marriage.

Nefertem chuckled. "I admit my parents usually do not take no for an answer."

Peering at Cleo, Kendra found her fast asleep. "She's off again." Nefertem moved to take the baby from her. She shook her head. "Cleo is going to sleep in the crib. You might like her sleeping on your chest for hours on end, but she needs to get used to sleeping in the crib."

*

Backing away, Nefertem made room so Kendra could stand. As his wife tucked their daughter into bed, his thoughts wandered. His brother's absence bothered him more than he was willing to let on. Mahes was missing not only from their home, but from the immortal realm as well. Nefertem could not shake the feeling that what had happened to him ten months before had now become Mahes' fate. Mahes had so far not replied to any of his calls, which was not a good sign.

If indeed Mahes' fate was the same, Nefertem hoped when the end came, Mahes found the happiness he himself now had with Kendra. That was all he could hope for.

The End

MAHES

Dana's one-time friend, Ellie, sends her an ancient scroll from Egypt. Not knowing there would be consequences for doing so, she opens it. Having a god pass judgment was the last thing she expected. That it's Mahes, the one Egyptian god she is obsessed with, makes it that much more unbelievable.

Mahes, the protector of maat, is sent to the mortal woman who has broken universal order by opening the Book of Thoth. He soon finds himself in a difficult position as his attraction for Dana grows.

With the help of his brother god, Nefertem, Mahes and Dana set out to return the book before Dana is tempted to read from it, and in doing so, condemns herself to death.

CHAPTER ONE

Plunking herself down onto her chair, Dana James stared at the cylindrical tube on her desk. The courier had delivered it a few minutes earlier. Even though she was curious to see what was inside, it was the sender who piqued her interest more. The point of origin stated on the courier's slip that it'd been sent to her by one Ellie Marstan. The sender's address was somewhere in Egypt.

Dana scowled at the cylinder, wondering why Ellie would have sent her a package. They hadn't exactly been on speaking terms for the last couple of years, but Dana had known Ellie was in Egypt on a dig. Working in the Egyptian antiquities department at The Nelson-Atkins Museum of Art in Kansas City, Missouri, Dana liked to keep herself up-to-date on any digs being done in that country.

She broke the seal around the top of the cylinder and gingerly slid out what was packaged inside. She pulled away the layers of bubble wrap, and was surprised to find a papyrus scroll in the center. It was in excellent condition, showing no signs of age. She drew a blank as to why Ellie would have sent her, in particular, the scroll. It couldn't have been from the dig. The Egyptian government would never allow anything excavated to be sent out of the country.

With her fingertips, she gently ran them across the papyrus. A tingling sensation shot along them, and Dana pulled her hand away. *That was weird.* To see if it would happen again, she lightly touched the scroll again. Nothing. Thinking she must have imagined it, she gently took hold of the edge of it and slowly unrolled it.

As she scanned the hieroglyphs that filled the length of it, an intense wave of foreboding rose inside her. She yanked her hand back, and the scroll rolled up. Dana had no idea what was written on it, since she hadn't had enough time to read the hieroglyphs, but she couldn't help feeling she'd done something wrong by opening it.

She sat back in her chair. Dana tried to still her racing heart. She was being ridiculous, but she couldn't shake the feeling of uneasiness that gripped her. She stared at the scroll sitting innocuously on her desk and sensed there was something more to it, something powerful about it.

With care, she replaced it in the bubble wrap and then returned it to the packaging it had arrived in. She retrieved her purse from her desk drawer before she picked up the cylinder. She had no intention of leaving it at work. Ellie had sent it to her for some reason, and she felt leaving it lying around for her co-workers to see didn't seem like a good idea. Dana locked her office door. It'd been a long day, and she looked forward to a quiet night at home.

* * * *

Mahes arched a brow at the woman who stood before him. "You know, if you wanted to speak to me, all you had to do was call and I would have come to you of my own violation. It really was not necessary for you to summon me and flash me to your temple, Ma'at."

The goddess Ma'at was beauty personified. Everything about her was perfect. Her long, black hair fell in waves down her back. Rich brown eyes rimmed in kohl stared at him. Even though she was slight in build, her looks were deceiving. Ma'at was one of the most powerful goddesses of the Egyptian pantheon. It was her duty to keep the universe in order, to not allow chaos to have free reign. She was charged with weighing the souls of the dead who came to the underworld. Her feather determined whether one would be allowed to go on to the afterlife or have his or her heart eaten by a demon for not having followed maat during life.

A small smile played on her lips. "I do like to keep you on your toes, Mahes."

"Now that you have me here, spill it."

"I think you have been spending too much time among mortals. You are beginning to sound like one now."

Mahes shrugged. "Thanks. With my brother living with his mate in the mortal world, I have come to enjoy my time there, which was where I headed when you so rudely summoned me."

His brother, Nefertem, at one time had been unable to walk among mortals unless summoned to judge them. That was all in the past. Nefertem now lived with his mate and baby daughter in Memphis, Tennessee. Mahes was supposed to be at his brother's house right now, watching the game on television while drinking large quantities of beer.

"I am afraid you will not be going to see your brother this day, Mahes. I have need of you."

Mahes dropped the gentle banter and grew serious. "You did not summon me on a whim, did you?"

"No." Ma'at stepped closer. "Maat has been broken. Universal order has been upset, and it must be corrected."

"What has happened?"

"The Book of Thoth has been found and opened. You

know that book is never to be read by a mortal. It contains knowledge only the gods are to have access to. The spells inside it are too powerful to be used by a mere mortal. Whoever reads from the book, must be punished in order to set things right."

"So, you are sending me to punish this mortal who opened the book?"

"It is what you do, Mahes. I realize the mortals no longer worship us as they did in the past, but maat must be kept in balance. The one who has the book has not read from it. Knowing your closeness with the mortals, I will allow you to decide what the punishment will be as long as the book remains unread, but there are some stipulations you must follow. The Book of Thoth must be returned to the place from where it had been taken. If this mortal does read from it, the punishment will be death."

"I will do what needs to be done."

"I knew you would not shirk your duty."

Mahes really had no choice in the matter. Ma'at would not allow him to say no. As she reached out and placed her palm on his cheek, he closed his eyes as a jolt of energy surged through him. He felt most of his powers drain away, leaving him as mortal as the one he was to judge. He opened his eyes and found Ma'at smiling. He was about to ask who the mortal was when a picture of a woman appeared in his mind. A split second later, he found himself in the middle of a street with a car heading straight for him, and no time to move out of the way. He swore as he jumped to throw himself onto the hood before it hit him head-on.

*

Dana felt as if her heart was now permanently lodged in her throat. She couldn't believe she'd actually hit someone, but the proof was there, lying on the hood of her car. She had no idea where he'd come from. One minute the street was clear, and the next he stood in front of her oncoming vehicle. As the man moaned, she put the car into Park and then quickly got out to see how badly he was hurt.

She was grateful the street they were on was a quiet one and not in the downtown core. As the man tried to get up, she quickly pushed him back down. "I think you should stay still until we're sure you aren't badly injured."

He turned his head to look at her, and Dana forgot to breathe. He was gorgeous. Male-model gorgeous. With her hand still pressed to his shoulder, she skimmed her gaze over his face. It was all planes and angles. His lips were firm, and she couldn't stop herself from wondering what they would taste like. She looked higher and encountered deep amber eyes that matched the color of expensive scotch. Along with those, he had longish black hair and tanned skin, which only added to his good-looks. The corners of his eyes crinkled as he smiled with oozing with sex appeal.

Dana tore her gaze from his face and tried to bring her raging body back under control. "I'm so sorry. I didn't see you. Where are you hurt?"

"I cannot tell. Maybe you should check for me." His voice was deep, and his words were accented as if English wasn't his first language.

Dana stifled a gasp as she placed her hands on the middle of his chest. She'd been a lifeguard at the local pool when she was a teenager so had a little bit of first-aid. That being the case, she knew he had to be checked for any major injuries before being moved. The only way for her to do that was to run her palms over him, feeling for any broken bones.

The thought of touching his well-muscled body thrilled her more than it should have. She was supposed to be seeing how badly he was hurt instead of admiring how well the tight, white T-shirt and blue jeans he wore showed off his hard body. Giving herself a mental shake, she got down to the business at hand.

Gently, so as not to hurt him, Dana ran her hands down each of his arms. His skin was warm beneath her fingertips. Finding no broken bones, she moved to his legs. She skimmed her palm down one and then back up the other. Unable to stop herself, she found her gaze pulled to the crotch of his jeans. There was no mistaking what the bulge there was. He seemed to be just as large in that area as the rest of him.

Looking back up at his face, Dana's heart pounded. Arousal slammed into her, causing her body to liquefy. The way he stared at her said he knew she'd been checking him out, and he liked it. Her pussy throbbed, wanting to have the full, hard length of his cock deep inside. Flustered, she took a step back, trying not to read too much into the way his gaze followed her movements.

She cleared her throat, and said, "You appear to be okay. No broken bones."

"Good to know."

As he slowly sat up, Dana noticed the stain of blood on his side, marring the pristine whiteness of his T-shirt. With a cry of exclamation, she stepped closer and lifted his shirt to examine the cut across the lower part of his ribs. It wasn't deep, but it needed to be cleaned.

"It doesn't look as if it'll need stitches, but you'll have to have it taken care of." Knowing what she was about to suggest was foolish to the extreme, she pushed on anyway. "I only live a couple of blocks from here. If you come to my place, I can take care of that for you. It's the least I can do."

He seemed to consider her offer. She'd be taking her chances by inviting a total strange to her house, but her gut told her to not let him go, and not because she found him extremely attractive. It was something much deeper than that. Something inside said she'd been meant to meet with this man. It was her "gift," as her mother had liked to call it. Dana had always been able to sense things others around her couldn't. She didn't know if it was just good instincts or really was a "gift" as her mother had said.

The man nodded. "I think I will take you up on your offer. I am starting to feel as if I was hit by a car."

He stiffly slid off the hood. Quickly, Dana came around to the passenger side before she opened the door for him. He was a lot taller than he looked lying down. He had to be at least six foot four. He towered over her five feet four inches. Seeing how stiffly he moved, she stepped to his side to help him into the car. He leaned into her, pressing against her. With her bottom lip between her teeth, she got him inside and then closed the door. Back at the driver's side, she took a deep breath to slow her rapidly beating heart. She acted like a lovesick teenager with her first crush. The feel of him leaning along her had sent her body into overdrive. Without looking down, she knew her nipples had hardened into tight little buds.

Dana slipped the car into Drive and concentrated on the road as she drove the short distance to her place. She felt him watching her. To distract herself, she asked, "What's your name? I'm Dana, by the way."

"My name is Mahes."

Dana turned to take a quick look at him. She now recognized Mahes' accent. "You're Egyptian?"

"That is correct."

"How do you feel about your parents naming you after an ancient Egyptian god?"

"What do you mean?"

"Mahes was an Egyptian god. He was the son of Ptah and Sekhmet, who were part of the Memphis triad of gods along with their other son, Nefertem."

"You seem to know a lot about the ancient gods of Egypt."

"I should. I majored in Egyptian art and archaeology at the University of Memphis. I did my dissertation paper on Mahes. He's not as well-known as the other gods, but he was no simple one. He was known as The Lord of the Massacre. He was a feline deity, so the priests bred lions at his temple in Leontopolis."

Dana let her words trail off and mentally kicked herself. She'd done it again. She had a bad habit of talking too much whenever the subject of ancient Egypt, and most especially anything to do with Mahes, was brought up. She got so wrapped up in the subject it sounded as if she conducted a lecture. Usually, when that happened around men who weren't in the same line of work as herself, their eyes glazed over in boredom. She lost count of the number of first dates who'd never called for a second because of that very reason.

Taking a quick glance at Mahes, she was surprised to see her speech had the opposite effect on him. His gaze was riveted to her, staring at her with interest. After she reached her condo apartment, Dana parked her car in the underground parking garage before she went around to his side. He was already out and waiting for her. She wrapped her arm around his waist and let him lean on her as she headed for the security door.

*

Mahes relaxed against Dana's side, letting her support some of his weight. His injuries were not as bad as he made them out to be. Granted he was a bit sore, but he really was not that badly hurt. Having her offer to look after his injury had worked out all the better for him. She was the one Ma'at had sent him to judge. Dana had been the one who had opened the Book of Thoth, and she had it with her. He could sense it in the car with them. Almost as if she knew what he thought, she stopped their progress.

"Are you going to be okay alone for a second? I forgot something in the car."

At his nod, she quickly returned to her vehicle and reached into the backseat. She pulled out a cylindrical tube and then locked the car back up. She tucked it under her left arm and returned to his side. There was no question in his mind that inside that tube was the book.

Mahes allowed Dana to lead him through the security door she had unlocked, and into the elevator. He drifted his gaze over her as she pushed the button for her floor. She was not the type of woman he was normally attracted to. He usually liked his beautiful to the extreme with a body that matched her good-looks. Dana was pretty, but she would not be considered a raving beauty. She had high cheekbones, a small pert nose, eyes that looked more gray than blue, and full, lush lips that were made for a man to kiss for hours on end. Her best feature was her hair. At first glance, he thought it was brown, but with the light inside the elevator shining on it, he saw the coppery-red highlights shot throughout it. She wore her it down, so it hung in coppery waves. There was something about her that drew him to her.

The elevator soon dinged once they reached her floor. Mahes stepped into the hallway and smiled at the top of Dana's head. She really was a small thing, but she was stronger than she looked. She allowed him to lean on her as she struggled with her keys while trying not to drop the cylinder still held under her arm. Finally able to open the door to her condo, she walked him into her living room and gently helped him to sit on her couch.

"Just sit there while I get the things I'll need from the bathroom to clean your cut."

She bustled off down the small hallway that was connected to the living room. Mahes looked around. Though her place would not be considered large, by any means, he found it warm and inviting. The walls were painted light beige and matched the color of the plush carpet beneath his feet. There was not much furniture to clutter it up. There was only a couch, loveseat, television, and a medium-size coffee table that sat in the middle of the room. A few pieces of artwork hung on the walls.

Mahes skimmed over the scenes that were painted on the papyrus. They appeared to be copies of originals found on the walls of ancient Egyptian tombs. He made a mental note to watch what he said around Dana. She knew too much about the ancient past of his country, and more importantly, about him. Hearing her return to the living room, he pushed his thoughts aside.

Dana sat next to him and placed the items she carried on the coffee table. She seemed to have brought everything in her medicine cabinet. He warily eyed the bottle of rubbing alcohol. Silently, he watched as she soaked a cotton ball with the disinfectant. He braced himself as she lifted his T-shirt and pressed it to his skin. He hissed in pain as she gently dabbed the cut, cleaning away the small amount of blood.

"Sorry. I know it stings, but you don't want an infection."

"It is okay. Just do not take your time about it."

"All done."

Dana picked up a tube of ointment, squeezed some onto her finger, and carefully spread it over the wound. A rush of desire surged through him. He found her simple touch arousing. Even though she was not touching him in an intimate way, it did not stop his blood from pounding, or his cock from growing hard. He wanted her. He had to resist the urge to grab her and pull her under him so he could bury himself deep inside her body. He closed his eyes and concentrated on bringing himself back under control. He needed to take things slowly. It would not do to scare her away.

She covered the wound with gauze and tape, then gave

it a final tap before she pulled his shirt back down. Mahes could tell Dana was just as affected as he by their closeness. Her face was slightly flushed, and her breathing was accelerated.

"Thanks for taking care of me." His voice sounded husky even to his own ears.

"As I said before, it was the least I could do. Is there anywhere you want me to drop you off?"

He was not ready to leave yet. He had to make sure she did not read from the book. There was the small matter of figuring out where he would go when he left, and where exactly there was. Not answering Dana's question, he got up and walked around the room, looking at the framed pictures on the walls. He had to think of a way to convince her to keep him around.

As he stared at the pictures depicting his ancient past, Mahes could only think of two things that would get Dana to allow him to stay. He turned back around as he pulled his shirt over his head and walked to the couch.

"Can I get my shirt washed? It is all I have at the moment. I am here on vacation, and the airport lost my luggage so I do not have a clean one to change into." Drawing on all the charm he possessed, he looked at her and said huskily, "I would also like to hear more about my namesake. You seem to know so much about him."

"Um...o-okay," Dana stammered. "I can do that."

Dana got off the couch, snatched the T-shirt out of his hand, and pointedly avoided looking at his bared chest. Mahes chuckled to himself as she hurriedly walked out of the living room and disappeared down the hallway.

CHAPTER TWO

Dana headed for her bedroom and quietly shut the door behind her. Leaning against it, she took a deep breath. She had to get herself under control. Tending to Mahes' injury had done wicked things to her body. Every time she'd touched him, a wave of awareness had rushed through her. She'd gloried in the feel of his warm, smooth skin beneath her fingertips. Sitting so close to him, she'd smelled the musky male scent that was all his own.

Without thinking, she lifted his shirt to her nose and breathed deeply. His smell filled her senses, making her wonder what the rest of Mahes would look like unclothed. The sight of him shirtless, with his broad, muscular chest bared for her to see, had almost been too much to resist. It'd been way too long since she'd had a man in her bed, and she'd never had one as good looking as Mahes show interest in her before. The man's sex appeal was through the roof, and well he knew it. Dana bet he had to beat the women off with a stick.

Dana shook her head at her own foolishness as she stripped off the dress pants and blouse she had worn to work. After slipping into a pair of gray yoga pants and a black T-shirt, she left the bedroom and went to the small laundry room next to it. She loaded Mahes' shirt into the washer, and told herself to stop acting like a ninny around him. Yes, he was gorgeous, but there was no way he could be that interested in her. Her looks weren't spectacular, by any means, and she didn't have the type of personality that would make her stand out. She was too bookish, too much of an academic, or so she'd been told by a couple of ex-boyfriends. She shouldn't read more into having Mahes ask her to tell him what she knew about his namesake. Being Egyptian, it made perfect sense that he'd be interested in the history of his country.

Back in the living room, Dana found Mahes on the couch, patiently waiting. Her gaze latched on to him. The man was pure sin. His wide chest was well-padded with muscle and free of hair. She lowered her gaze, and her mouth went dry as she feasted her eyes on the sight of his washboard stomach. He had a killer body. Looking lower still, her attention was drawn to the bulge in his pants.

"Are you hungry?" he asked.

Dana was hungry, all right. She would love nothing more than to strip Mahes naked and lick every inch of his hard body. Realizing what she did, she felt her face flush as she dragged her gaze back up.

"What did you say?"

"I asked if you were hungry. Since it will take a while for my shirt to be washed, and you have kindly consented to tell me all you know about Mahes the god, we could order some takeout. My treat."

From the look Mahes wore, Dana had a feeling he knew exactly what she'd been gazing at so intently. She felt her face grow even redder just thinking about it. She seized on to what he'd suggested, and said, "Sure. That's a great idea. What kind of takeout do you like?"

"I will eat just about…anything." There was no missing

what Mahes alluded to. "I am paying, so you can decide what to order. You have the advantage since you make your home here in…"

"Here in Kansas City?"

"Yes, Kansas City…" Mahes' words trailed off again.

"Kansas City, Missouri?"

"Yes. I had forgotten what city we were in for a moment. I still must be jet lagged."

"The time difference for Egypt and here is a lot."

Either he was jet lagged or he'd hit his head when she'd run him over with her car. She hoped it wasn't the latter, but just in case, she decided she'd better closely watch him. Concussions didn't always show up right away.

"So, what do you feel like eating?"

The image of a naked Mahes stretched out on her bed as she licked and kissed every inch of him flashed through her head. *Get your mind out of the gutter, Dana.* "Pizza. Why don't we order pizza?"

"Then pizza it is."

Dana turned and headed for the kitchen. Mahes followed her. She pulled out a bunch of restaurant flyers that she kept and flipped through them until she found a pizza place close to her condo. "What do you like on it?"

"Order what you usually get. I am not a picky eater. Having something new to try makes it more enjoyable for me since I rarely get the chance to explore different foods."

"Okay." Dana wasn't sure what to make of that. It made her wonder what he normally ate if he thought pizza was something that needed to be explored, as if it were some kind of new delicacy.

Dana picked up the phone and punched in the telephone number for the pizza place and then gave her order. The food would be delivered in a half hour. She hung up, then opened the fridge and peered inside.

"Would you like something to drink while we wait for the pizza to arrive? I have wine or beer, and not much else besides water."

"I will take a beer."

Mahes' voice came directly behind her. Dana jumped back in surprise. She slammed into him, and would have pushed them over if he hadn't managed to wrap his arms around her middle to steady her.

She turned and looked at him. "Sorry. I seem to be an accident waiting to happen today."

"No need to apologize. I startled you." Keeping his hold on her, Mahes reached around and pulled a beer out of the fridge. "Though I must say, it has given me an excellent excuse to have you in my arms."

His deep voice seemed to wrap around her like silk, holding her to him. Her gaze became riveted to his mouth as he'd spoken. She licked her lips as her body flared to life. Her nipples pebbled where they were crushed against his bared chest. She wanted to rub along his body and purr like a cat.

It wasn't until her lips were a mere inch from his that she broke the trance she found herself in. Dana pulled free of his embrace and grabbed a beer out of the fridge for herself. Before heading back to the living room, she took two large glasses out of the cupboard.

Hoping Mahes would overlook her little misstep, Dana sat on the couch and turned on the television. She poured her beer into one of the glasses before she took a big sip. From the corner of her eye, she watched him sit beside her. He took a swig from the bottle he held. He obviously was going to forego using the glass she'd brought for him. He acted as if nothing different had happened between them. Her heart still thundered. It would seem the attraction she felt was only one-sided. It was a bit of a disappointment, but who was she kidding? The man was so far out of her league it wasn't even funny.

Dana tried to sound as unaffected as he appeared to be as she asked, "So, what exactly do you want to know about your namesake?"

"Everything."

Dana shook her head. "I have to give you fair warning, once I get started, I can go on for hours without stopping."

"I have been told I possess that quality as well."

There he went again. Mahes seemed to have a lot of double meanings in whatever he said, and his words mostly had to do with sex. "Okaaay. If I start boring you with too many details, just stop me. You wouldn't be the first person I've bored to death."

"I promise you, I will not be."

"All right then. Mahes was the lion-god of war and guardian of the horizon. His job was to help Re fight the snake-demon Apep in the solar barque every night. He protected the pharaoh while he fought in battle. His real name was rarely used. He was referred to by several epithets instead."

"Like The Lord of the Massacre."

Dana nodded. "Yes, that was the one most commonly used. The others were Wielder of the Knife, The Scarlet Lord, Lord of Slaughter, Avenger of Wrongs, and Helper of the Wise Ones."

"Given those names, he must have been pretty bloodthirsty. Someone you would not want to cross."

"He wasn't really evil if that's what you're thinking. He was the punisher of those who violated maat. He promoted order and justice, therefore, the last two epithets. I guess if you were the one upsetting the balance of maat, you would take Mahes' coming as something you should be scared of."

"I am sure he struck fear in many wrongdoers' hearts."

"You would assume so. Personally, I think he was more protector than executioner."

"Why do you think that?"

"He protected the innocent and helped maintain order. I don't know why really. It's just something I feel whenever I think of him."

"Is that so? It sounds as if you truly admire Mahes."

Dana turned to look at the television, not really seeing what was on. She had no idea why she'd told Mahes that. She usually kept her "feelings" to herself, but on some level, she trusted him.

"I guess you could say I admire him."

Dana looked at her clasped hands where they sat on her lap. She wasn't about to tell Mahes she felt drawn to the god. What had started as a mere interest, had grown to a borderline obsession. Doing the research for her dissertation paper had set it off. By the time it was done, she'd spent many nights dreaming about him, only waking to an empty bed, yearning for the touch of a man who didn't exist.

Mahes shifted beside her. Dana looked at him and was surprised to see he watched her intently. If she wasn't mistaken, his expression was one of appreciation. That couldn't be right.

"Why are you looking at me like that?"

"Is it a crime for a man to admire a woman he finds attractive?"

"Let me check your head. I think you must have bumped it when I hit you."

Dana turned to face Mahes and tunneled her hands through his thick, black hair, searching for any signs of swelling. As her gaze met his, she stilled her movements, leaving her fingers where they were. His regard had changed from one of admiration to one of longing. His rich, amber eyes appeared almost black as they dilated with desire. His gaze drifted to her mouth, and stayed there. He was going to kiss her.

Mahes slowly lowered his mouth to hers. Just before his lips reached hers, he murmured, "There is nothing wrong with my head, Dana. I know exactly what I am doing."

Dana shut her eyes at the first brush of Mahes' lips. As

she leaned toward him, he claimed her mouth fully. He wrapped one arm around her waist and pulled her against his chest as his other came up to cup her cheek.

The man sure knew how to kiss. The feel of his mouth slanting over hers sent her senses reeling. He sucked on her bottom lip, and Dana fisted her hands in his hair. She pulled on it, letting him know she wanted more. Obliging her, Mahes licked the seam of her lips before pushing his way inside. She moaned softly. Getting her first real taste of him, her body come alive. Her pussy ached and grew wet as his tongue twined with her own. Her breasts grew heavy, and her nipples pebbled into tight buds as they brushed against his hard chest.

Holding her to him, Mahes slowly laid back on the couch until she was stretched out on top of him. The hard length of his cock pressed against her stomach. He let go of her mouth and made a trail to her ear with his lips. At her earlobe, he took it between his teeth and gently tugged. Dana shivered in response. He continued lower and nipped the sensitive flesh just below her ear. She arched her neck, giving him better access.

She released his hair, then placed her hands on his chest as she ground her pussy against the hard column of his thigh. Mahes shifted beneath her, pulling her up higher on his body so his erection was nestled between her legs. She ached for him to fill her.

Lost in the sexual haze that Mahes' kisses had created, Dana at first didn't hear the buzzer. It sounded a second time, and she reluctantly pulled out of his arms to stand beside the couch. "It's the pizza delivery guy. I have to let him up."

Dana walked to the door before she pushed a button on the small panel located next to it. After ascertaining it was indeed the delivery guy with their pizza, she pushed another button to let him into the building. Mahes come up behind her. She turned to face him, and her breath caught. He was still aroused. The hard length of him strained against the zipper of his jeans.

She dragged her gaze back up to his face. "He'll be up in a minute."

Mahes reached into his back pocket to remove his wallet. After taking out a couple of bills, he held them to her. "That should be enough to cover it."

Nodding, Dana accepted the money. "Thanks."

Dana turned to face the door. If she continued to look at Mahes, she'd be back in his arms in a matter of seconds. That wouldn't be a good thing. Yes, the man had kissed her senseless, but she'd let it go too far. If they hadn't been interrupted, she was almost positive they would have ended up making love, which was so unlike her. She never slept with a man she hardly knew. If she managed to make it past the first couple of dates, and the guy was still interested in her, then she considered it. That, sadly, didn't happen very often.

Once the delivery guy knocked on the door, Dana opened it and then handed him the money before accepting the piping hot pizza. Still unable to look at Mahes, she headed for the kitchen to get plates and napkins.

*

Dana walked away before Mahes followed her. His body was still very much aware of her presence. Now that he had tasted her and held her in his arms, he wanted more. What they had shared on the couch was far from enough. Her response had surprised him. On the outside, she acted timid, almost unsure of herself, but once her passion had been ignited, that uncertainty had disappeared. She was a woman who knew what she wanted, and was not afraid to take it.

Following Dana with his gaze as she moved about

opening cupboards, Mahes bit back a smile. She was doing her utmost to not make eye contact with him. The timid mouse had returned, it would seem. He decided to let her have her distance. For now.

Spying the cylinder that contained the Book of Thoth on the table, Mahes crossed to it and picked it up. The power inside it reached out to him. In this form, he was just as susceptible as any other mortal. Not that he planned on reading from the book any time soon.

Dana came to him and took it. "I'll take that. The item inside is very fragile."

"Is it something from your job? With your education, I assume you work with antiquities?"

"Yes. I work in the ancient Egyptian section at the Museum of Art. No, this isn't work related. A friend of mine sent this to me. She's on a dig in Egypt at the moment."

That explained how Dana had ended up with the book. Her friend, whoever she was, had to be the one who had found it in its resting place. "What is it?"

"A scroll. I haven't really looked at it yet."

If he had his way, she would not be getting any more chances to learn exactly what it was. "Put the scroll away. The pizza is going to get cold, and I am starved."

"All right. I'll just put this in my room. You can take the pizza and plates to the living room. We'll be more comfortable there. I think the washer is done as well, so I'll switch your shirt to the dryer on the way back."

With the pizza box in one hand and the plates in the other, Mahes returned to the living room. After making room on the coffee table, he flipped open the box. He took a deep breath, savoring the smell of pizza sauce and melted cheese. He only needed to eat while in mortal form. The last time he had been able to enjoy food had been almost a year ago, when his brother had changed him to a mortal, keeping him trapped in this world. He had not been too pleased with Nefertem at first, but his brother had had a good reason at the time.

In a matter of minutes, Dana had completed her tasks. She sat and put a piece of pizza on each of their plates. "I think the blood washed out of your shirt. It should be dry in twenty minutes or so."

"I thank you."

Mahes took a big bite of the fresh pizza and let the silence hang between them. He found he did not want to leave Dana, and it did not have to do with her having possession of the book. He wanted to stay and get to know her better, in every sense of the word. His sister-in-law, Kendra, would be overjoyed to learn that. She called him a man-whore because he was able to draw any woman to him. That he did nothing to discourage their attentions tended to irk Kendra to the extreme, especially when it was the most attractive ones he showed the greatest interest in. He being attracted to a woman who was no supermodel would thrill Kendra to no end.

While watching television, they managed to eat the whole pizza between them, with Mahes having more than half by himself. They washed it down with a couple of bottles of beer. Feeling nicely full, he sat back and sipped on his third. Dana valiantly matched him beer for beer, though she looked as if she felt its effects. Beer was his drink of choice, and he had to consume a large quantity of it to feel it.

Dana sat curled in the corner of the couch. Her eyes drooped. He could tell she was soon going to lose the battle to stay awake. It was not all that late, only ten thirty, but he could tell she was not going to last much longer.

"Would you like to go to bed, Dana?" She looked at him questioningly, and he added, "I mean, do you want to go to sleep, alone?"

"Sorry. I had a long day, and the beer is making me sleepy. I usually don't drink that much of it. Do you want me to call you a cab?"

Mahes hesitated before he answered. "Would it be all right if I stay the night here on your couch? The hotel where I had originally booked a room messed up my reservation. I was unable to find one before I met you. You are the only person I know in this city that I could ask, and I promise it will only be for one night."

He watched Dana's face as she considered his request. He held still, not wanting to give her any reason to say no. After a minute, she nodded.

"Even though I just met you, I feel as if I can trust you. I don't get the feeling you would murder me in my bed at night while I slept. You can stay on the couch for one night only."

He smiled, turning the full force of it on Dana. Her gaze locked on to his mouth. "It is a deal. Why don't you get some sleep? Do not feel as if you have to stay up and keep me entertained."

Dana stood, looking a little unsteady on her feet. "I think I'll do that. Let me get you a pillow and a blanket first."

Mahes followed Dana down the hallway, then waited while she opened the linen closet before she pulled out a pillow and blanket for him to use. She shoved those into his arms and then showed him where the dryer was so he could get his shirt, which was now dry.

They stood at the door to her bedroom. Mahes knew all it would take to have Dana invite him to share her bed would be to kiss her as he had done earlier, but he held back. He had her trust now, and he wanted to keep it. Forcing his way into her bed when she was not ready, would be a sure-fire way to lose what ground he had gained with her. So instead of dragging her into his arms and kissing her the way he wanted to, he settled for a light kiss on her forehead.

"Have a good sleep, Dana, and I will see you in the

morning."

"You as well, Mahes."

After backing into the bedroom, Dana pushed the door closed. With a deep breath, Mahes retrieved his T-shirt before he headed back to the living room. It was going to be a long night.

CHAPTER THREE

After waiting an hour, just to make sure Dana would be asleep, Mahes picked up the phone and made a collect call to Nefertem. He was glad Kendra had insisted he and his brother learn how to make calls such as that.

Nefertem answered and accepted the charges. "Where the hell are you, Mahes?"

Slipping into Egyptian, he said sarcastically, "Hello to you as well, Nefertem. I have missed you too."

"Knock it off. When you did not show up tonight, I knew something was wrong. That you are calling me collect proves I was right in my suspicions. What have you gotten yourself into now?"

"It was not anything I did. Ma'at summoned me."

There was a knowing silence on the other end of the line before Nefertem spoke again. "What did she want you to do?"

"I have to pass judgment to reset the balance."

"On a mortal?"

"Of course on a mortal. A woman, to be exact. She opened the Book of Thoth."

Nefertem let out a low whistle. "That is not good. How did she manage to get hold of it? I thought the book was hidden."

"It would seem Dana has a friend who's an Egyptologist, who also happens to be in Egypt on a dig. She must have found it and then sent it to Dana. Why she sent it to her, I have not been able to determine yet."

"Dana, is it?" Nefertem chuckled. "Do I detect a bit of interest on your part when you speak her name?"

"If you tell Kendra, I am going to make you regret it."

"Yes, you are definitely interested in this woman."

Mahes ground his teeth in exasperation. "Let us move on, shall we? I need your help. Ma'at turned me mortal, then stuck me in the mortal world with nothing but the clothes on my back. The book needs to be taken back to Egypt, and I refuse to travel by plane. It was horrendous enough the first time."

A year ago, Kendra had accidentally summoned Nefertem, using the pendant to which he had been bound, not knowing what would happen once he was in the mortal realm. His coming had meant their mother was soon to follow. She had passed judgment on all mortals and found them in need of punishment. To stop her coming, they had had to go to Egypt and find the spell that released Nefertem from the hold the pendant had over him. It had been housed in a hidden library in a chamber buried deep in the earth between the Sphinx's feet.

"Where exactly are you?"

"Kansas City, Missouri."

"That works out perfectly. Missouri is right next to Tennessee. If you want me to get you to Egypt, I want you to come here to Memphis, then I will do what you ask."

"You want me to come to you?" Mahes snapped. "I think it would be easier all around if you just popped in here and got me once I get the book from Dana."

"No."

"What do you mean no?"

"How do the mortals say it? Payback is a bitch? I finally can get even with you for all those tests you have put me through. Time for you to squirm a little, Mahes. If you want to get to Egypt, you will have to drive to Memphis. Oh, and bring Dana with you or the deal is off." With that said, Nefertem hung up.

Mahes pulled the phone from his ear and stared at it, stunned. Nefertem had actually hung up on him. There was no point trying to call his brother again. Nefertem would only refuse the charges. He had stated his terms, and he would hold Mahes to them.

He placed the phone on its base and wished he could strangle Nefertem. Yes, maybe he sometimes went a little too far with his tests, but he did it for the other person's benefit. Maybe Nefertem had a right to be a little pissed off with him for testing Kendra to see what her true feelings for him were. It had all worked out well in the end. Her feelings had been true. No harm, no foul. She had even managed to put him in his place. It was obvious Nefertem was not going to let this opportunity to get even with him slip through his fingers.

Sitting back, Mahes leaned his head against the back of the couch. He had had this all planned out. It was going to be so simple. He would get the book from Dana and have Nefertem pick him up and take him to Egypt. Once the book was returned, he would regain his immortality, and he could carry on with his life as usual. Now Nefertem had complicated matters. Mahes would have to somehow convince Dana to drive him to Memphis, Tennessee, to see his brother.

* * * *

After rolling to her side, Dana squinted, trying to see what time it was. The bright red numbers on her digital clock said it was nine o'clock in the morning. Groaning, she went to her back and threw an arm over her eyes. It was Saturday, and usually she slept in at the start of the weekend, but that wasn't going to happen today. For one thing, she found she couldn't sleep any more. She'd gone to bed too early the night before. As usual when she drank more than one beer, it made her sleepy. The other factor that kept her from falling back to sleep was the thought of Mahes asleep on her couch.

She'd enjoyed the night they'd spent together. She couldn't remember ever feeling as comfortable around a man as she had with Mahes. Not once had he talked down to her or made her feel like the biggest nerd on the planet. Just that in itself made her want him more than she already did. She'd lost count of the number of times she'd had wanted to push him down onto the couch and have her way with him. Her fingers had itched to touch all that bronzed skin that was easily in reach.

The sound of the phone ringing made Dana jump. She quickly picked it up after the second ring, hoping it hadn't awakened Mahes in the other room. "Hello?"

"Hi, Dana, it's Ellie. I hope I didn't wake you up. I waited as long as I could before calling you."

Doing the mental math, Dana calculated the time in Egypt to be around five o'clock in the evening. "No, I was awake already."

"Good. The reason I'm calling you so early is to see if you got the package I sent you."

"Yes, I did. It was delivered yesterday to my work."

"Great. Can you do me a favor and just stick it in a corner somewhere at your place? I'll be coming back to the States in a few weeks."

"I don't mind holding on to it for you, but I have to wonder why you sent it to me in the first place. The last time I heard anything from you was a couple of years ago."

"I know. I apologize. It didn't have anything to do with you, honestly. I've been working on a project that has demanded most of my time. It's something really big. I think all the time and money I've spent working on it has finally paid off."

"Does the scroll have anything to do with it?"

Ellie fell silent for a few seconds before she spoke again. "No. No, of course not. The scroll is something different all together. Did you open it, Dana?"

"No. I just opened the packaging to see what you had sent me."

"Are you telling me the truth?"

"Why would I lie about something like that?" Dana didn't like the way Ellie's voice had grown harsh-sounding as she'd questioned her. It came across almost like a threat. That if she had opened it, Ellie would have been more than displeased with her.

"You have to promise me you won't open the scroll, Dana. It's mine, and I don't want you damaging it. It has great meaning to me."

"I give you my word. I won't open it."

"Excellent." With that assurance, Ellie was back to being cheerful-sounding. "I owe you one. Sorry to cut this short, but I have to run. I promise we'll have more time to catch up once I get back. Bye."

Dana barely had enough time to say bye in return before Ellie broke the connection. She hung up and shook her head. Ellie was definitely acting strange. With her being all friendly again, Dana had to wonder if there was more to it than only renewing old acquaintances.

She threw back the covers, then softly walked to the closed bedroom door. Dana pressed her ear against it and listened for any movement coming from the other side. She didn't hear anything so quietly went back to the bed and pulled open the drawer in the small table next it. She reached inside and pulled out her Egyptian tarot cards.

She really wasn't the type of person who was into all things supernatural, but tarot cards, and the Egyptian tarot cards in particular, were her weakness. Her mother had taught her how to read the cards when she was still young, as her mother had taught her. Dana's great, great-grandmother had been half Egyptian, and supposedly was more "gifted" than Dana. She'd taught her daughter how to use the tarot cards and to believe what they revealed. In Dana's case, she found she couldn't turn her back on that part of her heritage. For her, the cards were usually right on the money when she did a reading for herself.

Dana pushed the covers back even more and sat crossed legged on the bed. She shuffled the cards, being careful not to bend or kink them. She cut the deck, then drew the top card and placed it face up on the mattress. The Egyptian tarots could easily be considered pieces of art. They were a reproduction made from the deck devised by a famous occultist who had linked the tarots to the Book of Thoth. The scenes depicted ancient Egyptian life, religion, and culture. Each one was designed to look as if the images were painted on papyrus, which in turn sat on a black background.

When something in her life bothered her, Dana usually used the tarots for a mini-reading. She looked at the card. She'd selected one of the major arcana—Judgment. In the Egyptian deck, the Judgment card had two figures on it. The first one was the god Anubis—the god of death. Anubis was the gatekeeper of the underworld, and directed the dead either to Osiris, if they were found to be pure, or to Ammit to face a much worse fate if they were not.

The second figure on the card was a person dressed in pure white with a kilt that fell to the ankles. Anubis seemed to be looking back at the figure as he faced forward. The way they stood with their arms outstretched to each other, crossed at the wrists, it looked as if Anubis led the person by the hand.

The Judgment card could mean either of two things. It could be interpreted as good or bad. It could be a reminder that sometimes it was necessary to be judged and to learn from it. It could also mean a person had to put past mistakes behind them, and that they were ready to start fresh, cleansed of all guilt. Dana wasn't sure if either of those scenarios matched any aspect of her life at the moment, but it was something to remember and watch for.

Dana cocked her head toward the door, still not hearing any noise coming from the other side. She replaced the Judgment card and quickly shuffled the deck once again. She placed her right hand on top of the deck and thought of the image of Mahes. After cutting the cards, she pulled the first one and placed it face up on the mattress. Mahes' card was a major arcana as well. His was The Emperor. It depicted a figure of a man sitting on top a cubical stone with his legs crossed at the knee. In one hand, he held up what looked like a scepter. On his head, he wore the red crown of Lower Egypt with a gold cobra sitting in the center of his forehead.

The Emperor card represented structure and order. He kept the forces in balance, bringing order out of chaos. In an archetypal role, he was a guide, protector, and provider. As with her card, Dana wasn't sure how it would apply to Mahes.

She gathered up the cards and then carefully placed them in their box before returning them to the drawer. Even though the tarots hadn't given her a definite answer, she always felt better for having done a reading.

Now that she was up, Dana wanted her morning tea. She opened the bedroom door before she quietly headed for the kitchen. At the end of the hallway, she took a quick look into the living room. It looked as if Mahes was still asleep. She cringed to herself at the uncomfortable position he slept in. He really was too tall for her small couch. He would probably wake up with a stiff neck.

In the kitchen, Dana filled the kettle and then plugged it in. She threw out the used tea bag she'd forgotten to get rid of the day before from the tea pot and rinsed it. Standing in front of the counter, she waited for the kettle to boil.

"If that is tea you're making, I will have some as well."

Dana yelped in surprise before she turned to face Mahes. "You almost gave me a heart attack. I thought you were still sleeping."

"Sorry." Mahes gave her a sheepish grin. "I did not mean to scare you. I tend to be quiet on my feet. I heard you in the kitchen, so I thought I would see what you were up to. I heard the phone ringing as well."

"I'll have to tie bells to you if you do that too often. I am making tea and there will be enough for both of us. Sorry about the phone. It was my friend calling."

"The one who sent you the scroll?"

"Yes. She wanted to make sure it arrived okay. When she gets back to the States, she'll come and get it." Remembering the strange conversation she'd had with Ellie, Dana grew thoughtful.

"I can tell something is bothering you about the whole situation."

Dana shrugged. "I don't know. It's just a feeling I have. Ellie and I haven't been close for a while now. I still can't understand why she picked me to send it to. It seems a little fishy. Even though she told me to just stick it in a corner and forget about it, I think I'm going to do some snooping and see what exactly she sent me."

"I do not know, Dana. If she wants you to leave it alone, maybe you should do as she asked."

"Any other time I would, but if the scroll ends up being more than it appears, I'd like to know before the police, or someone like that, come knocking on my door, demanding it back. In fact, I think now would be the perfect time to take a look at that scroll again."

"Leave it be, Dana."

She didn't heed his words and went to walk passed him. Mahes grabbed her around the waist, pulling her against his chest. Before Dana could protest, his mouth came down onto hers.

CHAPTER FOUR

Mahes had not intended to seduce Dana first thing that morning, but he could not think of anything else to do that would stop her from looking at the book. That he was going to seduce her at some point had been a given, but he had thought he would give her some time first. Now that he had her in his arms, he had no intention of holding back. There was something about her that called out to him, and he was unable to resist.

Claiming her mouth fully, he wrapped his arms around her waist and held her flush against him. His cock hardened where it nestled against her belly. No other woman had that kind of effect over him. Only Dana could bring him to full arousal in a matter of seconds.

Mahes continued to kiss her and licked her bottom lip until she opened for him. He slipped his tongue inside, savoring the taste of her. He could not hold back a moan as Dana sucked it deeper inside her mouth, wrapping her own around his. He crowded her and pushed her back until her hips hit the counter. She threaded her fingers through his hair and pulled his head down, increasing the pressure of his lips.

The same as the evening before, the timid mouse had been replaced by the demanding tigress. Dana rubbed against him as she sighed into his mouth. Knowing what she wanted, Mahes shifted his leg so it came between hers. She pressed down on his thigh as she rubbed her pussy up and down it. He let go of her waist and snaked his hands up the front of her shirt. She did not have a bra on to hinder his progress. Gently, he cupped her breasts. They were not large, but they were a perfect handful.

He needed to see more of her. Mahes grabbed the bottom of Dana's shirt and pulled it over her head. Bending to her neck, he nibbled a trail of kisses down its smooth column. He continued his downward path and cupped her breast once more. Her rosy nipple was hard, just begging for him to taste it. He swirled his tongue around its turgid peak. She pressed against his hand as she bit back a moan. With his teeth, he tugged gently before sucking the tight bud deep inside his mouth. She ground herself on his leg as she fisted her hands in his hair, holding him to her.

His fully engorged cock pressed against the zipper of his jeans, which now seemed too tight. He shifted once again and lifted Dana, positioning her so he was in contact with the opening to her body. He moved to her other nipple and pumped his hips into her. She wrapped her legs around his waist and ground on the hard length of his cock. She felt too good.

Mahes released her nipple and stared at Dana. Her face was flushed and her lips were swollen from his kisses. She had her eyes closed, but they slowly drifted open under his regard. As he looked at her, he gave her one last chance to stop what they had started. In way of an answer to his silent question, she brought his head down and kissed him thoroughly.

He slid his hands down to the twin globes of her bottom. He picked Dana up and quickly headed for her bedroom. Still holding her to him, he placed her on the center of the bed, then came down on top of her. She pushed on his shoulder until she had him positioned beneath her. She straddled his thighs, took hold of his shirt, and pulled it up his body. Once he was free of it, she bent down to place small kisses across his chest. Mahes kept his hands at his sides, allowing her to have complete control. He sucked in his breath as she ran her tongue across each of his flat nipples.

Sitting up, Dana trailed her fingers down his stomach until they came to rest on the top of his jeans. With ease, she popped open the button and then unzipped his pants. She pushed at them, moving them down past his hips until they were as far down as she could get them. Mahes kicked them off the rest of the way. She licked her lips as she stared down at his hard cock that jutted out from his body. With her index finger, she rubbed the bead of liquid that sat on the very tip into his skin. He fisted his hands in the sheets beneath him.

With the same finger, Dana ran it down his full length. His cock jumped at her touch. She appeared fully engrossed in what she was doing, and wrapped her hand around the base of his shaft and squeezed. She released some of the pressure, then slid her fist up and down his full length. In response, Mahes pumped into her hand. At the rate things were going, he was not going to last long. It was only a matter of time before his body demanded he bury himself deep inside her welcoming heat.

Dana made short work of removing her pajama bottoms. Now naked, she straddled his hips so his hard cock nestled between the lips of her pussy. She rubbed her core up and down his shaft, coating him with her juices. Mahes closed his eyes for a second, savoring the feel of her against him. Once he thought he had reached his limit, she took her bottom lip between her teeth and slid up his body until the tip of his shaft pressed against the opening to her body. She pushed down, sheathing him to the hilt. They groaned.

Dana slowly rode him. Mahes relaxed his grip on the sheets and reached up so he could cup her breasts, tugging on her nipples. She increased the pace as she arched her back, causing his shaft to rub her clit with each downward stroke. He was in so deep her inner walls squeezed around his entire length.

His climax built. Wanting Dana to come first, he reached to where their bodies were joined and stroked her clit. She moaned as she rode him faster. The feel of her inner walls clamping around him, milking him, as her climax rose to claim her, sent him tumbling over the edge. With a loud groan, Mahes arched his hips, almost lifting her off the bed, and emptied deep inside her. Breathing hard, she collapsed onto his chest. He kissed the top of her head and tightly wrapped his arms around her. Only with her had sex ever been that satisfying. He pulled the covers over them, then his eyes drifted shut.

*

Dana tried to slide off Mahes, but he kept his arms firmly around her waist. His cock was still buried deep inside her. Small tremors continued to rock her body. Making love to him had blown her one and only boyfriend's bed play out of the water. Not that that relationship had lasted long, but she'd thought the sex hadn't been half bad. Obviously, she'd been totally in the wrong with that assumption.

She ducked her head under Mahes' chin, feeling her face flush, as she remembered how aggressive she'd been. He hadn't acted as if he'd minded, but with her limited experience when it came to sex, she wasn't sure. As his lips had touched hers, something had come over her, something that had wanted to claim him as hers. Thinking of how she'd acted, Dana became a little self-conscious.

Mahes must have sensed the change in her. He put a hand under her chin and forced her to look up at him. "Are you okay?"

She nodded. "Yeah. I'm sorry."

"For what?"

"For sort of taking control and not giving it back. I don't know what came over me."

Mahes held Dana to him and rolled her beneath him. He propped himself up on his elbows on either side of her head, then kissed the tip of her nose. "Do not dare to say sorry. I liked it. If anything, I should be apologizing to you for going too fast."

"You're not just saying that?"

"No, I am not. You can have your way with me any time you like just so long as I get to have my way with you in return."

"It's a deal."

Dana smiled and wrapped her arms around his neck. She was having a hard time fathoming that this gorgeous man was in her bed and actually wanted her. If she wasn't mistaken, he still wanted her. His cock hardened inside her. "Already?"

"I guess I cannot get enough of you. If I do not watch it, I will not want to leave you when I have to return home."

Dana didn't want to think about Mahes having to go home to Egypt. When he left, she would miss him a great deal. Even though they'd only just met, she couldn't help feeling she knew him on a deeper level. It wasn't because they'd made love, either. She'd always been attracted to tall, dark, and handsome men. That Mahes was Egyptian as well only made him that much more attractive. Maybe it was her Egyptian heritage calling out to his. She only knew she wasn't ready to think about him leaving.

Mahes brushed her hair off her forehead and placed a tender kiss there. In no hurry, he kissed her temples, her eyes, and the corners of her mouth. Dana resisted the urge to take control and forced herself to lie there and enjoy what he was doing to her. His gentle kisses were arousing, making her want him to possess her again.

Dana turned her head to the side to give him better access to her neck. He kissed his way down to the big vein there. He nipped her before dragging his tongue across it. He moved a little higher and swirled his tongue inside the shell of her ear. She shivered as her body broke out in goosebumps. He tugged on her earlobe with his teeth before he claimed her mouth.

He swept his tongue inside as he slowly pulled back until he was almost free of her body. With equal slowness, he slid back into her. Dana's eyes fell shut, and she moaned. Mahes was hard, stretching her to accommodate his thick shaft. With her feet flat on the mattress, she lifted her hips, matching his agonizingly slow strokes. He was in so deep the tip of his cock hit her cervix as he sheathed himself to the hilt.

She clutched his back and tried to urge him to increase the pace. She needed him to go faster, harder. She groaned in frustration and dug her nails into his well-muscled butt. Mahes lifted himself up onto his hands and positioned himself higher on her body. He pumped his hips faster, his shaft stroking her clit, pushing her ever closer. Dana wrapped her legs around his waist, matching his strokes as she squeezed her inner muscles around him. She panted and held on to him as her orgasm surged through her. As her body continued to clutch his shaft, he threw back his head and groaned. A rush of warmth filled her as he emptied himself inside her.

Mahes rolled to his back and pulled Dana against his side. "I think you have worn me out. A nap is looking pretty good right about now."

Dana giggled as she placed a kiss on his muscled chest. "I could do with one as well, though I must say my day is looking good so far."

"I will try to make it an even better one after I recoup my strength."

"I'll hold you to that."

Snuggling closer, Dana listened to Mahes' heart thumping under her ear. Soon his breathing evened out as sleep claimed him. She looked at him. She'd planned on taking him to find a hotel, but that wasn't something she wanted any more. If she was only going to have a short time with him, she wanted to make the most of it. He could stay there with her until he had to leave. As for clothes, a quick trip to the mall could easily solve that problem. With that settled in her mind, she closed her eyes. She fell asleep with a smile.

* * * *

After a quick nap, Dana suggested they each take a shower and then head to Oak Park Mall. Mahes had in turn suggested they shower together. She'd quickly shot that idea down. She knew very well washing would be the furthest thing from their minds. She wanted to use the shopping trip to bring up the idea of him staying at her place. She was pretty sure he would accept her offer, but until he said yes, she wasn't going to count on it a hundred percent.

It wasn't until she'd finished her shower that Dana remembered she'd filled the kettle earlier to make a pot of tea. She wrapped the towel she wore around her tighter and took a quick peek into the kitchen. The kettle was cool to the touch. She had to be thankful she'd bought a one that automatically shut off when it reached boiling point. Who knew what kind of state she would have found her kitchen without that little feature.

She returned to the bedroom. Mahes still laid on the bed. As she entered the room, he flipped back the sheets in invitation. "I have kept the bed warm for you."

Dana chuckled. "A very tempting offer, but I must decline. Take your shower. I think I saved some hot water for you."

"Having a cold one might not be such a bad thing."

Mahes slipped out from under the covers, then crossed to where Dana stood. He was semi-aroused. After seeing where her gaze strayed to, he added, "We can still go for round three."

"No. Round three will have to wait until later." Dana reluctantly pulled her gaze from his manhood.

"Something to look forward to then."

On his way out the door, Mahes claimed Dana's lips in a searing kiss, leaving her breathless. The man seriously had one of the nicest asses she'd seen. There was nothing like a toned butt on a man. She gave herself a shake before her thoughts could go any further down the gutter than they already had. She quickly donned a matching bra and panties. Thinking of what the night held in store for her, she'd chosen the sheer, lacy set she'd treated herself to a few months back. Over those she pulled on her favorite low-rise jeans and a black T-shirt that had a golden eye of Re across the chest done in glitter.

After combing her hair, she picked up Mahes' clothes, which were scattered all over the floor. She couldn't resist smelling his T-shirt before she placed it on the bed with his jeans. There was something about his scent that she found irresistible. It smelled like man and something that was his own.

Mahes returned to the bedroom with a towel wrapped around his waist. He'd slicked back his wet hair. "Do you think I could borrow your comb?"

"Here you go." Dana retrieved it off the dresser and handed it to him. "While you're dressing, I'll make some tea."

"Sounds good." Mahes' gaze landed on her chest, and

he cocked a brow at her. "Nice shirt."

Dana smiled. "Thanks. Anything that has to do with ancient Egypt, I love. My great, great-grandmother was Egyptian. That's part of the reason I got into the field I did."

"Hmm, I'm Egyptian. Does that mean you love me too?"

Dana felt her face rush with blood. "I said ancient Egyptian, and you're nowhere near that old. As for loving you, time will tell." Mahes' deep-sounding laughter followed her out of the room.

CHAPTER FIVE

The Oak Park Mall was one of Dana's favorite places to shop. It was Kansas City's largest indoor shopping center. With close to two hundred stores to choose from, she could find practically anything she wanted in one place.

Mahes turned out to be a bigger window shopper than she was. He held her hand with their fingers linked as he pulled her from one store front to another. Dana was thoroughly enjoying herself, except for one small thing. She found herself hard-pressed not to notice all the looks the women who passed them shot his way. It wasn't only one or two, either. It was more like all the women they encountered, young or old. Dana, not normally a jealous person, would have felt like ripping out the other women's eyes if he paid them the least bit of attention, which he didn't. He seemed to only be interested her.

At one of the bigger department stores, Dana led Mahes to the menswear section. He quickly browsed the racks of clothes. Once he found something he liked, he passed it to her to hold on to while he continued looking. She soon found herself loaded down with six pair of jeans and twice as many shirts, ranging from long to short-sleeved. After he placed yet another shirt across her arm, she spoke up.

"Ah, Mahes. Don't you think you have enough clothes already? I don't think they'll let you take all this into the fitting rooms."

Mahes looked at the pile of clothes Dana held and seemed a little surprised to see how weighted down she was. "I guess that should be enough. I am a bit of a clothes horse, or so my sister-in-law, Kendra, tells me. I just like to look good."

Heading in the direction of the fitting rooms, Dana asked, "You have a brother who's married? Is he older or younger than you?"

"He is older, and yes, he is married. He and Kendra have been for just a little over a year. They have baby daughter as well."

"Do they live in Egypt?"

"No. Actually, they live in Memphis, Tennessee."

"Aren't you going to go visit them while you're in the States?" Dana realized it was a bit rude on her part to be asking that particular question. She really didn't know Mahes all that well to be questioning him about his family. "Sorry, I shouldn't have asked that."

Now at the fitting rooms, Mahes smiled and lightly brushed his lips across hers as he took the mound of clothes he'd chosen. "I do not mind that you asked. I do have plans to go visit my brother at some point. I have not really picked a set day yet when I would make the trip to Memphis. Now that you have brought it up, how would you like to come with me?"

"You want to take me to meet your brother and his family?"

"Yes."

Dana mulled it over. Getting the time off work wouldn't be a problem. Sally, her boss, had been nagging her for months to take a vacation. Dana hadn't taken a full week from work for over a year. There really hadn't been any reason to use up her vacation time. It wasn't as if she had anyone waiting at home for her.

"I haven't been back to Memphis since I left university. Sure, why not? I'd love to go with you."

"Great. Let me try this stuff on and then we can go to your place and plan when to make the trip."

Mahes ended up not taking very long to try on all the clothes he'd picked out. He was in and out of the fitting room in a matter of minutes. After helping him carry the items he decided to keep to the cashier, Dana dumped her load onto the counter next to his. Much to her dismay, the girl spent more time sending him flirtatious looks than ringing in his purchase. Dana tried her best to ignore the sickening display. That they were all one-sided did do her heart good. He passed the cashier his credit card once all the items were rung up. The girl brushed her fingers against his hand when she gave him the receipt.

Dana split the bags of newly purchased clothes between them and suggested they go to a coffee shop in the mall. With coffees in hand, they sat at one of the small tables.

She picked up the carton of cream that sat on the table and poured some into her coffee. Mahes pushed his closer so she could add some to his as well. Over the rim of her cup, she watched him take a cautious sip. She had to bite the inside of her cheek to stop from laughing as he just about gagged.

"What's the matter, Mahes? Is there something wrong with your coffee?"

"Is it supposed to taste this horrid? I cannot understand how mor...people can drink something this bitter." Mahes scowled as he stared at the contents of his cup.

"Coffee can be bitter if you don't put any sugar in it. Myself, I don't mind it this way. You can't tell me you've never had it before."

"If all coffee tastes like this, this will be my first and last cup of it."

Dana chuckled. "Here, try adding some sugar before you pass final judgment." She pushed the glass bowl that held sugar packets toward him.

In fascination, she watched Mahes add six packets of sugar to his coffee. After stirring it vigorously, he lifted it to his mouth to take a sip. Dana thought to warn him that he might have gone too far the other way, but decided not to say anything as he took a huge gulp. He shuddered as it went down.

"Was that any better?"

"Not really. There is not enough sugar in the world to make that disgusting brew taste good. I think I will stick to tea. It is only slightly better than this, but at least I can tolerate the way it tastes."

First it was pizza, now coffee. Dana was pretty sure Egypt had those things. She couldn't help but feel it was strange that a man Mahes' age hadn't experienced either of them before now. Since she didn't know exactly where he lived there, she really had nothing to base her assumptions on.

Dana finished her coffee in record time and decided they had all they needed from the mall. As they walked to her car, she thought it wouldn't be such a bad idea to meet his brother. Having to make the road trip to Memphis would be the perfect time to learn more about her lover. Being confined in a car for hours at a time tended to bring people closer, or drive them crazy. Either way, by the end of it, she would know him better than she did now.

* * * *

Mahes watched the scenery go by. He could not believe how easy it had been to get Dana to agree to meet Nefertem. He had been racking his brain about how he was going to suggest the trip to her. Who knew it would be that simple?

Turning to look at Dana's profile, he followed the line of her jaw to the slim column of her throat. He felt drawn to her. None of those other women who had tried to catch his attention in the shopping mall compared to Dana. He had seen the way they had looked at him, but for the first time in his long existence, he felt uncomfortable with the unwanted attention. He had known if he had reacted in any way, Dana would not have taken too kindly to it.

He shifted his gaze farther down her body and rested on the outline of her breasts. They were the perfect size. Just thinking about how it felt to caress them, to suck them deep inside his mouth, made him want to taste them again. His body swelled to aching point, making his jeans suddenly too tight. With reluctance, he pulled away from Dana's chest. Mahes noticed she gave him a quick look before she once more focused her attention onto the road.

"Stop doing that, Mahes."

"What exactly was I doing that you want me not to do again?"

"You stared at me as if you wanted to devour me."

Mahes was not going to deny he was thrilled Dana felt uncomfortable under his regard. "I cannot help it. Is it a crime that I want to taste every inch of you?"

Dana's fingers tightened on the steering wheel, causing her knuckles to turn white. "It is if you make me have an accident, and I total somebody's car."

"Then I suggest you get us back to your place quickly. I want you again." Mahes' voice came out sounding husky with need.

Dana swore under her breath and slammed her foot down onto the gas pedal. In what seemed like record time, she pulled into her parking space in the underground garage at her condo. Mahes collected all the shopping bags from the backseat before coming around to her side.

With his free hand, he hauled her against his chest and

claimed her lips in a demanding kiss. After pulling away, he simply said, "Hurry."

With shaking hands, Dana tried to get the key into the lock of the security door that opened to the inside of the building. Mahes was tempted to push her aside and do it himself, but she managed to turn the lock on her second try. They raced to the elevator, then both of them pushed the up button at the same time. Luckily, a car was already at the ground floor. The doors slid open, and they hurried into it.

Once inside Dana's condo, Mahes kicked the door shut behind them and dropped the shopping bags where he stood. One big step was all he needed to reach her and roughly pull her to him. He groaned as he pushed his way inside her mouth. He could taste the coffee she had consumed. He found he did not mind it as long as it had been in her mouth first.

They were not going to make it to the bedroom this time. The urge to take her, possess her, rode him too hard. He backed her toward the couch, then pushed her down onto it so she half-lay, half-sat on it. Going down on his knees between her sprawled legs, he made short work of removing her shirt and jeans. With his heart thudding in his ears, Mahes stared down at Dana. His roamed his gaze over the sheer lace bra and panties she wore. He could just barely see her nipples through the lacy scraps of material.

He bent forward and swirled his tongue around each nipple, dampening the see-through material. Dana arched beneath him. He licked down the valley of her breasts. It was then he found her bra did up at the front. It did not take much effort on his part to work the hook free, baring her breasts to his view. He pushed the straps down her arms, freeing her of it, before he once more turned his attention back to her chest.

Using his teeth, he tugged on a peaked nipple, causing it to tighten even more. Mahes swirled his tongue around it once, then sucked it deep inside his mouth. Dana moaned and arched her back, pushing herself against him.

Mahes ran his hand down across her ribs to her flat stomach, then worked his hand under the waistband of Dana's panties. He dipped a finger between her nether lips and found her pussy already wet. She was more than ready for him, but he wanted to taste all of her. He moved out between her legs only long enough to pull off her underwear before pushing her thighs farther apart. He lifted her slightly off the couch and stroked her with his tongue. She jerked her hips in response. He wanted to push her to her limits and beyond. He flicked her clit with the tip of his tongue. She gasped and clutched his head, threading her fingers through his hair.

He continued to lick as her scent and taste filled his senses. His cock, already fully erect, ached to be inside her, but he wanted her to reach her pleasure first. Using his fingers to open her even more to his attentions, Mahes moved his tongue in and out of her wet core. Dana's moans grew more fevered the closer she came to her climax. Once she was almost at the point of no return, he pushed two fingers deep inside her slick core as he sucked on her clit. She bucked her hips as her orgasm ripped through her.

Not giving her a chance to recover, Mahes shed his jeans, pulled her bottom closer to the edge of the couch, and sheathed his aching cock inside her with one stroke. With hands on her hips, he kept her from moving as he fought the urge to spill inside her. He groaned as she squeezed his shaft with her inner muscles.

After he finally allowed himself to move in her, he pulled back until only the very tip of his cock was inside her welcoming heat. Inch by slow inch, he pushed back inside until he was sheathed to the hilt. He continued the slow pace until they he wanted more. Mahes increased it by slow degrees as he thrust into her, rubbing his pelvic

bone against her clit. His climax rose ever higher. Wanting
Dana to come the same time he did, he leaned forward and
sucked greedily at her breast.

Mahes pumped his hips faster as Dana's inner walls
clamped along the length of his shaft, milking him. He
rode her until his climax tore through him. Breathing hard,
he collapsed on top of her, thinking sex had never been so
good. As she wrapped her arms around him, holding him
tight, he realized he never wanted to let her go.

* * * *

They'd moved from the living room and were now
snuggled together on Dana's bed. Even though Mahes had
his eyes closed, she could tell he wasn't asleep. She rested
her chin on his chest and stared at him. She was afraid she
was falling for him hard. He was everything she'd ever
wanted in a man. He listened to her and never made her
feel as if she said something she shouldn't have. That he
was incredible in bed was an added bonus. Smiling, she
ran her finger along his firm jaw.

Mahes captured it and led it to his mouth, gently
nipping. "What are you smiling about?"

"Nothing specific. I just feel like doing it."

He took hold of her arm and pulled until she ended up
sprawled across his chest. He smiled. "I will take full credit
for putting that smile there."

Dana shook her head. "Not very conceited, are we?"

"I do try."

"I refuse to make your ego any bigger by praising your
prowess in bed. Let's change the subject."

"If we must," Mahes said with a hint of amusement.

"How about you tell me more about your brother and
his family? You never did tell me what his name is. I know
his wife's, but I don't know your brother's."

"It is Nefertem."

"You're kidding, right?"

Mahes shook his head. "No. My brother's name is really Nefertem."

"So just like the god you're named after, you have an older brother named Nefertem as well. Your parents must really love ancient Egypt to have named their sons after gods."

"You could say that."

"You said they have a baby daughter?"

"Yes. Her name is Cleo. She is a month old, and already has Nefertem wrapped around her little finger."

"As it should be. Will he and Kendra mind if I show up unannounced? I would hate to put them out when they have a small baby to look after."

"They will not mind. Knowing Nefertem, he would be very upset if I showed up without you."

"I find that hard to believe, considering we just met. As far as I know, you haven't even been in contact with your brother since you arrived here."

"Then you thought wrong." At Dana's questioning look, Mahes added, "I phoned my brother last night after you went to bed. It was a collect call, so you do not have to worry about the long-distance charges."

Dana was a little surprised Mahes had made the phone call while she'd been asleep. Not that she minded, though. If she'd been more on the ball last night, she would have asked him whether he wanted or needed to call anyone. She'd assumed there wasn't anybody he wanted to talk to when he'd told her she was the only person he knew in the city.

"So you told Nefertem about me when you talked to him on the phone?"

"I told him I stayed at your place, but he got the feeling I was interested in you and insisted I bring you along."

"I have to say your brother is very astute."

Mahes scowled. "More than I like him to be at times. In

this case, I do not mind, but there are instances when I wish he was not so in tune with others around him."

"Maybe he feels as if he has to keep an eye on his little brother."

"I hope not. I can take care of myself without the added burden of Nefertem constantly looking over my shoulder."

"At least you have a brother. I'm an only child. When I was growing up, I would have loved to have a sister or brother."

Mahes ran his hand up and down her back in a comforting motion. "That must have been hard. What about your parents? What were they like?"

"Actually, it was just my mom and I when I was growing up. As for my father, I have no idea who he was. Mom never told me his name."

"Where is your mom now?"

Unable to look at Mahes, Dana shook her head. "She passed away six years ago. She had cancer. Once the doctors diagnosed her, she only lived a couple of months after that. I still miss her."

"I am sorry. Do you have any other family?"

"No. I come from a long line of women who only have one child, and the child is usually a girl."

"You are all alone in the world then."

Dana looked back at Mahes and shrugged. "It's something I've gotten used to. Feeling bad about it isn't going to make it any different. I don't mind being alone."

"As long as I am here, you never will be."

She lay her head on Mahes' chest as he wrapped his arms around her. She could easily get used to him being around all the time, but she had to tread carefully. After he left, she would have to be on her own again. A small voice, buried deep inside, said it was already too late for that. She only hoped she was strong enough to give him up when the time came.

CHAPTER SIX

They spent the majority of the day in bed, only surfacing long enough to eat. In between bouts of lovemaking, they talked about anything and everything. Dana had never experienced that type of male companionship. It was exhilarating to be able to say what was on her mind with no repercussions. She could be as silly as she wanted with Mahes. He was only too happy to join in. She even found naked pillow fighting highly arousing.

During the night, they planned out their trip to Memphis. Mahes wanted to leave on the following Monday. That gave her all of the next day to pack and talk to her boss about having some time off. Dana brought up the subject of him staying with her until they left since she had forgotten to do so while at the mall. He had more than happily accepted her invitation and kissed her senseless afterward.

It was going to be a long trip for them. It was four hundred and eighty miles from Kansas City to Memphis. Apparently, she would be doing all the driving since Mahes didn't have a driver's license and didn't know how to drive. She figured it was going to take them almost eight hours to reach their destination. She'd never been on a long road trip before. She'd taken the train when she'd moved to Memphis to start university. She was a little nervous, but she did have a GPS.

The following morning, Dana got out of bed and quietly walked to the shower. Even though it was late, she left Mahes to sleep. He'd more than earned it. She couldn't quite manage to wipe the smile off her face as she thought of all the ways they'd made love during the long night.

Dana slipped into the bedroom and pulled on some clothes as silently as possible. On the way out, she picked up the scroll Ellie had sent her, then softly closed the door behind her. She put tube on the coffee table as she picked up the phone and called her boss. As she'd predicted, Sally was more than willing to give her a couple of weeks off work. Before Dana hung up, Sally had even suggested she take a third week as well. She shot her down on that one. The two weeks would be long enough to be away.

Mentally ticking that chore off her list, she sat back on the couch and stared at the cylinder that held the scroll. She couldn't shake the feeling it was something more than what Ellie had said it was. Even though Ellie, and then Mahes, had told her to leave the scroll untouched, Dana's gut told her she needed to know exactly what she'd gotten herself into by agreeing to look after it.

Before she could talk herself out of it, Dana picked up the cylinder and carefully withdrew the scroll. Just like the first time she'd touched it, a tingling sensation shot through her. Gently taking hold of the edge of it, she prepared to open it. One minute she was about to, and the next, the scroll was no longer in her hands.

In shock, she looked up to find Mahes before her, holding the scroll out of reach. She gasped at what she saw. It wasn't his nakedness she found disturbing, it was his eyes. They were no longer their usual color. They were now gold, but that wasn't the only thing that had changed about them. His pupils were mere slits, giving them a cat-like appearance.

"I told you not to open the scroll." Mahes didn't raise his voice, but Dana could hear the suppressed anger in his tone.

"Mahes, your eyes."

He ignored what she said. "I told you not to open the scroll," he said again. "You do not know what you are dealing with. It was never meant for mortal eyes."

"What are you talking about?" A shiver of fear ran down her spine as Mahes growled in the back of his throat. It sounded like one a large cat would make.

"You will never look at the book again. If you do, you will suffer the consequences of your actions."

Dana couldn't shake the feeling Mahes would be the one to mete out the punishment. Right now, the way he looked, she believed him capable of it. "Calm down, Mahes. I promise never to look at the scroll, I mean, the book, again."

Mahes glared at her for a few seconds as his cat-eyed gaze bored into her before he nodded. He picked up the cylinder and put the book back inside it. "I cannot wait any longer. We will leave for Memphis today, the sooner the better. You will only be tempted to do what you should not the longer I wait."

Not feeling comfortable having to look up at Mahes from her position on the couch, Dana stood. "I'm starting to think I might have made a mistake agreeing to go to Memphis with you. If you really feel as if you have to leave today, I don't mind taking you to the bus station."

"No. You have to come with me, along with the book."

"I don't understand what's happening here, Mahes. Your eyes are normal one minute, and the next, they change color and shape. I think I'd have to be insane to even think of spending almost eight hours stuck in a car with you. It's a little creepy."

Mahes took a step toward her. He narrowed his eyes when she took one back. "You should have listened to me when I told you to leave the book alone. If you were to read from it—"

Dana put up her hand. "Would you stop lecturing me about the damn book for a minute? I get it. You don't want me to go near it. Fine, but that doesn't give you the right to take something that doesn't belong to you. Ellie will want that back. Will you at least tell me what the hell is happening to you?" Her voice grew louder as she'd spoken and she'd ended up yelling the last part.

He seemed to come back to himself. He no longer stood as if he were ready to attack her. Unbelievably, his eyes slowly changed to their normal state. "I did not mean to frighten you, Dana. Believe me, it is the last thing I want to do. It is because you touched the book. Please, I need you to come to Memphis with me. Your friend took something that does not belong to her. I need to make things right again. The book must be returned."

Dana no longer sensed the leashed anger inside Mahes that had been there mere seconds before. He was back to being the man she'd welcomed into her bed and body. She hoped she didn't come to regret it, but when he looked at her, pleading with his eyes for her to do as he'd asked, she placed her hand in his once he reached out to her.

"Fine, I'll go, but I want some answers, Mahes. I at least deserve that much."

"It will have to wait." He pulled her close and kissed the top of her head. "I promise to explain everything, but not now. We need to get the book to Memphis." Mahes released her, then gave her a little shove in the direction of the bedroom. "Pack what you want to bring while I take a quick shower."

With a nod, Dana returned to the bedroom. She grabbed her suitcase from the closet and then packed. As an afterthought, she took out her Egyptian tarot cards and slipped them into the suitcase as well. By the time Mahes had finished showering and dressing, she'd finished. All set to go, she left him to gather up his belongings. It was going to be a long eight hours.

* * * *

In the car, Mahes watched Dana walk into the convenience store at a gas station. Once she disappeared inside, he leaned his head back and blew out a breath. Everything had gone to shit. He could not believe how close he had come to losing her. If she had opened and read from the book, he would have been unable to stop himself from striking her down. As Ma'at had commanded, he would have killed her for daring to read from the Book of Thoth. The cat-side of him would have risen and taken full control. Unlike Nefertem, Mahes' cat heritage was not usually so close to the surface. It had reared its ugly head when she had touched the book, causing his eyes to change.

During the night, he had decided he would tell Dana who he actually was. He did not want to let her go. She being mortal and he an immortal did not matter. It had worked out for Nefertem and Kendra. It could work for him and Dana. That their father, Ptah, had changed Kendra into an immortal, Mahes thought was irrelevant.

He had not planned on having to tell her quite so soon, though. He had wanted to wait until they reached Memphis. With Nefertem and Kendra present, he had figured Dana would be more accepting. That was no longer an option. She wanted answers, and he had a feeling if he did not explain everything to her, and very soon, she would turn from him.

As Dana returned, he sat straighter. Once in the car, she passed him a paper bag. He looked inside and found a couple of bottles of water along with some bags of chips and other things to munch on.

They drove in silence until Dana merged onto the east I-70. Once she reached the speed limit, she turned to take a quick look at him. "Okay, talk. I really need to know what's going on, Mahes."

"I want you to know. I am just not sure how well you are going to accept as the truth what I tell you."

"Well, you'll never find out unless you do."

Mahes shifted in his seat and turned to look at Dana's profile. "If you were to look deep inside yourself, you would know who I am."

"What kind of answer is that? I'm going to say this once. If you don't stop talking in riddles, I'm going to take the next exit off the highway and drop you at the nearest bus station. Just tell me already."

"It is not a riddle, Dana." Mahes took a second to collect his thoughts before he forged on. "You already know me, more than most people in this day and age, I might add. I could call you a stalker for all the digging into my life you have done." She shot him a look that said she still did not understand where he headed with that speech. "You are going to make me say it straight out, are you not? I'm *the* Mahes."

Dana snorted. "Yeah, like I'm supposed to believe that. You're *the* Mahes, the ancient Egyptian god Mahes."

Mahes ground his teeth in frustration. It obviously was going to take some work to get Dana to believe him. "I *am* the god Mahes. I was sent to restore the balance. When you opened the book the first time, you broke maat. As you know, it is my job to set it right again."

"Okay, so what's so special about that book," Dana motioned to the backseat with her head where the scroll sat, "that me opening it broke the universal law? You can't tell me Ellie never looked at it before she sent it halfway across the world to me."

"It is no ordinary book. It is the Book of Thoth. Since I was not sent to her, but to you instead, I assume that no, she did not open the book before shipping it to you."

"The Book of Thoth? You're saying that innocuous-looking scroll is the Book of Thoth?"

"Correct. Do you know much about the book?"

"Only that tarot cards are supposed to be linked to the Book of Thoth, and if you actually read from it, it would grant you special powers. That it's filled with spells only the gods are to know and use."

"Then you know why I must return it to its resting place. It belongs to the gods, and no mortal is allowed to possess it."

"You're telling me you're an immortal? If that's the case, why do you have to eat and sleep like any other mortal on the planet? I thought higher beings, such as you, didn't need to do any of those things."

"When the goddess Ma'at summons me, she takes away my immortality so I can more fairly judge humanity."

"Thanks go to Ma'at for wanting to keep things fair while her judge and jury punish we mere mortals."

"There is no need to be sarcastic about all this. I am telling you the truth."

"Sorry if I'm finding this too much to swallow."

"Fine then. What about my eyes? How do you explain them changing into a cat's?" Mahes got the feeling he had gotten to her with that one when she sat stoned-faced, looking out the windshield.

"I can't," Dana shot back.

"I can. You have researched me and my family. You know who my mother is. Sekhmet is truly a lion-headed goddess. The cat is in my blood, as it is in my brother's."

"So, why did your eyes change into a cat's this morning?"

"They only do that when maat has been broken and I must punish the offender to set the balance right."

"What would have happened if I'd actually read from the Book of Thoth?" As he remained silent, Dana asked in a sterner voice, "What would have been my punishment?"

Mahes did not want to answer, but she had to know exactly what would happen if she did not leave the book alone. "It would have been death."

"I see. You would have killed me without a second thought. Struck me down, not allowing me to plead my case."

"That is the way situations such as this have been dealt with for thousands of years."

"Well, sorry, I don't find that acceptable. I hate to tell you, but this isn't ancient Egypt. Your laws don't have any bearing here."

"It is universal law. It comes from a higher power than your mortal ones."

"I still think it's bullshit."

"The main thing is you did not read from the book. Now you know why I want you never to touch it again."

"Your concern for my wellbeing is so very touching, considering you would be the one to put me to death."

"Dana, please understand I—"

"Enough! I don't want to hear any more explanations. I don't know what to believe. Either you're telling me the truth, or you're a total nut job who somehow managed to make me see what you wanted me to see. Right now, I want you to stop talking. I have a lot of driving to do today, and I would really appreciate it if you would leave me to do it in peace. Once we get to Memphis, there will be more than enough time for you to convince me you're no loon."

To make sure he remained silent, Dana turned on the car stereo loud enough to make conversation impossible. Sighing, Mahes turned around in his seat and looked out the windshield. He had blown it. He hoped to hell Nefertem would be able to bail his ass out or he would lose her for good.

* * * *

The miles slowly crept by, leaving Dana nothing to do but think about what Mahes had told her. She so wanted to believe he was who he'd said he was. To actually know the Egyptian god she'd come to admire was real was more than a dream come true. The downside was he'd been sent to seek her out and punish her for something as trivial as opening that damn book. It wasn't as if she'd read anything from it and gained the powers it was purported to give. Right now, all she wanted to do was scream in frustration.

Dana glanced at Mahes out of the corner of her eye. He sat with his head turned from her, watching the scenery go by. She sighed to herself. He looked like any other normal mortal man. Nothing on the outside showed what he claimed to be. She couldn't help thinking once they arrived at his brother's place she'd be proven right in her thinking. That Mahes was not an Egyptian god. If that was the case, she didn't know what she'd do. She had strong feelings for him, but if he was truly delusional, she couldn't stay with him.

They entered the city of Memphis later that evening. They hadn't exchanged a word since Mahes had revealed his true self. Dana was the one to break the silence that hung between them when she asked for directions to get to his brother's house. In monosyllables, Mahes told her what streets to take.

After pulling into the driveway of a modest two-story home, Dana stayed behind the steering wheel, wondering if she should just turn back around and go home. Mahes didn't give her a chance to even try. He came around to her side of the car and then opened her door. Once he helped her out, she remained at his side as he took everything from the backseat, including the book.

She silently followed him to the front door. Mahes didn't ring the doorbell. He opened the door and stepped right in. That he felt at home there was obvious. He dropped what he carried in the hallway and called to see who was home.

A woman carrying a small baby appeared. Dana could only assume this was Kendra, Mahes' sister-in-law. Kendra smiled when she saw Mahes and rushed to embrace him. Dana took a step back, giving them space to greet each other. She was a little surprised to hear Mahes and Kendra speaking in Egyptian.

Kendra was the first one to focus her attention on Dana. Stepping around Mahes, smiled, and introduced herself. "Hi. I'm Kendra. Let me be the first to say how happy I am to see you. When Nefertem told me Mahes had met someone, I was overjoyed."

Mahes broke into the conversation before Kendra could say any more. "I am sure you were. Sorry to cut the introductions short, but where is Nefertem? He needs to see Dana."

Kendra looked first at Dana, then at Mahes, seeming to pick up on the tension between them. "He's upstairs. Let me get him."

Once Kendra had disappeared up the stairs, Mahes took her by the elbow and led Dana into the living room. She pulled her arm free and sat on the couch to wait. He went to stand a little away, giving her some space.

It wasn't long before the sound of someone coming down the stairs could be heard. The man who entered the room drew Dana's gaze. He was tall, just as Mahes was, and had the same exotic, dark good-looks. The only difference was his eyes. Nefertem's were pure gold. As he turned to look at her, a jolt shot through her. There was something different, powerful even, about Nefertem. She couldn't explain what she felt when his gold-eyed gaze skimmed over her. She just knew he wasn't like anyone she'd ever met before.

She stood as Nefertem came closer. He smiled. The first thing she noticed was how pointed-looking his eyeteeth were. The second, was he was even better looking close up.

Nefertem turned to look at his brother. "I did not think you were going to arrive for another few days." He spoke with the same accented voice as Mahes.

"We had to come today. Dana almost read from the book this morning. It has to be taken back." Mahes shot Dana a quick look before he continued. "She is having a hard time believing who I am."

Nefertem chuckled. "Is that so? I wonder why." He wrapped his arm around Dana's shoulders and pretended to whisper conspiratorially to her loud enough for Mahes to hear as well. "Knowing Mahes, he probably expected you to know the answer already. Being what he is, he likes to drive everyone insane with his tests. That you do not believe he is well and truly a god would mean you failed. Let me guess, he probably started off by saying you should know who he is without him having to explain in great detail."

"Actually, yes, he did."

"I thought as much."

Mahes glared at his brother. "Nefertem, you are walking a fine line. What exactly is the point you are trying to make?"

"The point I am trying to make is that you probably just dropped it on Dana. Of course she would not believe you. Most mortals would think you were a little crazy if you walked up to them and told them you were an ancient Egyptian god. They need to see the proof before they accept what you are telling them."

"You know Ma'at took my immortality away."

"I know, but I have mine." Nefertem pulled Dana closer

to his side. "You can thank me after we get back."

In a blink of an eye, Dana found she was no longer in Nefertem's living room.

CHAPTER SEVEN

This place was like none she'd seen before. The temple was lavishly decorated in jewel tones, painted on the walls and in the fabrics used throughout. Solid gold was used as accent pieces, giving the temple a rich appearance. Once she saw the woman seated on a gold throne that was placed on a dais, she knew Nefertem had indeed given her all the proof she needed.

"Who do we have here, Nefertem?"

"This is Dana, Mother. She had come to visit with Mahes."

Dana kept her hands in front of her, tightly clasped, as Nefertem's mother walked to them. This was the goddess Sekhmet, mother of the gods Nefertem and Mahes. Dana found she could only stare at the woman. Being a cat-goddess, Sekhmet was indeed part cat. She had the body of a woman, but the head of a lioness. Her beautiful, gold cat-like eyes studied Dana from head to toe. A smile spread across Sekhmet's lips, revealing fangs.

"It is nice to meet you, Dana. It would seem my sons have now found their mates."

Dana was about to say she wasn't Mahes', but Nefertem didn't give her the chance. "That might be a little too early to say, Mother. I brought Dana here to help her understand a few things Mahes has told her."

"Understand what, dear? Why is it you who have brought her here and not Mahes?"

"He could not. He was summoned by Ma'at. That is why Dana is having a problem believing Mahes is a god."

"Ah, I see. I get the feeling, Dana, you are involved in whatever Mahes has to set right. Is that how you met him?"

Dana nodded. "Yes." Her voice cracked. Clearing it, she tried again. "Yes, you could say I was the reason Mahes was summoned."

"Well, you have piqued my interest." Sekhmet linked her arm through one of Dana's. "Shall we see Mahes now? I want to see my gorgeous granddaughter as well."

Once again, Dana found herself back in the mortal world. Mahes, who'd been pacing the length of the living room, was brought up short upon seeing they had returned. He came to Dana's side and wrapped an arm across her shoulders.

His eyes shot daggers at Nefertem. "Do not ever do that again."

Sekhmet interrupted before the conversation went any further. "Calm down, Mahes. Your mate is fine. Nefertem only did what he thought was best."

"I do not think taking Dana to the immortal realm was what she needed to see right now."

"Actually, Mahes, it was." That was exactly what she'd needed. She'd sensed Nefertem was different, but it wouldn't have been enough to convince her. She was the type of person who needed tangible proof before believing, especially something of that caliber. It wasn't every day she learned the Egyptian gods were in fact reality.

Mahes looked at her. "So, you believe me now?"

"Yes." Dana nodded. "Your mother isn't exactly someone I can overlook or explain away."

"You are not kidding." Mahes said softly.

"I heard that," Sekhmet shot back. "Now that we have that all settled, I am going to look in on Kendra and Cleo. Then I want to hear what Dana did to have Mahes sent to her. Since I am here, I might as well see if I can help in some way." Not waiting to hear what her son thought of her suggestion, Sekhmet left the room in search of her daughter-in-law.

* * * *

Kendra and Sekhmet joined the others a short while later. Sekhmet held baby Cleo. Mahes still found it hard to believe his mother and Kendra could get along so well, considering their past history.

When Kendra had summoned Nefertem, it had released another side of their mother. She had turned into Re's destroyer. Luckily for mankind, they had been able to circumvent her coming to the mortal realm. Sekhmet had not been pleased. Their mother had tried to take revenge by trying to kill Kendra. Ptah, their father, had managed to undo the damage Sekhmet had done by healing Kendra and turning her into an immortal.

That was all in the past. Re had changed Sekhmet back to her normal self, once more subduing the destroyer side of their mother. Usually a caring, nurturing person, she had welcomed Kendra into their family with open arms. Kendra had been slow to forgive Sekhmet, but in the end, for Nefertem's sake, she had been able to.

Once Sekhmet sat and pinned him with a look, Mahes knew she was ready to hear what was going on. "Mahes, why were you summoned to Dana?"

In way of an answer, he got up and retrieved the

cylinder that held the book. With care, he removed it before he placed it in his mother's hands. She scowled as she looked at the book, then handed it back to him.

"I can see you know what this is." As Mahes had spoken, he'd placed the book back inside the cylinder out of sight.

"Of course I know what that is. It is the Book of Thoth." Sekhmet turned to look at Dana, who sat next to Mahes on the couch. "How exactly did you come to be in possession of the book?"

"A friend of mine sent it to me. I had no idea what it was until this morning when Mahes took it from me."

"Be thankful you did not read from it. Any mortal who does will suffer. Do you know the story about the Book of Thoth?"

"To be honest, I know very little about it. I only know tarots are supposedly based on it."

Sekhmet nodded. "You are correct. The Book of Thoth holds powerful spells and knowledge, meant only for the gods. It was buried in the City of the Dead with Prince Neferkaptah, the son of the pharaoh Amenhotep. Neferkaptah had been a scribe and a magician. He was the first mortal to find the book and read from it. Once he did, he learned the language of the beasts, was able to see the wind, hear the sun, and learned the secrets of the gods as well as the songs of the stars. The book had been safely hidden in the Nile, which was where he'd found it. Snakes and scorpions had guarded it. It had been placed in a golden box, which in turn was inside a silver one. That was placed inside an ebony box, then an ivory, then a wooden, then a bronze, last being an iron box. The price for his transgression was to watch his wife and son die. His son, Merab, and his wife, Ahura, drowned themselves in the Nile. Neferkaptah died in the end as well for his misdeed."

Dana's face had gone a little white. Mahes pulled her

closer against his side. "I think Dana knows enough about the book, Mother."

Sekhmet smiled reassuringly at Dana. "I did not mean to scare you. I only wanted you to understand what could happen if you read from the book. Your friend did you no favors sending it to you. Once the book has been returned to Neferkaptah's resting place, the balance will be restored."

"It will be returned tomorrow," Mahes assured his mother. "With Nefertem's help, the book will be back where it belongs, then Dana will have nothing to worry about."

* * * *

By nightfall Dana was drained, but at the same time exhilarated. Being able to talk with Sekhmet had been an enlightening experience. The goddess had answered all her questions about the gods and life in the immortal realm. Nefertem and Mahes had chimed in from time to time as well. Once they'd finished, the hour had grown late, and Dana's head had been spinning.

She and Mahes had been given Kendra's brother's bedroom to sleep in. Markus was away on a business trip and wouldn't return until the following week. Dana put her suitcase on the floor by the bed. Mahes had his back against the closed door, watching her. She still found it hard to believe this man, this god, was hers, at least for the time being. She didn't know what would happen after the book was returned. She'd been too scared to ask. After the balance was restored, Mahes would have his immortality restored. Whether he'd still want her, a mortal woman, after that, was a question she feared to face.

Mahes crossed the room and came to stand in front of her before he cupped her face in his hands. "What is going on in that mind of yours, Dana? I know you are thinking about something."

She tried to smile, but failed miserably. "It has been a lot for me to take in."

"I know. You should know me being a god does not change anything."

She so wanted to believe him. "How can it not? I'm mortal. You're a god. I know my feelings for you won't change, but yours might."

Mahes dropped his hands to the tops of her shoulders. "No, they will not. Did you not hear my mother? You are my mate."

"Fine, I'm your mate. How will you feel when the years aren't as kind to me as they are to you? I'll grow old and eventually die."

"It does not have to be that way." Mahes lowered his head until he looked Dana squarely in the eyes. "Once I have my immortality back, I can make you like me. You will not be a goddess, but you will be immortal. You will be like Kendra."

"Kendra is immortal?" A spark of hope flared inside her.

"I guess we forgot to mention that. Ptah made Kendra immortal after my mother shot her with an arrow." At Dana's shocked expression, he quickly added, "That is a long story, and one I will tell you another day. Suffice it to say, it worked out well for Nefertem and Kendra. It can work for us."

"Truly?"

"Truly. I have waited thousands of years for you. I just did not know it until I met you. I have never told another woman this. I love you, Dana."

"I think I've loved you for years, Mahes. I fell in love with the god back when I was in university, but now I'm in love with the man too." As Mahes moved to claim her lips, Dana gently pushed him away. "Wait. I have to do something first."

After going to her suitcase, Dana fished inside it until she found her tarot cards. Mahes arched a brow. "Don't laugh. When I get stressed or feel unsure about something, I like to do a reading for myself. It makes me feel better afterward."

Mahes took the box of cards from her and smiled. "Egyptian tarot cards. Why am I not surprised?" He handed them back.

Dana sat on the bed and took the cards out of the box before she shuffled them a couple of times. She put her hand on the deck and closed her eyes for a second. She cut it and turned the top card face up. It was The Lovers. On it were three figures—a man in the middle of two women. The women looked to the side while the man faced toward the front. Above them was another figure inside a sun, aiming a nocked arrow at them.

Dana smiled. "The Lovers card represents love and sex. It refers to a relationship based on strong love. Of the force that draws two people together. You see the man and women?" Once Mahes nodded, Dana continued. "The man is supposed to be torn between them. One is supposed to be virginal, and the other a temptress. He has to decide between the two. Make a choice between right and wrong."

Mahes leaned closer. "What do you choose, Dana?"

"I choose you. For me, that's the right decision."

Mahes picked the cards up and put them on the small table beside the bed. "There is no other for me."

This time when Mahes claimed her mouth, Dana met him halfway. The feel of his firm lips moving under hers made her shiver with longing. She wanted him with every fiber of her being. She slipped her arms around his neck and kissed him back, putting everything she felt into it. Knowing exactly who he was made it more intense.

He seemed to sense she wanted him with no long, slow love play before their joining. He took hold of the bottom of her top before he stripped it off her and then dropped it to the floor. Her bra soon followed. She needed to have his bare skin pressed against her. She pulled at his shirt. Mahes chuckled at her impatience.

Mahes released her mouth, then licked a trail down her chest to her breasts. Dana caught her bottom lip between her teeth as he sucked a taut nipple deep inside. With each pull, the pressure built inside her core, causing wetness to pool between her legs.

Dana held Mahes to her and leaned against him until he lay back. She pulled out of his grasp and made short work of removing the rest of their clothes. She gave him a wicked smile as she crawled back onto the bed, straddling his hips. She took his lips in a fierce kiss, pushing her tongue inside his mouth to taste him, before moving on.

She kissed a path down the side of Mahes' neck. She worked her way across his chest, swirling her tongue around his flat nipples before she blew on them. He shivered. Dana continued her downward path, licking her way to his hard, full cock. Her pussy clenched as she thought of how good it felt to have that part of him buried deep inside her.

She took hold of his shaft and pumped her hand up and down his length until a bead of moisture appeared on the very tip. Still holding him firmly, Dana swirled her tongue around the head of his cock. Mahes groaned and bucked his hips. Liking the effect she had over him, she licked him from base to tip before she opened her mouth and took as much of his length inside as she could manage. Alternating between sucking and swirling her tongue around the tip, he grew even harder.

Mahes only allowed her a few moments more to pleasure him in that way before he grabbed her by the arms and dragged her higher up on his body. He positioned her above him, then with a moan, buried his throbbing cock inside her with one thrust. With her hands on his chest, Dana slowly rode him. She clamped her inner muscles around his shaft as she arched her hips. His hard length stroked her clit with each thrust.

Her climax slowly built. Leaning forward, she offered Mahes one of her breasts. He cupped it, laving her taut nipple with the flat of his tongue. He took it between his teeth and tugged on it. As he sucked greedily, Dana rode him faster, harder, pushing her orgasm nearer. As it rose to engulf her, she closed her eyes and moaned as wave after wave of pleasure surged through her and her inner walls clutched his hard shaft.

Taking hold of her hips, Mahes kept her pace steady as he strove for his release. He grew still harder. He met her downward strokes and thrust into her. Once his orgasm took hold of him, he arched his hips, almost lifting her off the bed as he emptied himself deep inside her.

Dana collapsed onto Mahes' chest. They breathed hard. His heart loudly thumped beneath her ear. Content, her eyes drifted shut. The long day of traveling, along with everything else that had happened, had finally caught up with her. As she drifted off to sleep, he kissed the top of her head before he pulled the covers over them.

CHAPTER EIGHT

In the morning, Dana woke up to find the spot next to her empty. With her face in Mahes' pillow, she took a deep breath. She gloried in his musky, male scent. She rolled onto her back and stretched. Her stomach growled, giving her another reason to get out of bed, other than going in search of Mahes. Hoping no one was already in the shower, she quickly slipped on the clothes she'd worn the day before heading for the bathroom. Luckily for her, it wasn't occupied.

After a quick shower, and having put on fresh clothes, Dana went downstairs. A voice came from the kitchen. The only ones there were Kendra and her daughter, who sat in a baby bouncer lounge chair on top the kitchen table. Kendra had been talking to Cleo, but turned when she heard Dana enter the room.

"Good morning. Did you sleep okay last night?"

"Yes, thanks." Dana crossed the room before she sat at the table next to Kendra. "Where is everybody?"

"You just missed them. Nefertem and Mahes have gone to make their plans. They went to see where exactly Nefrekeptah's tomb is, and to find out what, if any, damage has been done to it."

Dana nodded. She hadn't thought of that. Ellie had to have dug out the tomb to find the book. There was no telling what state she'd left it in. She would have more than likely buried the entrance once she'd retrieved what she'd wanted, but in her haste to get it out secretly, Ellie might not have been as careful as she would have been at other dig sites.

Kendra went to the fridge. "You must be hungry. How about I whip you up something to eat? Are eggs and toast okay with you?"

"Sure, that's fine."

As Kendra went to the stove to start cooking the eggs, Dana looked at baby Cleo. She found her watching her as Cleo happily chewed on her fist. Dana smiled. Cleo was a gorgeous baby. She could see a lot of her father in her features. What hair she had was dark, but her eyes were a beautiful gold just like Nefertem's. Stretching out a finger, Dana gently stroked the infant's soft cheek. Cleo took hold of it before she could pull it away and stuck it into her mouth. Dana chuckled as Cleo gummed her finger.

Finished cooking, Kendra put a plate of eggs and toast in front of Dana. She shook her head and grinned when she saw her daughter gnawing on Dana's finger. "If you're not careful, Cleo is likely to gum your finger off."

Dana worked her finger free. "I don't mind."

She picked up her fork and ate. After making short work of her meal, she turned to look at Kendra. Now that Mahes had told her Kendra was immortal, Dana noticed there was a slight difference about her, an aurora that she hadn't noticed before. It wasn't the same as when she looked at Nefertem, but there was something that her "gift" picked up on.

Sensing Dana watching her, Kendra picked Cleo up and motioned for her to follow her. Once they were settled comfortably on the couch, Kendra said, "I see Mahes told you about me being immortal. I'm sure you have questions."

Dana nodded. "Yes, I do." She took a minute to collect her thoughts before she continued. "Mahes said after this is all over, he could make me like you. I'm willing to take that next step, but…"

"But you aren't sure what to expect."

"Exactly. Mahes didn't go into much detail. To be honest, I have no idea what he'll be like once he has his immortality, his godhood, restored."

Kendra shifted the baby in her arms and chuckled while she shook her head. "That sounds like Mahes. First, let me tell you it does my heart good to see he has at long last fallen in love. Before you, any pretty face would turn his head. Going shopping with him, let me say, was distracting. Women flocked to him in droves, and he did nothing to discourage their attention."

"I know what you mean about women being drawn to him, but when I took him to the mall, he acted as if he didn't notice they panted after him."

Kendra stared at her, then burst out laughing. She slowly brought herself back under control. "I'm sorry. I didn't mean to be insulting. You have to understand that Mahes is, was, a huge womanizer. I called him the man-whore. That he has fallen for you, and doesn't look at anything else in a skirt, well, I thought I'd never see the day."

"He was that bad, was he?"

"Yes, but if he wants to give you immortality, it would seem he has chosen you as his mate. He wouldn't have offered it if his feelings weren't true."

"So, what's it like being married to a god?"

"It has been interesting. Life is never boring, I'll give you that much. In some ways, it isn't all that different from being married to a regular man. We've had our disagreements, as any other married couple does.

Sometimes I forget Nefertem is an Egyptian god. To me, he's just Nefertem. Then there are other times I can't help but remember who he is. He doesn't need to sleep, whereas I still do. Nor does he need to eat. I enjoy cooking, so I'm happy my brother lives with us and I can at least cook for him."

Not being able to sleep in Mahes' arms as he slept next to her would be a drawback. After sleeping in an empty bed for years, she was getting used to having a warm body to turn to during the night. She would miss it, but it wasn't the end of the world.

"Okay, I can handle that. Anything else I should know?"

"Other than you won't ever grow old and will live basically forever with the man you love, there isn't much else I can tell you. Mahes, I'm sure, will help ease you into the Egyptian god way of life. They do have their own hierarchy, and it can be a bit confusing at times, but you'll do fine, especially since you majored in Egyptian art and archeology in university. You have a better understanding than I did in the beginning. I've had to learn a lot as I went along." Kendra sniffed her daughter's bottom and grimaced. "I'd better change, Cleo. Where is Nefertem when I need him?"

As the other woman left the room, Dana thought over everything she'd told her. Once Mahes had his godhood back, she would be more than happy to accept the gift of immortality he'd offered.

* * * *

Nefertem and Mahes returned to the house an hour later. Dana still found it a bit of a shock that Nefertem could pop in and out of places at will. When Mahes saw her, he came and gave her a kiss before sitting next to her. He slung his arm around her shoulders and pulled her against his side.

"Well, what did the two of you find out?" asked Kendra, who'd been sitting next to Dana on the couch before Mahes came to sit between them.

"You can see signs near the tomb entrance where the earth has been disturbed," Nefertem answered. "Only if you know to look for it. The tomb itself was not disturbed in any way."

Dana was pleased to hear something so ancient hadn't been damaged. "I guess Ellie kept a modicum of professionalism when she robbed the tomb. I'm still finding it hard to believe she would have done something like that. She's known for doing everything by the book. Yet it has been a few years since we really had any interaction. It would appear Ellie has changed, and not for the better if she's sunk so low as to steal an antiquity from a tomb, and then smuggle it out of the country."

Mahes squeezed Dana's shoulder. "I have a feeling the book is responsible for the changes in your friend. To some people, finding it becomes an obsession. The Book of Thoth, and the power it holds, can take over the one who searches for it."

"I think you're right. When Ellie called to see if the book had arrived, she did say the reason she hadn't been in touch with me was because she'd been working on a really big project, and that she'd had a breakthrough of some kind recently."

"The breakthrough would have been finding the actual book."

"So, what do we do now?"

Nefertem spoke next. "We return the book. There is a dig going on nearby so we will have to be careful. The ideal time will be at night when there is no one about."

"Okay. When?"

"Today." Nefertem smiled knowingly at his brother. "I think Mahes would like to have this over with as quickly as possible. I have the feeling he is anxious to start the new life the two of you have planned."

Dana grinned at Mahes like a love-sick fool, but she couldn't seem to stop. "Today works for me."

* * * *

They had to wait until four o'clock in the afternoon before they could go to the tomb in the City of the Dead. With the eight-hour time difference, it put the time in Egypt at midnight. Dana found it a bit disconcerting to see the sun shining brightly one moment, then to be plunged into darkness.

The City of the Dead was steeped in ancient history. Situated in the necropolis of Saqqara, it was the oldest cemetery in unified Egypt. Rich and poor alike were buried there. Each one made the same journey to a final resting place. With the dawn, a burial party would have left the sprawling capital of Memphis to cross a shallow lake by boat to reach Saqqara. Climbing from the floodplain, they would have walked up to the desert plateau. There, tombs of nobles from the first dynasty would be the first thing they encountered. To the south loomed a step pyramid, the tomb of King Djoser, the builder of Egypt's first pyramid.

Thousands of tombs were spread across Saqqara, making it an archeological gold mine. Dozens of digs, originating from different countries, could be taking place at any given time. It was estimated that only half the tombs there had been discovered, which explained how the Book of Thoth had lain hidden for centuries undisturbed until now.

Any other time, Dana would have wanted to wander around the many dig sites and see what artifacts had been unearthed, but not this night. With her fingers laced through Mahes', she silently walked beside him as he led her to Nefrekeptah's tomb. She carried the book, still inside its cylinder, in her other hand.

Nefertem waited for them at what Dana guessed was the entrance. There was nothing to see that would mark it as such. It looked like any other patch of desert sand in the area. "Tell me again what I have to do once we're inside?" she asked Mahes.

"Once Nefertem and I have the sarcophagus open, you have to place the book back on Nefrekeptah's chest."

"Then the balance will be restored?"

"Correct."

Taking a deep breath, Dana carefully removed the book from the cylinder. "No time like the present I guess. Let's get this back to where it belongs."

"I'm afraid I can't let you do that."

At the sound of Ellie's voice coming from behind her, Dana turned to face her one-time friend. She was shocked to see the changes in Ellie, not only in her appearance, but in her demeanor as well. Ellie had always been thin, but now she was too skinny, as if something slowly ate away at her from the inside. Her clothes hung on her loosely. Her eyes were over bright and had immediately focused on the scroll Dana carried.

"What a surprise to see you, Ellie."

"I could say the same about you. Last I knew you were at home in the States."

"Well, when I was offered an opportunity to come to Egypt, I jumped at it."

"Oh really? You also felt it was necessary to bring my scroll along with you?"

Dana dropped the pleasantries. "It isn't yours, Ellie."

"I found it. It's mine."

"That doesn't make it yours. Do you have any idea what this is?"

Ellie rolled her eyes, then shook her head as if to say Dana had asked a really stupid question. "Of course I know what it is. It's the Book of Thoth. Do you think I would have gone to so much trouble to sneak it out of Egypt if it weren't something as powerful as that?"

"If you know what the book is, you have to know what the repercussions are if you read from it."

"Sorry if I don't believe all that crap about the gods punishing a mortal for reading it and gaining its powers. I never took you for a superstitious person, Dana."

Dana shot Mahes a quick glance. "Let's just say I've had to change my way of thinking when confronted with irrefutable proof."

Ellie, for the first time, seemed to notice Mahes and Nefertem. "Who are they?"

"They're Nefertem and Mahes. If you believe in the Book of Thoth's existence, then you'll know exactly who they are." Ellie's show of bravado seemed to falter. "Maat has been broken, and returning the scroll is the only way to correct the balance. Mahes was sent to make sure it's done."

Ellie said nothing further. Dana turned away and started to walk to Nefertem. The feel of something cold and hard pressed against the base of her skull suddenly brought her up short. She turned her head slightly. Ellie had moved up behind her and now held a gun at her head. She shivered with fear. Ellie's mind had gone, and she was likely to do just about anything to keep the book in her possession.

"It didn't have to come to this, Dana. All you had to do was store the damn book at your place until I came to retrieve it. I've worked for too many years to find it to have you put it back in that tomb to rot. I want everything it'll grant me. The day of the gods ruling over mortals is over. We have every right to know what they know." Ellie jammed the gun harder against her head. "Now hand over the book."

Not knowing what else to do, Dana slowly passed it to

her. Ellie lowered the gun before she opened the book. As Dana made to step away, Ellie aimed the gun at her once again.

Dana froze in place. "Don't read from the book, Ellie. Please."

Ignoring Dana, Ellie read. The wind picked up and swirled in circles around them. Before Ellie could finish, Mahes made a loud, animal-like growl. His eyes had once again changed to those of a cat. As he growled again, he curled his lip. His eyeteeth had lengthened to sharp points. Dana had nothing to fear from him. It was Ellie who'd incurred his wrath.

Dana quickly stopped Ellie before she could read once more. "If you value your life, you'll stop. Now. Mahes will strike you down if you continue."

She must have noticed the change that had come over Mahes. Ellie quickly placed the barrel of the gun against Dana's temple. "I think not. Tell him to back off."

"I can't. This is what he was sent to do. To punish those who upset the balance."

"Let's see what your precious Mahes does when you read from the book. I know you've been obsessed with him since university. I can see the way you're looking at him with longing in your eyes." As Ellie shoved the open book in front of her face, Dana closed her eyes, refusing to do what the other woman wanted her to do.

The wind suddenly became stronger. Nefertem's voice seemed to be closer as he spoke to her. "Keep your eyes closed, Dana. Do not open them until I tell you."

As the wind swirled around her, Dana felt the sting of sand it'd picked up. More and more of it buffeted her, making it feel as if a thousand bees stung her. With her eyes tightly closed, she put her hands over her face. Finally, by slow degrees, the wind died, taking the abrasive sand with it.

Once Nefertem told her it was safe to open her eyes,

Dana slowly lowered her hands and cracked an eye open. She realized there was no longer a gun pressed to her head, and Ellie was nowhere to be seen.

"What happened?"

"I sent Ellie to a place where she can learn what happens when you mess with the gods," Nefertem replied.

"The book?"

"Mahes took it from her."

Mahes stood a little distance away with his back toward her. The book was tightly clutched in one of his hands. He breathed hard, as if he fought a battle inside himself. "What's wrong with him, Nefertem?"

"When I whisked Ellie away, he did not get to do what he was summoned to do. Punish the one who took the book. The cat has a hold of him and will not let go until the book is put back."

Dana took a tentative step toward Mahes and held out her hand. He spun around so quickly she almost lost her footing in surprise. His lip curled back in a snarl.

Nefertem stepped between them. "I would keep my distance right now, Dana."

Dana nodded. The only way she could describe how Mahes acted was feral. Not wanting to set Mahes off, she quietly watched as Nefertem took the book from him and passed it to her. Once he took hold hers and Mahes' arms, they flashed inside the tomb. The men easily removed the lid of the sarcophagus. Dana took a deep breath and looked inside.

The mummy of Nefrekeptah lay with his arms crossed. Not wanting to take any longer than was necessary, Dana reverently placed the book on his chest. After she'd stepped away, Nefertem replaced the stone lid of the sarcophagus, sealing the mummy and the Book of Thoth inside.

The change in Mahes was instantaneous. The cat side of him receded as quickly as it had risen. After stepping inside his open arms, Dana laid her head against his chest as Nefertem flashed them back outside. She took a deep breath of the night air and looked at the face of the man she would love for eternity. To claim him, this ancient Egyptian god, as her own was a dream she never thought would be realized.

Dana reached up to brush her fingers against his cheek, then on tiptoes and kissed his firm lips. As the stars shone upon them, she poured all she felt into the kiss. She had the man of her dreams. What more could she want?

The End

ABOUT THE AUTHOR

Marisa Chenery was always a lover of books, but after reading her first historical romance novel she found herself hooked. Having inherited a love for the written word, she soon started writing her own novels.

She now writes young adult books and erotic romances.

Marisa lives in Ontario, Canada, with her boyfriend, Steve, four children, four grandchildren (she's a young grandma in her fifties) and rabbit and dog.

www.marisachenery.com

www.ingramcontent.com/pod-product-compliance
Lightning Source LLC
Chambersburg PA
CBHW020331180626
46812CB00001B/141